Praise for Elaine Everest

'A warm tale of friendship and romance'
My Weekly

'Captures the spirit of wartime'
Woman's Weekly

'Heartwarming . . . a must-read'
Woman's Own

'A lovely read'
Bella

The Teashop Girls at War

Elaine Everest, author of bestselling novels *The Woolworths Girls*, *The Butlins Girls*, *Christmas at Woolworths* and *The Teashop Girls*, was born and brought up in north-west Kent, where many of her fiction books are set. She has been a freelance writer for twenty-five years and has written widely for women's magazines and national newspapers, both short stories and features. Her non-fiction books for dog owners have been very popular and led to her broadcasting on the radio about our four-legged friends. Elaine has also been heard discussing many other topics on the airwaves, from her Kent-based novels to living with a husband under her feet when redundancy looms.

You can say hello to Elaine on
Twitter: @ElaineEverest
Facebook: @ElaineEverestAuthor
Instagram: @Elaine.Everest
Website and blog: www.elaineeverest.com

Elaine Everest

The Teashop Girls at War

PAN BOOKS

First published 2024 by Macmillan

This paperback edition first published 2024 by Pan Books
an imprint of Pan Macmillan
The Smithson, 6 Briset Street, London EC1M 5NR
EU representative: Macmillan Publishers Ireland Ltd, 1st Floor,
The Liffey Trust Centre, 117–126 Sheriff Street Upper,
Dublin 1, D01 YC43
Associated companies throughout the world
www.panmacmillan.com

ISBN 978-1-0350-2064-5

3 5 7 9 8 6 4 2

A CIP catalogue record for this book is available from the British Library.

Typeset by Palimpsest Book Production Ltd, Falkirk, Stirlingshire
Printed and bound by CPI Group (UK) Ltd, Croydon, CR0 4YY

MIX
Paper | Supporting
responsible forestry
FSC® C116313

Visit **www.panmacmillan.com** to read more about all our books
and to buy them. You will also find features, author interviews and
news of any author events, and you can sign up for e-newsletters
so that you're always first to hear about our new releases.

To friends and family.

Hoping you stay healthy and young of heart xx

Prologue

~

June 1942

'I will never again complain about unpleasant customers who tell me the bread is stale and neither will I tell Flora I hate the fish pie when she serves it up at Sea View. In fact, I will ask for second helpings and eat it with a smile on my face,' Anya told her friend as she held her hand.

The friend did not reply. In fact, she'd not uttered a single word for a while, not since Anya had laid the woman's head in her lap while she sat on the cold concrete floor of the warehouse by the docks. Stroking the woman's face, Anya tried hard to remember the good times at Sea View with the wonderful people she thought of as her family. The moon shone through a hole in the wooden roof. 'Are you watching the moon and thinking of me, Henio? My thoughts are often of you, and if you are safe,' she whispered.

The sound of waves lapping against the building made her think of Ramsgate somewhere across the sea. What would her friends be doing now? Perhaps Lily had taken them dancing and they had stopped on the way home to buy a bag of chips; she could almost smell the vinegar and taste the salt on her lips. Why, oh why, did this have to happen?

Angrily she closed her eyes. Now was not the time for tears. 'Do not cry,' she hissed to herself through gritted teeth. 'We will come through this; there are people who rely upon us both to return. To fail is not an option.'

Footsteps approached from behind them. 'It is too late, Anya; it is too late for you both,' a familiar voice called out. 'I will have the chance of a new life, but you and your friend will not.'

Anya turned to see a gun pointing at her head from only a few feet away. Her nose wrinkled as a familiar perfume reached her, and she closed her eyes. If she could have fought back, she would have done, but there was no time. She swore, thinking that she should have found a hiding place where they wouldn't have been discovered. Life was for living and she had failed. There was no time even to pray as the gun fired . . .

1

March 1942

Flora Neville looked around her, taking in the busy Margate branch of Joe Lyons' teashop and her daughter, Rose, handing out instructions to two young waitresses. Her heart almost burst with pride as she thought of Rose's achievements since starting work as a young Nippy at the Ramsgate branch. Now here she was, a manageress and a married woman to boot.

The Margate tearoom was spread over several floors, with a veranda where diners could gaze out over the beautiful sands when the weather was good. The main dining room was awash with beautiful chandeliers and highly polished brass fittings that gleamed on the oiled wooden counters. Close to the door was a counter where shoppers were able to purchase bread, pies, biscuits, cakes and tea. Joe Lyons kept his tearooms well stocked even though there was a war on.

'Mum, what a lovely surprise,' Rose said, coming across the room. 'Why are you here? Not that I'm not glad to see you,' she hastily added, as Flora was shown to a table by the window.

'I'm meeting Ruth. It seems she is in the area on business and she invited me to have lunch with her. Here she is now.' Flora waved in the direction of the door, where a glamorous woman had entered and was looking around.

'I'll have someone serve you,' Rose said after greeting her sister-in-law. She wondered why Ruth hadn't mentioned she would be visiting their seaside town. Ruth worked as a secretary in London, where she lived with her mother, Lady Diana.

'Do come and join us for coffee if you can. This is just a flying visit,' Ruth said, as if reading Rose's mind.

'I'll try,' Rose promised. 'I must keep an eye on a couple of trainees, and we are rather short staffed today. So many of the women are now doing war work; it pays so much better than working here,' she sighed before hurrying away.

'Rose looks tired,' Ruth said as she removed her gloves and picked up the menu. 'I simply adore dining here; it's so different from the kind of places I'm usually taken to. Shall we have the Spam fritters, or perhaps fried fish?' she asked, running her finger down the main courses.

Flora smiled at her. Apart from speaking posh and wearing wonderful clothes, there were no airs or graces about Ruth Hargreaves. She was the spit of her mother, Diana, and Flora loved them both dearly. 'I'll have the same as you,' she said, hoping Ruth didn't choose the Spam fritters, as she'd made them for her guests at Sea View yesterday. There again, they were tasty, and it wasn't as if she had to cook them herself this time.

Ruth didn't reply; her gaze had moved to the window and she was looking out to sea, apparently deep in thought.

'A penny for them?' Flora asked.

Ruth frowned as she turned her attention back to Flora. 'I beg your pardon?'

'A penny for your thoughts; you seemed miles away for a moment there, although it is lovely to sit and look out over the beach. I asked for this table because it has such a wonderful view.'

'That's so kind of you . . . no, I was thinking about work, that's all. Shall we order?' Ruth asked, as a Nippy in her smart black and white uniform arrived at their table, pencil in hand.

Flora wasn't fooled. Ruth was always quick to tell them she was just a simple secretary working in a boring office, but Flora had often thought there must be more to the girl than that.

'Tell me, is Anya on duty today?' Ruth asked, looking towards the counter where the staff known as Sallys sold baked goods.

Flora checked the dainty watch on her wrist. 'She should be here any time now. She only works part time since giving birth to her son; she fits her work hours around Joyce Hannigan, who cares for him when not at work herself.'

'Is there anyone living at Sea View who doesn't work?' Ruth chuckled before giving their order to the Nippy. 'Fried fish and chips, I think, and a large pot of tea. Real seaside food,' she said, again looking out to sea.

'The view was so much better before the war and the beach defences,' Flora sighed. 'I can't wait for the day our children can play on the sand again and holidaymakers return to Thanet. There was always something special about having visitors for a week or two. I know I have my permanent guests, but . . .'

'You want your life to return to normal,' Ruth finished her sentence.

'Do you think it ever will?' Flora asked as the Nippy appeared with a tea tray. She helped the young woman place the items onto the table before thanking her.

'We will damn well try,' Ruth assured her, again making Flora wonder about the part Ruth played in the war.

The women tucked into their meal, making small talk until the door opened and in walked Anya, the Polish woman who had resided at Sea View since escaping her country in search of her pilot husband, Henio. Ruth's eyes lit up.

'Did you wish to have a word with Anya?' Flora asked, dabbing at her mouth with a napkin.

'Is it that obvious?'

'I'm not daft,' Flora grinned. 'I'll fetch her for you and then go have a word with Rose in her office.'

'Thank you; ten minutes should be enough.'

Flora left the table and hurried to the staffroom, where Anya was removing her coat. 'Ruth would like a word with you,' she said quietly, not wishing the other staff to hear.

Anya looked hopeful. 'Does she have news of my Henio?'

'I don't know; I'll tell Rose you will be a little late to your workstation,' Flora said, patting the worried woman on the arm. She'd had more than a soft spot for the girl from Poland ever since she'd rescued her when Anya had been chased by young lads throwing stones and calling her a German spy.

'Please do sit down,' Ruth said as Anya approached. 'There's tea in the pot if you would like some?' she added, putting her hand on the teapot to check the heat.

Anya waved her hand to dismiss her offer. 'You have news of my Henio?'

Ruth was expecting this question. Even though she had no knowledge of personnel movements, she'd been able to find Henio's whereabouts once before by pulling strings among her colleagues and friends. She couldn't afford to upset Anya. 'I'm putting out feelers; rest assured no stone will go unturned in order to find him.'

If truth be known, she had no idea where Henio was since his plane had gone down over France; she doubted it would be good news, as it wasn't often pilots were lucky enough to escape from the German-occupied territory more than once. For Anya's sake she hoped Henio was safe, but time alone would tell. She looked at the dark-haired woman with high cheekbones, who was gazing at her directly. Anya's eyes seemed to bore through her.

'Then why do you wish to talk to me? I have bread to sell,' Anya said, turning towards the queue building up by the counter.

'I need your help.'

'Then speak, before I am dismissed for being away from my workstation.'

'I can't speak to you here. I wonder . . . would you come to my office?'

A puzzled expression crossed Anya's face. 'In London? Where you are . . . a secretary?'

Ruth smiled. 'Yes, in London. I can arrange a travel pass and someone will meet you at Victoria station to escort you.'

'Does this have something to do with the war?'

Ruth looked about her. They were always being warned that walls have ears. She couldn't believe that this Lyons teashop on the Kent coast could be a dangerous place, but then, one could never be too careful. 'I'm not at liberty to say. I can explain more when we meet.'

Anya remained silent for several seconds before giving Ruth a brief nod. 'If Rose gives permission for me to leave my job for the afternoon, then I will say yes.'

'I'll square it with Rose,' Ruth promised as Anya pushed her chair back to leave. 'There is one thing. Can you . . .'

'I'll keep it mum,' Anya said curtly, before rising and leaving Ruth alone.

Ruth poured a cup of lukewarm tea, smiling to herself. She only hoped that when Anya learned what was expected of her, she would indeed 'keep mum', as lives depended upon it.

'What's going on, Mum?' Rose asked, watching through the small window of her office as Ruth and Anya were talking. 'I doubt Ruth is offering to knit an outfit for young Alexsy.'

'I don't know, but it's unlikely Ruth is here for a social visit. I used to think she was a rich butterfly flitting from party to party, but these days . . .'

Rose agreed. 'I like her a lot but . . .'

'Still waters run deep?'

Rose chuckled. 'Let's not think about it too much. Hopefully Ruth has heard something about Henio's disappearance. She tends to move in circles where people know such things. How long has it been now?'

'Hmm; it must be fifteen months, as he knew Anya was expecting but went missing before the baby was born,' Flora said sadly.

'I don't know how Anya copes. I know I'd be in pieces if that was my Ben. That's why I'm pleased we've decided to put off having children until this beastly war is over.'

Flora wanted nothing more than to see Rose and Ben with their own children; it had been a while since they went to stay with Lady Diana in Scotland. 'Don't leave it too late, you never know what is going to happen,' she said, expecting the familiar outburst.

'Oh, Mum, we've had this conversation so many times. If anything should happen to Ben, I will remember him not as the father of my children but as the thoughtful, loving man he was. No number of children would change that. Besides, I could always adopt, like you have,' she smiled, thinking of young Daisy, who was loved and spoilt rotten by everyone who lived at Sea View guesthouse.

'Darling, that's different and you know it,' Flora said, thinking back to when she had pulled the little girl from a bombed-out house. Daisy had been the only survivor of an air raid close to their guesthouse in Ramsgate.

'You're right. But believe me, there will be grandchildren aplenty for you and Ben's mother when the time is right.'

'Let's hope that whoever makes the decisions in this universe falls in with your plans,' Flora said good-naturedly.

'I've had a letter from Ben,' Rose said, reaching into her desk drawer.

Flora looked at her daughter's radiant face. 'I hope he is safe?'

Rose opened the envelope and handed the letter to her mum.

Flora was shocked. 'Oh no, I can't read your personal correspondence,' she said, flapping away the letter.

Rose giggled and held it up. 'There is so much the censor has crossed out that I can't make head nor tail of much of it. He sends his love to everyone and is doing his utmost to keep well; apart from that, your guess is as good as mine. However, I will cherish it,' she sighed, holding the letter close to her heart before putting it safely back in the drawer.

'Make sure you take it home with you,' Flora said as she got to her feet. 'It looks as though Ruth has finished her chat. I'd best go back and finish my lunch. Will you come to mine for your dinner this evening rather than go home to an empty house?'

'I'd love to. I have something for Daisy and want to see her face when she opens it.'

'Then stay the night and we can have a good catch up,' Flora said, giving Rose a kiss on the cheek. 'I do like your perfume,' she added, sniffing the air close to her daughter.

'Ben sent it to me for our wedding anniversary. It seems strange to think we've yet to enjoy a Christmas as husband and wife.'

'There will be plenty more for you to enjoy once this war is over,' Flora said as she made to leave the office, praying she wasn't tempting fate with her comment.

'I don't know about you, but I could do with a fresh pot of tea and possibly a bowl of jelly and custard,' Ruth said as she took a menu from a hovering waitress. 'By the way, do you have any idea why these delightful waitresses are called Nippies?' she asked as the girl took down their order.

'No, I'm sorry, I have no idea,' the young girl blushed. 'I'm new here.'

Flora gave her a sympathetic smile; no doubt Rose was too busy these days to tell her new staff the story. She would have to remind her to do so. 'It is a simple story. A while ago, well-to-do women would call all their female servants "Gladys" because it was easier than remembering names,' she said apologetically, looking towards Ruth.

'Goodness, some of my mother's friends still do that,' Ruth exclaimed.

'Lyons decided to run a competition to give a more suitable name to their waitresses and the most popular was "Nippy", as the women were forever nipping about between tables. That was when your uniform was designed,' she smiled to the young girl. 'And very smart you look, too.'

The girl blushed again. 'I much prefer to be called a Nippy as Gladys was my grandmother's name,' she said, before thanking Flora for the information and hurrying away.

'You learn something new every day,' Ruth said, stubbing out her cigarette before lighting another from her fancy gold lighter. Her hands were shaking slightly.

'Did you have a nice chat with Anya?' Flora asked, too impatient to wait for Ruth to say anything.

The smile left Ruth's face as if she had suddenly shut down. 'I just wanted to know how she was coping, nothing more,' she said.

Flora remained silent but nodded her head knowingly as Ruth looked away, unable to hold her gaze.

'This damnable war,' Ruth whispered as again she looked out at the sea. 'Will it ever end . . . ?'

Flora reached across the table and patted the younger woman's hand. 'Any time you need a friendly ear, you know where I am.'

Ruth remained silent as she reached for her handbag. Removing a gold powder compact, she checked her reflection before dabbing the tip of her nose. 'That's better,' she smiled.

'You may prefer not to answer but I do mean what I say. You are part of my family since your brother married my Rose, and for me, that means I'll be here for you night or day,' Flora assured her. 'Promise me you'll never forget that.'

Ruth nodded her head, but wouldn't be drawn. 'Oh, good, here comes our pudding.'

2

Flora looked around the large table in her kitchen at the guesthouse. This was where her long-term guests congregated each day, not only for their meals but also to chat and feel at home. A large room that ran the length of the back of the house, it was kept warm by the heat of the stove she used for cooking. Flora had managed to fit in several shabby old armchairs to make the room cosier and one of her residents, the elderly Miss Tibbs, had crocheted brightly coloured blankets to cover them and for snuggling under. A row of windows looked out over a small yard and garden area, where Flora kept a few chickens and attempted to grow vegetables. At present the windows were covered in a criss-cross of anti-blast tape that she found ugly, so she had closed the heavy brocade curtains. These had originally been used in the formal dining room, but had now been requisitioned as a way of brightening up the room where they all spent the most time. Since the war, Flora had turned the formal dining room into a bedroom to accommodate Miss Tibbs, as her arthritis made it hard for her to climb the stairs to the bedroom she'd inhabited for many years. Flora's own small private sitting room-cum-office was now a bedroom for Daisy, her adopted daughter, who was currently parading around the kitchen showing off a cardigan knitted by Rose. There was even a knitted dolly that fitted into the pocket, which, when discovered, had the child squealing with joy.

'I unravelled one of my own cardigans after I scorched a sleeve and thought it too wasteful to throw away. But don't look too closely, as there are a few mistakes. I am far from a perfect knitter,' Rose said, secretly thrilled that the young child was delighted with her gift.

'Waste not, want not,' Miss Tibbs called out from her armchair set by the stove. The guests adored the old lady. To everyone's concern, she seemed to be becoming more frail of late and her memory was not what it used to be.

'Very true,' Flora called out loudly. 'It was knitted with love; you taught Rose well,' she smiled as the other women in the room agreed. 'Now, who is ready for their tea? Mildred brought home enough fish to feed us for nearly a week. I insisted she take some to the children's home to help them eke out their rations. There's plenty of mashed potato to accompany it if any of you aren't so keen on fish,' she said, noticing Joyce's daughter, Pearl, wrinkle her nose.

'She will eat what you put in front of her and be grateful for it,' Joyce declared. 'Some children would be thankful for such a tasty meal.'

A chastised Pearl apologized to Flora. 'I'm sure it will be very nice,' she whispered.

Flora leant close to the child. 'I can fry you an egg if you prefer?'

Pearl licked her lips but refused, noticing her mother's raised eyebrows. 'The fish pie will be nice; please don't go to any trouble on my account.'

Flora made a note not to put too much fish on Pearl's plate. There were a couple of slices of madeira cake in the tin. Once the girl's mother had gone out for the evening, she would share it with Pearl. She liked to treat the child.

'Are you going anywhere nice this evening, Joyce?'

'Derek is taking me to the cinema; there's no need to look like that, Pearl. The film is for adults, so you won't miss anything.'

'What is the film?' Rose asked as her friend Lily came into the room holding the hand of her two-year-old daughter, Mary. Rose turned to greet her, sweeping the child up into her arms and kissing her warm face. Mary was like a miniature version of her mother, with the same light brown hair and pink cheeks.

'It's called *The Black Sheep of Whitehall*,' Joyce said as the women started to fuss over Mary. 'It's supposed to be a comedy.'

'A strange title for a comedy,' Miss Tibbs muttered from her chair.

'Then I'd best dish up, or your gentleman friend will be here to collect you before you've eaten,' Flora fussed, as everyone mucked in laying the table. Rose helped her mum to serve the pie. 'Check the cabbage is cooked properly,' Flora instructed as Rose lifted the lid of a large saucepan while Pearl let out a loud 'Yuck!'

'We can't start without Katie and Mildred,' Miss Tibbs said as she watched Flora dish up the food. 'It would be rude.'

'Katie's on a late shift at the Ramsgate teashop,' Rose explained, wishing her friend could have joined them. It was an age since they'd had a good chat.

'She did say she would pop in later so we could walk home together,' Lily said as she sat Daisy into a highchair and tied a bib around the child's neck. 'Rose, why don't you come back with us to Captain's Cottage? You could catch the bus to the Margate teashop in the morning?'

Rose was tempted. The home she shared with her husband Ben felt empty while he was away, but she had already promised to stay at Sea View for the night.

'Go back with Lily and Katie; I don't mind at all,' Flora smiled. 'Do you think I should put some food aside for Katie?'

'No, she's going to eat during her break and said not to worry about her.'

Flora waved the spoon she was using to serve the pie. 'I'll never stop worrying about any of you. Speaking of which, can someone call Anya? She took Alexsy and went straight up to her bedroom when she came home from work. I hope she's not going down with something, as she didn't look herself. Now, do I save some for Mildred . . . ?'

'I'll go,' Rose said, and she hurried out of the cosy kitchen and up to the next floor, where their Polish guest shared a room with her child. She tapped gently on the door.

'Come in,' Anya called very softly, 'but be quiet, he is sleeping.' Rose crept into the room. 'He has had a busy day with Joyce and Pearl. They took him to the park and then down to the air-raid shelter in the tunnels. He enjoys it down there,' Anya whispered as she gazed adoringly at the small carved wooden bed her husband had made.

Rose wondered if it was the same for all children: that in this awful war they were used to playing in the tunnels under the town, where it was safe from enemy bombs. She knew deep down that no child of hers would be born during the war; that was why she and Ben had decided to wait to start their family.

'He's adorable,' she sighed. 'Would you like me to sit with him while you go downstairs to eat your dinner?'

'There is no need, with the bedroom door open I will hear if he cries out. However, he is like his father and once asleep will not wake for hours.'

Rose raised her eyebrows. These days, Anya hardly ever mentioned Henio. 'Is there any word?'

'Nothing, but I go to London tomorrow so may find out something then. I have arranged for someone to cover my shift at the teashop and apologize for not speaking to you about it.'

'I found your note on my desk. It is my turn to apologize, as I was holding a training session for the newer Nippies and was not available to speak to you. I take it this has something to do with Ruth visiting the teashop with my mother?'

'Beware, the walls may have ears,' Anya whispered, looking around her.

Rose shrugged her shoulders. 'We are safe here in Sea View. Come on, let's go and eat our meal before it gets cold.'

Anya left the door ajar and followed Rose downstairs. She sat next to Joyce at the table, thanking everyone for waiting for her. 'I wondered if someone would be able to take care of Alexsy tomorrow afternoon, as I have to go to London?' she asked, glancing round the table.

'Oh dear, I'm on air-raid duty tomorrow,' Flora apologized. 'And I believe Joyce is at work.'

Joyce nodded her head. 'We are short staffed so I can't change my shift. I'm sorry,' she added, seeing Anya's disappointed face.

'Me too, I'm afraid. But I know Katie isn't working, as she has offered to care for Mary for the day. I reckon she'll jump at caring for two kiddies. You know what she's like with small children,' Lily said as the women looked at each other. It was no secret that Katie and her husband, Jack, were desperate to have their own family, having both been brought up in a local children's home.

'It would be a relief if she could,' Anya said, tucking into her fish pie with gusto. 'It is a very important meeting, and I cannot miss it.'

Flora hoped that whatever it was, it would be good news for Anya.

Katie arrived as they were clearing the table, sighing as she sat down. She was manageress of the nearby Ramsgate Lyons teashop and often popped in to see her friends rather than go straight home to Captain's Cottage, where she lived with Lily and young Mary.

'That was a tiring day; we had someone down from head office inspecting the teashop. Even though I know we are ship shape, it plays hell with my nerves.'

'If it was the same chap who came to inspect us, he was a miserable so-and-so. If he'd smiled once, he'd have cracked his face,' Lily said as she poured tea for all the women apart from Joyce, who was already on her feet and preparing to go out.

'Now, you're to be a good girl while I'm out and no

being cheeky to Aunty Flora,' Joyce instructed Pearl. She adjusted her hat, using a small mirror that hung on the wall where all the inhabitants of Sea View tended to check their lipstick and hair before they went out. 'And you're to go to bed when told to do so; you have school tomorrow.'

Pearl sighed and opened her mouth to reply, pausing as she saw Flora give her a wink and a nod towards the cake tin. 'Yes, Mum, I promise,' she chanted, even though she didn't like her mother's new man friend. She crossed her fingers behind her back, hoping Derek would not be around for long.

Katie coughed for attention, waving a letter above her head. 'I've heard from Jack and he's coming home,' she said, beaming as widely as her pretty face would allow. 'But I have no idea when,' she went on, looking around at the women's questioning glances. 'The censors have crossed out so much of his letter I can't make head nor tail of it. Can you read it, please, Rose?'

Rose took the letter and started to work out what it said. 'I do wish the censor wasn't so keen to make our lives so difficult. He is coming home, as that's in the first line of the letter . . . after that, things become a little strange. There's something about the weather and the food – it could be good or bad; it's so hard to tell . . . I can read this line: he says that when you are together again . . . Oh dear,' she said, quickly folding the letter and sliding it back across the table. 'I don't think I ought to have read that.'

Katie blushed as laughter erupted around the table. 'Oops!'

'He must miss you a lot,' Anya said, looking solemn.

The women fell silent.

Katie rushed to where Anya was sitting and folded her arms around the Polish woman. 'I'm so sorry. Here I am wittering on about my Jack, and poor Henio . . . I take it there is no news?' she asked, searching Anya's face for any tell-tale sign. Anya was good at hiding her feelings.

'Nothing, but I must beg a favour of you. Can you look after Alexsy tomorrow? It is your day off, no? No one else is available.'

'Of course. I can collect him mid-morning, if that is convenient?' Katie replied, not showing any sign she was upset at being the last person Anya had asked. 'I have a little shopping to do, and then we can go back to Captain's Cottage and play in the garden if the weather is fine.'

'And the Luftwaffe behave themselves,' Lily sighed.

'They are such a problem. If I ever meet Mr Hitler, I will tell him so,' Anya huffed.

'God help the man,' Lily said, making them all laugh.

Later, when the cake had been eaten and Pearl was tucked up in bed, Flora turned to Anya, who had just returned to the kitchen after checking on baby Alexsy. 'Don't think I'm being nosey, but . . . I hope there's nothing wrong?'

Anya frowned. 'Wrong?'

'Your important meeting tomorrow, and not being able to take Alexsy with you. I hope you are not ill?'

Anya laughed airily, waving her hand as if to brush away the suggestion. 'No, my health is . . . what you say . . . rude?'

A relieved Flora tried not to laugh. 'You mean you are in rude health, and I'm pleased to hear it. I do worry about my residents and would hate any of you to be poorly.'

'I will tell you if I am off colour. However . . .'

Flora frowned. There was something wrong. 'Please tell me.'

Anya paused for a moment before shaking her head. 'No, there is nothing. I am becoming fanciful like you English. Let us have another cuppa.'

Flora chuckled, but she could tell there was something on her lodger's mind. 'I'm here if ever you wish to talk.'

3

Anya looked around her at the busy railway station. She'd only visited London twice before, and one of those times she'd been hidden under the floorboards of a truck, as her entry into England was unofficial. She'd seen little of the capital city, and could only recall the stench of fuel and the discomfort of being squashed into a small space. This time she wore a smart green tweed suit over a cream silk blouse Rose had insisted she borrow, with her travel permit safely tucked inside a brown leather handbag lent to her by Flora. The only similarity between her two visits was the butterflies that were playing havoc in her stomach.

All the world and its neighbour seemed to be waiting for a meeting under the clock. 'A silly place to meet a stranger,' Anya muttered to herself, stepping aside and giving a uniformed man a look of disdain as he pulled a young woman into his arms. He kissed her in a way that spoke of many unsaid words. If only Anya had been able to meet her Henio and kiss him in such a way; but it wasn't to be. He had simply vanished and there'd been no word since.

Looking at her wristwatch, she sighed; the person she was meant to be meeting was five minutes late. She wondered whether there was another clock in the station. Stepping closer to the couple, who were still locked in a tight embrace, she tapped the man on his shoulder and coughed politely. 'Excuse me. Is there another clock in this station?'

They pulled apart; the woman stared hard at Anya as the man straightened his uniform tie. 'I'm not sure you should be asking such questions,' the woman said. She threw her companion an apologetic glance. 'I think she's German.'

'I am a proud Polish woman,' Anya replied, looking round to see that several people had stopped as they heard the word 'German'. 'My husband is a Polish pilot flying with your RAF.' She raised her chin proudly. 'He is currently missing in action while fighting for your freedom,' she added, knowing even as she spoke that she shouldn't be saying it.

'That just proves she's a German; otherwise, she'd know we mustn't speak of such things,' the woman said, smirking at the growing crowd.

Anya held up her hand to show a simple gold ring on her left hand. 'I am proud to wear this band that ties me to my husband. It will never leave my finger, unlike the one you have taken off to meet this . . . person,' she spat back, pointing to a pale mark on the woman's finger where a ring had recently been removed.

The crowd chuckled knowingly before dispersing.

'Anya Polinski?' a woman asked from behind her left shoulder.

'Yes,' Anya bristled, reluctant to turn away from the brassy woman, who was clearly squaring up for a fight.

'I'm sorry to be so late. Would you come with me? I have a car waiting.'

Anya fell into step beside the older woman, who was dressed in a faded tweed suit. She wore a navy blue felt hat on top of greying shoulder-length hair which was clipped back at either side, showing a plain face with cheeks adorned with lines. If Anya had been asked to describe her, she'd have been hard pressed to say anything other than 'a plain woman, easily forgotten'.

'May I ask where we are going?' she asked as the car nudged its way through bustling streets. If not for the windows criss-crossed with sticky tape and the sandbags heaped against walls, Anya thought there would have been surprisingly few signs there was a war on; until they turned a corner to see collapsed buildings that had once been shops and homes, while up above, barrage balloons dotted the skyline.

Soon their car approached a row of important-looking buildings. Anya would have been interested to know what went on behind the grand doorways, but dared not ask in case the woman sitting ramrod straight next to her thought she was a spy; so many people seemed to think such a thing since she'd arrived in England. Instead she gripped her borrowed handbag, waiting for the car to stop. Why did Ruth wish to see her? she wondered for the umpteenth time.

After climbing from the car, she waited for her companion to join her. There was no sign of what the building in front of her contained. Four small holes drilled into the Portland stone showed where a brass plaque had once announced what was behind the oak double doors. A tremor of antici-pation ran through Anya as the woman said, 'Follow me.'

She tried to keep up as the woman hurried her up a

wide staircase to the next floor before guiding her through several identical corridors. Occasionally they would pass someone coming out of one of the rooms and Anya would hear the clacking of typewriters from inside, before the door closed and the person hurried away. So many people are in a hurry, she thought to herself.

Eventually, the woman stopped so abruptly that Anya collided with her. 'Sorry,' she muttered as the woman tapped on a door and opened it without waiting to be called.

'She is here,' she said to a younger woman who sat behind a desk, busy at her typewriter. The first woman turned and left the room.

The girl behind the desk picked up a telephone. 'Your appointment is here, ma'am. Shall I send her in?'

Anya watched. There was one other door; she presumed that was where she would go.

'Take a seat and you will be seen shortly,' she smiled before returning to whatever the important work was on her desk.

Anya looked around her, knowing she could never work in such a place. Although the Nippies in the Margate teashop drove her up the wall at times with their incessant chatter during their breaks, she'd rather have that than work in this bleak place. She just hoped that if she had been called to do war work, it wouldn't be as a typist as she had yet to learn the English language properly, let alone how to use a typewriter. She was inwardly rehearsing how to turn down the job when the internal door opened and Ruth appeared.

'Anya, thank you so much for coming to meet me,' she said, giving her a warm hug. 'Joan, would you be a dear and organize some tea, please? Make sure it's good and strong. Anya here works for Joe Lyons, and we can't let our side down with the dishwater that usually passes for tea around here.'

Anya, who would have preferred coffee but didn't like to say, followed Ruth into a small office and sat down in an armchair set in front of a frosted window. Ruth sat opposite. The time had come to hear what the other woman had to say. In her heart of hearts Anya prayed it wasn't news of her Henio; or, worse still, that she wasn't about to be sent back to Poland for having arrived without proper papers. She prayed they would allow her to take her child back with her. Henio would have to seek them out once he came back from wherever he was – if he was still alive.

Katie sighed as she looked at the two sleeping children tucked up under a knitted rug on her large bed. She yearned for the day when she would be able to look down on her own children. It seemed so unfair that she and Jack had so much love to give to their own family; both being orphans, it had always been their plan to start a large family as soon as possible after their wedding. So far, she'd been unable to fall for a baby, and it worried her so much; would Jack still love her if she was barren? However, he was due home soon and hopefully things would start to happen. She blushed at her thoughts.

For now, she would love and care for her friends' children; it would be good practice for when her own came along. Just now there were nappies to hang on the line, then she could settle down to her knitting until they awoke. The sun was shining; she planned to sit in the garden and let the sun do its best to warm their bones and lift her spirits – that's if the air-raid siren didn't start to wail. Mary hated to be cooped up in the damp underground shelter, preferring to run around in the garden like the free spirit she was – so like her mother, Lily. Although Alexsy was too young to understand what was happening, he did become miserable; picking up on her own fears, no doubt. She had planned to put them both in Mary's pram and walk along the cliff top to visit Flora in Ramsgate, but Flora was on air-raid duty today. It was a shame because if the sirens kicked off they could have dashed into the tunnels that threaded under the main part of the town, where residents took shelter against the bombs raining down on them. These days many people stayed in the tunnels as much as possible, almost setting up home there to be safe. Some of them no longer had homes to live in following the destruction caused by the Luftwaffe to their seaside town.

Tucking the wash basket under her arm, she hurried out to the line that stretched from the house to the old apple tree, thinking as she did of the time an RAF pilot's parachute had become caught up in the tree and they had rescued him. Peter was a frequent visitor to the cottage these days, enamoured as he was with Lily. The girls often served him with apple pie when he visited in case he forgot his unusual arrival to their property, while their friend Mildred would grumble that in all the time she'd lived there before giving Katie, Lily and Rose the deeds to the house, having no living relatives herself, she had never witnessed such a strange event.

Katie stopped to breathe in the fresh air before picking up the empty laundry basket and heading back indoors; it would only take her Jack's ship to arrive back from foreign shores and her life would be perfect. She sighed with delight as she looked around the kitchen of the thatched cottage. It would be a wonderful place to bring up her own children when she had them. A long mullioned window looked out over the garden to where the Anderson shelter sat surrounded by pots of pansies. The girls had been determined to make the place where they would spend many hours as attractive and welcoming as possible. Upstairs the children slept in the same room, in wooden beds that matched handmade wardrobes and cupboards – a gift from Mildred when Mary was born.

'Katie, I'm home, and guess who I have with me,' Lily called out as she entered the cottage.

All thoughts of the sleeping children were forgotten as Katie rushed into the hall, expecting to see Jack. 'Oh, Jack,' she cried, then came to a stop. He wasn't there. In front of her were Peter the pilot and a ginger-haired RAF officer she'd not met before. 'I'm sorry, I thought you were someone else.' She blushed, glaring at Lily. 'Be quiet, the children are taking their afternoon nap,' she told her, before nodding to Peter. 'I'm pleased to see you've taken the normal way into our home; are you here for tea?' She was thankful she'd brought home some of the stock from the Ramsgate tearoom that wasn't likely to last another day, after distributing the rest to her staff. Without it, the cupboard would have been almost bare.

Peter kissed her on the cheek. 'Hello, Katie. If it's not too inconvenient, we'd love to join you for afternoon tea. And I can contribute,' he said, handing over a small cardboard box.

Katie peered inside to find two tins of ham along with packets of butter and tea. 'I'll not ask any questions as to how you came by them,' she grinned. 'Would you like to join us?' she asked the other airman, who stood wringing his cap in both hands. 'We won't bite,' she added, noticing his discomfort.

'Only if it's not inconvenient,' he said in a quiet Scottish accent, stepping forward to introduce himself. 'Daniel Stewart; my friends call me Stew.'

Katie gave the ginger-haired man a gentle smile. She knew what it was like to be the quiet one in a group, and Stew seemed less forward than his mate Peter. 'Welcome to our home, Stew. I take it you're not from around here?' she asked as they went through to the lounge.

'I don't think I'm giving anything away to say I'm from the Scottish Highlands,' he grinned. 'You certainly have a comfortable home here,' he added appreciatively, looking around the cosy room with its inglenook fireplace.

'We can't accept the praise for furnishing it, as it was like this when our friend Mildred gave us the property. Lily, why don't you tell the story and show Stew round while I make tea? The children will be waking shortly, so keep an ear open for them,' she said, noticing how Lily was cosying up to Peter.

She was busying herself in the kitchen when Stew joined her. 'Can I help?' he asked.

'Goodness, no, but thank you for offering. I'll not have a guest helping with a meal,' she said, giving him a smile. Up close she could see that he stood a little taller than her Jack, with broad shoulders and an upright frame; she supposed it came from his upbringing. Weren't RAF officers typically picked from the privately educated upper classes?

'Is there something wrong?' he asked, bringing Katie back to the present.

'I'm so sorry; I was miles away. My husband is due back any day soon and I can't help wondering how far away he is at the moment. He could even be here in Thanet and be knocking on the door at any moment . . .'

'Ah, that could be rather awkward for you,' he frowned. 'Perhaps I should leave.'

'There's no need, honestly; besides, you've not even had a cup of tea, let alone anything to eat. Here,' she said, holding out a plate of paste sandwiches. 'Carry this through to the living room while I fill the teapot. My Jack is used to people coming and going; with the three of us girls owning the house we tend to entertain a lot, even though Rose has now moved out. She married Ben Hargreaves and has a home in Pegwell Bay, although she will pop by and stay with us when Ben is away; he's in the army,' she explained, before clapping a hand to her mouth. 'Perhaps I shouldn't have said that? Honestly, they could have been thinking of me when they designed that poster about loose mouths and keeping mum. You aren't a German spy, are you?' she asked, smiling sweetly.

'As if I'd tell you if I were,' he laughed.

They were still laughing as they returned to the kitchen after laying out the food. Lily and Peter joined them, holding the children, who looked sleepy.

'Yours?' Stew asked, glancing towards Katie.

'Goodness, no. Mary belongs to Lily and this is Alexsy, whom I'm looking after today for a friend.'

'It's not for want of trying, though,' Lily winked as she passed a fractious Alexsy to Katie. 'I think his nappy needs changing.'

Katie looked embarrassed. 'It's my dearest hope that before too long Jack and I will have a family of our own. I'm grateful that we have good friends to fill the gap. Although you can go off some,' she said, wrinkling her nose as she sniffed Alexsy's nappy.

'I'll help you; I have three of my own,' Stew said, reaching out to take the child.

'You don't look old enough,' Katie gasped before apologizing. 'You must think me so rude.'

He chuckled. 'That's my Scottish genes. We live long and healthy lives in my family.'

'And have lots of kiddies, by the sound of it,' Lily chipped in as she passed him a basket containing nappies and a clean romper suit. 'One is enough for me . . . for now, anyway,' she added, giving Peter a coy glance.

'Let's get stuck into this food, shall we?' Peter said, rubbing his hands together.

'But Stew . . .' Katie started to say.

'I'll not be long,' he called over his shoulder. 'Don't wait for me.'

'Now, that's a man who would make a perfect father for your children,' Lily grinned, nudging Katie.

'I have no idea what you mean,' Katie huffed.

'We have drunk too much tea and I have told you about my life in Poland. Now, will you tell me why I am here?' Anya said. She was getting fed up with all the small talk. Checking the gilt-framed clock hanging on the wall, she could see that an hour had already passed, and still she was none the wiser as to why she'd travelled to London. 'Tell me, is my Henio dead?'

Ruth shrugged. 'That is not why you are here, although I will continue to make enquiries. Now, if you have finished your tea, we need to be somewhere else.' She went to her desk and picked up the telephone. 'Have the car ready in five minutes, please.'

Anya was puzzled; wherever was she being taken?

'I have to be back in Ramsgate to collect my son,' she pointed out as Ruth reached for her coat.

'I'll make sure you are home in plenty of time,' Ruth assured her. 'Now let's get cracking, shall we?'

This time, Anya was shown down a back staircase and out into an alley just wide enough for a car to access. It was a squeeze for them to climb inside.

'We prefer to take this route,' Ruth explained as she offered Anya a cigarette, which the Polish woman declined.

Anya had a feeling she was being kidnapped and wished she'd had the foresight to inform Flora whom she was going to meet. She knew little about Ruth, apart from her being Rose's sister-in-law and someone who did not appear to work very much for her living, what with having wealthy parents. Anya felt disloyal in her thoughts and was reminded of one of Flora's favourite sayings: 'It takes all kinds of people to run the world.' But what kind of person was Ruth?

Try as she might, Anya could not identify any of the roads on the route the car took. Neither Ruth nor their driver spoke a word, which alarmed her even more. She thought of jumping out and running away but there was never an opportunity to do so, and by the time the car stopped she was a bag of nerves, convinced something awful would happen. She even prayed for the air-raid sirens to start so she could get out of the car and make her escape.

With her mind working overtime it was some seconds before she realized the car had pulled up and the driver was getting out, ready to open the door for them. Allowing herself to be directed through a single door, she followed Ruth up a narrow staircase and was ushered into an office not unlike the one they'd sat in earlier.

'I'm sorry for all the subterfuge, Anya, but what I'm about to talk to you about is top secret. This office is more secure than where we were before, but I wasn't able to bring you straight here for security reasons.'

Anya nodded her head slowly as she took in Ruth's serious face and after a few seconds knew she had to ask the question that was foremost in her mind. 'Is this legal, or are you working against the government?'

Ruth guffawed loudly. 'My dear woman, nothing could be further from the truth. I work for the government.'

'As a secretary?'

'If that is what you wish to believe. However, the truth is, I work for the SOE.'

'What is this SOE? Why does everyone speak initials? It is most confusing. Flora tells me about ITMA and ENSA – I am so easily confused.'

Rather than laugh at Anya's comment, Ruth sat opposite the woman, lacing her fingers together as she thought carefully about her next words. She would have preferred to remain at her own office, but Kenneth had wanted to meet them here; he had some strange ways, but she went along with him most of the time rather than argue. There were enough problems in the world without her acting up because she didn't like this dusty, impersonal room with its old desk, unmade fire and out of date calendar on the wall.

'Anya, what I am telling you must go no further than this office; in fact, you will be expected to sign a document to that effect . . .'

'I don't understand.' Anya looked around the room and for the first time focused on a man who had come in with them and was now standing by the door, smoking a pipe. She turned back to Ruth. 'Why do you want this of me?'

'Because, Anya, you are very important to the safety of this country and also the safety of your homeland,' Ruth started to explain. Anya's eyes grew wide with astonishment. Ruth continued, 'The SOE stands for the Special Operations Executive, Mr Churchill's secret army. We believe you can identify a woman who is collaborating with the Germans. We want you to confirm her identity and we can do the rest.'

Anya shook her head in denial. 'I know the same people that you know: Flora, Rose, Miss Tibbs, Lily, Katie, and people we sit with in the tunnels during air raids . . . Are you saying one of those is a col– a collab—'

'A collaborator,' the man with the pipe said as he came closer, perching himself on the edge of Ruth's desk. 'No, Anya, it is not one of your friends – it is someone from your past.'

'Who are you to know of my past?' she spat back at him.

'Anya, this is one of my colleagues, Colonel Kenneth Parry,' Ruth explained. 'He can tell you more.'

Anya looked between Ruth and the tall, thin man with unkempt salt and pepper hair, whose pipe seemed almost glued to his lips. She noticed how scruffy he looked, in a sagging jumper that had seen better days, with fraying cuffs and darned elbows. She shook her head wildly and got to her feet, her chair scraping on the linoleum floor. 'I'm not sure I wish to know. I will go home now, if you do not mind? I promise not to say a thing about this.'

'Please, Anya, identifying this woman would bring the war to an end so much sooner. You have no idea how important this is.'

Anya chewed on her fingernail as she thought about what Ruth was telling her. 'If I was to do this for you, will you find my Henio and bring him home to me?'

Ruth looked to Kenneth, who had started to puff on his pipe. He nodded his head. 'We will do our very best.'

She sat down again, ready to make her point. 'Your very best is not good enough. I want him home to Ramsgate alive, or in his coffin so I can grieve, and our son has a place to visit where he can say his prayers by the grave of the father he has never met.'

Ruth reached across the desk and squeezed Anya's hand. She tried not to think of all the women she had sent away who had never returned. How would she face her sister-in-law, Rose, if Anya died on this mission?

'I promise I will do my utmost to help Alexsy by getting both of his parents home to him safely. Will you take a short journey and identify the woman for us?'

Anya thought for a few seconds before saying, 'I will be proud to help Mr Churchill. Will I wear a uniform and stop working for Joe Lyons as a Sally?'

Kenneth laid his pipe down on the wooden desk and sat down in a vacant chair. 'Anya, we want you to go home and continue in your work as you usually would. It will be arranged for you to have training and you will be accompanied; you should have nothing to fear. We will, however, ask you to put your affairs in order, and quickly, as this mission will occur very soon.'

Anya frowned. 'You mean, I must find someone to care for my son in case I am killed on this mission and my Henio doesn't come back alive? Where am I to go?'

'It will be disclosed closer to the day you depart,' Kenneth explained.

'Am I to return to Poland? It can't be anywhere else as I do not have the language . . .'

'Please, Anya, don't ask, as we cannot tell you at this time,' Ruth begged.

'Then I will return to Ramsgate and carry on as normal until you call me.' She looked at her wristwatch. 'If I do not hurry, I will miss my train; I cannot expect Katie to care for my son overnight.' She stopped, thinking about what she had just said. 'Katie would make a good mother to my boy . . .'

Ruth picked up the telephone and asked for a driver to take Anya to the station as Kenneth shook her hand. 'I'll walk you downstairs,' Ruth said, taking her arm.

Outside, as they waited for the car, Ruth gave Anya a big hug. 'Katie is the ideal person . . .'

4

'I've not seen you in here before,' a smartly dressed young man said as a young Nippy handed him a menu.

'I can't say I've seen you in here either,' she replied cheekily, looking behind her to check she hadn't been overheard.

He nodded appreciatively before giving her a wink. 'What's your name, or are you a Gladys like all the rest?'

'Gladys?'

The man tutted. 'Dear me, you must be new not to know about the company you work for . . . I'll have a pot of tea, the Spam fritters followed by syrup pudding and custard,' he said, brushing away the proffered menu.

'My name is Jennie. I've worked for Lyons for a while,' she said, giving him a defiant look even though she was taken with his appearance. He wore a smart suit, which was different to most men, who were in uniform, and he smelt of soap as though he'd not long had a bath. She'd noticed as he walked into the teashop that he wasn't over tall and held himself confidently, as if he was used to women watching him.

'My, my, you're a cheeky one. I bet you keep your boyfriend on his toes.'

'I don't have a boyfriend; I live in digs and answer only to myself,' she answered, chin held high, not adding that no lad had ever asked her out.

He raised his eyebrows. 'So if I asked you out for a drink at the end of your shift, you'd not be interested . . . ?'

Jennie was caught off guard. She'd never been invited out by a young man before now. Although she kept herself clean and tidy, she always thought there were other Nippies ahead of her in the queue for the attentions of the male customers; who'd want to go out with a younger woman who wasn't yet twenty? Even so, she was proud of her shiny light brown hair and large brown eyes. There again, perhaps it was time she started to make more of herself and accept invitations to walk out with men.

'I'll get your order, sir,' she replied, giving him a smile before she hurried to place his order. 'That's a cheeky one,' she couldn't help saying to the cook, who was standing at the service station taking the Nippies' orders.

'You'll be for it if you get caught being over friendly with the male customers. You know Mrs Jones doesn't like that sort of thing going on during her watch,' the cook sniffed.

'Well, Katie isn't here,' Jennie retaliated. 'Besides, she knows me, so I won't get the sack. All the same, can you give him an extra dollop of custard? I want to keep him sweet in case I accept his offer . . .'

The cook tutted but made a note with the stub of a pencil on the order form Jennie had handed to her. 'I don't know, you girls will chase anything in trousers.'

Jennie ignored this. 'By the way, what is a Gladys?'

'It's what the waitresses used to be called here before the bosses decided they was to be called Nippies; but that was a good few years ago. What made you ask such a thing?'

'The young man mentioned it. He seems quite charming.'

'They are all charming when they're after something, so you be careful and mind he only gets extra custard.'

Jennie glared at her. 'I know how to take care of myself, thank you very much.'

'On your head be it,' the cook said. 'You'd best get his pot of tea over to him before he forgets you and starts chatting up one of the others.'

Jennie hurriedly did as she was told; was that how it worked when a man was interested in you? She didn't know much about courting and such like, although she was keen to experience such things. She wasn't about to tell the cook she was innocent of the ways of men; she would have to learn – and quick.

The man looked over the top of his newspaper, surveying the tearoom. It was a quiet day with not many staff on duty and he began to feel easier about entering the premises, but he was beginning to feel more comfortable. He'd not been back to the area in a while since leaving the town in a hurry several years before.

'Here's your tea and food, sir,' Jennie said as she placed a heavy tray onto the table and started to remove the silver teapot along with the hot meal. 'I'll bring your pudding when you have finished your first course so it's still nice and warm.'

'Thank you.' He placed his newspaper to one side. 'Tell me, is there a Nippy working here called Lily?'

Jennie frowned, wondering what Lily was playing at. The last she'd heard, there was an RAF pilot in her friend's life. 'Why do you ask?'

He could see she was miffed at him mentioning another woman. So she was interested in him . . . He'd found in the past that entertaining a Nippy made for a cheap night, as the women tended to have eaten at work. A glass or two of gin wasn't a great expense. 'No reason, she's a friend of the family; as I was passing, I thought I'd say hello. Not to worry.'

Jennie relaxed; the last thing she wanted was to attract the wrath of Lily. God forbid! She was grateful that Lily now worked at the larger teashop in Margate with the veranda that looked out over the beach. Here at the Ramsgate branch it was cosier, and she had more chance of talking to the young men who came in for a meal. 'I'll leave you to eat your food before it goes cold,' she said as he lifted his knife and fork. She picked up the silver tray to walk away. 'I finish my shift at five o'clock, if you fancy a walk and a bag of chips?'

He nodded, his mouth full of Spam fritter. A glass of gin and a quick fumble would be more to his liking; he'd soon bend her to his ways.

She waited for him to swallow his food. 'By the way, what's your name?'

'Tom . . . Tom White.'

Jennie felt lightheaded but happy. Tom had treated her like a queen as he escorted her into the pub, guiding her to a seat out of view of the bar while he looked about as if seeking someone. She was confused, until he explained that he wouldn't want her embarrassed by the landlord asking her age. Perhaps now she was courting she should think about dressing more appropriately and wearing a little make-up, she thought. Some of the other Nippies kept make-up and a change of clothes in their lockers as they went out straight from work. She would do the same from now on, as she wouldn't like anyone to think Tom was taking out an underage woman. She'd hoped they would take a walk and stop for chips as she'd suggested, as her stomach thought her throat had been cut; there hadn't been time to stop and eat at work as they were so short of staff. She just hoped Tom couldn't hear her tummy rumbling. After a glass of port quickly followed by gin, she began not to care.

'I think I ought to be going home,' she said as he helped her on with her coat. Although she was enjoying herself and feeling special for the first time in her life, she knew her landlady, Flora, was relying on her to come home and keep an eye on the children. Flora was going out with the other women of Sea View to their weekly bingo session, which was held in the tunnels beneath the town.

'There's no need, the night is still young. Why not come back to my hotel? I happen to have a couple of bottles of brown ale we can enjoy together,' he said as he tucked an arm around her and steered her out of the pub and up the street, pausing by an alleyway to pull her in and press her against a wall. He stopped any excuses with a hard kiss, leaving Jennie breathless. As much as she was enjoying her first ever kiss with a man, she pushed him away, laughing. She'd heard it never paid to be too keen.

'No, I have something I promised to do this evening,'

she said, straightening her hat and pulling her handbag and gas mask over her shoulder from where they'd slipped during the embrace.

'As long as I can see you tomorrow,' he said, breathing heavily against her as he tried to kiss her once more.

Jennie almost burst with excitement. He wanted to see her again! She would make sure to eat something next time and wear some make-up; she'd dash out during the day and see what there was to be had in Woolworths. They might even have stockings on sale if she was lucky. 'I'd like to see you again,' she said, feeling shy as she stood on tiptoe to give him a quick peck on the cheek. 'Would you mind walking me home? I'm feeling a little unsteady on my feet.'

He grudgingly agreed and walked along holding her close to his side, which made walking harder. She pointed the way. 'It's this way, up Madeira Walk; Sea View is at the top.'

Tom frowned. Where had he heard that name before?

They set off at a brisk pace. He was keen to deliver her home now he wasn't going to get any further with her. Besides, there was someone at home that would suit his needs, and she was older and worldly wise. Jennie was sweet enough, but sweet girls were hard to woo. He much preferred an older woman. His thoughts went to Lily; it had been an age since he'd seen her and although he wasn't the marrying kind, he knew he'd be happy with someone like Lily warming his bed each night.

'Nearly there,' Jennie said as they crossed the road. 'Oh, there's Flora. Hey, Flora, wait for us,' she called out, hurrying Tom towards her landlady. 'I want you to meet Flora.'

A feeling of dread ran through Tom and he held back. Now wasn't the time to come face to face with one of her fiercest defenders. Why, oh why had he come here with the idea of finding Lily?

'I really ought to get back; I have things to do. You'll be fine now you have someone to walk with,' he said, struggling from Jennie's grasp. 'I'll see you tomorrow.' He turned and hurried down the sloping Madeira Walk, disappearing from sight in the dark night.

'Oh, I wanted you to meet my boyfriend,' a disappointed Jennie said as Flora joined her from where she'd been crossing the top of the road towards Sea View.

'Boyfriend? When did this happen?' Flora asked, watching the retreating figure as he walked away. He looked familiar, but she couldn't be sure why. She cursed the blackout and lack of moon as it also meant she couldn't see enough of the departing man to tell if he was really who she thought he might be.

'This afternoon. He came into the teashop; he took me for a drink after work. We're going to meet again tomorrow.'

'That's nice, dear, but don't appear too eager or he may get ideas. Why not bring him to tea on Sunday? I'd like to meet him,' she said, feeling protective of the girl who had no family of her own. 'What's his name, is he from around here?' she asked, wondering if that was why she recognized him.

Jennie giggled and seemed to be unsteady on her feet. 'He used to be, but for now he's visiting. I do hope he comes back to live here,' she said with a loud sigh. 'His name? It's Tom White; he said his family knows our Lily. Isn't that funny?'

Flora was pulled up short and couldn't think of a word to say. It was as she had feared. Why was Tom White back in Thanet and what did he want?

5

'I'm home,' Flora called out as they entered Sea View, removing her coat and hanging it on a tall mahogany hall stand along with her gas mask and hat. She kicked off her shoes and stepped into a well-worn pair of slippers. 'That's better,' she sighed. 'Come along, Jennie, with luck the kettle is on the hob, and someone has peeled the vegetables.'

Jennie wrinkled her nose. 'We aren't having fish, are we?'

Flora laughed. 'I hope not. I know Mildred is generous with her catches, but even I am starting to grow fins, the amount we've eaten lately. Come on, let's go and find out,' she said, linking arms with the young girl and walking down the short flight of steps to the cosy kitchen.

'You couldn't have timed it much better if you'd tried,' Miss Tibbs chuckled from where she stood at the stove, swathed in one of Flora's crossover pinnies and stirring the large stew pan. 'Mildred here queued at the butcher's and managed to get some scrag end. We will eat royally tonight.'

'Even I was getting sick of fish,' Mildred said as she poured their tea from a large Brown Betty teapot. 'I do have to confess to bartering with the butcher,' she added wryly.

'No doubt the poor butcher's family have fish pie for their tea,' Anya said, looking glum.

'And no doubt they will eat it with relish; not everyone is as fortunate as we are to have someone like Mildred in our large Sea View family. We should be grateful,' Flora said, thinking she should not have joked about eating so much fish; she made a note to think before she spoke in future. 'Now, where are our babies?'

'Joyce has gone to collect Pearl from her Girl Guides meeting and will be back very soon. She said to tell you to save her some dinner and she still wants to go to bingo with you this evening,' Miss Tibbs said, waving the serving spoon. 'She'd best hurry, as I'm about to add the dumplings.'

'I've put Daisy down for a sleep as she was dead on her feet. I took her out on the boat for a couple of hours to tire her,' Mildred said. 'She ran me ragged.'

'My Alexsy is still at Captain's Cottage with Katie,' Anya said, looking at the clock on the wall. 'It is past his bedtime.'

'Once we've eaten, I'll drive over and collect him; someone will have to come along to help me,' Mildred said. 'I can't steer my van and hold a wriggling child.'

'I can come with you,' Anya said.

'No, you look all in, stay here and tell Flora about your day in London,' Mildred instructed her. 'Jennie here can help me. We'll only be fifteen minutes, then we can all go to bingo together while Jennie looks after the kids.'

'Please thank Katie for helping me out at late notice,' Anya said. 'She is worth her weight in stone.'

'Gold!' they all said together. Even Anya laughed.

'I need many lessons before I am English,' she said.

Flora patted her on the shoulder. 'Please never change, Anya. We love you as you are.'

To their surprise, Anya took a handkerchief from her pocket and began to weep into it. 'You have no idea how grateful I am for your caring,' she sniffed.

Flora gave her a hug. 'What's brought this on; have you received news of Henio?'

'No, it has just been a long day. I will feel better once I've cuddled my son and had a good night's sleep.'

Flora knew she needed to persist; there was something troubling Anya and she was determined to get to the bottom of it. 'Anya, I don't wish you to think that I'm interfering in your private business. It's just that you haven't been the same since Ruth visited; you seem deeply troubled. You know what they say: a trouble shared is a trouble halved.'

Anya looked away from Flora. 'If you will excuse me, I am going to change out of these clothes so that Alexsy does not make sticky marks on the jacket.' She reached for the handbag Flora had lent her for the day and removed her purse, scarf and handkerchief. 'Thank you very much for lending me your best handbag; I took great care of it,' she said, passing it to Flora.

'You are welcome to use it any time,' Flora said as she stroked the brown leather. 'Rose and Ben gave this to me for my last birthday; wasn't that generous of them?'

'You are so fortunate to have a caring daughter,' Anya said, not smiling as she stood up.

'Your son will be the same when he is older. That is the joy of motherhood, seeing our offspring grow up to be caring and loving people.'

Anya's face grew pale. 'I only hope . . .' She couldn't finish her words before hurrying from the room.

They'd not long finished their meal when the front door slammed closed and Joyce rushed into the room. 'We're back,' she said, almost collapsing into the kitchen as she gasped for breath. 'I never thought I'd make it in time; have the others left yet?'

'Left . . . ?' Flora asked, distracted by thoughts of Anya.

'Wake up, you look as though your thoughts are elsewhere,' Joyce smiled as she checked her dinner, which was waiting for her on top of a pan of boiling water on the hob. 'Oh delicious, I'm famished,' she added, using a tea towel to carry the hot plate to the table. 'I'll eat as quickly as I can, as we don't want to miss the first game. Would you like to share this, Pearl?'

Her daughter, who'd been intently watching Flora, peered at the plate of stew. 'No thank you. I had my tea before I went to Girl Guides, although I'd quite like to share one of your dumplings.'

Joyce went to get a dish for her daughter.

'Aunty Flora,' Pearl said earnestly, 'I hope you don't mind my asking, but are you going down with something? You don't look quite the ticket, as Miss Tibbs would say. I'm learning first aid at pack meetings. Can I help you?'

Flora tried to smile, giving a small chuckle. 'It's just been a long day and I'm feeling my age, but thank you for the offer. I'm sure a trip to the tunnels with your mum to play bingo will lift my spirits. Who knows, perhaps we will win something. Rumour has it there's a tin of pineapple in among the prizes.'

'Ooh!' Pearl said. 'Shall we have it with custard, or

perhaps a sponge cake . . . ?' She licked her lips in anti-
cipation.

'We've not even played a game yet, and you're dreaming
of what to do with the winnings. Here, sit and eat your
dumpling; I've added a spoonful of gravy for you,' Joyce said
as she put the food on the table and sat down to eat her own
meal. 'I do like that handbag. Have you been somewhere
nice to use it?' she asked, noticing Flora's bag on the table.

'No, I lent it to Anya as she had an important appointment.'

'I hope it wasn't to hear bad news about Henio. I can't
believe it must be almost a year since he went missing.
Having lost my husband when Pearl was so young is heart-
breaking enough, without having a child grow up not
knowing one of its parents.'

'I can't remember my dad,' Pearl chipped in, licking her
spoon clean. 'That was tasty. I'll go and change out of my
uniform before it gets grubby.' She jumped up and put her
bowl into the sink. 'And I'll do our washing up when I've
changed so you aren't late going out. Can I put your
handbag upstairs, Aunty Flora?'

'That's very kind of you, my dear; just leave it on my
bed. Will you knock on Miss Tibbs' door to tell her we'll
be leaving soon?'

'Will do,' the girl said as she gently placed the bag over
her arm. 'It smells of leather and perfume,' she said as
she unclipped the clasp and peered inside. 'Oh, you've
left a piece of paper,' she added, passing it to Flora before
skipping from the room.

'That daughter of mine – one minute she is a child and
the next a young woman. It saddens me that she cannot
recall her father . . . Whatever is the matter, Flora?' Joyce

asked, looking at the puzzled expression on Flora's face as she read the piece of paper Pearl had handed to her.

'It's a travel permit for Anya to travel to London – it's signed by my Rose's sister-in-law, Ruth.'

'Why would Ruth wish to see Anya in London when she's only just been down here? You mentioned you'd met her for lunch?'

'I've as much as asked her what's going on, but she's being so secretive.'

Joyce was thoughtful. 'I wonder . . . no, I'm being daft . . .'

'Please do say,' Flora begged. 'I really have no idea what's happening and I want to help Anya and Alexsy if I can.'

'When I applied for my job at RAF Manston recently, it was made clear to me that I would not be allowed to speak to anyone about my work or, come to that, even tell them where I worked. They even had me sign something. I thought it rather fanciful and told them so, as it was only for part-time work in the canteen. I don't think Hitler especially cares what we have on the menu, do you?'

Flora frowned. It had been a long day and she couldn't make head nor tail of what Joyce was getting at. 'Please explain . . .'

'Well, these days plenty of people are working in jobs that have to be kept a bit confidential, even if the work itself is quite ordinary. Perhaps Ruth is helping Anya to get some sort of new job in London and they can't tell you about it.'

'I suppose it could be something like that. It would be one thing if Anya seemed happy in herself, but she was in tears just now. Something isn't right about all this; and I know she won't want to ask for our help even if she needs it.' Flora squared her shoulders, a determined look on her face. 'I shall have to send my own spy to find out,' she said. 'My Rose will have to speak to Ruth; I'll put this back in my handbag for safety.'

'Good grief, Flora. I feel you are overreacting to Anya being a little quiet of late.'

'It's more than that; I can feel it in my waters. And I must see Rose anyway because of young Jennie.'

'Why? Rose manages the Margate teashop, so surely if Jennie has done something wrong it is Katie you should be having a word with?'

'It has nothing to do with her work, apart from the girl having met a man while she was on duty.'

'What man? You can't stop a girl Jennie's age from courting.'

'I can if it happens to be Tom White . . .'

'Bloody hell,' Joyce exclaimed, not noticing her daughter enter the room.

'Mother, language!'

Rose grabbed her mother to stop her in her tracks. 'Here, let me take Daisy,' she said, sweeping the child into her arms. 'Come on, let's hurry before we're blown to smith-ereens. Why you wanted to go back for your handbag I don't know; it's not like you to take your best handbag down into the tunnels. I'm not saying anyone will pinch it, but . . .' she scolded as they reached the entrance to the tunnels and were ushered inside.

'I've brought it along for a reason. There's something I want to show you,' Flora said as she did her best to catch up with Rose, who was striding along briskly. 'Once we've dropped off our things with the girls, along with Daisy, do you think we could find a quiet corner where we can talk?'

Rose stopped and turned so sharply that Flora nearly walked into her. 'Is there something wrong, Mum?' she asked, concerned.

'Not as such, although I'm worried about something and you may be able to help me.'

'All right, let's go down to our space in the tunnel and if no one else is there we can chat.'

They moved along smartly, at times almost propelled along by the stream of other families hurrying towards their places in the tunnels to settle down for what could be a long stay. The two women had only just found their bench and bunk beds when Miss Tibbs joined them, huffing and puffing. 'I was calling out to you,' she said once she could catch her breath. 'Didn't you hear me?'

'I'm afraid not, with all the commotion down here,' Flora said, helping the old woman clear a space where she could sit. 'I'll make a brew in a minute . . .' she said, digging about in a large shopping bag that had seen better days. 'Ah, here it is.' She pulled out a glass bottle with a cork stopper. 'If we're careful, there should be enough milk to last, even if we end up down here for a long stay.'

As if on cue, there was the earth-shattering sound of a bomb hitting its target not far away. Few people took any notice, as by now they were used to the sound of the bombing raids, although there was still the very real fear of emerging from the tunnels that ran under Ramsgate town to find their homes had been reduced to a pile of rubble.

'How anyone can sleep through this din,' Rose said, glancing to where an elderly man was snoozing in a deck-chair.

'He's as deaf as a post,' Miss Tibbs said, giving him a disdainful look. 'Honestly, he gives us old folk a bad name.' She delved into a battered tin they kept under the bunk. 'Did you bring any biscuits, Flora? This tin's almost empty.'

'Bless her, she'll never change,' Flora smiled as she helped Rose settle Daisy onto one of the beds. It was a little early for the child to go to sleep, but she was clearly tired out by all the activity. At last the two women sat down, and Flora sighed. 'Well, so much for our plan to play bingo.'

'What was it you wanted to talk to me about?' Rose asked, watching her mum pull out a paper bag containing home-made biscuits. Flora murmured that they were a little burnt around the edges but beggars can't be choosers, and tipped them into the tin. She glanced about her and then leant closer to Rose. 'Look in my handbag and tell me what you think; but keep it to yourself. I brought it with me for you to check; I'd not usually bring my best bag into the tunnels.'

Rose frowned. Whatever was her mother talking about? She lifted the bag from where it had been placed on the bunk bed and peered closely at it. There was lighting in the tunnels, but it was dull; they often found it was better to rely on candles or the light from their torches.

'There appears to be some scuffing on the underside, but that's to be expected. A little brown boot polish will cover it.'

'Oh dear, I never noticed that.' Flora stepped closer to examine the marks. 'I meant for you to open the handbag and check inside . . .' she said in a low voice, turning away to see if anyone was watching.

Rose snapped back the pearl clasp and looked inside. Apart from a piece of paper there was nothing to see, although she could smell the scent from Flora's powder compact. 'What am I looking for?'

'Read the piece of paper,' Flora hissed before calling hello to a neighbour who was setting up nearby.

'It's just a travel pass,' Rose retorted as she unfolded it.

'Oh, for goodness' sake,' Flora said, taking it from her and holding the typed side close to Rose's face. 'Read the words – but quietly,' she scolded, as Rose opened her mouth to speak.

A few seconds later Rose stared at her mother. 'Why has Ruth supplied Anya with a travel pass to go to London?'

'That's what I want you to find out. You're related to Ruth, so can you ask her?'

'Why can't you ask Anya?' Rose said. 'After all, it's her business, and it could be something to do with Henio.'

Flora shook her head. 'No, Anya would have told me if she'd heard news of Henio. This is something else. She's been acting strangely ever since that conversation she had with Ruth at the teashop.'

'Even so, surely we've no reason to interfere?'

'She was awfully upset earlier,' Flora said emphatically. 'I can't help feeling something out of the ordinary is going on. And if anything were to happen to her, with Henio still missing . . . well, what would become of little Alexsy? We're all Anya's got at the moment and I'd just like some reassurance that things are all right. Won't you please speak to Ruth?'

'I suppose so, but I can only do it when I have a good reason to go to London. Perhaps when Ben is home and has a twenty-four-hour pass. Last time we took in a show and stayed in a posh hotel, so we could have some time alone; but it could be weeks, probably months, before he is on leave again.'

Flora sighed. 'We've got to find out sooner than that, in case Anya needs our help.'

'What do we need to find out and who are you helping?' a booming voice asked from behind Rose, causing both women to almost jump out of their skins.

'Oh, Mildred, you gave me such a shock creeping up like that.'

Mildred gave a belly laugh. 'The pair of you were so intent on disagreeing with each other, I'm surprised you even heard me. I only popped out to check the boat hadn't been hit. Now, what are you two falling out about?'

Flora shared a glance with Rose and hoped her daughter wasn't about to spill the beans. She thought quickly and decided that although she wasn't keen on announcing it here, she had no choice. 'Tom White is back,' she said, raising her eyebrows.

'Good grief, what does that man want?' Mildred groaned. 'Didn't he cause enough problems for our Lily before he got the sack from Lyons?'

Rose made an effort to conceal her surprise, aware that Mildred would assume her mother had just been telling her the same news. She simply shook her head. 'Surely he knows he's not welcome in these parts. I thought he'd been carted off to the army when his so-called ailments were found to be fake? The ones that kept him from joining up?'

Mildred had gone red in the face. 'What happens now and who is going to run him out of town?'

Flora did her best to placate her. 'Mildred, dear,' she said, placing her hand on the fisherwoman's arm and hoping there was no grease on the sleeve of Mildred's boiler suit. Although she always took off her work overalls on arriving home at Sea View, Mildred seemed to feel it was sensible to wear them while down in the tunnels. 'Do please try to calm down. It will do you no favours to get het up over the situation.'

'How did you find out, Mum?' Rose asked. She was wondering if Tom was likely to walk into the Margate teashop and confront Lily. He had such a high opinion of himself, he was liable to do anything.

'Oh, well, you are bound to find out before too long. It seems he is courting our Jennie.'

'Oh, for goodness' sake,' Mildred spluttered with anger. 'He must be twice her age. Does she not know about what happened between him and Lily?'

'We tried to keep everything quiet, and as Jennie had only just moved in with us around that time, I doubt she knows anything. Young Mary's father has never been discussed and with Lily living at Captain's Cottage while Jennie is living with us, we don't really talk about Mary's parentage; it just hasn't come up in conversation.'

'If you don't have a word with Jennie, I will,' Mildred said. 'Goodness knows what will happen if he gets his dirty mitts on her. To my knowledge she's never had a boyfriend; this man will be the ruin of her. Where is she now? There's no time like the present for putting her straight.'

'She came down to the tunnels with us. We never did get to the bingo. She's further down the tunnel with Joyce and Pearl, so please, Mildred, be sensible and stay here with us,' Flora urged. 'Rose, we should have a little sing-song. It will lift our mood and we need that so much at present.'

6

'*I'll be seeing you in all the old familiar places . . .*' Rose closed her eyes as she sang her heart out, her voice echoing through the Ramsgate tunnels where, yet again, the residents were taking shelter. There had been a number of further air raids since the one that had interrupted the bingo outing a few days earlier. With every trip down into the tunnels, Rose felt it all the more important to do whatever she could to keep everyone's spirits up.

Rose was always moved by the familiar words of heartwrenching longing for those who dreamt of their loved ones on faraway shores. Her own thoughts were of her husband, Ben; although they'd been married since Christmas 1940, they'd only spent scattered weeks together while he served in the army helping to bring this war to a conclusion. His family involvement in the food business meant that he was often called upon to advise the War Cabinet on the distribution of food to the masses. So many people who worked in industry did similar work; in fact, Rose had heard that Joe Lyons and

Co. did it too, but that was only a rumour discussed behind closed doors.

Finishing the song, she opened her eyes to a round of applause and cheering. 'What would you like to hear next?' she called out as the elderly man sitting nearby at an old, battered piano started to flick through the sheet music on top of it.

'There'll Always Be an England,' called one woman, while another shouted, 'Can we have something to dance to?'

The pianist pointed to the open page and, after Rose nodded enthusiastically, played several chords. Everyone soon joined in as Rose jollied them along, singing '*Run rabbit, run rabbit, run, run, run . . .*' They sang even louder as bombs rained down nearby, with the elderly raising their fists upwards towards the German planes while youngsters skipped around, weaving in and out among women who'd started to dance.

'That done us the world of good.' Several women stopped Rose to thank her as she returned to where Flora had been singing along with Miss Tibbs.

'Phew, I've sung myself hoarse,' Rose said as she accepted the cocoa Flora poured into an enamel mug from a thermos flask she'd brought from home. 'That looks familiar,' she added, peering more closely at the flask as she settled down on a bench next to her mum. Like many people, they had made their part of the tunnels into as cosy a little home as possible. Some old curtains and pieces of wood partitioned off the bunk beds allotted to the Sea View residents and a small paraffin stove meant they were able to warm food or boil a kettle.

'It's mine,' Mildred was quick to say. 'It was left on my boat and I thought it would be of use at Sea View.'

'How strange, it looks like army issue. My Ben has one. Why would someone leave it behind?'

'They probably pinched it,' Miss Tibbs butted in. 'There's plenty of black-market stuff around these days.'

'Well, I never. We'd best keep it out of sight in case someone thinks we have links to the black market,' Flora said.

'You can use it whenever I don't take it with me for an overnight fishing trip.'

'It must be so lonely and cold on your fishing trips, Mildred. Have you thought about retiring and doing something else?' Rose asked as she sipped her drink.

'I've thought about it from time to time, when I'm battling the waves to get back to the safety of Ramsgate harbour, but fishing is in my blood; I'd not know what to do with myself. Perhaps you could take me on as a Nippy?' Mildred chuckled.

'You would have to wear a uniform and smart footwear for a start. I couldn't have you turning up for work in your wellington boots, reeking of fish. Somehow, I can't see you as a landlubber. We would have to style your hair; perhaps give you a perm,' Rose added, warming to the subject as Mildred started to scowl. They all loved Mildred as she was: slightly overweight with short, greying hair and a stubborn streak. She was reliable and a friend to them all.

'I prefer to stay as I am, thank you very much.'

'Perhaps you're right. I adored coming out with you on your boat when I was younger, apart from when the waves were choppy.'

'And you were violently sick, so we had to come back to port so I could hand you over to your mother,' Mildred said as Flora raised her eyebrows.

'I feel quite queasy just thinking about it. Now, shall we play a game of cards to pass the time? But no gambling, Mildred . . .'

It was much later when the friends made their way back up the road to Sea View. 'Thank goodness the house is in one piece. I can't stop the fear that one day our home will be a pile of bricks and memories,' Flora shuddered.

'Don't even think about it,' Rose said. 'But if it should happen, you can move in with me – you as well, Mildred, and Miss Tibbs, I'll make room for you all. Pegwell Bay doesn't seem to attract as many air attacks as Ramsgate.'

'I'd rather sleep on my boat if it's all the same to you,' Mildred said, turning to peer out to the harbour to see if the *Saucy Milly* was safe.

Flora delved into her bag for the door key as they reached the top of Madeira Walk.

'Is that someone sitting on the doorstep?' Mildred demanded suddenly.

'Well, I'll be blowed!' Flora said as she crossed the road to greet Ruth. 'Hello, Ruth, we didn't expect to find you here. Why didn't you take shelter?' she asked, kissing the younger woman on the cheek before giving her a hug. 'How is your mother?'

'Mother is fine, she's up in Scotland with her grand-children, and doing her bit, as they say,' Ruth replied, producing a packet of Player's cigarettes and offering them around before lighting her own. 'I could kill for a drink; it would challenge the patience of Job sitting through an air raid on your doorstep,' she laughed, although her hand shook as she took a deep drag on her cigarette.

'You mean you've been here for . . .' Rose started to ask,

amazed at how chic Ruth looked in an olive-green silk dress than fitted her to perfection. It was most certainly couture.

'. . . Hours,' Ruth chuckled, full of bravado.

Flora scolded her as she opened the door. 'You could have guessed where we were, so why not seek us out down the tunnels?'

Ruth got to her feet, shaking out the matching coat she'd been sitting on. 'You know me . . . I like to live dangerously, and I love a bit of fresh air.'

'But you could have been killed, you silly girl,' Miss Tibbs said, tapping her on the arm. 'We had a lovely sing-song in the tunnels as well as a mug of cocoa; there would have been plenty if you'd joined us.'

Ruth shrugged her shoulders. 'Not to worry, I'm here, and no damage has been done. Let me help you get the kettle on, Flora,' she said, ignoring Mildred's shocked expression.

'I'm not saying it's not nice to see you,' Flora said as she checked through a bag she kept handy in case of air raids before repacking it ready for the next time. 'But why are you here? And do you plan on staying overnight? I do have the box room spare; it's not much but you're welcome to it. I've only got to put fresh sheets on the bed.'

'Don't bother on my account; there will be a driver picking me up in two hours. I only came down to Ramsgate to have a word with Anya. Is she not at home?'

Mildred shook her head. 'She's still at work, like most people, although I would think she spent most of the afternoon in the cellar of the teashop. She has a late shift so I'm afraid you'll miss seeing her, unless you would like to go there? I can give you a lift in my van, or there's a bus to Margate. However, it won't get you there and back before your driver collects you,' she added.

'That would be delightful, thank you, Mildred. I'll just have a cup of tea and a biscuit with Flora and then I'll be ready to go, if that suits you?'

Flora could not believe what she was hearing. 'You do know that Mildred's van is used to carry her catches once she's been fishing?'

'It's dirty and greasy as well,' Miss Tibbs joined in, looking the smartly dressed Ruth up and down.

'A little bit of muck never hurt anyone,' Ruth said. 'Can I help set out the cups?'

'No tea for me. I want to clear out the front seat to make room for madam here,' said Mildred as she left the women to their tea.

Miss Tibbs was soon snoozing in her armchair by the stove, and Flora took the opportunity to have a few words with Ruth. 'I hope you don't mind me asking – it's only because I care, and you can tell me to mind my own business if you wish . . .'

'Goodness, this sounds serious,' Ruth chortled. 'Fire away.'

Flora wiped her hands on her apron and sat across the table from Ruth. 'It's Anya. I'm so worried about her. She's not said anything to me, but I'm aware that she went to London the other day and met you while she was there. No, please don't make any excuses,' she said, before opening her handbag and producing the travel pass as Ruth opened her mouth to speak. 'I can only assume this has something to do with Henio being missing for so long. She says very little – it's her way of coping – however, if you let me know whether there is bad news, I'll do my best to be there for her.'

Ruth was silent for a few moments, trying to choose the right words. 'You have an extremely tight community here at Sea View; it is rather like a large family with multiple generations, and I envy that. The last thing I want to do is walk in and disrupt this happy environment, but there's a war we need to win, and I want you to understand that whatever happens in the months ahead, it is for the good . . . I'm sorry I cannot say any more than that. In fact, my boss would have my guts for garters if he knew I'd spoken with you.'

Flora was thoughtful, taking in what Ruth had said; or rather what she hadn't said. 'I take it, then, that this has nothing to do with Henio being missing in action?'

'All I will say is that from what I've heard, everything is being done that can be done to trace Henio's whereabouts. If we have any news, good or bad, Anya will be the first to know, and I will tip you off that she needs the support of her friends more than ever.'

Mildred knocked on the back door before stepping into the kitchen. 'I'm ready to set off for Margate if you are, Ruth?' If she noticed any tension in the air, she didn't say so.

'Good grief, is that the time? Thank you so much for the tea and chat,' Ruth said as she collected her coat from a hook behind the door that led to the hall. 'My driver may be knocking on your door before I get back from going to see Anya. If that is the case, will you tell him I'll be as quick as I can and to wait for me?'

'Your driver – yes, of course,' Flora assured her, although there was the tiniest hesitation in her voice as she said it.

'You're an angel,' Ruth said before hurrying after Mildred.

*

'I take it you are not here to give me news of my husband?' Anya said, as she looked up from serving a customer to see Ruth standing at the other side of her counter.

Ruth allowed a woman behind her to be served before leaning over the counter, keeping her voice low. 'I need to speak with you – it's urgent. Is it possible for you to take a few minutes off?'

Anya had a few words with the other Sally working alongside her before leading Ruth towards Rose's office. 'Rose isn't on duty so we will take the liberty of using her office,' she said, closing the door behind them and pointing to a seat. 'It is best we sit, as we won't be spotted as easily through the window.' She nodded towards the large window that looked out over the restaurant and the Margate seafront beyond. 'Are you here with news of Henio, or is it something to do with what we discussed in your office?'

'I'm sorry, I don't have news . . .'

Anya nodded her head thoughtfully. 'Perhaps people should be given a hard push. I do not think I am the only wife waiting to hear if her husband is alive or dead. Do these men not realize this fact?'

Ruth tended to agree with Anya, but her loyalty to those above her caused her to hold back. 'Believe me when I say, I will do all I can for you.'

'So, you are here to give me more information about the task you wish me to undertake?' Anya said, looking directly into Ruth's eyes.

'I am. However, I must insist that you be more careful about what you are about to do. It is imperative your journey is kept a secret.'

Anya frowned. 'You speak as if I have told all and sundry? I can assure you I have spoken to no one. If you do not believe me, go find someone else to carry out your dirty deeds. Has someone told you otherwise?'

'Somebody who is quite trustworthy has discovered that you travelled to London to meet me and they're curious as to why,' Ruth said, keeping her tone pleasant so that Anya wouldn't feel she was being scolded.

'I do not understand . . .'

Ruth sighed. 'You left your travel pass inside the handbag Flora lent you.'

Anya was shocked. 'Then I hold my hands up and admit I did wrong. I will be more careful next time.'

'So, there will be a next time?'

'Yes. I owe it to my son, for him to grow up in a free world. If my Henio can put his life on the line, then so can I. You must promise me one thing.'

Ruth felt relieved. She knew there was no one else who would be capable of carrying out this task; if Anya refused to help them, it would fail.

'I have chosen someone I would like to care for my son,' Anya continued, 'and to bring him up in a respectable household. Can you assure me this will be done? I would also like this person to care for him while I am carrying out your orders.'

'Flora would be the perfect person to care for Alexsy; she has a big heart and open arms.'

'No, as I said before: as much as I love Flora, it is Katie I want to be the mother to my child. Katie is a respectably married woman, and my thoughts are that she may not be able to have children. If anything happens to me and I do not return from wherever you plan to send me, my gift to Katie would be my son to bring up as her own child; she would help him to grow into a thoughtful, respectable young man. And she would also be able to tell him about his true parents and how they laid down their lives for England, his new home.'

It took all of Ruth's strength to stop herself from dissolving into tears, or throwing herself at Anya and hugging her tightly. Anya was facing the task ahead with such remarkable fortitude. Even before she knew exactly what was expected of her, she was looking to the future, something many of Ruth's operatives had not done.

'I will make sure your wishes are carried out,' Ruth assured her, unable to say much more.

'There is something else: when I return, I do not wish my colleagues to ask questions and, being the gossiping women they are, they are bound to want to know where I've been.'

Ruth nodded. 'I've already thought of that, and I have devised a credible plan. We will arrange for it to appear that Joe Lyons has requested you go to London and help with training the new Sallys.'

Anya beamed. 'That is an excellent plan.'

Ruth suddenly felt so much better. Anya was thinking logically about what lay ahead, and the requests she had made were ones Ruth would easily be able to grant. 'We'll arrange for a letter to be sent here, to Rose, to make it official. After that you must speak to Katie, but don't give anything away to her; simply tell her that as you will be away in London for a while, you would like her to be your son's guardian.'

'I understand,' Anya replied seriously. 'Now, I must

return to my counter before the other Sallys complain about me and I get the sack. What would you do with me then?'

Ruth thought that it would in fact be quite a bit easier if Anya wasn't employed, as there wouldn't have to be so much subterfuge, but she kept this to herself. 'Once you are informed by Rose about your transfer to London, you will be issued with details of when and where to go. At that point I'll be in touch with more information about your training and, in time, the details of your mission.'

'Can you tell me more about this training?'

'All of our operatives are trained in the art of self-defence,' Ruth said carefully, not mentioning that Anya would also be taught how to kill the enemy if push came to shove.

'I'm not sure I will need to defend myself, as I will only be identifying someone and then returning home,' Anya said. 'Let me do this mission and then we can forget all about it.'

'We will see,' was all Ruth would say, knowing that Anya would have to follow orders and go into the field as a fully trained member of the SOE.

7
~

Flora had helped Miss Tibbs to her bedroom and settled her comfortably there, with her knitting near to hand and her private wireless set tuned in to *Workers' Playtime*. All the hours they'd recently been spending down the tunnels had tired the old lady out. Then she returned to the kitchen to clear away the last of the supper items. Rose had taken little Daisy out for a walk between the sudden rain showers and Flora had just decided it was the ideal time to settle down and read *The People's Friend*, when she heard a knock at the door.

If it had been Ruth returning with Mildred, her lodger would have used her own key; and they were more likely to have entered through the kitchen entrance via the small back garden. No, it was most likely Ruth's driver turning up as expected, ready to collect her and drive her back to London. With a reluctant glance at her unread magazine, Flora went to the front door, conscious of a faint flutter of apprehension that she firmly repressed. She resisted the impulse to remove her functional apron and tidy her hair at the mirror.

'All right, I'm coming,' she called out as the driver knocked for a second time. 'For two pins I'd make you wait out there in the rain,' she sighed as he started to knock again. Turning off the hall light before pulling back the blackout curtain, she opened the door, glaring at the man on the doorstep.

'That's no way to welcome an old friend,' a familiar voice said.

Flora sighed as she took in the sight of him standing in the miserable early evening gloom. 'John. I did wonder if it might be you coming to collect Ruth.'

'None other,' he said as he stepped over the threshold.

Flora looked up at him standing in her doorway, tall and broad-shouldered. Even in the poor light she could make out the colours of his brown hair and warm hazel eyes. Her heart was already starting to melt, and she reprimanded herself for being so weak. 'You'd best get yourself inside so I can draw the curtain and turn on the light,' she said, turning her eyes away.

She wasn't sure if she was angry with John, or simply disappointed that the friendship they'd had at one time had petered away and they'd never spoken since. 'Come down into the kitchen and dry yourself off. It's warmer there,' she said, ushering him ahead of her. She did pull off her apron and run her fingers through her hair, telling herself she'd have done the same whoever the visitor had been.

John crossed over to the stove to warm himself. 'You'd have thought the weather would be warming up a bit by now,' he said, rubbing his hands together.

'It was chilly down the tunnels today,' Flora replied, going through the motions of laying out her best cups and teapot rather than look him in the face and put into words the question she'd wanted to ask him for over a year. 'Sit yourself down,' she said, nodding towards the armchair set by the coal fire stove while she carried the tea tray to the table, taking a seat as far away from him as possible.

The room fell silent, the only sound being the coals as they settled in the stove. The air seemed thick with unsaid words.

'Look, Flora . . . I meant to contact you, I really did. Then, as time moved on, I . . . I . . .'

'You thought it would be better to keep away? I thought we were friends, John. Even if you no longer cared for me, didn't we still have a good friendship?' Flora looked at him properly for the first time, noting the lines around his eyes and a face that was thinner than she remembered. 'You know I picked the telephone up endless times, thinking of ringing you, before putting it down again. Think how that made me feel – a woman running after a man. Women aren't supposed to do that. You could have said you didn't care . . . if you couldn't face me, a note would have sufficed,' she managed, before her throat started to constrict and the words refused to come. She picked up the teapot and poured their tea, her hand shaking so violently that the hot liquid slopped into the saucers.

'Here, let me,' he said, taking it from her and filling the cups before pouring milk. 'Just as you like it,' he smiled, sliding the cup and saucer towards her.

'You remembered that at least.'

'Please, Flora, I can explain. Let me do that,' he begged, impulsively moving down from the armchair to kneel in front of her.

'After all this time? Let's just leave it, eh?' she asked, feeling her heart flutter at his closeness. 'Let's just say hello when we bump into each other and leave it at that . . .'

'Oh, this damned war,' he said as he reached out to her.

'We're home,' Rose called from the back door. Entering along with Daisy, she made enough of a commotion for John to get safely back up and return to the chair by the stove, where he picked up his tea.

Daisy rushed to hug Flora while Rose beamed at John. 'Hello, stranger, long time no see. Is there any more tea in that pot? I know, I'll make a fresh one,' she said as she tuned in to the highly strung atmosphere in the room. 'Daisy, tell Mummy what we've been up to. We've had such fun watching the boats in the harbour until the rain started, then we hurried to the teashop and had a milk-shake each.'

'Toast,' Daisy said shyly, watching John while holding onto Flora's arm.

'Katie gave her some buttered toast; it was such a treat.'

'She's grown,' John said, smiling down at the child.

'It happens with children if you don't see them for a while,' Flora answered, noticing how shocked Rose looked at hearing her speak so sharply. 'John is here to collect Ruth; she's gone over to the Margate teashop to see Anya.'

John stood up, preparing to go. 'It would be best if I collected her from there, but thank you for the tea. It was good to see you again, Flora.'

'No, wait,' Flora said, causing him to stop in his tracks and look at her with hope in his eyes.

'What I mean is . . . don't go . . . Mildred will no doubt be driving Ruth back by now and you may miss her.'

'Mum's right,' Rose said. 'Here, have a fresh cup of tea and warm yourself; you look drenched to the skin.'

It was only then that Flora noticed John was still wearing his wet coat. 'I'm sorry, I should have dried your coat for you. Give it here and I'll lay it over the back of a chair. It won't take long to dry in front of the stove.'

As she draped the coat over the chair it was all she could do not to hold it against her face, breathing in the smell of John's tobacco and his shaving soap. Why, oh why, did he have to come back into her life, if only for a couple of hours? She'd done her best to forget him after being rejected, and now here he was and all the old feelings of longing had returned.

'Damn you, John Bentley,' she murmured to herself.

'Mum, whatever is going on?' Rose asked later, after John had left with Ruth. 'I've never seen you look so distraught. You've never really said why he disappeared from your life; I thought perhaps the pair of you had decided to remain friends and not pursue a romance . . . ?'

Flora held her arms out to Rose for a hug, and Rose held her mother tight.

'My goodness, I feel better for that,' Flora said after a few moments, taking a handkerchief from the sleeve of her cardigan to wipe her eyes. 'Isn't it supposed to be the mother comforting her daughter, not the other way round?'

Rose was a little tearful herself; she didn't like to see her mum so distressed. She led her over to an armchair before sitting on the arm and stroking Flora's head. 'Tell me all about it, please.'

'There's really nothing to tell you. It was as if he vanished.

We had that lovely Christmas and your wedding – after that, I never saw him again. As you know, when Ben's mother came to stay, she travelled by train and didn't require a driver; John was never mentioned. You know me, I'm not one to force myself on people, and let's face it, at my age I'm rather long in the tooth for romance. Perhaps he found someone else, someone younger. I plucked up the courage to ring him several times, but I always ended up putting the receiver down before anyone answered. I feel such a fool.'

'Oh, Mum, you're not a fool. You are just a woman who fell in love; and don't say otherwise,' Rose added.

'Let's forget all about him, shall we?' Flora said, forcing a smile onto her face.

'If you say so,' Rose replied, although she felt John had been good for her mum and would have liked nothing more than to see them as a couple. He had seemed strong and dependable, and that was something to be admired. He was hardworking, too, running his own garage and also chauffeuring Lady Diana. Rose decided she would leave it for now and have a word with Ben whenever she saw him; he and John Bentley were good friends, so he might have an idea of what was going on. 'Now,' she said to her mum, 'tell me what was so important that Ruth had to go rushing off to Margate to speak with Anya? Surely she could have waited for her to come home at the end of her shift. Do you happen to know what's going on yet?'

Flora fell silent.

'Mum?'

Flora shrugged her shoulders; it had been a tiring day. 'I don't know what to think any more. Let's leave it for now, eh?'

'If you say so; but I'm going to ask Mildred if she knows anything. After all, she drove Ruth to Margate and back. I'll go and ask her right now, before she either turns in for the night or goes off fishing. She keeps such odd hours of late. Do you think she's up to something?'

'Like what?' Flora asked, too drained to give much thought to Rose's question. 'It's her occupation and she works with the tides.'

'I don't know . . . perhaps she's dabbling in the black market, or up to no good?'

'Oh, for goodness' sake, you have such fanciful thoughts at times,' laughed Flora.

'I'll ask her all the same. I'm glad I made you laugh, though.'

'I'm glad too, darling.'

'It's only me, Mildred. Can you spare a couple of minutes?' Rose asked, tapping on Mildred's bedroom door.

'Come along in,' Mildred said as she opened the door dressed in a flowing Japanese kimono. 'There's no need to look at me like that. Just because I own and work on a fishing boat, it doesn't mean I can't dress like a woman sometimes. This was given to me by a good friend many years ago . . .' She held out the silky fabric and began twirling around, then staggered against her bed. 'Oops!'

Rose didn't know whether to laugh or be shocked; she'd never seen Mildred act this way. 'Have you been drinking? And what's all this on your bed?' she asked, looking at a heap of clothes and other items strewn across the counterpane. As a rule, Mildred's room was as spick and span as her boat, with a place for everything and everything in its place. The single bed was always made, and a small bookcase held well-thumbed copies of the classics. On the walls were oil paintings of coastal views.

'I may have had a little something,' Mildred said, picking up a bottle of brandy from her dressing table. 'Would you care for a tipple?'

'Oh, why not . . . it would finish the day off nicely. Can I help you put this all away? Otherwise you'll never be able to get into bed.'

'I'm having a sort out; I should've done it ages ago. Much of this will have to go,' Mildred said, putting a hand on her hip as she surveyed the heap of clothing.

'Whatever made you decide to have a sort out this late in the day?'

Mildred shrugged her shoulders. 'I felt it was time to sort out my life.'

'Has anything happened? . . . You're not ill, are you?'

Mildred almost choked as she started to laugh and couldn't stop. 'I'm as fit as a fiddle!'

'But all of this . . .' Rose said, pointing to the mess in what was normally a tidy room.

'I've decided I want to travel light from now on, in case . . .'

'In case what?'

'In case someone has to clear up after me when I'm no longer here,' Mildred replied as she spied a small pile of freshly laundered overalls. 'These I do need to keep.'

'But you're not that old; what are you, fifty, fifty-one?'

'I'm fifty-eight. But it's not the years you have to count, but how you feel inside. Why, I'm no more than thirty-six in my head.'

Rose shook her head. 'I have no idea what you're up to,

but if I can help then please do ask me. You know, Mum can pass on any clothing you no longer need; with so many people being bombed out, the WVS is only too glad of clothing to distribute.'

'I'll keep that in mind. Now, what did you want to see me about? I'm not daft; you don't usually visit me in my room,' Mildred grinned as she poured a drink for them both before clearing a place for Rose to sit down.

'Mum and I are worried about Anya . . .'

'It seems to me you worry too much.'

Rose ignored Mildred's jibe. 'She seems so out of sorts of late. At first, we wondered if she might have had bad news of Henio; but then we've noticed Ruth has been to see her a few times. We're starting to think something odd is going on and Ruth might be involved, but none of it makes much sense . . .'

Mildred began picking up items of clothing from the heap on the bed and folding them. She didn't say a word.

'I wondered . . . as you drove Ruth to the Margate teashop this afternoon, whether she might have said anything . . . about Anya, I mean . . .'

'Have you asked Anya?'

'No . . . she's not home from her late shift yet. It's hard to know what to ask her. She seems to hold her cards so close to her chest.'

'I suggest you speak to her directly, because if I say anything, I may be betraying a confidence. And don't even ask,' Mildred added, seeing a light in Rose's eye.

'Well, Mum will have to talk to her. I need to sort out my own pile of laundry for the morning. Goodness, there's always so much to do; I never seem to catch up.' Rose stood up to go. 'Good luck with your sorting out,' she said, glancing again at the mess on the bed.

Mildred was thoughtful as she watched Rose leave the room.

'May I have a word, Flora, if it is not too late?' Anya asked as she returned to Sea View later that evening.

'Of course you can. Would you like a hot drink?' Flora asked, starting to get up from the armchair where she sat knitting a cardigan for Lily's daughter, Mary.

'No, not for me. I am full up to here with tea and coffee,' Anya said, waving her hand up to her forehead. 'You look tired, Flora. Has it been a long day for you also?'

'You could say that,' Flora replied, trying not to recall John standing on her doorstep and how much her heart had ached at the sight of him. 'What is it you would like to talk to me about?'

'I may have to go away for a while, to London,' Anya said, 'but I'm unable to take Alexsy with me. I would like to arrange for him to be looked after.'

'Alexsy will be well cared for with us, for as long as you need him to be.'

'No,' Anya said abruptly. 'I have given this much thought and, with there being much bombing in London, I need to make long-term plans in case my Henio never returns and something happens to me. I feel Alexsy should go to Katie as she will have the time to bring him up as her own son . . . he would be my gift to her and Jack,' she said, looking away from Flora so as not to show the tears that were threatening.

'Oh, Anya . . . I don't know what to say. Of course, Katie would make the perfect mother for Alexsy, even if only for a week or so. May I ask what you will be doing while you're away?' Flora asked.

Anya pulled herself together and looked Flora in the eye. 'I will be doing some work for Joe Lyons, training the Sallys.'

All kinds of questions occurred to Flora in response to this. Why had Rose, as Anya's manager, not seemed to be aware of any such plan? And did the Sallys, the women who served at the teashops selling bakery items, really need such dedicated training that staff would be relocated in order to provide it? At that moment, though, it seemed best not to confront Anya with any of this.

'I will help all I can,' she said. 'Be assured Alexsy will be in safe hands. Your room will be kept for you and please don't worry about the rent. Whatever you are doing, we want you to come back to us safe and sound.'

For the first time since the two women had known each other, they hugged, both of them knowing there were secrets that could never be shared.

8

Rose looked around her; she always enjoyed this time, when staff were occupied in the kitchen preparing for a busy day ahead while the Nippies checked each table was correctly laid ready for when diners started to arrive. At the counter, Anya and the other Sallys were laying out the first delivery of fresh bread, pies and cakes sent from the London bakery department. Rose was proud to work for Joe Lyons' company, who by hook or by crook managed to stock the many teashops and Corner Houses around the country, despite rationing and shortages. True, the menu wasn't as extensive as it had been before the war started, but all the same the staff at Lyons did their utmost to ensure the show went on as before.

A thought crossed Rose's mind and she hurried outside to check the windows, making a mental note to book the window cleaner for a visit. Really, what they needed was to have him commit to a regular schedule of cleaning, as she'd hate someone from head office to drop in and find the teashop not looking its best.

'Why don't you ask Flora if she knows someone who could clean the windows? The company sign could do with a polish as well,' Lily said, coming up behind Rose. Gazing up at the 'J. Lyons and Co. Ltd' sign, with its gold lettering on a cream background, she tutted. 'It's all that dust and muck from the air raids, along with the sea spray . . .'

'At least the building is still standing. I fear one day the bus will turn the corner and all that will be here is a pile of rubble.' Rose shuddered.

'Or worse still, it could happen while we're inside the building along with the customers,' Lily said. 'I'd best get inside and put my uniform on before the manageress catches me. I've heard she can be a tyrant.'

Rose shook her head and smiled as she watched her friend enter the teashop. She was used to Lily pulling her leg since she'd been promoted to manageress, but overall, her friend didn't abuse her position and was a hard worker. Making another note to place a telephone call to her mum and ask if she knew a window cleaner who hadn't yet been called up to serve, she went inside. In ten minutes the teashop would be open and she'd yet to inspect the Nippies in their uniforms; regardless of there being a war on, standards shouldn't drop.

'She's coming,' one of the younger Nippies whispered as Rose entered the staffroom to see them all shuffling into a line, ready for her instructions.

'Good morning,' she smiled, putting them at their ease. 'I'm pleased to say we have a full complement of staff with no one off sick, so you can all continue with your usual duties today. Anya, was the order correct?'

'Everything was delivered as requested,' Anya replied, handing over a stock sheet. 'I have ticked everything off.'

'In that case, you can return to your counter,' Rose replied, giving a nod to Anya and the other part-time Sallys. She had no need to check them, as Anya was very strict with her fellow counter staff; they never had a hair out of place and always looked smart in their dark blue dresses.

Rose next walked along the line of Nippies, who showed her their nails and turned around so she could check their black lisle stockings were free of holes and runs. 'Very good, ladies. I don't need to remind you there is a nail brush over by the sink, and in the drawer of the table there is black darning thread for your stockings as well as red thread to secure any pearly buttons that have worked loose on your uniforms. We have a plentiful supply of aprons in case any should be dirtied during a shift. Lastly, keep your hair clean and brushed and your shoes polished. I'm proud of you all and want us to have the best Lyons teashop in Thanet. Now, let's have a pleasant day and keep smiling, as no one wants to be faced with a grumpy Nippy when they come here to enjoy a meal.'

Lily joined Rose as the other Nippies headed out to their workstations. 'You'd best not let Katie hear you say we are the best teashop in Thanet,' she grinned.

'A bit of competition will keep us on our toes,' Rose chuckled. 'Oh, blast, I meant to ask one of the girls to tidy up the cellar in case we have another air raid. Would you . . . ?'

'Of course I will, but do ask someone to keep an eye on my tables in case customers are sitting there waiting to be served.'

'Take a tray with you, as there's bound to be cutlery and God knows what else left down there.'

Rose cast an eagle eye around the teashop as she made

her way across the floor to her small office. Hopefully, if the weather picked up, they would be able to open the upstairs veranda that looked out over the sands, even if it was to view barbed wire and signs telling people to stay off the beach due to mines. She smiled as she thought of how Lily was adamant it was safe, and the army were bluffing; she wasn't going to be the one to test her friend's theory.

She had just sat down at her desk when one of the Nippies brought in a tea tray and the post. 'Thank you, Anna,' she smiled, reaching for the engraved letter opener Ben had given her. She ran her fingers over the wording that she never showed her staff. *To my Rose: I hope I never become a thorn in your side.* 'Oh, Ben, I long to see you – it's been far too long,' she sighed as she started to open the envelopes, beginning with the one from head office. She gasped as she read the letter inside informing her that Mrs Anya Polinski was to be sent to London for an indefinite period of time, to help train a new intake of Sallys.

'Oh gosh, why is this happening?' Rose said out loud. 'I'm already short on Nippies and now I have one less Sally; whatever am I going to do?' She sat with her elbows on her desk, holding her fingers to her temples, closing her eyes as she tried to think through the problem. This news had come right out of the blue – and why Anya? Opening her eyes and flexing her shoulders, she raised a hand to get the attention of a Nippy who was passing the window of her office.

'Yes, Mrs Hargreaves, did you want something?'

'Thank you, Fran, please ask Anya to come to my office once the queue for bread has shortened.'

'Of course, and would you like a fresh cup of tea?' the young woman asked, nodding towards the untouched tea on Rose's desk. 'It must have gone cold by now.'

'Please, but only when you have time; don't go out of your way just for me,' Rose smiled.

'I'll bring some biscuits as well,' the girl replied before scurrying away, which made Rose think how 'Nippy' was the perfect name for her waitresses.

Rose was sipping her fresh cup of tea and reading the letter from head office for the umpteenth time when Anya tapped on the door and walked in without waiting to be asked. 'You wished to see me?' she asked, looking worried as she spotted the letter in Rose's hand emblazoned with the Lyons heading.

'Take a seat,' Rose said, giving her a warm smile. 'I've received a letter from head office; they would like you to go to London to help train a new intake of Sallys. It seems to be happening in rather a hurry, as they would like you to start after Easter Monday and that is not long away. How do you feel about this? If you aren't keen, I can write and refuse the position on your behalf.'

Anya was quick to answer. 'I would enjoy the opportunity, thank you. Will you tell them I agree?'

Rose's eyes shot open in amazement; she had never seen Anya answer a question so quickly without chewing it over and asking lots of inconsequential questions. 'You do understand this will mean living in London for a few weeks, and you can't take Alexsy with you?'

'I understand, but it would be a good opportunity for me to help my adopted country.'

Rose thought that was a little strong; it wasn't as if Anya

was joining the forces. 'The letter doesn't say anything about the position being permanent. I will need to ask head office how long they expect you to be in London, as we'll have to find a replacement while you're away.'

'That is fair. Perhaps I should go back to my counter while you make enquiries? Thank you for being understanding,' Anya said, getting briskly to her feet and leaving Rose on her own.

Rose reached for the telephone on her desk and dialled the number shown on the letterhead. After a little while it was answered and she asked to speak to Mr Percival Montgomery, but was told he was not available. She quickly explained her reason for ringing and was promised that somebody would call her later in the day. Then, unable to settle, she again lifted the telephone receiver and dialled the number for Sea View.

'Hello, Mum, I'm glad I caught you; something has cropped up . . . No, it's nothing you should worry about, it's more . . . Well, I'm not sure what to think,' she said, going on to explain about the letter and Anya's attitude.

'But dear, this is all rather confusing, because Anya told me yesterday evening that she was going away.'

'Oh . . . ? We must have got our wires crossed,' Rose said. 'I really don't know what to think. Perhaps something was mentioned to Anya to sound her out the day we had the inspector visit. All the same, it is highly unusual for Lyons not to have let me know first.'

'I'm going to put my coat on and catch the bus to see you, so we can have a chat about this in your lunch break. I have something here I want to give you as soon as possible. It's a letter.'

Rose groaned. 'I hope it doesn't contain another problem.'

'I hope not, dear, as I recognize Ben's handwriting.'

Rose stopped herself from shrieking in case the diners heard her through the thin wall of the office. 'Oh, I wonder what he has to say?'

'If you get off the telephone and allow me to get on, I'll catch the bus that's due in five minutes; I'll be with you within the half hour.'

Rose busied herself working through the rest of that morning's post before heading back through the teashop, greeting familiar diners with a ready smile as she went to the door to place a card in the window advertising for serving staff. She prayed under her breath that at least one applicant would come forward before Anya left for London; otherwise she would be donning a uniform and working in the teashop herself. As a Sally. Much as Rose had enjoyed her time as a waitress, she now had far too much work to do as a manageress. She was also aware that trying to cover both roles herself was unlikely to go down well with the new area manager, whom she was yet to meet.

Rose's excitement grew as she waited for Flora to arrive, keeping an eye on the clock as she worked. What might Ben's letter say? . . . Perhaps he was coming home to work in England, which would mean she would see much more of him than she had in over a year. If that was the case, she would have to give their little cottage in Pegwell Bay a spring clean and make it welcoming for the master of the house. With her head full of ideas for brightening their home, she went back into her office to write them down. Of late she'd been staying with her mum at Sea View when on a late shift, rather than travelling the couple of miles further along the coast to an empty house; the buses were unreliable, especially if there was an air raid. It would be different with Ben back home . . .

She still had her head in the clouds, dreaming of having her husband home again, when the telephone rang. 'Lyons teashop, Margate, Mrs Hargreaves speaking,' she answered politely.

'Mrs Hargreaves, I am returning your earlier call requesting more information about the duration of Mrs Polinski's transfer.'

'Thank you for returning my call so promptly,' Rose replied, crossing her fingers. It would be all right if they only needed Anya for a matter of weeks; in that case, Rose might just be able to cope without taking on anybody new. 'It's just that we are understaffed now, what with so many women doing war work and our new area manager not having joined us yet. I feel rather out on a limb.'

'I do understand. Unfortunately, the most I can tell you is that Mrs Polinski's new position will be open-ended. It could be two weeks, or it could be two months . . .'

This wasn't what Rose wanted to hear. 'How am I to cope? I've placed enquiries with the labour exchange for new staff, without one application. So many women have been evacuated with their children or are chasing war work, which can pay double what they would earn here . . .' There was silence at the end of the line, making Rose wonder if she had gone too far in making her feelings known. At least they couldn't sack her with there being a staff shortage, she smiled to herself.

'I appreciate that this does make things difficult for you, Mrs Hargreaves, and I apologize for whisking Mrs Polinksi away, but she is perfect for the task in hand. May I suggest you liaise with your fellow manageress at the Ramsgate teashop and create a work rota? We can add a budget for overtime if any of your staff would like to work longer hours. When your new district manager arrives, they may have other ideas that will help you to manage the situation.'

Rose thanked the woman before hanging up, only then belatedly realizing that she didn't know her name. Feeling rather as though head office had passed the buck, she stepped out of her office to give Anya the news that her new position was open-ended.

'I just hope they allow you leave to come home and see Alexsy, otherwise he may forget what you look like,' she said, once she had passed on the rest of the information. As soon as the words left her lips, it occurred to her that they had been rather tactless.

Anya was adamant that she would take up the new opportunity. 'I will put my acceptance in writing,' she told Rose, before turning to help a customer who was asking about the availability of gypsy tarts.

'I need to escape for a little while,' Rose said when her mum appeared. 'We'll only be interrupted if we sit here in the teashop, even if we're in my office.'

'Let's take a walk along the seafront and stop for lunch somewhere,' Flora suggested. 'You are entitled to take a lunch break, you know,' she added, seeing Rose's troubled look. 'We have a lot to discuss, and I want your undivided attention.'

9

Ruth stubbed out her cigarette in an already full ashtray and straightaway lit another. 'This job is going to be the death of me,' she said to Kenneth Parry, who was puffing on his pipe as he lounged in a threadbare armchair in the corner of her office. 'Everything is going to plan; I just hope Anya is up to the mission. She's the only one capable of confirming our suspect's identity.'

'There must be somebody else,' he said thoughtfully, examining his pipe.

She passed a plate of biscuits to him, which he declined. 'Believe me, Anya is the only person from that woman's past life who can one hundred per cent identify her; the subject has completely reinvented herself in recent years.'

Kenneth nodded in acknowledgement. 'If we are certain it is her, then our next step will be to convince her she needs to work for us rather than enjoy being the conquest of a Nazi.'

Ruth agreed. 'She seems to be a tricky customer. I pray Anya is up to this.'

He let out a deep sigh. 'It's such a big risk, and her part in the mission must run smoothly or God knows what will happen. It troubles me that she's never done anything like this before, and I'm concerned about her not knowing the French language.'

Ruth reached for a biscuit, then remembered she had a cigarette in her other hand and replaced it on the plate. 'There will be someone else with her, a woman who I know is a reliable courier; I've used her a few times. Together they should be able to complete the mission. I have yet to explain everything to the courier but I've warned her she may be needed at a moment's notice. We'll wait until Anya has completed her training; she will be with us next week.'

'So much can go wrong. I've never felt so unsure of anything in my life; I don't even have a contact on the other side to meet them. Have you had any luck?'

'There is someone I can use. He'll be there to meet them and help if the going gets tough. He is important to the next part of the plan.'

'It doesn't seem enough,' Kenneth said. 'I'm considering cancelling this mission.'

'We can't do that,' Ruth pleaded. 'Think of how valuable it will be if Anya is able to identify the target.'

He chewed the stem of his pipe thoughtfully. 'She mustn't be involved in anything at all beyond making the identification. It could be dangerous for her, and for us, if she's found out.'

Ruth pushed her point home. 'Let's just say Anya knows our target very well, and if we can secure the target's confidence it could be invaluable in discovering more information about the Nazi Party. Her father is a scientist who is working for them . . . We've got to risk it, whatever the outcome,' she said through gritted teeth, pushing aside the thought of young Alexsy being left without a mother if anything should go wrong.

'You think this will go to plan? We've never worked at such short notice before.'

'I pray it goes to plan, as I know Anya's friends very well. One of them is married to my brother, Ben.'

'It's not the perfect situation. But of course, if you hadn't found out about Anya's background, we would not have been able to carry out this mission.'

Ruth felt a surge of pride; it was the first time she'd been praised since joining the department.

'I suggest you distance yourself from her friends,' Kenneth added, 'so that you can keep a clear head.'

'I'll do my best,' Ruth promised, feeling decidedly sick at the thought of what lay ahead. 'God, I could kill for a drink.'

'Let's sit here while you read your letter from Ben,' Flora said, indicating a wooden bench that faced out to sea. 'I'll knit for a while so as not to disturb you.' She took out a ball of wool and started to concentrate on her knitting.

'There's no need, Mum. I have no secrets to keep from you.'

'All the same, I'd prefer not to watch you read Ben's words; they're private between the two of you. It's quite pleasant here, isn't it? And only a short walk from the teashop. You should come out here more, it would do you good.'

Rose chuckled as she slit open the envelope with her finger, pulling out the single sheet of thin paper. She fell silent as she read her husband's words; the only sound was the crashing of waves onto the shore and the seagulls crying overhead.

Flora dared not look at Rose; was it good news, or would her daughter be disappointed? 'Knit one, purl one,' she breathed in and out. 'Please God, let it be good news. Knit one, purl one; please, please, please . . .'

'He's coming home,' Rose squealed with delight. 'Look, he says he is coming home; it's only for a short while, but I'll see him at long last.'

Flora completely forgot whether she was supposed to knit or purl and abandoned her knitting to take the letter now being flapped in front of her face. 'Why, this is wonderful news, and you will only have to wait a couple of weeks – although . . .'

'What have I missed?' Rose asked, seeing her mum's concerned face and taking back the letter. 'I know I will have to go to London to meet him, as by the time he travelled down here it would be time for him to leave again . . . we can use his mother's home while she is away, so we'll be alone.' She blushed at the thought of her first time with Ben, when they were alone in his mother's London apartment.

'It's just that this will be while Anya is away. Who will stand in for you at the teashop? I don't want to put a dampener on your happiness, but they are going to struggle with both you and Anya not at work, and already being short staffed . . .'

Rose turned pale. 'I can't go, can I? The teashop is my responsibility and if the new area manager turned up to find I'd abandoned my duties, I'd be sacked on the spot. Oh well, it was a lovely thought while it lasted.'

Flora stuffed her knitting back into her bag. 'There must be a way round this, let's not give up too soon. Can't Lily stand in for you? Surely she knows the ropes by now, as she's worked for Joe Lyons as long as you have.'

'It would still leave us short on Nippies and counter staff with Anya having gone to London. You know, I was surprised how quickly she accepted the appointment,' Rose said, going on to tell Flora what had transpired that morning.

'Honestly, Rose, I don't know what to think, with her so ready to rush off to London. My mind's in a whirl trying to fathom what is happening, and poor Alexsy left behind.'

'It does make you wonder what happens to all the children whose parents are killed in wartime.'

'Look no further than Sea View and our Daisy.'

Rose clamped her hand to her mouth. 'Gosh, how could I have forgotten Daisy? She's become such a big part of our family, I'd forgotten she lost her own family during a bombing raid when she was a baby. If anything should happen to Anya and Henio, you will have two adopted children to care for.'

'No, just the one. Anya was adamant that she would want Katie to take Alexsy. In fact, he is to go to Captain's Cottage and be cared for by Katie while Anya is away in London.'

'Meaning the Ramsgate teashop will be short staffed as well if Katie isn't able to go into work. It gets worse and worse.'

'You must speak to head office,' Flora said, looking concerned.

'Oh, Mum, I did just that before you arrived. They advised me to liaise with the Ramsgate branch to see if we could sort out a rota to share staff between us. Don't they realize our staff have families and commitments? Many of the women's husbands are serving overseas and they have sole responsibility for their children.'

'A lot of the children have been evacuated, but even so, it would be asking a lot of your staff. Let's go and have a cup of tea while we think about how we're going to get you to London to see your Ben. If we don't come up with anything constructive, I'll wear a Nippy uniform and do a few shifts myself. Perhaps we could talk Mildred into being a Sally . . .'

They both snorted at the thought of Mildred in a Sally's uniform, being polite to customers.

Rose became serious. 'That's something else I wanted to mention. When I went up to chat to Mildred last night, she was acting as if she was preparing for her own demise: clearing out her cupboards, talking about giving things away . . .'

'Don't you worry,' Flora said, tucking her arm through Rose's as they dashed across the busy road to a cafe, 'I'll have a word with her when we get home. She's probably just having a sort out to help the war effort. Do you fancy sharing a plate of chips?' she asked as they sat down at a table. 'It'll make a change from eating at your teashop.' She looked up at a chalked board on the wall of the cafe.

'I'd love to. I feel as though I can make sense of my thoughts when I'm away from work and have you to guide me,' Rose said, waving the waitress over to place their order. 'Let's have a fried egg as well.'

'You look a lot happier than you did earlier,' Lily said as she greeted Rose.

'Yes and no,' Rose replied. 'Can you come into my office for a minute or two?'

'Lead the way,' Lily said, giving a small curtsey. 'If you want a full report on what has happened in your absence, we had a case of a dropped tray and a full-scale tantrum when a child's mother wouldn't let him have an adult-sized portion of bubble and squeak. Apart from that, it has been very quiet.'

Rose closed the door and filled Lily in on what had been happening, explaining that she had made some notes to help things run smoothly while Anya was away, and that Katie would care for Alexsy. 'Even though she has no idea at the moment,' Rose added. 'Will you be home this evening? I want to speak to you and Katie together.'

'I have nothing planned. Peter is on duty, so I was going to stay in and wash my hair. Katie, as far as I know, is free.'

'Good. I'll ring her shortly for a chat and then we can all put our heads together to see how we're going to cover the next few weeks. With luck I'll be able to take a couple of days off, as Ben is coming home.'

Lily squealed with joy before apologizing in case the customers had heard. 'In that case, by hell or high water we will make sure you can spend a few days with him. Even if I have to bring Mary along with me while I work an extra shift.'

'Hopefully that won't be necessary,' Rose said, trying hard not to imagine what head office would have to say about it.

'I'll have one of the girls bring you in a tea tray so you can telephone Katie in peace. I'm thrilled Ben is on his way home,' Lily said before leaving the room.

*

'May I have a word?' Anya said after knocking on the door to the office.

'Come in and take a seat,' Rose said, noticing Anya's worried expression. 'Is there anything wrong?'

'It is with me going away; I am worried for my son if anything should happen. You may think me silly but with no news of Henio for so long, I am thinking the boy may never know about his parents. I have spoken to your mother about this.'

Rose nodded her head as she listened, not liking to ask how Anya had known last night that she was leaving Ramsgate when the letter from head office hadn't arrived until today.

'We live in dangerous times, Anya, and any one of us could be killed by enemy action at any time. I can understand how worried you are about being in London, when the enemy seems to be targeting it so often. I was there at the start of the Blitz and it was horrendous; I still wake up thinking I'm in another raid and calling out for Ben. My advice would be to always have your gas mask with you, and know where the nearest public air-raid shelter is.'

'I will do that, thank you. If anything should happen to me, I would like you and Lily and Katie to tell my Alexsy about Poland and read him the stories from the books I have collected. I want him to know his culture and what has happened to his homeland that made his parents flee at the start of this war. Tell him, also, how much his mother's friends meant to her, and how England is a good place. He must learn to speak Polish and one day return to help build his country into the wonderful place it once was. I have photographs for him and will trust you with them before I leave.'

Rose couldn't stop the tears from running down her face as she listened to this. She left her seat to go to Anya and give her a hug. 'I promise that whatever happens – and even if, as we hope, you are only away for a couple of weeks – I will do all I can to keep Alexsy happy and remind him of you and Henio.'

Whatever was happening in Anya's life, Rose now understood why her friend felt the need to make plans for the future of her child. She would be the same if she was ever in the same position. She would also tackle Ben to pull as many strings as he could in the search for Henio.

10

5 April 1942 – Easter Sunday

'You'll need a cardigan before too long. It's not that warm,' Flora said as she watched Lily stretching out on a blanket, enjoying the sunshine.

'I'm fine for now,' the younger woman grinned back, wriggling the skirt of her cotton frock a little higher over her knees. 'Lily by name and by colour,' she said, looking at her pale skin. 'I hope this sunny weather holds out so I can look a little healthier.'

'Cover yourself up, girl. Someone might see you,' Miss Tibbs said from where she sat next to Flora on an old carved garden seat, dressed in her very best outfit and hat. They were out on the flower-bordered back lawn of Captain's Cottage. 'What if your young man comes to visit?'

Lily roared with laughter. 'He's up there somewhere flying his plane; I doubt he can see me down here, even if he has a pair of binoculars. Captain's Cottage is free from prying eyes. With only the coast road to Ramsgate out the front, we hardly see anyone.'

'I can see you from the gate,' Peter said, as he appeared in the garden followed by Stew.

'Oh my God,' Lily shrieked as she jumped to her feet, quickly smoothing down the skirt of her pink floral frock before racing into his arms. 'What are you doing here?'

'We've been given a couple of hours off, and knowing you were celebrating Easter Sunday, I thought I would come and join you. I brought this miscreant along,' he added, as Stew gave a shy nod to the women.

'I'm Flora Neville, Rose's mother,' Flora said. 'You are very welcome to join us. I take it you've come to visit the apple tree you landed in?'

He gave a belly laugh, his eyes twinkling. 'I'll never live that down. I'm lucky I fell into the right garden, with a bevy of beautiful ladies to help me.'

'The silk parachute came in handy as well,' Lily grinned.

'I aim to please. We come bearing gifts,' he said as Stew handed a box to Lily, who placed it on the ground before calling young Pearl over to help her unpack it.

Pearl's eyes lit up. 'How wonderful, proper chocolate as well as hot cross buns. Delicious!' she exclaimed, before looking shyly at the two airmen to make her thanks.

'You are welcome,' Stew said. 'Traditionally we should have eaten the hot cross buns on Good Friday, but the chef at our base made so many that we'll be eating them into next month.'

'Would you like to join in with our egg hunt?' Pearl asked. 'We don't have any chocolate eggs, but there are some spiffing homemade cardboard ones as well as a couple of carved wooden ones. I helped make some of them,' she added proudly.

'I couldn't think of anything better,' Stew said as he handed his cap to Flora, who took both his and Peter's to a nearby wooden garden table that had seen better days. 'You will have to tell us what to do,' he said. 'It's been a few years since I went on an Easter egg hunt.'

Flora left Pearl explaining how they had to use one of the straw baskets Katie had made and search throughout the garden until each person had found two; any more, and they had to pass them to another person. She picked up the hot cross buns and took them into the kitchen, where she found Katie and Rose deep in discussion. 'I take it you are planning your staff rotas?'

'It's going to be tricky,' Rose replied as she peered at a large sheet of paper covered in names and scribbled-out words.

'Why don't you both leave this for a little while and come into the garden to enjoy our party? It is such a lovely day, it's a shame to miss having the sun on your face for a change. And we have more visitors; look what they brought,' she said, passing the box of buns to Katie.

Katie inhaled deeply when she saw what the box contained. 'I know I work in a teashop and should be used to it, but I adore the smell of hot cross buns. Who brought them?'

'The young airman and his Scottish friend,' Flora said. She could have sworn that Katie blushed slightly at this.

'In that case, it would be rude of us to hide away in here,' Katie said. 'I wonder if we have enough margarine to do these buns justice? Butter would have been lovely,' she sighed.

'I agree, but let's see what we can do with what we have. Don't forget that we brought over a portion of our rations; I didn't expect you girls to feed us for nothing.'

'If you look in the pantry, you will see my contribution,' Rose said. 'I gave all my staff a small bundle of food that would have gone over and been no good when the store opens after the weekend. There should be some extra margarine in among the loaves, and a few teacakes.'

Katie laughed. 'Great minds think alike. I too share the perishable goods among my girls, and I've left myself a few bits and bobs this weekend as well.'

'We shall have a feast!' Flora cheered. 'Why, even Mildred and Miss Tibbs are here, and Jennie will be along shortly – we have everyone together for once.'

'Apart from my Jack, Anya's Henio . . .' Katie started to say, and Rose piped in:

'Not forgetting my Ben.'

'Oh dear. Me and my big mouth,' Flora said, looking glum.

Rose gave her mum a big hug. 'Don't feel bad about it. Any one of us could have said the same thing. It's been so long since the menfolk were with us that we do tend to forget once in a while that there was a time when we were all together.'

The women fell silent until there was a polite cough from the open kitchen door. 'I thought I'd return some of these; if you can point me towards the kitchen sink, I'll wash them up,' Stew said as he entered the room carrying a tray of empty cups and saucers.

'Oh, bless you,' Rose replied. She took the tray from him. 'There's no need for you to help in the kitchen; you've done enough bringing these delicious buns to add to our afternoon tea. Sit yourself down and relax.' She nodded towards one of the bentwood chairs set around the kitchen table. 'I'll go and check if there are any more and then get stuck in.'

Flora got to her feet. 'I'm going to see how the children are getting on with the egg hunt. I just hope they aren't too disappointed with the lack of chocolate eggs.'

'Peter brought along a few bars, so that will help to keep them happy,' Stew said.

'Oh, bless him, I completely forgot even though I was standing there; silly me,' Flora chuckled, and she too headed out of the kitchen.

There was an awkward silence as Katie found herself alone with the shy Scottish pilot. She had taken to him the first time they were introduced and told herself that it was probably because he was a family man and many miles from home. For something to break the silence, she went to the kitchen sink and poured hot water from the large kettle sitting on the stove into an enamel washing up bowl, then sprinkled soap flakes on top and ruffled the surface with her fingers to create a lather. She froze for a moment as she found Stew standing by her side; then he reached for a tea towel and began to dry the plates already stacked on the wooden draining board.

'I miss doing things like this,' he said.

'There's always plenty of washing up to do here, as well as baskets full of items waiting to be ironed,' Katie smiled. 'Lily's Mary gets through clothes so quickly! Honestly, she seems to miss her mouth every time she eats. Then of course she has discovered the garden and enjoys nothing more than digging holes everywhere.'

'It would be my pleasure to help with all of that, if you like. One of my children is about Mary's age and he's just the same.' Stew smiled fondly.

Katie turned towards him and, without thinking, placed a hand on his arm. 'I was only joking about inviting you here to do housework, but all the same you're welcome to pop in any time you are passing. I can't begin to imagine how you must miss your home life,' she said, then snatched her hand back as she realized it was still resting on his sleeve. For a moment, their eyes met; then a noise from the kitchen door announced Rose's return with more cups and saucers to be washed up.

Katie started to chat about anything that came into her head just to break the moment between them, but it was still there, the feeling that they had connected in some way; and even though she should have stopped her thoughts then and there, she couldn't help hoping that Stew would be a frequent visitor to Captain's Cottage.

'What is all this?' Stew asked politely, as he spotted Rose and Katie's lists lying on the kitchen table.

'We've been trying to sort out staff rotas so that both the Margate and the Ramsgate teashops have enough staff,' Rose explained. 'Not only were we short staffed before, but now Anya, she's the Polish lady who lodges with my mum, will be away for a while; and I was so hoping to be able to take a few days off when my Ben comes home on a short leave.'

'We have to account for childcare, too, so that someone can look after Mary as well as Anya's little boy,' Katie added.

'And we can't expect my mum to care for them, as she has so much war work on at the moment. Not to mention she also has little Daisy to look after,' Rose finished with a sigh.

Stew laid his tea towel across the back of a chair and picked up the paperwork, reading it thoughtfully. 'I see you have a problem. My advice would be to ask all your current staff if they would like to put in extra hours as well as keep advertisements for staff in both shop windows.'

'We are doing most of that,' Rose said, moving over to join him in scanning the rotas. 'There are also a couple of ladies we may be able to move between branches; that's if they are agreeable. I would dearly love to have Lily back at work full time, but it is the lack of childcare that's our biggest problem.'

Stew nodded, thinking through the situation. 'Have you considered having someone move in here temporarily, to look after the children while you're at work? And perhaps even do a few shifts at the Margate teashop as it's the closest?'

'Gosh, that's an excellent idea,' Rose said. 'Thank you so much. I don't suppose you could fit in a shift in between flying your planes, could you?' she asked with a grin.

'Sadly not, although I miss my old job – I was an under-manager at Woolworths and often took care of the staff rotas. If you wish to chat about your management problems, I'd be happy to help. Both of you,' he added, looking towards Katie.

The three of them were still talking about work when a flustered Flora joined them. 'I am so annoyed,' she said, sinking into one of the seats at the table. 'Joyce has just arrived back from her duties at the Sunday school. It seems she popped into Sea View before coming back here, as she thought she'd need a cardigan, and caught Jennie with her young man. And had the sense to send him packing, and almost dragged the girl here screaming and shouting. I tell you, Jennie will be the death of me. Now she's threatening to move out of Sea View, and of course I can't stop her; but I do fear what might happen to her if she's left to the devices of Tom White.'

'What's this about Tom White?' Lily asked as she joined them.

Flora exchanged looks with Katie and Rose as a silence descended in the kitchen. She'd not wanted Lily to find out that Tom was back in town, hoping the man would soon move on. He'd caused far too much grief for poor Lily in the past.

'I'll join the others in the garden,' Stew said, knowing that whatever was going on wasn't any of his business.

'Thank you for your help,' Katie called after him, then blushed as Flora gave her a questioning look.

Lily stormed past Stew as he left the room and stood with her hands on her hips facing her friends. 'What the hell is going on and why have you not told me Tom White is back in town? Don't you think I deserved to know? What if he had walked into the teashop, because you know, that's the sort of thing he would have done, even though he was sacked from the company . . .'

'Sit down, Lily, and I will explain,' Flora said. 'You don't want your guests hearing, do you?'

She was referring to Peter, and Lily got her drift. She took a deep breath. 'It was a shock to hear Joyce telling Miss Tibbs. How is Jennie involved?'

Flora explained how Jennie had met Tom in the Ramsgate teashop when Katie wasn't on duty.

'Believe me, if I had been at work that day, I'd have sent

the man packing. And I'd have warned you he was back in town,' Katie was quick to say.

Flora continued, 'It seems Jennie took a shine to him and went out with him when her shift finished. I spotted them as I returned home; the pair of them were strolling up Madeira Walk, hand in hand. I think the penny must have dropped when he saw me and recognized where Jennie was heading, as he scarpered before I could say anything.'

Rose shook her head. 'It doesn't seem right. He must be at least fifteen years older than her. I have a gut feeling he's up to something.'

'Perhaps he's here to see Mary?' Lily said, with panic in her voice. 'I don't want him having anything to do with her. What can I do?' She looked around wildly. 'Have you said anything to Jennie about this?'

'Don't start worrying,' Flora said, patting her hand to calm her down. 'Jennie has no idea about Tom's connection to you and Mary. From what Joyce has just told me, her head has been turned by his attention and he's taken her out a couple of times. I intend to nip it in the bud as soon as possible, even if it means moving Jennie away from the area. We don't want her ending up with a baby, as that seems to be the lot of many girls this Tom has met in the past.'

Lily looked embarrassed. 'And I'm one of them; I know I was foolish, but it happened at a time when I'd lost my mum and my stepfather was . . .' Tears welled up in her eyes.

'Don't upset yourself by thinking about that time in your life,' Flora said, passing Lily a handkerchief as she started to weep. 'We all know you were an innocent victim.'

Rose was thoughtful. 'I do believe I have the answer to our problem. Mum, you can't have Jennie living at Sea View if there's a risk of Tom visiting her while you aren't there. And, Katie, you don't want this happening at the teashop while your back is turned. Am I right?' she asked, looking between the two women.

'You are, love, but of course we don't want to see her back living on the streets,' Flora said. 'I'd like the chance to help her understand that she can't carry on with any man who shows an interest in her. She's not a bad girl, just has her head easily turned. She's had so little attention in her life, poor kid . . . But I've a feeling that trying to tell her a few home truths about Tom White will have no effect at all.'

'I feel the same,' Katie joined in. 'Besides which, we are so short staffed I can't afford to lose her. I'll have to make sure that when she is on duty I'm there, or one of the older Nippies; not that I want to ask my staff to keep an eye on her, as that's not part of their job description.'

'So, what's your idea?' Lily asked Rose.

'Well,' Rose began, 'if we had someone living in here at Captain's Cottage, we would all be able to work full shifts . . .'

Lily went red in the face with anger. 'Am I getting this right? You're thinking of moving Jennie in here to look after my Mary? That is sheer madness. Imagine, the minute our backs are turned she could have Tom White in here with my daughter – whatever are you thinking?'

Flora raised her hand to stop Rose speaking and calm Lily down. 'I can see some sense in what Rose is saying. If Jennie understands that this is her only chance to stay in gainful employment and keep a roof over her head, it might shock her into behaving. We are only thinking of her,' she said, as Lily began to object. 'Of course, we have yet to discuss the care of Anya's son while she is away.'

'I'd have thought he would stay with you?' Lily said, looking puzzled.

'Anya has made a request,' Flora said, looking this time at Katie. 'The poor girl is worried something will happen to her while she is in London, and with Henio still missing in action, she feels she should plan for the long-term care of her son in case he should become orphaned.'

The girls gasped. 'What an awful situation to be in,' Katie said. 'I don't know how I would cope; does she really have to go to London to train the Sallys? Couldn't someone else go?' She turned beseechingly to Rose. 'Speak to head office, they would listen to you.'

Rose shook her head, glancing at Flora to back her up. 'Anya wouldn't thank us for interfering.'

'That's right, she wouldn't,' Flora agreed. 'That is why she has decided that she'd like you, Katie, to become Alexsy's guardian. And if anything does happen to her and Henio, you and Jack will become his parents.'

'Oh my,' was all Katie could say for a little while as she absorbed Flora's words. 'I would adore caring for little Alexsy, and I know I speak for my Jack as well when I say that. You all know how much we want a family of our own, and if anything should happen to his parents, we would make sure he never forgot them,' she promised, her eyes glistening. 'Under the circumstances, we should take in Jennie; don't you think so, Lily?'

'All right; but let me state here and now,' Lily said, 'I don't want her knowing anything about me and Tom White.

Or that he's Mary's father. God only knows why he's come back, and the last thing I want to do is encourage him. I have a feeling in my gut that he's up to something.'

'That makes sense, and even though I no longer live here, I will do my best to help out when I can,' Rose said; but even as she spoke, she wondered if they were really doing the right thing.

Flora got to her feet. 'I'll leave you three to chat among yourselves,' she said. 'I want to have a word with Jennie and put her straight on what we've decided. Shall I tell Anya you understand her wishes for Alexsy, and that you accept?'

'That would be lovely. Thank you for all you've done to help,' Katie said, giving Flora a kiss on the cheek. 'Who ever would have thought I'd be a temporary mum to Alexsy?' she smiled. 'I just pray that it really will be temporary, however much I'd love a child of my very own.'

'Jennie, stop making eyes at those men and come and talk to me,' Flora said. She led the girl towards the bottom of the garden, stopping by the entrance to the Anderson shelter.

'I was only chatting, there's nothing wrong with that,' Jennie answered belligerently.

Flora looked her in the eye. 'I want to have a word with you about bringing men back to Sea View when no one is at home. I'm disappointed to hear you felt that was a good idea.'

Jennie faltered under Flora's steely gaze. 'I never thought . . .'

Flora shook her head. She felt sorry for the young girl and partly blamed herself for the situation; after all, Jennie had been not much more than a child when she moved into Sea View. It was time Flora took her under her wing and guided her.

'In a way, I blame myself for not keeping an eye on you,' she said. 'You are young and have a lot to learn, especially when it comes to older men paying you attention. You know their intentions are not always good, don't you?'

'It was nice to have a boyfriend, like the other Nippies,' Jennie said. 'I felt I could hold my head high at work and be just like them.' She was starting to look apologetic.

'Jennie, dear, there are better men who will love to court you in years to come. You are a personable young lady, so please don't let men like . . . like that person you were with mess up your hopes of a decent future.'

Jennie frowned. 'Do you know him?'

Flora didn't want to say too much of what she knew about Tom White. 'I know of men like him; I saw him when he walked you home one day. He is far too old for you. Why do you think he wanted to be on his own with you this afternoon? I take it he knew there was no one home?'

'He did ask me, and I wanted to show him where I lived. I'm very proud to live at Sea View; I feel as though everyone there is part of my family. I didn't expect . . .'

Flora took a sharp breath. 'He didn't do anything to you, did he?'

'No; we kissed a lot and he suggested I show him my bedroom. I didn't want to, so I offered to make him a cup of tea instead, just as you would have done with a guest. That's when Joyce came home and sent him packing.'

Flora chewed the inside of her cheek, trying hard not to smile. A cup of tea would have been the furthest thing from Tom White's mind. 'I take it you don't plan to see him again?'

'He was rude to Joyce when she told him to leave; I was shocked. It made me see a different side to him. I just hope he doesn't turn up at the teashop again,' Jennie said miserably, 'or I could get the sack.'

'Then what I have to suggest to you could be your salvation. However, you must understand that if something like this happens again, I will have to ask you to leave Sea View, and no doubt you could also lose your job.'

Jennie turned pale. 'I'm such an idiot; I'm sorry, it won't happen again. What is your suggestion?'

'We all make mistakes in life; what we must do is learn from them and move on. Now, I need your help, but it is rather a big favour to ask.'

'Oh, I'll do whatever you ask; thank you for forgiving me,' Jennie said, giving Flora a big smile.

'Well, Anya is going away for a while to help train the new Sallys in London. She can't take Alexsy with her, so she has asked Katie to look after him here. As you know, Katie works long hours at the Ramsgate teashop, and with Lily working part time at the Margate branch, they already find it difficult to arrange their shifts so that someone is always here to care for Mary.'

Jennie cocked her head on one side, not sure what Flora was getting at. 'I can see that that's a problem, but how can I help?'

'I suggested that if you wouldn't mind moving into Captain's Cottage for a few weeks, you could look after Mary and Alexsy while the girls are at work. There's a very nice room you could have, and Rose thought that as this cottage is closer to the Margate teashop, you would be able to do the odd shift to earn some money – as long as it fits around caring for the children. What do you think?' Flora held her breath and crossed her fingers behind her back, expecting the girl to complain and go into a sulk. Jennie's reply surprised her.

'I'd adore to help out, as long as I can move back to Sea View later on. You wouldn't let out my room to someone else, would you?'

Flora breathed a sigh of relief. 'No, of course not; the room will remain yours and you can keep your possessions there if you wish. I believe the girls will also pay you, as we don't want you out of pocket. However, there is one thing you must promise me.'

'Oh, anything,' Jennie said, clasping her hands together in glee. 'This will make me feel like I'm part of the family.'

'Bless you. I've always thought of you as part of my extended brood,' Flora replied, wondering if this longing for family was the real reason Jennie had been so ready to respond to attention from an older man. 'If you ever see that chap again, you are not to tell him where you live – and you are never to mention who you live with. Do you understand? Believe me, he is trouble.'

'I promise,' Jennie said as she threw her arms around Flora. 'Thank you, Flora. I promise to do all I can to help.'

As Flora hugged the girl back, she couldn't help but wonder if they had really seen the back of Tom White.

11

'It is good to sit with my friends at Easter and watch the children play,' Anya said to Joyce, Mildred and Miss Tibbs. They were sitting on a rug laid out on the grass in the garden of Captain's Cottage. 'I cannot remember the last time we were all together in such a pleasant way.'

'It would have been Rose's wedding two Christmases ago,' Miss Tibbs said, 'although the weather was not as warm as it is today.'

'It was perishing cold and snowing,' Mildred exclaimed.

'But beautiful all the same,' Joyce added as she raised her face to the spring sunshine. 'It was so good of Rose, Katie and Lily to invite the children of their colleagues to afternoon tea and the egg hunt; it seems to have become an annual event since Mildred gave them the ownership of Captain's Cottage. It has done my Pearl good to meet a few new faces. With so many children being evacuated, she's not made many friends in recent years. Everyone is so kind to her at Sea View, but it's not the same.'

'A child should not have to be with a group of old

biddies all the time,' Anya observed as she watched Pearl help Alexsy find a carved wooden egg donated by Mildred. 'I hope my Alexsy makes many friends and enjoys his childhood.'

'Why, you talk as if you won't be here. The war will soon be over and things will return to normal; then our children will be able to enjoy a normal childhood again.' Joyce smiled at Anya, who was known for her negative comments. They often raised a smile among her friends, who put them down to the difference in languages.

'They said it would be over by Christmas 1939 and it wasn't,' Miss Tibbs huffed as she sat propped up by cushions. 'Isn't it time for another cup of tea?' she called out, as Flora approached from where she'd been talking to Jennie.

'It won't be long,' Flora said as she joined them, sitting down next to Mildred. 'I must say that is a very fetching dress, Mildred; it makes such a change from your work attire. I've not seen you in it before.'

'I came across the frock when I was having a sort out the other day and thought I may as well get some wear out of it while I don't have to wear my boiler suits as much. I'm not sure I like wearing dresses, though. They can be a bit draughty around my nether regions,' Mildred said. She tucked the skirt closely around her legs, although they were well protected in thick lisle stockings.

Joyce and Flora exchanged a grin. 'Why aren't you out fishing so much at the moment?' Joyce asked. They all adored Mildred, although her mannish ways and work as a fisherwoman seemed eccentric to the other women of Sea View. It did at least mean they were kept plentifully supplied with fish; Mildred was one of the few boat owners who had been allowed out to fish from Ramsgate harbour since the war began.

'I'm having her engine seen to and a bit of an overhaul; it is long overdue. While she's in dry dock I've been helping my friend go out in his boat.'

'You should take some time off and have a little holiday; you do enough for the people of Ramsgate supplying fish and crabs, God knows you deserve a break,' Joyce said.

'I'd not know what to do with myself. That's why I've been having a bit of a sort out while I have time on my hands. However, perhaps I could go and visit an old friend for a few days,' Mildred added thoughtfully.

'I must say, it seems strange you not going out at night to fish. Although I like to know all my ladies are tucked up safe in their beds; I hate to think of you out at sea in the dark.'

'I'm fine; it's what I'm used to,' Mildred said, looking a little embarrassed by Flora's concern. 'I wonder, could I have a quiet word with you when we get back home? It's something and nothing,' she added as the other women showed interest.

'Of course, come down to the kitchen and we can chat over a mug of cocoa,' Flora said, wondering what Mildred wished to talk about. She was a woman who never spoke much about her private life. It had been a big shock to them all when she'd signed over ownership of Captain's Cottage to Rose, Katie and Lily, saying that the girls were like family to her and she wanted them to enjoy the property now, rather than after she had passed away and bequeathed it to them.

'I need to ask you, Flora, if you spoke to Katie about looking after my Alexsy?' Anya asked. 'You may think I am being foolish, but I was too nervous to ask her myself as I feel it is a big imposition.'

'Indeed I have, and she will be delighted to do so. I suggest you have a chat with her now and tell her all about Alexsy's routine.'

'I will do that right now, thank you, Flora.'

Flora reached out and touched Anya's arm. 'You should never fear asking any of us for help. We all think of you as part of our family and love you and Alexsy very much.'

Anya blinked away tears. 'I'm a very lucky person,' she said, getting to her feet and marching across the lawn towards the cottage.

They watched her disappear inside. Joyce shook her head. 'I'm not sure I could go away to London and leave my Pearl, and she is quite grown up. Have you sorted out Jennie? I was telling the ladies how I caught her with a man this afternoon.'

'Yes, I have, and she is quite contrite. I put a proposition to her, and she agreed; it will suit all concerned and solve the problem of the man . . .' The others listened with interest as Flora explained what had been planned.

'Nothing beats cocoa after a day out,' Flora said as she placed a mug in front of Mildred and sat down opposite her at the Sea View kitchen table. They were the only residents still awake, and apart from the usual creaking of the old house there was silence.

'Pure bliss,' Mildred said as she sipped the hot drink. 'Even though I'm partial to cocoa while on board the *Saucy Milly*, it's here, at the end of a fishing trip, that I enjoy it most.

I'm getting old,' she said, kicking off her stout brogues and wriggling her toes.

Flora sighed. 'We are all getting older, but this war seems to have made it feel so much worse. At times it drags me down.'

'What, you? Why, we look to you to buoy us up and keep us going.'

Flora laughed. 'And there was me thinking my residents kept me going; perhaps it's a bit of both. Now tell me, what is it you wanted to talk to me about?' She pushed the biscuit barrel towards Mildred. 'There may be a few fig rolls left.'

'It's about getting old. And before you say anything, remember I'm a good few years further on than you.'

'Not much older,' Flora said quickly.

'I'm fifty-eight,' Mildred said, which surprised Flora.

'Well, I never. I must say, you look good for your age; it must be all that fresh air. Even so, you are only five years older than me.'

Mildred shrugged. She wasn't one for compliments. 'To be honest, that's what I want to talk to you about.'

'But Mildred, we all must grow old at some time. Rest assured there will always be a home here for you and if your rent ever becomes a problem we can come to some kind of arrangement,' Flora said, giving her friend's hand a reassuring squeeze. 'Perhaps you shouldn't have given Captain's Cottage to the girls?'

'I'm grateful for your generous offer, but honestly, money is not a problem. As you are aware, I did well from my father's will even though we'd been estranged. I have invested my money wisely, and never marrying has meant I've been able to live frugally. That's one reason why I wanted the three girls to enjoy the cottage – apart from never wanting to live there myself, because of my unhappy memories of childhood. The place feels very different now that they're there, of course. It was a joy to see it come alive today at the tea party.

'No, what I really want to discuss is what will happen when . . . when I'm no longer here,' she continued, reaching for a large, well-worn envelope she'd placed on the table earlier. 'My solicitor has a copy of my will, but I need someone to oversee the process and make sure everything is done properly; I need an executor. I would like you to be that person.' She looked at Flora to see her reaction to the request.

Flora was lost for words. 'I don't know if I'm up to doing such a thing. Of course, I'm honoured you think I'm competent, but all the same I'm just a seaside landlady; I've had very little to do with paperwork or dealing with property and money. Perhaps you should ask someone else who knows more about such things?'

'I don't want anyone else to look after my affairs,' Mildred insisted. 'My solicitor can guide you, but it's the personal things I want you to take care of.' Opening the envelope, she pulled out a few sheets of handwritten notes as well as a copy of her will and a bundle of folded papers tied together with a faded red ribbon; it looked like the official deeds to a property. 'I will run everything past my solicitor to make sure it's in order. Perhaps you should come along with me, so that we both know everything is shipshape. Please say you will do this for me.'

'As long as your solicitor is in agreement, I will say yes,' Flora said, looking at the documents. 'Would you please take me carefully through all of these documents? But first let me top up our mugs; there's plenty of warm milk left in the pan. I'm used to catering for more than two people,' she smiled.

'I won't say no,' Mildred said, draining her mug and sliding it across to Flora. She began to lay the paperwork out on the table. When Flora returned with refilled mugs, Mildred picked up a faded sheet of paper. 'This is the ownership of my fishing boat, the *Saucy Milly*. I want the boat to go to Katie's husband, Jack; he has shown a lot of interest in the fishing business since he was a young lad. If he comes back safe from the navy, I intend to offer him a partnership. If he dies before me while in service to our country, then the boat will go to a friend who will get a good price for it and the money will be added to my estate.'

'That is very generous of you,' Flora said, thinking how much the young man would enjoy working as a fisherman. 'Katie and Jack will have a good life thanks to your generosity.'

'In case I'm not around to show him the ropes, I've made provision for a colleague to teach him. However, if I should go down with my ship, so to speak, there is insurance which will cover the purchase of another vessel.'

Flora felt a shiver run down her spine. Mildred was talking as though she really expected something to happen to her. 'Tell me, Mildred, are you ill? I've noticed you have been rather quiet lately. There was a time you were always out fishing at night and only had a few hours' sleep before going out again early the next morning. These days, though, you seem to be onshore much more. You can tell me; I won't let it go any further.'

'I'm fine,' Mildred assured her. 'Just the usual aches and pains of someone my age. I simply feel as though it's time to get my house in order. After all, no one else is going to do it for me.'

'That makes sense, but it seems so final . . . what else do you have there?'

'These are the deeds to a house I own in Deal. It's nothing special: two up, two down and a small outside toilet. I have a long-term tenant living there, the wife of a fisherman I knew who died at sea some twenty years ago. She was left penniless with a small child. I charge her a peppercorn rent, but whenever she decides to move on I want the house to go to you, Flora.'

Flora gasped. 'But why? I'm truly grateful, but I am very comfortable here at Sea View and hope to see out my days in Ramsgate.'

'You forget that I know this house belongs to your Rose, and it may be that she'll want to move back here one day. Or even sell up and move away.'

Flora was lost for words. She took a sip of her drink as she tried to put her thoughts in order. 'I'm at a loss what to say. Rose is very happy living with Ben in the cottage in Pegwell Bay; I doubt she would turf her old mum out into the street.' Even so, she was smiling in appreciation of Mildred's generosity.

'Who knows what is around the corner?' Mildred said. 'I most certainly don't. Think of it as a nest egg for your golden years. I very much want you to have the house. You have looked after all of us for so long; it is time you were cared for.'

Flora couldn't speak as tears welled up and her throat

became dry. At that moment there was the sound of a nearby air-raid siren starting to whine, getting louder and louder. 'So much for a peaceful night,' she sighed. 'I'll get the flasks filled while you rouse everyone; and don't forget to put that paperwork somewhere safe, in case we take a hit. Oh, and Rose is staying the night, so don't forget to bang on her door,' she added as she stood up and prepared to get organized. Before hurrying away, she stopped and put a hand on Mildred's arm. 'Thank you, Mildred. It means a great deal that you've entrusted me to see your last wishes are fulfilled.'

'There's another list here; we can go through it later,' Mildred replied as she gathered the documents together. 'It's just to say who gets my bits and pieces. I've already cleared out my bedroom, so I only have the essentials I need to live with; I want to make things easy for everyone. We can see my solicitor on Tuesday morning to get everything finalized.'

Flora nodded as the sound of sirens continued to fill the air. Despite Mildred's reassurances, something about all this still didn't seem quite right. What had really prompted Mildred to start putting her house in order at this particular time?

'These night-time raids are the worst,' Joyce said as she stroked Pearl's hair; the child lay asleep on a wooden bench with her head in her mum's lap.

'Especially when they amount to nothing,' Miss Tibbs agreed. 'Although I'd not wish a raid on anybody.'

'I'm good for nothing the next day,' Anya put in, 'yet we are supposed to keep smiling to show the Germans they do not worry us. Pah! I hate them all,' she said angrily.

'Shh,' Rose whispered. 'The children are sleeping. Shall I pour us a hot drink from the thermos, Mum? I managed to collect a few of the leftover buns from this afternoon and there's enough for half each.'

Flora nodded her agreement and watched as Rose took a knife from the old biscuit tin they kept under a bench for cutlery and other items. Whenever there was a night-time raid, Flora always tried to bring along a couple of thermos flasks and something to eat as they whiled away the night, praying they would be back in their beds within a couple of hours. As they'd been at Captain's Cottage all day, she hadn't packed the two bags and dry blankets she usually kept ready by the kitchen door to be grabbed at a moment's notice. She leant over to feel the blankets on the two bunk beds.

'Things get so damp down here. I should have brought some fresh coverings,' she whispered to Joyce. 'These can come home with us later and I'll dry them out ready for next time.'

'Let me take charge of the blankets; you do too much for us,' Joyce replied, making Flora think of Mildred's comment earlier in the evening. She felt embarrassed at the unexpected praise from her tenants.

'That's very good of you, thank you. I meant to ask: how you are getting along with your job at the airfield?'

'It's not too bad, but I hate the hours and the travelling. If it wasn't for workers being picked up in a truck each day, I'd have to cycle all the way there. I like working in the canteen . . . apart from when we hear about planes going down,' Joyce added with a deep sigh.

'You do a good job helping to look after the pilots' stomachs,' Anya said.

'I'm not a great cook, I mainly serve and clean up,' Joyce replied.

'Then why not do the same for Joe Lyons?' Anya said as she tapped Rose's arm. 'Rose, give Joyce my job; she can easily be a Sally as it does not require great brain power.'

Joyce laughed out loud at Anya's words before checking she hadn't woken Pearl. 'I'd love to work closer to home. But don't you have to be trained at one of the big teashops in London?'

'Not necessarily,' Rose answered. 'We have done some of our own training in this area since war broke out. You've been in our teashops enough times to see what is required of a Sally serving at the front of shop counter.'

'Would it not be easier for me to work at the Ramsgate branch?' Joyce asked.

'They have a full quota of Sallys at the Ramsgate branch; it is Anya's job we are trying to fill, if only for a few weeks. After that, I could use you as a Nippy if you wish to be trained? I don't have enough mature female staff. Why not come into the teashop on Tuesday and we can chat some more?'

'I'll drive you over there after I've finished some business I must see to,' Mildred offered.

'That's if you do not mind stinking of fish,' Anya said before turning to Rose. 'I too need to talk with you. I leave for London that day, and I will need to take my son and all his belongings to Katie tomorrow; he is to share a room with Mary, which he will like very much. Captain's Cottage is such a pretty house, Jennie too will love living there.'

Rose agreed. 'The girls are very fortunate to have the property. They each have a bedroom and Jennie doesn't mind squeezing into the box room. Now, we must find time to talk tomorrow,' Rose replied, starting to divide up the buns while Flora handed round the drinks.

So much was changing with her friends at Sea View, she thought. Would life ever be the same?

12

Looking back over the past couple of days, Anya had no idea how she had coped, especially when it came to handing over her precious son to Katie. She hadn't wanted a fuss and had intended to keep the news of Alexsy's first birthday a secret; however, once he'd had his afternoon nap and joined everyone in the garden of Captain's Cottage, she'd been taken by surprise when Katie had appeared carrying a small birthday cake, courtesy of Joe Lyons. Not only that, but there had been gifts galore for the birthday boy. The memory of his smiling face would stay in her heart for ever more.

She settled back in her seat on the train and closed her eyes for a while. She had the carriage to herself. The sun shone through the smoke-smudged window, making it rather stuffy, but she felt too tired to get up and open the window; it had been enough of a struggle to lift her small suitcase up onto the luggage rack.

Now she was on her way, she started to wonder what lay ahead. Ruth had mentioned training but Anya was still none the wiser about what this meant. If they expected her to train as a soldier, then they were in for a surprise, she thought to herself. She'd been brought up by strict parents who believed fighting was for boys while daughters remained demure and home-loving. It had been her journey from Poland that had taught her to use her sharp mind and at times a sharp tongue. She'd learnt early on to be a survivor, and she had a feeling this would be a skill she'd need to make use of during the weeks to come. There were many questions buzzing in her head; the sooner she met Ruth and had them answered, the sooner she'd feel more confident with her mission.

Arriving in the capital, she again stood under the clock at Victoria waiting for someone to take her on the next leg of her journey. This time there was no one to call her names and no sign of romance; she was disappointed, as she would have liked to see a couple bidding each other goodbye with a farewell kiss. It would have reminded her of her Henio, when he would kiss her farewell before going back to his base at Manston to carry out more missions. She raised her fingers to her lips, remembering that last time . . .

'Anya?'

She jumped as she saw Ruth approaching.

'You were miles away.'

'I was remembering . . .'

'That's good, we want you to recall as much as possible; it will help your mission.'

Anya shook her head. What was the point in correcting Ruth? She didn't look like the kind of woman who would have fallen in love and suffered such loss. From what Anya had seen, Ruth lived with her rich parents and never had to worry about a thing. 'Where are we going?' she asked as she fell into step beside the other woman.

Ruth raised her eyebrows but said nothing until they reached her car, an Austin 7 parked in a side road behind the station. She placed Anya's suitcase on the back seat and gestured for her to climb into the passenger seat. 'I am taking you to your training base in the south of England. You do not need to know where it is, as you won't be able to leave the grounds until it's time to head off on your mission. I will remain there for a few days, as I have work to do.'

'You aren't always in London?' Anya asked.

Ruth didn't answer, instead asking questions about the tea party at Captain's Cottage and saying that she'd hoped to be there, but something had come up at the last minute. 'I work strange hours,' she replied when Anya asked what had kept her busy on a religious holiday.

Soon they were out of the capital and driving past green fields and small villages. Anya felt she was no longer in Kent, as the one time she'd travelled from Thanet when she went to Biggin Hill, there had been hop fields and strange buildings with pointed roofs which she had been told were where the hops for brewing beer were stored. How little she knew of her adopted country. But something she was certain of was that England was beautiful, even when under attack from Germany. Perhaps when the war was over, she would be able to travel with Henio and Alexsy to visit more of it.

Ruth braked sharply as the sound of an air-raid siren pierced the air. She swore and started to get out of the vehicle. 'Quickly, we need to get clear of the car in case it is targeted,' she shouted to Anya.

They ran back down the lane, away from the car, and threw themselves into a dry ditch edged by tall grass. Anya's heart was beating twice as fast as usual. She raised her head slightly to look for the enemy, spotting a small formation of aircraft high in the sky.

'They must be aiming for one of the airfields round about here,' Ruth explained. 'They aren't far away . . .'

They watched as an air battle commenced, with Spitfires from the base fighting off their attackers. One enemy plane spiralled out of control, crashing into a field no more than a mile away, followed by a mighty explosion. 'I suppose the bombs on board that plane were meant for the airfield?' Anya asked, remembering that Manston airfield close to Ramsgate had suffered in similar ways.

'At least this time the airfield was saved. Come on, we may as well move on or we could be in this ditch for the rest of the day.'

'Is it safe? The all clear hasn't been sounded.'

'I would think so,' Ruth replied, getting to her feet and brushing down her tweed suit. 'You will have to get used to taking risks,' she called over her shoulder as they hurried back to the unscathed vehicle.

They journeyed onwards in peace. Half an hour later, Ruth pulled in through two large pillars and followed a long driveway up towards a large ivy-covered house. Anya had no idea where they were, as the road signs along their route had been removed to fool the enemy; not that she would have recognized the names of the villages and towns in any case. She could see huts in the grounds of the property, and rows of tents. Ruth gave nothing away.

'There used to be a lovely old pair of gates at the entrance, but they were donated to the war effort to build more planes. Such a shame,' Ruth said.

'The war is more important,' Anya said, wondering if her husband's plane had been made from people's gates. 'This is a very grand house; do the owners allow us to stay here?'

'It's been taken over by the government for the duration, so they've moved away.'

'If I owned such a place, I would never leave,' Anya said as she collected her suitcase and followed Ruth up the broad steps to the double doors, wide-eyed as she looked around her.

'Oh good; we're just in time for tea,' Ruth said, as if it were the most natural thing in the world to turn up at a mansion in the countryside with a woman from Poland in tow.

Rose looked across her desk at Joyce Hannigan. 'I very much feel you would fit in as a Sally if you wished to have a two-week trial; that would give us both time to decide if you really would be happy working here. Perhaps a week as a trainee Sally and another week as a trainee Nippy? I don't often give this option to potential employees, but knowing you so well and appreciating I somewhat dumped the interview on you at short notice, I'm prepared to bend the rules. What do you say?' she asked the middle-aged woman seated in front of her.

'I'm grateful for the opportunity. To be honest, I never expected to be able to train for a job at my age. As a widow with a young daughter, I thought I would be drifting from job to job until I was too old to work. And that perhaps

Pearl would marry well and look after her old mum in her dotage,' Joyce laughed.

Rose joined in with her laughter, although she felt Joyce was worth more than she was saying. 'Had you never thought to train for office work, or perhaps try shop work? I almost went to work for Woolworths when I left school, but then I fancied wearing a Nippy uniform and working with food.'

'I can see the attraction of the uniform but I wonder if I could cope, nipping about all day long; I'm no spring chicken.'

Rose looked down at the application form Joyce had completed before being given a tour of the teashop. 'You are only forty-one, that's no age at all. I have several Nippies who are in their fifties, and we do not expect them to be running about all the time. There is also the option to move into management if an employee is so inclined.'

Joyce fanned her face. 'Steady on. I was only thinking of a part-time job to fit around my daughter's schooling.'

Rose smiled. 'I'm sorry. I do tend to get carried away when I see a suitable candidate. Why not start as a Sally while you get the feel of the place? You won't be working on your own.'

'Thank you, I'd like that; but tell me, will there still be a vacancy when Anya returns? As much as I dislike my current job and the travelling, I'd hate to be out of work after a few weeks.'

'I can assure you we have permanent positions at this teashop. As for travelling here from Sea View, the buses are reliable and often Mildred will drive this way and collect us. Of course, air raids somewhat interfere at times, but we do our best,' Rose said with a reassuring smile. 'There could come a time when Katie has a vacancy at the Ramsgate teashop . . .'

'I'm sorely tempted,' Joyce dithered.

'Why not have lunch in the teashop and have a think about it? It's on the house,' Rose added, knowing Joyce might not have money to waste on treating herself.

'Thank you, I would like that very much and should be able to give you my answer afterwards. I've had a lot to take in today, even though after living at Sea View for so long I've heard so much about Lyons.'

'I hope it was nothing that would put you off,' Rose chuckled. 'Let me find you a table and have a word with your Nippy so she can answer any questions you may have,' she suggested, deciding that she would seat Joyce at a table where an older Nippy would be waiting on her.

'Before I go, may I ask you something?'

Rose nodded.

'It's probably something and nothing, but I spotted that Tom White hanging about at the bottom of Madeira Walk when I set off to catch the bus earlier. I assumed he was waiting for Jennie to come out of Sea View.'

'He will have a long wait, as we moved her into Captain's Cottage yesterday. But if he continues to hang about, there may be a problem,' Rose replied, pursing her lips. 'Perhaps we should have a word with him?'

'I'm afraid I've already done that. He said good day as I passed by, so I stopped to ask him if he was waiting for Jennie. After all, he does know me from when I booted him out of the house the other day.'

'Don't worry, I'd probably have done the same. Did he give you an answer?'

'If you can call a nod of the head and a grin an answer. He riled me so much, I asked if he knew Jennie was only fourteen – that wiped the smile off his face. Thankfully she looks young for her age and no doubt had added a couple of years on to impress him.'

Rose was confused. 'Why would you say that?'

'Don't be so naive, Rose; no man wants to be seen with a child, let alone seduce one.'

'Some do . . . However, when he worked for Lyons, he had the pick of the Nippies at most teashops; I saw that with my own eyes. Lily was vulnerable at the time and fell for his charm, the result being young Mary. No, there's got to be another reason he is sniffing about. Do you think you frightened him off?'

'I hope so,' Joyce said. 'He's an odious man.'

'I agree. I'm pleased Jennie is at Captain's Cottage taking care of Alexsy and Mary. From all accounts she did so well yesterday that Katie and Lily decided to have her take care of the children this morning. If she has a problem, she has strict instructions to use the telephone and get in touch with Lily, who will be back at the cottage in a shot. We are planning our work rotas so that between the two teashops, someone can always be at the cottage at different times to care for the children. I've put my name down even though I don't live there now; it's not as if I go to my own home very often. It'll be different once the war is over and my Ben comes home for good.'

'I pray that is soon. I hope I'm not speaking out of turn . . .'

Rose smiled at the woman, who wasn't known for giving opinions. 'Feel free to say what you think.'

'If I'm fortunate enough to work here, I wonder if you could add me to the rota to help with the children? I've had some experience, having brought up my Pearl; and it might mean I would have her with me at times, but she's a good girl and loves playing with the little ones.'

'Gosh, would you really do that for us?'

'You've all been so good to me, and Pearl too; I'd like to pay you back in a small way. And I promised Anya that I'd help you all if I could.'

'Everyone is being so generous,' Rose said, feeling more than a little emotional.

13

14 April 1942

'This way,' Flora shouted to a group of distressed women calling for help. 'Come inside, and for goodness' sake try not to touch your eyes or they will sting even more.'

Her voice was muffled by the gas mask strapped to her face. Inside she was fuming: what should have been a simple drill, instructing the people of Ramsgate about what to do in the event of a gas attack by the enemy, had deteriorated into confusion and panic.

'Why is this happening?' Miss Tibbs asked, looking at Flora through streaming eyes. 'We were only queuing at the butcher's. Is there an invasion?'

Flora nodded her thanks to the Nippy who was pulling people into the Ramsgate teashop while doing her best to close the door after each person in case gas crept inside. Pulling off her mask, she addressed the crowd. 'I repeat: do not rub your eyes or you will exacerbate the pain. Have none of you seen the posters all around the town, or indeed thought to carry your gas mask, let alone wear it?' she fumed. 'What if this had been a real enemy attack? Or worse, an invasion? How would you be able to fight back in the state you are in now?'

The women fell silent; one opened her gas mask box and pulled out the mask, along with a lipstick and a powder compact. 'Is it too late to wear it?' she asked, looking at Flora, her face smudged from where she'd rubbed the mascara lining her eyes.

Flora felt suddenly deflated. 'I apologize for shouting at you all, but this exercise has been planned for a while now and there's been plenty of notice. It is for your own safety.'

'Lesson learnt,' Miss Tibbs said as two of the Nippies handed out damp napkins for them to dab at their eyes. 'Shall we have a cup of tea, now we are in here?'

Flora shook her head and looked around the teashop. It seemed some of the other women had had the same idea and were sitting down at tables. She waved to Katie, who'd come out of her office to check all was well. 'I suppose you've heard what happened?'

'I couldn't help notice,' Katie said, looking back towards the window set in the wall of her office. 'At least we won a few customers. It's been dead quiet all morning with so many people staying home.'

Flora sighed, raising her hand to her forehead. 'I don't feel the council put nearly enough thought into this exercise. And as for the local bobbies, running about making a racket with those wooden rattles! My head is throbbing.'

Katie looked concerned, taking her arm. 'Come and sit down over here where it's quieter, and perhaps we can have a chat over a hot drink. It's about time I had a break.'

'Miss Tibbs . . .' Flora turned back to look for her elderly friend.

'Miss Tibbs has joined the other ladies and is putting the world to rights,' Katie said, steering Flora to a less busy part of the teashop and waving to a Nippy to serve them. 'How do you feel?'

'I'll be fine in a minute or two.'

'You do look rather pale. I wonder if you are sickening for something? How did you sleep last night?'

'To be honest, I was having a bad night even before we had that air raid. I know it was over and done with within a couple of hours, but I woke up with such a feeling of foreboding . . . I just couldn't shake it off.'

They fell silent as the Nippy approached with a tea tray. 'I've added some toasted teacakes as well,' she said, placing the tray onto the table and giving the ashen-faced Flora a sideways look as she left them alone.

'You've had a lot to cope with lately,' Katie consoled Flora as she lifted the lid of the silver teapot and stirred the contents. 'You need to put your feet up and rest more. With Anya away and Jennie and Alexsy staying at Captain's Cottage, at least you don't have so many residents to run after. I hear Joyce is doing well at the Margate teashop.'

Flora smiled her thanks as she was given her tea. 'Yes, it seems she loves working as a Sally; Rose wanted her to experience being a Nippy, but she is set on staying behind the counter and serving customers. The customers seem to like her as well. Oh, I received a postcard from Anya yesterday.'

'How is she getting on? I had wanted to let her know that Alexsy has settled in, but she never gave me an address.'

'Oh, you know Anya. She doesn't say much apart from that she is learning a lot, and the food is terrible, and to send her love to her son. There is an address – is says *care of*, but I'm sure it will reach her,' Flora said, holding out the letter for Katie to copy the address. 'It does seem strange for her to say the food is terrible when she is working for Joe Lyons . . .'

'Perhaps she has to dine in the staff canteen?' Katie chuckled. 'Lily has some photographs from the Easter Sunday tea party. I'll pop one in my letter to Anya; I'm sure she would love to see Alexsy's smiling face while she is working hard training the new intake.'

'She most certainly would . . .' Flora stopped speaking as Katie stared straight past her, looking out of the front window that faced the street. 'Whatever is wrong?' she asked, turning round to follow the girl's gaze. 'Oh goodness. I had hoped we'd seen the back of him after Joyce gave him a talking to,' she said angrily, spotting Tom White looking into the teashop.

'I've seen him hanging about a few times in the past few days. He never comes in and seems to be looking for something . . . or someone. What do you think we should do?'

'If it's Jennie he is looking for, he's out of luck, since she was moved to work at the other teashop. I do wonder, though, if the penny will drop and he will check there instead.'

Katie agreed with her. 'He's not going to go away, is he?'

Flora got to her feet, placing her napkin on the table. 'Something needs to be done before he goes to the other teashop and causes a scene. The last thing we want is Jennie, or come to that Lily, being sacked if there is a confrontation in front of customers. I'm going to have a word with him right now.'

'Be careful,' Katie said, looking worried. 'He has a vicious temper.'

And so have I if pushed, Flora thought to herself as she hurried towards the door, noticing that Tom was starting to walk away towards the harbour. Rather than call out, she increased her pace until she caught up with him as he waited to cross the road. Grabbing the sleeve of his jacket so he couldn't move away from her, she smiled sweetly. 'Hello, Tom. Do you remember me, Flora Neville from Sea View guesthouse? I wonder if we could have a few words.' She began leading him towards a nearby bench, not letting go of his sleeve until they had sat down.

Tom looked confused. 'What do you want with me?'

'You do know Sea View, don't you? Where Jennie lives, and where Lily Douglas used to live.'

His face paled. 'Where is Lily now?'

Flora shrugged her shoulders. She wasn't about to tell him, nor would she start to tell lies; she wasn't one to do that. 'Why are you taking such an interest in a girl who is still a child? Some would say it was rather unhealthy.'

Tom's eyes flashed as he pulled away from her. 'What do you think I am? I'm not that kind of man.'

'I think you are up to something,' Flora spat back. 'And I want to know what it is.'

'I was just being friendly to the child; I thought she might be able to tell me something about my daughter, Mary. I want to see her.'

Flora couldn't believe her ears. 'Excuse me for asking, but why, after you caused all that rumpus after the child was born, do you now want to see her?'

'I've been thinking about how I messed things up and I want to try again, if Lily would allow it.'

'Sorry, you are confusing me. Kindly explain how courting Jennie gets you closer to our Lily and her child?'

'I went into the teashop one day and she was there; we got chatting, that's all. She's a nice kid. I meant to ask her if she knew about Lily's, I mean our daughter, but it went out of my mind after we started chatting.'

'So much for wanting to become a doting father,' Flora said.

Tom thought for a while, choosing his words carefully, which didn't go unnoticed by Flora. 'I left under a bit of a cloud, and I didn't want Mr Grant to hear that I was back in case it caused problems for Lily.'

'Mr Grant has retired due to ill health,' Flora answered, before belatedly realizing that it might have been better to let Tom think the kindly area manager was still working in the Thanet area.

'I'm sorry to hear that. He was a decent sort, until he got the wrong end of the stick over my romance with Lily.'

Flora laughed. 'What romance? From my understanding, you had a sordid one-night relationship with Lily at a time she wasn't quite herself, and then you wriggled out of your responsibilities.'

Tom raised his hands in protest. 'It wasn't like that, believe me. Who is the area manager now?'

'Rose hasn't told me, but it has nothing to do with you. I thought you had been reported to the draft board?'

He gave a cynical laugh. 'It turns out I do have a problem with my health – my dicky ticker has kept me out of the forces. I've tried to find war work but there's nothing going for a man of my calibre. I'll keep looking, though,' he said, seeing her angry glare. 'That's why I've not been around. I wanted to find a decent position before I reacquainted myself with Lily.'

'Why don't you try at the airfield? I believe there is one position going begging in the staff canteen,' Flora said, thinking of the job Joyce had recently left.

He looked hurt. 'I couldn't do it. Imagine wanting above anything else to work for one of the services and, due to ill health, not being able to, and then seeing all those brave pilots going off to do their bit when I couldn't? I'd be too ashamed to face them.'

Flora was thoughtful. Perhaps she should give him the benefit of the doubt . . .

'Where are you living at the moment?'

'I'm presently staying in Boundary Road. It's all I could find at short notice,' he said, noticing her wrinkle her nose. 'Perhaps you could tell me of something more suitable; do you have a vacancy?'

I know what you're thinking of, my laddie, and I'm not that gullible, Flora thought to herself. If every room was empty at Sea View, I'd still not have you under my roof; but I do want to keep my eye on you. They do say, keep your enemy close . . .

'The air force is still billeting servicemen in the town, but I'll put the word out,' she replied. 'But you will have to find work, if only to hold your head high and show the world you are a reformed person – even if you say you did nothing wrong,' she added quickly, seeing he was about to protest. 'Get yourself off to the labour exchange and see what they have to offer. I'll meet you here this time tomorrow to hear what you've done to improve your lot. At that point, I may encourage Lily to let you see your daughter.'

Tom's eyes lit up. 'You'd do that for me?'

'I like to give everyone a second chance. But don't let me down, you hear me?'

'I promise,' he said, before shaking her hand and walking away.

Flora was deep in thought as she walked back to the teashop to collect Miss Tibbs, who would be wondering what had happened to her.

Katie was waiting for her at the door. 'What was all that about?' she asked. 'I could just about see you talking to that horrid man who made our Lily's life hell.'

Flora put a finger to her lips. 'I don't want anyone else to know, but I've arranged to meet him tomorrow. I want to keep an eye on him,' she grinned before going over to where Miss Tibbs was still holding court, talking animatedly about the first war. 'Come along, it is time we got ourselves back home; there are potatoes to peel and this beef shin to stew to feed the five thousand.'

'I'll make the dumplings,' Miss Tibbs replied quickly, draining her cup and hurrying after Flora.

'Don't forget this,' Katie called after her with a chuckle, holding out her gas mask.

14

'There's a problem,' Kenneth Parry said, throwing himself into a chair opposite Ruth in the lounge of the training centre where Ruth had come to visit Anya. He pulled out his pipe. 'Domino informs us the target will be moving on. The mission will have to be brought forward in case it becomes too risky.'

'It has always been risky,' Ruth replied, reaching for a cigarette. 'We need at least another week; she's not ready.'

'She will have to be, we have no option. She goes the day after tomorrow, or we call off the mission.'

'For goodness' sake, we can't do that, and you know it,' she spat back at him. 'So far it has only been gossip and hearsay about the damned woman.'

'Winston's expecting a confirmed sighting so our operatives can move in and do their stuff. If Hitler gets wind of Anouska being Jewish, he could arrange to obliterate her at any time, and then we'd be no further forward.'

'But Anya isn't ready . . .' Ruth repeated as she thought about how close she had become to the Polish woman. A voice deep inside had warned her this would never work out well; Anya was much too close to Rose's circle of friends, making her almost feel like a part of Ruth's extended family.

'She's only got to go in and take a look at the woman to confirm it is someone she knew from the old days in Poland, then get out.'

'She doesn't know any French. That was to be the next stage of her training . . .'

'She will only be in France for a matter of hours, and our courier will be with her. The château is close to the sea where they will be dropped off; what can go wrong? Anya just needs to confirm the identity of the woman, and then she can return to Ramsgate and forget she ever left our shores.'

'Shall I tell her, or shall you?' Ruth asked as she weakened. She knew it would be a feather in her cap if they could pull this off. Anya's part in the operation was small but crucial.

'You can tell her she will be on the boat the day after tomorrow, in the evening. We can give her the information we have just before we take her to meet the courier.'

Ruth shuddered. 'That soon? In that case, I'll take her. My brother's back in town and I don't want to miss him.'

'Take a few days off, you deserve it. We can cover everything from here.'

'Don't talk to me as if I don't pull my weight,' she snapped.

He raised his hands in surrender. 'No offence meant. I know if my brother was only home for twenty-four hours, I'd like to see him.'

Ruth gave a mocking laugh. 'You know everything, don't you? I only said he would be home, but still, you know the details . . .'

'It's my place to know everything,' he said, giving her a crafty wink. 'I'll tell Anya to come in and see you. I spotted her sitting in the garden with a book.'

Ruth shook her head as he left. She liked Kenneth a lot, but his apparent knowledge of everything that went on gave her the shivers. What else did he know about her, she wondered, as she opened the folder he'd given her containing details of Anya's mission. She was deep in thought when the Polish woman entered the room.

'Mr Parry told me to come straight in,' Anya said, looking worried. 'Have I done anything wrong? Everyone seems to shout at me in this place,' she said glumly. 'Perhaps it is best if I go home to Ramsgate and my son.'

'Sit down, and stop feeling so sorry for yourself,' Ruth said, giving Anya a gentle smile. 'You've been through a lot these past days; we've rather thrown you in at the deep end.'

'Deep end? I am drowning! I honestly cannot do this; you picked the wrong woman.'

'Oh, Anya. You can be certain that we have picked the perfect woman for the job,' Ruth assured her, thinking it was more that there was no other person who could carry out the mission. 'However, you will be pleased to know your training is nearly at an end.'

Anya frowned. 'How can it be, when I have yet to learn how to kill someone with a knife, I have yet to understand any of the French language, and I only know six letters in the Morse code?'

'Let's just hope they are the right six letters,' Ruth said, and both women burst out laughing. 'Seriously, your mission shouldn't involve killing anyone or sending messages by Morse code. You simply have to confirm the identity of the woman you will see and then report back to us, so we have up-to-date identification.'

'It sounds simple when you say it like that, but I know there will be more. When will I know who this woman is, and why she is so important to the British?'

Ruth closed the folder in front of her and reached for her cigarettes, offering them to Anya, who refused. 'All I can tell you at the moment is: the day after tomorrow, in the evening, you will be driven to the coast, where you will be taken over the Channel and dropped off at a point where you will be met. The person who meets you will take you to where you will watch and wait until you see the woman we need to identify, and then you will carry out your mission.'

Anya stared into Ruth's eyes. 'You make it sound simple . . . will it be simple? Will I see my son again?' she asked, reaching into the pocket of her cardigan and bringing out a photograph. 'This was him as a baby; he has grown so much and looks so like his father. I fear he will be an orphan soon.'

Ruth's heart ached for Anya. She'd done very little to find out about Henio and vowed to start hounding her contacts. 'The mission should be simple, but we must be realistic, because there is so much that could go wrong. You will have the best people with you; I promise they will take care of you. Your knowledge will do much to help bring an end to this war.'

Anya was thoughtful. 'I'm not afraid to die. I just need to know if my Henio is alive. Katie and Jack will be good parents to my boy if he is left alone. I wonder, would you . . .'

'I'll do anything at all if it will give you peace of mind,' Ruth promised, knowing Anya would need to be single-minded during her mission and not be thinking about her son.

'I would like to write letters to my husband and my son, in case I should not return. Also, I want to write to Katie and tell her more about Alexsy. Perhaps one day she can take him to visit his homeland . . .' Anya said, gazing past Ruth towards the window, where the sun shone down on the mansion's extensive gardens.

'I can take your letters and make sure they get to the right people if . . . if anything should happen to you. But I expect you to return, and then we will burn the letters together and forget you ever undertook this mission. Do you agree?'

'I agree,' Anya said through glistening tears. 'I'm not crying,' she added as she cuffed her eyes, giving Ruth a broad smile. 'Let us get on with defeating the enemy who killed my family and brought destruction to my beautiful country. I want revenge,' she said forcefully.

Ruth reached into a drawer in her desk and passed writing paper and envelopes to Anya. 'Use these to write your letters. Shortly you will be given a new identity and clothing suitable to your task. Do not talk to anyone apart from those supervising your mission; we can never be too careful at this stage.'

'Do not worry,' Anya said, getting to her feet. 'No one here speaks to the strange Polish woman.'

Ruth watched her go before lifting the telephone receiver. It was time to contact the people who would be assisting Anya in her task.

*

Katie let herself into Captain's Cottage. It was late evening, and after a long day she wanted to sit down and rest for a while. At least Jennie and Lily would have put the children to bed, and it would be peaceful. As much as she loved the two little ones, she was grateful someone else would be caring for them this evening.

She hung her coat and hat on the hallstand, hooking her gas mask holder on top of the coat where it could be grabbed at a moment's notice. Kicking off her shoes, she walked into the living room in her stocking feet to be brought up short. 'Jack?' she whispered before shrieking in delight and throwing herself into his arms. 'I knew you'd be home soon but didn't expect to see you today. Oh, I've missed you,' she cried before being silenced as his lips sought hers.

Several minutes passed before she stepped back, gasping for air and trying to calm her beating heart. 'Oh my goodness; I can't believe you are here,' she said, taking in his shining blue eyes and sandy-coloured hair. He only stood a few inches taller than her, but in Katie's eyes he was a giant among men. And she loved him dearly. 'But where are the others? It is past the children's bedtime.'

Jack took her hand and led her to the comfortable settee, pulling her onto his lap. 'They are upstairs. When they heard the gate open, they all decided to help put the kids to bed so I could greet you on my own.'

'Bless them all, but they can't stay upstairs,' she giggled. 'As much as I want my husband all to myself, I should call to them to come down.'

'In a couple of minutes,' he said, nuzzling her neck and kissing her throat.

'Why, Jack Jones, I've never known you so keen. I suppose it is having a girl in every port; I've heard about you sailors.'

Jack laughed before holding her at arm's length to gaze at her. 'Why would I even look at another woman when I have you to come home to?'

'Oh, Jack,' she sighed. 'I've been looking forward to you being home, but we have a houseful of people; it's not very romantic, is it? Perhaps we could book into a hotel for a couple of nights – that's if we can find one that's not too expensive?'

'Rose is one step ahead of you. She's arranged for Mildred to drive over and pick them all up; they are staying at Sea View for the two days I'm home.'

'She is such a good friend. But I still have my work.'

'Ha! No, you don't,' he grinned. 'Lily is going to cover for you while Jennie, Flora and Miss Tibbs take care of the children.'

'I can't believe this has been planned in such a short time. Our friends are so good to us. That must be Mildred,' Katie said as there was a loud thumping on the front door. 'You can all come downstairs,' she called out as she went to let Mildred in.

Lily, Rose and Jennie rushed down the stairs, full of excitement, hugging Katie and congratulating her on having her husband home. Mildred walked in and shook Jack's hand, welcoming him back. 'Come on, ladies, let's get you and the children loaded in my van and get on our way. Are the children awake?'

'Alexsy is out for the count, but Mary is awake,' Lily said. 'I've packed a bag for them, and they're in their night-clothes; we can wrap them up in blankets and hold them in our laps. That way they can be popped into bed as soon as we get to Sea View.'

'Are you sure Flora doesn't mind everyone descending on her like this?' a worried Katie asked as everyone began filing out the front door towards Mildred's van. 'Perhaps we two should go to Sea View instead?' she said, pausing on the doorstep and turning to Jack. He blanched at the suggestion.

'No,' Rose almost shouted. 'The idea is for the pair of you to have some time alone before Jack goes back to his ship. Besides, I'm off to London tomorrow to meet my Ben at his mother's home, so there will be more than enough room for this lot,' she said, nudging Lily to agree.

'Yes, have a great time,' Lily grinned, giving them a wink, which caused Katie to blush.

'We certainly will,' Jack replied as he took his wife by the hand and led her inside.

15

'I didn't expect our romantic night to be spent down the air-raid shelter,' Katie said as she cuddled up to Jack.

'I haven't heard you complain,' he replied as he stroked her hair. 'I must say, my back is aching from being in this tiny bunk bed. I just hope I'm fit enough to go back on duty later tonight.'

Katie giggled. 'The bunk is only meant for one person; perhaps we should have slept separately?' she said, wriggling even closer to him, if that was possible.

'I prefer it this way. Oh bugger, there's the all clear,' he said as they heard the wailing siren notify them that all was well and the raid was over.

She started to pull away from him. 'I suppose we'd best go back to the house and check everything is all right.'

'There's no rush, is there?'

'But there is; I'd like a bath to freshen myself up before I put on my good nightdress . . .'

'Perhaps you're right,' he said, giving a throaty laugh. 'But do you honestly think you're going to be wearing it for long?'

Katie shivered at his words. She'd expected to feel shy with Jack after they'd been apart for so long, but their first night back together had been perfect. Then tonight, even though they'd been forced to spend most of it in the shelter, had somehow made her feel even more at ease in his arms. 'Honestly, Jack, I'm glad nobody can hear what you're saying; you make me sound like a wanton woman. Come on, let's make you presentable and get back to the house.'

'After you, madam,' he said when they'd tidied up and collected what needed to be taken back to the cottage's kitchen.

She squealed as he chased her the length of the garden, catching her as she stopped to unlock the back door. 'Oh, Jack, do you have to go back this evening?' she asked, melting into his arms. 'We'll never be able to start a family with you away so much. If this war carries on much longer, I'll be a childless old maid.'

'God willing, it won't go on that much longer. At least we have the rest of today; who knows what will happen?'

She crossed her fingers, praying that he was right, as he lifted her into his arms and carried her upstairs.

Flora was pleased she'd held on to her large pram even after Daisy had grown out of it. With a seat fastened behind the front handle for the little girl, she would be able to take young Alexsy out in the pram and bring Daisy along too. Jennie helped her down the steps to the pavement, lifting Daisy onto the seat and fastening her reins to a clasp on either side.

'I'm not sure how long I'll be, as I have quite a list of shopping,' Flora told the young girl.

'I'm going into work later, as is Joyce,' Jennie replied. 'Lily will be here with Mary, so take as long as you please. At least the sun is out, and with luck there won't be an air raid this morning.'

'We can only pray,' Flora replied, and, laughing as Daisy started to wave goodbye to Jennie, she set off towards Madeira Walk. She had to take the slope down to the shops with care in case the heavy pram took off without her. She peered past Daisy to check Alexsy was happy. The little lad was sleeping soundly. 'Shall we go to the greengrocer's first and see what he has for our dinner?' she asked Daisy.

'Carrots and spuds,' the child suggested, making Flora laugh.

'Let's hope the butcher has something tasty to go with your carrots and spuds. Liver and onions perhaps, or sausages?'

Daisy wrinkled her nose at this suggestion.

'Sausages it is, then, that's if he has any. What a shame Mildred hasn't been out fishing lately or we could have had fish for our dinner.'

'And chips,' the child said, clapping her hands together with glee.

'Let's see,' Flora smiled. She loved her adopted daughter and couldn't imagine life without the little girl, even though she was sad at the thought that the child's blood relatives had all perished in the bombing when Daisy was a baby two years ago.

'Flora,' a masculine voice called out to her from across the road. She looked up to see Tom White waving to get her attention before hurrying over the road to join her. 'I wondered if you'd like to join me for a cup of tea?' he asked, staring at Daisy.

'I'd like that, but not for long, as I have a hundred and one things to do.'

'Is this . . . ?'

'Mary?' she asked, shaking her head. 'No, this is my youngest daughter, Daisy.'

Daisy gave him a shy smile before pointing into the pram where Alexsy lay. 'Mary sleep,' she said, putting her thumb into her mouth.

'Everyone's a bit tired this morning after last night's disturbed sleep,' Flora said. She turned to Tom. 'I'm sorry Hitler put paid to us meeting the other day; I had no way of contacting you. A cuppa would certainly hit the spot, but perhaps not at the Lyons teashop. There's a small cafe up the road a little where we can sit and look at the sea.'

'Boats!' Daisy shouted, before putting her thumb back into her mouth and staring at Tom.

'She's a beauty,' Tom said as they walked slowly along the pavement, avoiding people coming the opposite way.

'A little young for you,' Flora said, before catching herself and apologizing.

'Please, no apologies. I deserve all you say. How is Lily?' he asked, out of the blue.

'Fine,' was all Flora would say, not wishing to add that Lily was currently living at Sea View.

Tom helped her move the pram into the cafe and parked it close to the window. 'I'll get these,' he said, going up to the counter to place their order and coming back with two teas and a cup of milk. The cafe owner followed shortly after with a round of toast. 'I hope you don't mind; I didn't bother with breakfast.' He bit into the toast as Daisy held out her hand to him.

'Please,' she said sweetly.

'Can she . . . ?' he asked as Flora nodded approval. He tore off a piece of toast and gave it to Daisy; she tucked in with relish. 'How about . . . ?' he said, looking to the pram, which still had its hood raised against the sun.

'Let sleeping babies be,' Flora said. 'Like I said, it was a rough night without much sleep.' She kept her tone neutral. No matter how conciliatory Tom was being, she knew she would have to keep an eye on him; he wasn't to be trusted.

'I wondered if you'd spoken to Lily yet about me seeing our baby?'

'Good grief, with everything that's been going on I've not even thought about it. You'll have to give me a little longer. I might be able to let you know in a day or two.'

'The thing is, I've found a job and I'm moving away tomorrow. And my mother . . .' He looked away, apparently unable to speak.

'You can tell me,' Flora said, seeing how sad he looked.

'My mother doesn't have long, and she would love, just once, to see her only grandchild before she passes away.'

Flora was torn. How could she let a woman go to meet her maker without seeing her only grandchild? There again, was Tom telling the truth? 'I'll speak to Lily and see what she has to say. That's all I can promise.'

'Mary,' Daisy said, pointing to the pram as she chewed the last of her toast.

'Yes, dear, that was Mary's pram. Tom, I'll do my best, but don't expect miracles,' she said, getting to her feet and bending to take the brake off the pram. 'I must go, as I have a lot to do. Thank you for the tea,' she added as she tried to get out the door with the large pram.

'Here, let me help you,' he said, deftly manoeuvring it out into the street. 'Which way are you heading?'

'Up to the greengrocer's and then to the butcher's,' she said as he started to steer the pram in the direction she pointed. 'There's no need; I can manage from here,' she said, but he ignored her protest until they reached the first shop. 'Thank you,' she said as she took over and parked close to the shop front, kicking the brake on the wheel to stop it rolling away. She unclipped Daisy from her seat and set her down on the pavement. Peering into the pram, she could see that Alexsy was sleeping contentedly. It wouldn't be too long before he was too big for the pram and it could go back into storage; hopefully Katie would be able to make use of it before too long, Flora thought to herself. 'Thank you so much for your help,' she said to Tom as she started to enter the shop. 'I could be some time,' she added nodding towards the queue.

Daisy started to pull away, crying out 'Mary'; Flora hushed her as one or two shoppers turned to look. She bent down to have a quiet word with the little girl. 'You can play with Mary when we get home. It is Alexsy sleeping in the pram.'

Daisy nodded and placed her thumb into her mouth. Flora straightened up, thankful the child was not going to make a fuss.

The queue twisted around the greengrocer's shop; Flora was glad that at least they were inside, as it was decidedly cold for April. Daisy charmed the other shoppers, while some who recognized Flora asked her questions about the fiasco of the recent gas drill exercise. She occasionally looked over her shoulder towards the window, which was shrouded with boxes and posters, and could see the pram was where she'd parked it, safe and secure along with several others left by shoppers.

'Morning, Flora,' the shop owner said when she reached the front of the queue.

'Good morning, Bert; how is your Annie today? On the mend, I hope?'

'Bearing up, thanks for asking. She's out of bed now and managed to sit in the garden for a bit yesterday; I'm glad she wasn't caught up in that gas attack the other day, as it would have put her back weeks. She's always been a martyr to her bronchials.'

'Three pounds of potatoes, a pound of carrots, and half of onions, ta. You are lucky to have a decent sized garden; we've done the best we can with ours but there's no room to grow much in our small patch. That's why I'm always in here,' she added with a laugh.

He leant close as she tipped the potatoes into her bag and laid a piece of newspaper on top to protect the other vegetables. 'I've just heard that Nobby Clarke is giving up his allotment; it's got too much for him. His missus asked me if I knew anyone what would take it on. I hate to lose a good customer, but it would suit you down to the ground. That's if you've got time to tend it?'

'Like it? I'd jump at the chance to have an allotment to grow our own food. I've thought about it for a while now but not done a thing about it. Who does he rent from?'

'No one, he owns the strip of land himself; been in his family for donkey's years. He doesn't want to sell the land, from what she told me, as it runs along the back of his house in King Street. A basket of veg to keep the pair of them in food each week and to keep it tidy is all he's asking, but he wants it to go to a local who would make good use if it. Oh, and if they decide to sell up and move away, it goes without saying the allotment would be part of the sale.'

Flora's mind started to run away with ideas of how useful it would be to have the allotment. 'Can you tell his wife I'm interested and will be over to see them later today, air raids permitting?'

'I'll do better than that; I'll knock on their door on the way home for my dinner. We close for an hour these days to give me a rest now I've not got anyone helping me.'

Flora had the fleeting thought that Tom was after a job, but quickly dismissed it. She couldn't see him wanting to get his hands dirty. As faint grumbles about waiting for so long echoed through the queue behind her, she quickly gave her thanks and left the shop.

'It looks as though Tom has gone,' she said to Daisy as she clipped her into the pram seat.

'Gone,' Daisy pointed to the pram hood, which was still raised.

Flora frowned. What had happened to the primrose yellow blanket Miss Tibbs had knitted for Daisy when she first came to live as a baby at Sea View? It brightened the second-hand pram a treat. She unclipped the hood, ready to retrieve the blanket if Alexsy had kicked it to the bottom of the pram.

'Oh my goodness, he isn't here,' she exclaimed, causing Daisy to start crying loudly. Trying to still her fast-beating heart, she looked around her. Nowhere could she see a man carrying a small toddler wrapped in a yellow blanket. Whatever could she do?

'Is there something wrong?' a woman in the long queue asked as heads turned to stare.

'The baby, he's been taken,' Flora said, starting to feel faint. She grabbed the handle of the pram as Daisy continued to howl.

Soon, women had congregated around Flora asking questions. Did she have any idea who took him? How long had he been left? Why would anyone do such a thing? Were their own children safe . . . ? A flurry of women checked their own babies, who were all sleeping peacefully in their prams.

Flora's head started to spin as she answered as many of them as possible. 'Please, we need to find him,' she begged.

The greengrocer joined them, closing the door to his shop behind him. He was carrying a chair for Flora. 'I've rung the police on the shop telephone and they're on their way. Now, sit yourself down, Mrs Neville; you look fit to drop. Ladies, if you would care to come back in, say, half an hour, it would give Mrs Neville here time to compose herself and speak to the police. Is there anyone who would like to help look for the child?'

'I think I know who took him.' Flora gave them the best description of Tom White she could manage, and added that Alexsy had been wrapped in the primrose yellow knitted blanket.

Two younger women offered to look for the baby and were instructed to be back in fifteen minutes if they'd seen nothing in the surrounding streets.

'He can't have got far,' said the greengrocer, who had taken charge.

'Whose baby is it?' asked a woman Flora vaguely recognized from her Women's Institute meetings.

'He's the son of my lodger, Anya Polinski,' Flora said, thinking miserably of how she'd let her friend down by not taking care of her little boy.

'That poor woman whose husband is missing in action?' another neighbour asked.

'God forbid,' several people muttered.

'Perhaps she passed by and took him out of the pram?' the greengrocer suggested.

'No, she's in London, doing some training for Lyons. She left him in my care,' Flora explained, her voice cracking as she started to sob. 'Why has that hateful man taken him?'

'Now, now; tears aren't going to help, are they?' the greengrocer said, patting her shoulder and looking uncomfortable.

'You are right,' Flora said, wiping her eyes and pulling herself together.

'Can we get your Rose to come and help you?' the lady from the WI asked. 'I'm sure we could use your telephone to contact her,' she added, turning to the shop owner.

'It's no use; she has gone to meet her husband. He's on twenty-four hours' leave. If you could contact Joyce Hannigan at the Lyons teashop in Margate, she will be able to help me,' Flora suggested, knowing Joyce had a sensible head on her shoulders and would be good in a crisis.

'I'll do that right now,' the greengrocer said. 'Look: here comes a policeman.' He pointed to where the local bobby was cycling towards them.

Flora breathed a sigh of relief as the police officer parked his bicycle at the kerb.

'Would we be able to speak inside your shop?' he asked the greengrocer, nodding towards the growing crowd.

'By all means; let's use my back room, then my wife can come out and serve these ladies,' the greengrocer said, holding the door open to assist them through. 'You can bring the pram as well,' he added to Flora, who was dithering over what to do.

'Please do; it will be part of the evidence,' the constable told her as he took over holding the door for Flora to enter.

Flora faltered. 'Evidence? Surely we should all be out looking for Tom White, as he is the person who took the baby?'

The constable looked confused. 'You can't go throwing allegations all over the place; it may offend the person you are accusing,' he tutted.

'I'm not throwing allegations anywhere. I have reason to know he has taken Alexsy Polinski, thinking the child is Lily Douglas's daughter, Mary.'

'Why would he do such a thing?' the constable asked as he pulled out his notebook.

The greengrocer's wife stopped tying her apron to listen to their conversation.

Flora stopped speaking.

'This way,' the greengrocer said as he ushered her through to a back room that formed part of his family's living accommodation.

'I'll leave you to it,' he said, nodding to Flora and the constable.

'Thank you for being so kind. I'm sorry to be such a nuisance.'

The greengrocer shook his head. 'I'm partly to blame. If I'd not kept you talking about that allotment, the child might not have been taken.'

Flora managed a weak smile to reassure him. 'Tom wouldn't have been slow to grasp the opportunity to take the child . . .'

'Now, Mrs Neville, shall we start at the beginning?'

The beginning? Flora thought to herself. All she could think of was what an idiot she'd been, leaving little Alexsy outside for Tom White to snatch.

16

Rose had hoped for some time to prepare before Ben arrived to meet her at his mother's apartment in London. As it was, she opened the door to be greeted by the seductive sight of a champagne bottle being uncorked, and her husband approached to greet her with two champagne saucers filled to the brim.

'Careful,' she shrieked as he tried to kiss her, fearful of tipping her drink all over Lady Diana's luxurious Persian rug. She put both glasses down on a side table, then returned to where he held out his arms to her. 'I can't stand you being away from me for so long. Can't you hurry up and finish this war, so we can settle down and never leave each other for at least the next fifty years?'

'Believe me, I'm trying,' he whispered into her hair as he ran his hands down her back, gripping her hips as he pulled her even closer. Slowly he pulled up the dress she'd chosen especially for their meeting, exposing her new stockings and suspender belt. Rose thanked God she'd worn her best underwear and not saved it for when he took her out to dinner. Ben was a caring and thoughtful lover, and she savoured his touch as he tried to ease her dress over her head. 'Why so many buttons?' he asked in frustration.

'I could ask the same of you,' she replied breathlessly, trying to unbutton his uniform shirt.

'It's not good,' he said, swinging her over his shoulder and heading for the bedroom Lady Diana kept at their disposal. There they spent the next few hours getting re-acquainted in the best way they knew.

Later, Rose raised her head from the pillow and looked at the clothes strewn across the room. 'So much for my plan to greet you in my new negligee and seduce my returning hero,' she sighed, running her fingers through the soft hair on his chest.

'You could go outside and we could start again if you like?' he suggested, gazing at her nakedness.

'I'd frighten the doorman,' she chuckled, pulling a sheet up to cover her breasts.

'Don't tell me you are embarrassed?' he smiled gently, pulling back the sheet. 'I've dreamt of this moment for months and want to gaze at your beauty for ever.'

She took his hand in hers and kissed each fingertip. 'You think I haven't? I'd like to retain a little mystery, if you don't mind.'

'Mystery be damned,' he growled as he playfully tore away the sheet and took her into his arms once more.

'But I thought you'd booked a table for dinner?' she asked, pretending to be shocked at his advances but in the end succumbing, as keen as he was to continue their lovemaking.

'The table's booked for the whole evening,' he mumbled into her ear. 'There's nothing we need to rush out for.'

The sound of sirens filled the air.

'You shouldn't have tempted fate,' Rose sighed. 'Come on, let's get down to the cellar, but put some clothes on first.'

'To be continued,' he said ruefully as he reached for his trousers.

'I never expected to be dining on cheese on toast washed down with champagne,' Rose said that evening, once the all clear had sounded and they returned to the apartment.

'Food of the gods,' Ben sighed as he topped up their glasses. 'You can wear your dancing shoes another time, when I have leave for more than twenty-four hours.'

'And my new nightdress . . . ?'

He looked up at the clock as its hands moved towards midnight. 'There's still time, if you're keen?'

'Give me five minutes,' Rose grinned, grabbing her suitcase from where it had been left in the middle of the lounge floor and hurrying to the bathroom.

'Can I help?' he called after her.

'Not this time, but perhaps later,' she replied, looking round the open bathroom door towards him and raising her eyebrows suggestively before disappearing as she started to sing, *I'm in the mood for love . . .*

'It's not five minutes since you came home,' Rose said, trying not to look sad; she didn't want Ben's last memory of her to be of a weeping wife. 'I don't even know where you're heading off to,' she added, straightening his tie and picking up his cap from where he'd left it on the sofa. 'Write as soon as you can?' She gave him a gentle kiss.

'I'm sorry I can't tell you where I'll be. It was so much simpler when I was seconded to the Ministry of Food, but now . . .'

'Just stay safe . . . do it for me. No heroics. If anything happens to you, I'll never forgive you – do you hear me?'

Ben smiled. He knew better than to argue with his wife. 'I promise, and now I must go, as my driver is waiting for me in the lobby. Knowing him, he will be pacing the floor. Goodbye, my sweetheart,' he said, pulling her close for one last hug. 'Ruth will be back later today, if you need company.' Ruth had very decently agreed to stay with a friend the previous night, to give Rose and Ben some privacy. 'We had the chance to have a few words before you arrived.'

'That was kind, but I doubt I'll see her as I must get back home; I'm on duty tomorrow.'

Rose watched the door close behind him. She'd promised to be brave and so she would, she thought, fighting back tears. I'll go find Anya and take her out to lunch, she decided as she went to pack her suitcase, ready to catch the late train home to Ramsgate. She stopped to look at the crumpled bed before straightening the covers. 'So little time . . .' she said out loud, before scolding herself. 'Think to the future and forget the present,' she muttered, seating herself at the ornate dressing table and peering into the mirror. 'I'm so lucky to be loved.'

After leaving Lady Diana's apartment, Rose hurried along the Strand towards the Lyons restaurant, where she was sure she'd find Anya working on the second floor. She'd attended the same training rooms herself when she had first been promoted to manageress, which seemed a lifetime ago now.

After stepping back to allow diners to go ahead of her, she turned right through two swing doors and, not waiting for the lift, almost skipped up the two flights of stairs. Seeing Ben, along with their night of passion, had certainly put a spring in her step. She'd best calm down, she told herself, as Anya would be sure to notice a difference in her and ask questions. She was as sharp as a knife at times. With Henio being missing for so long it wouldn't do for Rose to be talking about Ben being home for his short leave. She wouldn't wish to hurt her Polish friend when Anya was working so hard.

'How may I help you?' a receptionist asked as Rose entered the door to the training rooms.

'I'm Rose Hargreaves, manageress of the Margate teashop. I wondered if I could speak to Mrs Anya Polinski? She is here training the Sallys,' Rose said politely.

The woman looked at a list on her desk and frowned. 'If you would excuse me for one moment, I'll check; please take a seat.'

'Thank you,' Rose smiled. She sat on one of the comfortable armchairs at the side of the reception area. A group of women passed through, wearing the dark blue Sally uniform: it was like the Nippy uniform, but without the apron or smart cap. Even though Anya had only been gone for just over a week, Rose was looking forward to seeing her face. She missed Anya's quick wit and the way she kept the counter section of the teashop in order. Anya was such a reliable member of her staff. What would she do without her? She stood up as the receptionist returned.

'I'm awfully sorry, but there must be some mistake,' the woman said. 'Mrs Polinski isn't working here.'

Rose frowned. 'Are you sure? I received the letter from head office myself instructing Anya – Mrs Polinski – about this appointment; she's been here for nearly ten days now. May I speak to the manager, please?' she asked.

'Of course,' the woman replied, picking up a telephone and dialling a number. Rose turned away, not wanting to appear rude and listen in.

After a hushed conversation, the woman replaced the receiver. 'My manager will come out to speak with you in a moment,' she said to Rose. This time, she was not smiling.

Rose nodded her thanks and decided not to sit down again. A tight knot was forming in her stomach as she started to wonder what had happened. She knew she had the correct address; she recalled telling Anya about the building and this part of London. Come to think of it, Anya hadn't seemed very interested. Whatever had happened to her? Rose prayed her friend hadn't been caught up in an air raid. She could be lying in hospital somewhere, unconscious or, God forbid, something worse . . .

She jumped as someone spoke to her. So deep in thought had she been, she hadn't noticed a grey-suited man entering the room.

He held out his hand. 'Mrs Hargreaves, I am pleased to meet you. I'm Percival Montgomery. Let's talk in private.'

Rose shook his hand, but fear was gripping her so hard that she could hardly walk as he led her down a narrow hall to an office.

'Please take a seat. Can I offer you any refreshment?'

'Tea would be nice, thank you,' she said, trying to think why his name was so familiar. Of course: his had been the name on the letter that had been sent to her requesting Anya attend the training school.

They made small talk about the weather and her journey to London until a tea tray had been brought in. 'Will you be mother?' he asked.

'Of course,' she replied, before realizing in dismay that her hands were shaking uncontrollably. She did her best to pour but was horrified as tea spilled over into the saucers. 'I'm so sorry,' she said, replacing the silver pot on the tray. 'You must think I'm an awful Nippy if I can't do a simple task like pouring tea. It's just that I'm so worried about Anya – Mrs Polinski. I can't understand why she isn't here. Do you know anything about this? Could she have been injured in an air raid?'

Percival Montgomery looked uncomfortable and twisted his fountain pen between his fingers. 'This is rather difficult . . .'

Rose felt her temper rising. 'Please, just tell me, as I must think of her son. You know her husband is missing in action? This could make her little boy, Alexsy, an orphan.'

He raised his hand to stop her talking. 'Please, Mrs Hargreaves: Anya Polinski is not dead and neither is she injured. Well, not to my knowledge. I'm not at liberty to tell you anything, but believe me, she is doing a service for our country, and that is all I know. If I knew any more than that, I would not be at liberty to say.'

Rose was confused. 'Mr Montgomery, I am not going anywhere until I know what has happened to Anya,' she said, crossing her arms across her chest and giving him a stubborn look.

'Mrs Hargreaves . . . Rose, please don't make this difficult for me.'

'Oh, Mr Montgomery, believe me, I am going to be extremely difficult if I don't find out where my friend has disappeared to.'

He pulled a handkerchief from his pocket and mopped his brow. 'I can only direct you to where you may be able to find more information, and that is to speak to your family. Now, if you will excuse me, I have a meeting to attend. Please stay and drink your tea,' he said, getting up and leaving the room as fast as he could.

'I don't want tea – I want answers,' she called after him. After waiting for a while, she decided to go back to the apartment and use Lady Diana's telephone to speak to her mother. Surely Flora would know what to do.

17

Rose made her way as quickly as she could back to the apartment, hardly speaking to the doorman as he tapped the brim of his hat in recognition. Her hands trembled as she fumbled with her key, and once inside the apartment she threw her coat down and hurried to the telephone. She knew Sea View's number off by heart, but even so, she had to try three times as her fingers kept slipping into the wrong holes of the dial, such was her agitation.

At last she heard ringing on the other end of the line. She sat down on the side of a nearby armchair, breathing deeply to calm herself.

'Hello, Mum?' she asked when someone answered.

'No, this is Miss Tibbs – who may I say is calling?'

'Miss Tibbs, this is Rose. Please can you fetch Mum for me?' She prayed Miss Tibbs wouldn't want to chat, as she often did when Rose rang from the teashop.

'She's indisposed,' Miss Tibbs said importantly. 'Can you telephone later? She asked me to write down any messages.'

'I'm afraid I can't; this is very important.' Rose took a

deep breath; it would take something major for Miss Tibbs to get Flora to the telephone once she had told her she didn't wish to be disturbed. 'Someone has disappeared and I need Mum's advice,' she said clearly so that the old woman would understand. She didn't name Anya, as Miss Tibbs was prone to gossiping, which wouldn't do at all.

'We know, dear, that is why Flora is resting. It has been rather a shock to us all. The policeman has only just left. Joyce and Lily have organized a search party.'

Rose didn't understand: what was Miss Tibbs wittering on about? How could they all know about Anya, when she had only just discovered their friend was missing? 'Please bring Mum to the phone,' she begged. She was still waiting, nervously chewing a fingernail, when Ruth let herself into the apartment a few minutes later.

'Hello, Rose, where is my errant brother? Have I missed him?'

Rose put her hand over the receiver. 'He left a couple of hours ago; sorry, I'll be with you in a moment, Ruth . . . lovely to see you, by the way,' she managed to smile as she turned her back to speak to Flora.

'Mum, whatever is Miss Tibbs doing answering the telephone? You know how she gets confused. Look, I can't hang about, but wanted you to know that Anya isn't where she said she was. I've just been to the training school, and they say she's not working there. A manager told me to speak to Ben about it as he knows something. It was all a bit garbled, but I'm going to have to stay on here another day to find out what is happening. I'm about to ring the police to ask for help . . . Mum, are you there?'

'Darling, please stop talking, I can't get a word in edgeways.

I too have disturbing news; the police have just left. Someone took Anya's son this morning.' Flora went on to explain what had happened. 'The police won't believe me when I tell them it was Tom White. I believe he took the baby thinking it was Mary.' Now it was Flora's turn to call down the line, as it crackled and the sound faltered. 'Rose . . . can you hear me?'

Ruth stepped in front of Rose and held out her hand. 'Give me the telephone, Rose,' she said firmly. Surprised, Rose held out the receiver to her sister-in-law, who placed it back into its cradle. 'Now, let's sit down and have a talk, shall we?'

'I can't, I need to speak to the police. I don't know if you heard, Ruth, but I found out this morning that Anya isn't at work – and she never has been. Something terrible must have happened to her,' Rose stammered, her throat constricting with the tension of holding back tears. 'And now Mum says someone has taken Alexsy. She mentioned Tom White's name . . .'

'Oh God,' Ruth said, her hard exterior shattering as she put her arms round Rose and hugged her.

'Anya needs to know as soon as possible, but I don't know where she is. What a bloody mess! Mr Montgomery at the training school told me to look to my family. He didn't say any more and he seemed not to want to speak to me. He all but ran out of his office. I just don't understand,' she cried.

'It's me who knows what happened to Anya,' Ruth said, 'and I'm not able to tell you anything.' She reached for a silver cigarette box on a nearby occasional table, took out a cigarette with trembling fingers and lit it before offering it to Rose.

'I will, thank you; my nerves are shattered,' Rose said, taking the cigarette with shaking hands. 'I want to know what's happening, Ruth. It'll go no further. However, if you don't tell me, I'll blab to everyone I know . . .' She glared at her sister-in-law.

'I can say that Anya is safe and well at this very moment.'

Rose frowned. 'You make it sound as though she's being held against her will.'

Ruth gave her a pleading look. 'Don't ask me any more. I won't be able to answer without getting into serious trouble.'

Rose snorted. 'You mean to say, you care more about saving your own skin than you do about Anya's safety?'

'That's not the case at all. We are in the middle of a war, Rose, and although people laugh at the warning posters, it is very true that careless talk can cost lives.'

Rose turned pale. 'I don't begin to understand what is happening, but can't you at least get word to Anya that Alexsy is missing?'

Ruth shook her head, dismissing the idea at once. 'Anya needs to be one hundred per cent focused on what she is doing. If her mind should wander . . . I dread to think what would happen.' She went to the cocktail cabinet and poured two generous helpings of brandy. 'I think we both need this; go on, take it,' she insisted, as Rose started to refuse. 'Tell me more about this man who is supposed to have taken Anya's child.'

Rose sipped the amber liquid slowly, wincing as it burnt the back of her throat, and then began to tell Ruth about Tom White and what a bounder he was. 'Mum seems to think he took Alexsy by mistake, thinking he was Mary.

But why he wants the little girl after all this time, when he was so beastly to Lily, God only knows.'

'It does sound likely that Flora is right and he thought he was snatching Mary,' Ruth said thoughtfully. 'But why would a man take such a risk, trying to snatch a child he's never shown any feeling for and didn't even want to acknowledge? We all agree he is up to no good, but there must be a reason . . .'

'When he spoke with Mum yesterday, he got her to say she would ask Lily if he could see his child.'

Ruth raised her eyebrows. 'And did she do that?'

'No, I don't think she'd had a chance yet.'

'So it's possible that when he bumped into Flora today, he decided on impulse to make the most of the encounter and snatch the child?'

'That sounds about right, but you'd need to speak to her to check the facts.'

'Rather tricky, as she'd want to know why I was involving myself in the whole situation. I do sympathize, though. And actually, I know of someone who could turn up to help . . .'

Rose put down her glass. 'In that case, I'm going to head for home and see what I can do there. What shall I say about Anya?'

'Tell Flora she's been moved to Lyons' head office at Cadby Hall to help out there due to staff shortages. She's not likely to question you.'

'Good idea, but can you promise me that when you know something about Anya, you will tell me? My lips are sealed,' Rose said, running her fingers along her mouth as if to zip it closed.

'I'll do my best,' Ruth said, although she didn't make eye contact as she spoke. 'Let me get you a taxi to the station. I'll pay for it.'

'Thank you,' Rose said. That would mean she'd be able to catch an earlier train to get home and help with the search. 'When will the person you know turn up at Ramsgate? And should I say something to Mum?'

'Let's keep it between ourselves, so Flora doesn't get wind that I'm involved. It's best if as few people know as possible.'

Rose went to collect her suitcase from the bedroom, wondering what else Ruth wasn't telling her.

'It's been twenty-four hours and Alexsy is still missing,' Katie sniffed. 'What can we do to help that we've not done already?' she asked.

'Don't be disheartened,' Lily consoled her. 'I feel it in my gut that he will be found before too long, especially if Flora is right and it was my Mary Tom thought he had taken. Mind you, if I get my hands on the blighter, I'll knock him from here to next Tuesday and back again.'

Katie looked at Lily through unshed tears. 'Be careful. I wouldn't put it past him to be violent. The police wouldn't be impressed, either.'

'Pah to the police, they've done very little since it happened. If it wasn't for friends and neighbours, there'd be no one out searching for him.'

Katie turned away from Lily and took out her handkerchief to wipe her eyes.

'Please don't be upset, Katie. Alexsy will be found.'

'Anya trusted me to care for him. Whatever will she think?

There is something else . . . I wasn't going to say anything, but . . .'

'Come on, you can tell me.' Lily put her arm around her friend's shoulder.

'I hoped that after my Jack came home on leave, I'd be pregnant.'

Lily was puzzled. 'Surely it's too soon to know? It's only been a few days.'

'No,' Katie sniffed. 'Aunty visited hours after he left. I prayed that this time it would happen.'

'Oh, you poor thing,' Lily sympathized. 'No wonder you're so down. But you and Jack are young; you will fall before too long.'

'I hope so. I was hoping to be able to write to him in a few months and give him good news. He must think it is my fault.'

'It's no one's fault. You need to do something to take your mind off things. We both don't need to be in work until this afternoon, so why don't we go down to Flora's and help her put up some posters around the town? There's a bus due in ten minutes. Wash your face and let's get our skates on.'

'Do you mind going on your own? I want to wash my hair before I start work.'

'Of course I don't mind; and then let's have a lazy evening at home. I'll bring some leftover food home after work, so we won't need to cook.'

'That sounds lovely – you will be careful, won't you? In case Mary gets taken?'

'I'll guard her with my life,' Lily promised as she went to get Mary ready for her outing.

Katie put water into the largest of their pans and set it on the stove to heat along with the kettle; that would be enough to wash her hair, and then have a cup of tea afterwards. She felt rather a fool for breaking down in front of Lily, but she'd felt so low about not having a baby of her own. Watching both Lily and Anya with their youngsters, and Flora bringing up Daisy after adopting her, she felt left out.

Thinking of Anya spurred her on to wash and dry her hair as quickly as possible so that she could hurry to Flora's before her shift and collect some posters to put up in the Ramsgate teashop. She also had a photograph of Alexsy that she would show to customers. An hour later, having checked her hair and added a little rouge to her cheeks, she decided she was ready to go to work. After making sure the back door was locked she went to the front door, collecting her coat and gas mask from the hallstand. As she was buttoning up her navy blue coat and tying the belt there was a knock on the door.

'Hold on a moment,' she called out as she picked up her bag and mask, meaning to speak to whoever it was and leave at the same time. A smile crossed her face as she saw who was on her doorstep. 'Hello; are you on your own?' she asked, glancing past Stew for Peter.

Stew was struggling with a large box. 'He's on duty. I wanted to drop this by, but I see you are going out,' he said.

'I'm in good time, so I can catch the next bus,' she smiled, stepping back so he could come into the house.

'Shall I go through to the kitchen?'

'Please do, before you drop that,' she replied, taking off her coat and hanging it up. 'I'm intrigued as to what's inside.'

He pulled open the flaps of carboard and stepped back for her to look in. 'Oh my goodness, two chickens!' she shrieked, causing them to flutter their wings.

'I'm assured they are good layers,' he said as he closed the box. 'I can bring around another two, if you're keen?'

'I'm sorely tempted, as we can always share the eggs with the ladies at Sea View and the children will love helping to care for them. Will they be all right in the empty rabbit hutch until we build them a proper home? Mary has no idea that the rabbits went into the pot recently. We felt awful, but that was the idea for having them.'

'I don't see why not. Let's go out to the garden and see if it's suitable. I can come round and build you a proper house for them, if I can stay to tea and have boiled eggs and soldiers,' he grinned.

'That's a deal. My mouth is watering at the thought,' she said, unlocking the door and leading him out into the garden. Her mood lifted as Stew explained that he'd always had chickens at home, and hoped his wife was managing to care for them on her own.

'I'm eager to learn,' she smiled. 'Flora has been offered an allotment and we are all going to help maintain it. What with fresh fish from Mildred and our own vegetables and eggs, we won't have to worry about queuing and rationing quite as much.'

'Have you thought about organizing a pig club?'

'Crikey, no! I don't want a pig living in our back garden.'

'Think about it. I'm happy to help advise on that as well as running an allotment.'

'Do you have time, what with fighting a war?' she asked, thinking how generous he was being to a group of strangers.

'It's my pleasure; I miss growing and building things. My wife will have a list a mile long when I get home and I'll enjoy putting things right and helping look after our children when I can. Here, let me show you my family,' he said, reaching into his jacket pocket and pulling out a wallet containing several photographs. She was just about to take them when in the distance the sound of the air-raid siren started to grow, getting louder and louder until they could see something on the horizon. 'Enemy planes,' he said, cupping his eyes with his hands.

She grabbed his arm, a look of panic on her face. 'We've got to get into the shelter. It's this way,' she said, pulling him towards the bottom of the garden.

They almost fell into the Anderson shelter as the sound of planes droned overhead. Stew closed the doors, plunging them into darkness.

'We have some candles and matches,' Katie said, starting to feel around.

'Here, let me help.' He flicked on his cigarette lighter. The flame cast flickering shadows throughout the shelter, causing Katie to shiver as she reached under the bunk bed to retrieve a biscuit tin containing candles and matches. It was wrapped in oilcloth to keep them dry.

'Under normal circumstances I'd have brought the bag containing a torch and flasks that we keep by the back door. There was also a can of paraffin to top up the stove; it's enough to warm this small space,' she said, shivering. 'Everything gets so damp down here, we tend to carry blankets and rugs indoors to dry them out.'

'Don't tell me, they're in the kitchen,' he said with a rueful laugh, as she lit two candles and secured them on old saucers. 'Hopefully we won't be down here for long, but I'll go and get them.' He started to get to his feet to open the shelter door.

'No!' she shrieked, grabbing his jacket and pulling him back towards her. 'Don't be a fool. With luck they'll be heading for the airfield, but you can't take that chance.'

A look of pain crossed his face. 'I pray the lads got our planes up in time,' he said as he sank down onto the bottom bunk. Katie sat next to him, shivering, as the sound of bombs exploding could be heard not far away.

'Show me the photographs of your family,' she said, trying to distract them both from thoughts of his comrades fighting the enemy.

He reached into his pocket and took out the photographs. 'This is John, our eldest; he will be nine now, and Andrew is coming up seven years of age. Grace, our youngest, is three; it doesn't seem five minutes since she was born. In fact . . .' He pulled out his wallet and removed a smaller photograph. 'This is Moira, my wife, not long before Grace was born.' The photo showed a heavily pregnant woman laughing into the camera.

Katie felt a sob catch in her throat. That's all I've ever wanted, she thought to herself as she trembled uncontrollably.

'Here, take this,' he said, noticing her shivering and removing his jacket to place around her shoulders. She leant against him, feeling his warmth and comforting arms as he held her close while her tears flowed. Her grief for the family she so desperately wanted, and might never have, poured out like never before. Here in the dimly lit shelter, somehow it felt safe for her to let the feelings out while Stew held her close and whispered words of comfort.

18

'I know this woman!' Anya exclaimed, stabbing her finger at the grainy image of a woman on the arm of a German officer. 'It is Anouska Bartkowicz.'

'Are you sure?' Ruth asked. Kenneth puffed on his pipe, nodding thoughtfully.

'Did I not escape from Poland with her? You learn to know someone when you travel together hiding from the enemy for many weeks. Why is she with this man?' Anya added with a sneer. 'She hated these pigs.'

'Times have changed, particularly in her life,' Ruth said, looking sympathetic.

'They cannot have changed that much. She would never fraternize with the people who murdered the people from our village,' Anya spat. 'This must be an impostor.'

'That is why we need your help to identify her at close range,' Kenneth explained. 'I cannot tell you much more than that, apart from you identifying this woman will aid the war effort.'

Anya was silent for a moment as she digested his words.

'What happens next? I hope I am not to be dropped into enemy territory like others I hear of?'

Ruth shook her head. 'We don't plan to drop you by parachute due to your lack of training; instead you will meet someone who will take you there and bring you back. You will observe the target and once you are sure she is, or isn't, Anouska Bartkowicz, you will be brought back to England. Are you confident in your new identity?'

'A very nice lady is teaching me about my identity, Monique Breton, and I have clothes and papers; I am to have my hair cut after this meeting. I am not sure my Henio would approve as he prefers my long hair and would be surprised to see me use red lipstick, but I will do it if it helps the war to end.'

'It is to make you look more French and blend in with the other women, so you do not stand out. Your beautiful hair will soon grow, and I'm sure Henio would understand.'

'When do I go?'

'Very soon. I will take you to the drop-off point; you will travel at night. Your companion will instruct you about the destination when you meet. There will be an agent in the field who can assist if things go wrong – but they shouldn't,' she was quick to add, seeing a look of alarm cross Anya's face.

'I will trust you, not that I have much choice. The sooner I am home and with my child, the better,' she replied.

Ruth turned away in case her thoughts showed on her face.

*

Rose sat across the kitchen table from her mum, both barely saying a word as the mugs of tea in front of them grew cold.

'I blame myself; I've gone over and over my conversation with Tom White, and not once did I say that the child sleeping in the pram was Alexsy and not Mary. What a fool I've been,' Flora said, giving a bitter sigh.

'Oh, Mum, you mustn't think like that. I would have done the same in your shoes,' Rose said, trying to console her; although privately she knew she wouldn't even have given Tom White the time of day, let alone tried to help him. 'Shall I speak to the police again to see if there have been any developments? At least I will feel as though I've done something.'

'Very well, dear. This is the telephone number. Ask for Chief Inspector Atkins – I kicked up such a stink down at the police station, the desk sergeant called a superior.'

Rose took the piece of paper with the number and hurried up the short staircase to the hall, where the telephone sat on a shelf with a notepad and pen beside it. She prayed there was still time to find Alexsy before Anya returned from wherever she had been sent. Oh, if only Ben was home; he'd soon get the information out of his sister, she thought as she picked up the receiver and started to dial.

She'd only just got through to the inspector when someone knocked at the front door. 'Excuse me for one moment,' she said politely, expecting it to be one of the residents who were out looking for Alexsy. 'Oh . . .'

The man standing there, holding a wooden crate and a bunch of flowers, gave her a grin.

'I'm sorry, I'm on the telephone to the police. Mum's in the kitchen; you know the way,' Rose told him before returning to her call.

Down in the kitchen, Flora had started to tidy the kitchen and was wondering what to make for the evening meal. No one had had much of an appetite these past couple of days.

'Knock, knock,' a familiar voice called from the doorway, making her jump. 'I hope I'm not intruding?'

Flora felt her heart flutter. She'd told herself there was no future for her with John Bentley, but still he filled her thoughts and her dreams.

'Hello, stranger,' she said, trying to react as if it was perfectly normal for him to walk into her kitchen unannounced. As he placed the crate on the tabletop she pulled off her faded pinny and discreetly ran her fingers through her hair, attempting to tidy herself.

'Rose told me to come down,' he said. 'This is from Lady Diana – and these are from me,' he added, holding out a bunch of red roses.

'Oh my goodness; they are gorgeous,' Flora said, breathing in the heady perfume. 'Surely they aren't in season?'

'Let's just say I know a man with a hothouse,' John laughed.

'You've not changed,' she said, smiling. 'I know the perfect vase for these. It was a wedding present from the girls in the chorus line when I left the business; it seems so long ago now,' she sighed, kneeling down in front of the dresser and reaching to the back of one of the three cupboards. She pulled out a tall cut-glass vase. 'Perfect,' she said as she rinsed it under the tap before carefully filling it with the long-stemmed roses and placing it in the middle of the table. Finally, she stepped back to gaze at the display. 'Aren't they beautiful?'

'Not as beautiful as you,' he said, moving towards her.

'Now, John, we agreed to keep things platonic,' she said, wagging a finger at him, even though she'd have liked nothing more than to have him kiss her. 'Besides, my daughter could walk in at any minute.'

John laughed quietly. 'Rose is a grown-up married woman; I'm sure she wouldn't deny her mother a romance.'

Flora gave him a stern look. 'Is that your intention, John? Because you've a funny way of showing it. You vanish for months on end, then saunter in as if you were here only yesterday without an apology. I can't live like that, even if you can. I'd rather be friends and nothing more until such a time as you understand I'm not a woman who only wants a dalliance. I'm not talking of marriage, we've both done that – and I won't live in sin either,' she said as he raised his eyebrows. 'I just want some kind of commitment, so until you can make up your mind, then keep your kisses to yourself.'

'I'll put the kettle on, then, while you open the crate,' he said, without showing any kind of upset at her sharp words.

'Ooh, what is this?' Rose said as she joined them.

'A Red Cross parcel from Diana, by the looks of it. She's such a generous person. When did you see her, John?'

'I didn't. She sent the crate down by train from Scotland, I collected it at the station in London and delivered it in person as I'm down this way on business. Tea, Rose?'

'Please,' she replied, sitting close to where Flora was pulling back the lid and removing the straw packing. 'If you don't have a use for the crate, it would make a lovely toy box for Mary; that's if you don't want it for Daisy?'

'What a good idea. Daisy has a toy box, so I'll have Mildred drop it over to Captain's Cottage when she's passing,' Flora said as she pulled out the first of the items. 'My goodness, a Dundee cake; I didn't even think these were being made since the war started. And a bottle of whisky, and a haggis; I've not eaten that for years. It's delicious,' she said, seeing Rose's look of distaste.

'I almost forgot,' Rose said, reaching into the pocket of her dress and pulling out an envelope. 'This was by the telephone; I spotted it while speaking to the police. Your name is on the front, Mum.'

John looked puzzled as he brought the tea to the table. 'What's this about the police, if you don't mind me asking?'

'Anya's son has gone missing,' Rose started to explain. 'Everyone is out looking for him.'

'Not everyone,' Flora said, looking miffed as she continued to unpack the crate. 'Mildred has decided to go and visit a family friend, so won't be home for a few days. I'd have thought better of her, when we have an emergency on our hands,' she said, pulling out a beef joint and a shoulder of lamb. 'Gosh, Diana is so generous. In my next life I'm going to marry a man who owns a farm in Scotland and doesn't mind feeding his friends during wartime. Help me put these in the larder, Rose, then we can sit down and tell John what has happened. You never know, he may have an idea that can help us.'

Flora and Rose held nothing back, from Anya's mysterious absence to Alexsy going missing. They even explained how Jennie had moved into Captain's Cottage for a while to help care for the children so the girls could go to work.

'It's been like playing chess at times. We've even planned our shifts at the two shops around caring for the little ones,' Rose explained. She looked at her mum. 'I'm moving back in here for the foreseeable future. I'll let Ben know, and pop over to the house and shut it up for a while. I have good neighbours who will keep an eye on it and let me know if anything should happen.'

'Happen?' John asked.

'Air raids. We are at war, if you'd not noticed,' Rose ribbed him.

'Tell me more about this Tom White,' he said, taking a small diary and a pencil from an inside pocket of his jacket. He started to make notes as the women talked, and occasionally asked questions. 'Where does he tend to pick up his lady friends?' he asked, trying to be tactful.

'He found Jennie at the Ramsgate teashop, but we feel he was only in there to try to find out about Lily. From what I remember, when he worked for Joe Lyons, he did like to have a drink. If he is still in the area, no doubt he'll be visiting the pubs,' Rose said.

Flora looked concerned. 'He wouldn't take Alexsy to a pub, would he? People would ask questions, and with the number of posters we've pinned up around town he'd be a fool to even try it.'

'What if he isn't working alone?' John suggested.

'I can see no reason why he would work with someone else. Unless . . .' Flora started to speak, but hesitated and looked to John for guidance.

'Unless what, John?' Rose asked frantically. 'If you have an idea, please share it with us.'

'Well, perhaps he has someone lined up to take on a

little girl for the right price. There must be plenty of couples who would adore to be parents of a daughter he is not interested in. Why else would he come back to Ramsgate and ask about Lily and where she lives?'

Rose's eyes opened wide. 'You could be right. But what happens when he realizes it isn't Mary, and instead he has stolen a little boy?'

'I've been worrying about that all day,' Flora said miserably. 'Oh God, it's all so dreadful.' She leant her head into her arms and started to weep.

'Stop crying,' John told her firmly. 'We've got to keep thinking about what could have happened. Then we can go out and find him.'

Flora wiped her eyes and straightened up, apologizing. 'I'm fine,' she said as Rose looked concerned. 'John's right; let's keep thinking. I take it the police have not come up with anything, Rose?'

'They made all the right noises, but I didn't learn anything from the conversation. Our hopes lie with what we can do ourselves.'

John looked thoughtful. 'If he, or a possible companion, wanted to get rid of the boy, where would they take him? I'm not even suggesting they'd have killed him and got rid of the body. Tom White may be a bad one, but I doubt even he would stoop to killing an innocent child.'

'Perhaps he'd have left him somewhere?' Flora chipped in.

'We can forget about them leaving him on the doorstep of a police station, as we'd have heard by now.'

'Put yourself in his place: what would you do?'

'I would want to leave the child somewhere safe. And I'd also want to know who he was,' Flora answered.

'Mum, if he's still in the area, the chances are he will have found out who Alexsy is from all the posters and the locals gossiping. He's only got to overhear someone talking. I do believe he will leave Alexsy somewhere safe – somewhere where he will be found. Have you checked our back garden? The gate isn't locked. I doubt he would leave Alexsy on the front steps . . .'

The women looked at each other for a moment and then leapt up and dashed to the back door, flinging it wide open. There wasn't a child in the garden.

'That was a silly idea. He'd know he might be seen entering our small garden,' Flora said as she closed the door.

'It was worth checking, Mum. We don't know what he's thinking.'

Flora started to pace around the kitchen. 'We've got to work it out; I feel as though we are almost there.'

'It would help if we had a photograph of Tom that could be shown around town. Didn't the police ask if Lily had one?'

'They did, but Lily was so shocked at the idea of him trying to abduct Mary that she couldn't think straight at the time. There again, they didn't have the kind of courtship that she'd have kept mementos,' Flora explained to John. 'Would you agree, Rose?'

Frown lines creased Rose's forehead. 'Mum, do you have the family photograph album handy? I'm sure I gave you a couple of photos that were taken at the Margate teashop's Christmas dance round about the time Tom White worked for the company.'

'I put a lot of our photos into a biscuit tin and hid it under a floorboard in the cupboard under the stairs, in case the house took a hit during an air raid. I'll get it now,' Flora said as the ominous sound of the air-raid siren started to build from a few streets away. 'Trust Moaning Minnie to interrupt us,' she sighed. 'Rose, can you go and collect Miss Tibbs and Daisy? They are sorting out Miss Tibbs' button box,' she smiled. 'John, grab those bags by the door while I fill the flasks, and then we must hurry to the tunnels. I take it you will join us?'

'Try to keep me away,' he said, already on his feet and following her instructions.

19

Lily clambered down from the bus, holding Mary on her hip, as the driver shouted for the passengers to hurry and take cover.

'There's an entrance to the tunnels over the road,' he called after them. Most people didn't need a second bidding as they hurried to join a fast-moving queue of Ramsgate residents taking shelter underground.

Lily smiled to herself. This was such a regular occurrence these days that the conversations of those around her continued as they had done before the siren sounded.

'I've got this jumper of your dad's to unpick; it'll give me something to do while we wait for the all clear.'

'I was just about to put a pudding on to steam – bloody Hitler will ruin our dinner.'

'I hope no one's pinched our spot . . .'

'Has there been any news about that young boy who was snatched?'

Lily's ears pricked up as the woman who had asked the question turned to her neighbours, waiting for an answer.

She kept close to the group as they shuffled deeper into the tunnels.

'I heard a yellow knitted blanket was found along King Street this morning.'

Lily couldn't stop herself from interrupting. 'Do you know where in King Street?'

As if it was the most natural thing in the world, Lily was included in their conversation. 'Up by the chemist's. The owner had put it in the window in case someone claimed it. My neighbour spotted it and told him it could be the one the little lad was wrapped in; she told him to take it to the police, but he refused to get involved.'

Lily wanted to ask more questions, but the conversation moved on.

'Why would he not tell the police?' another woman asked.

'It seems his son had his collar felt for flogging things on the black market, so he's not keen on the plod, the silly bugger.'

Lily hurried on, hoping to find Flora and the ladies from Sea View; she had to give them this news as soon as possible. If the blanket was indeed the one Miss Tibbs had knitted, then it could mean Alexsy was still nearby. They would need to speak to the owner of the chemist's shop to find out when it had been handed in, as that might be a clue to where Tom White was heading.

She held Mary close as she weaved her way through the myriad of tunnels to where her friends set up home while underground. It was horrible to think that it could have been her own darling daughter who was missing. 'God forbid,' she whispered as she reached a familiar part of the tunnels. Her eyes, now acclimatized to the dim light, skimmed over the people setting up, ready for a possible long stay. She smiled as she heard Rose's sweet voice even before she'd spotted her friends.

'*There'll be bluebirds over the white cliffs of Dover . . .*'

'Thank goodness I found you,' Lily said, as Flora held out her arms to take Mary. 'I have some news.'

'About Alexsy?'

'Yes, I overheard someone talking just now,' she started to explain, stopping to catch her breath after the effort of carrying her little girl through the tunnels.

'Sit down and rest for a couple of minutes. I want Rose to hear this; she's almost finished leading the sing-song. John's helping Miss Tibbs make us a hot drink.'

Lily gave her a sly smile. 'He's back on the scene, is he?'

'Oh, it's nothing like that, he brought a crate of food from Diana and was helping me and Rose with some thoughts about where Tom White could have taken the lad – and what's happened since. He told me he has to leave soon and was only held up by the air-raid sirens going off.'

Lily smiled to herself. It was obvious John Bentley adored Flora, and it was time the woman started to think about her own life rather than caring for all and sundry.

'Hot drinks all round,' John said as he carefully carried three enamel mugs in each hand. 'Miss Tibbs spotted you and made an extra one,' he said as Lily started to protest that she was taking someone else's drink. 'Here you are, Rose,' John added as she joined them.

'Now listen, everyone,' Flora said, getting their attention, 'Lily has something to tell us.'

Lily explained what she had overheard as she entered

the tunnels. 'I doubt they know any more than that,' she said, as John suggested finding the women again to ask them for further details. 'Besides, I don't know how we'd find them with so many people down here. I last saw them up near the entrance, so they could have gone down any of the tunnels and be anywhere by now.'

'Not to worry, as I know the man who owns the chemist's shop; he can be a bit of a curmudgeonly old so-and-so. It's best I walk up there and have a word alone. I need to purchase a few bits and pieces anyway, so I can chat to him in passing, so to speak,' Flora said.

Lily nodded in agreement. 'That's a good idea. Much better than us all rushing in there like bulls in a china shop and him not telling us what we need to know.'

'What do we need to know, dear?' Miss Tibbs asked as she delved into Flora's bag and found a packet of cheese and pickle sandwiches. 'My favourite,' she beamed, offering them round.

'Nothing for you to worry about, dear,' Flora smiled at the old lady.

Katie woke to the sound of the all clear to find Stew looking down at her as they lay on the bottom bunk bed close together. Gradually, the memory of what had gone on between them came back to her. 'Oh my goodness,' she exclaimed, pushing him away and climbing from the bed, pulling her dress around her to cover her exposed breasts. 'Please don't say we . . .' But she knew they had, and she'd wanted him to make love to her as much as he'd wanted to. 'I've never done this with anyone else apart from my husband; what must you think of me?'

'I'm as much to blame,' he apologized. 'We are both

lonely and missing our loved ones. Being pushed together and alone, we let our emotions take over.'

She sat back down, buttoning up her dress and straightening her hair. 'It shouldn't have happened. We must never tell a soul,' she said, looking distressed. 'What would people think?'

'I'm not going to tell anyone. I'm not the kind of man who talks about his conquests to his colleagues.'

'Oh, you think of me as a conquest, do you?' she asked, feeling disappointed. It sounded as if he thought her no better than those women who hung about in pubs waiting to be picked up by men.

'No, you've got me all wrong,' he said, running his fingers through his hair in frustration. 'Until this afternoon I've only ever known one woman, and that's my wife. What a pair of fools we've been,' he said, giving her a gentle smile.

'I'm not sure how I can keep this from my husband,' Katie replied, more distressed than ever. 'We've never had a secret in all the years we've known each other. He knows me so well – he will guess that something has happened.'

'Please don't feel guilty. Perhaps you'll be able to forget about it and move on before he comes home on leave again. I do understand, Katie; I know I will find it hard not to tell Moira, and she will see that I've changed. Let's hope they will both think it's the war that has changed us. What do you say?'

Katie took a deep breath and decided. 'We mustn't dwell on this, and you aren't to come to the house alone ever again. In company with the others, we will both try to act as we have before. Do you agree?'

'Yes, I agree with you. I will forget it ever happened . . . and thank you.'

'And now I must go to work.' Katie pushed open the door to the Anderson shelter and took a deep breath of fresh air.

The problem was, she knew she'd never be able to forget their time together.

Flora walked purposefully through the town on her way to visit the chemist's shop. She felt newly optimistic that they would manage to find Alexsy – hopefully before Anya returned from her training duties. Her heart ached as she thought how the little lad must be missing his mother. She prayed he would be found soon and would have no lasting memories of this time in his young life. 'We have to find him and soon,' she muttered to herself.

Up ahead, she spotted Katie hurrying towards the Lyons teashop and called out to her. 'I don't know about you, but I feel all over the place after an air raid. I never seem to be able to catch up with my work. You look flustered,' she said, noticing Katie's flushed face and jittery manner.

'I'm fine; the bus took a while to come, that's all,' Katie said without smiling. 'I must dash; goodness knows what's going on in the teashop' – and she hurried away.

Flora shook her head. Hitler had a lot to answer for and if she ever met him, she'd give him what for, for messing up these young girls' lives. There was her Rose and young Katie without their husbands at home; and as for Lily, with no husband and a young daughter to bring up alone . . . not that that was Hitler's fault, of course. Flora found herself imagining the scene if she ever did meet him; but then, that would mean they'd been invaded. She gave herself a mental shake and returned her thoughts to the matter in hand as the chemist's shop came into view.

'Good afternoon, Mr Francis. I'm pleased to see you and your premises are still in one piece after today's raid. How is Mrs Francis?' she asked.

He nodded to her unsmilingly, apparently not very keen to make conversation. 'Did you want something? It's just that I have my stock taking to get on with.'

'Someone mentioned that you picked up a yellow knitted blanket that had been dropped on the pavement outside?'

'I did, it's over there by the window display. But before you take it, I'll need proof that it belongs to you.'

Flora wondered how she could prove the blanket had been knitted by Miss Tibbs as a gift when Daisy had been born – then it came to her. 'There's a small darn in the bottom left-hand corner where it brushed against a candle when we were down the tunnels. The wool I used is a slightly darker colour.'

He went over to the old-fashioned curved window and lifted the blanket from where it was draped over a large glass ornamental bottle filled with coloured water. Holding it up to the light from the window, he inspected the knitting closely. 'Yes, I can see where it has been darned. You ought to be more careful in future. Someone else might have put it into a dustbin.'

'I will,' she promised, resisting the urge to hold the blanket to her face and inhale the baby's scent. 'I wonder, can you recall exactly when you spotted it?'

He sniffed disapprovingly. 'It was when I'd opened up after lunch yesterday, before I went out to clean the front windows. Does it make any difference?'

'It does.' She needed him to tell her more. 'What time would that have been?'

'It was twenty-five past two. I called after the couple who dropped it, but they were too busy arguing. I went back into the shop to leave it somewhere safe, as there was someone walking their dog and I didn't want the disgusting animal cocking its leg, if you get my drift.'

'Oh, I do, I do,' she said, trying to fight the urge to give him a big kiss. 'I'll be off now. Thank you for hanging on to it.'

He followed her out of the shop. 'Tell me why that couple had it, if it belongs to you?'

Flora pretended not to hear him as she hurried back towards Sea View to share the news with the others.

'Well done, but you could have asked him what the woman looked like and if they had a child with them,' Rose said once she'd listened to what Flora had to say.

'Oh God, I never gave it a thought; I was so pleased to know it was Alexsy's blanket and that someone had dropped it. What a fool I am. I could kick myself,' Flora said, looking glum. 'Shall I go back and ask Mr Francis?'

'I wouldn't; he might find it rather strange. I know I'd be worried if I was him,' Rose said, trying not to laugh when the situation was so serious. 'However, if a detective was to walk in there with his notebook . . .' she suggested. They both looked over to where John was checking what he'd written in his diary.

'He's wearing a suit and looks official,' Flora said to Rose.

John looked up at them and smiled. 'I really ought to be getting back to London and my work, but I'll go and speak to your Mr Francis and see what I can find out.'

'Wonderful!' Rose exclaimed. 'Thank you. I'll stand you a meal at the teashop when you're next down here.'

The smile dropped from John's face. 'It may be a while before I'm back.'

20

Anya looked about her as she stood on the stony shore, trying to keep her balance in the strange shoes she'd been given to wear. Heavy, laced-up brogues were not what she was used to, and the leather was already rubbing on her little toe. She would kick them off once on the boat and see what she could do to make them more comfortable. Steeling herself to forget about her discomfort and take notice of her surroundings, she tried to recall all she been told.

But where was she? It wasn't Ramsgate or Margate, she knew that for sure. It had been hard to distinguish landmarks while Ruth was driving her to the Kent coast, where she was to meet the boat and the person who would accompany her to France. Thinking it must be Seasalter, or perhaps Reculver, which she'd seen on a map that Flora kept in the hall of Sea View for the residents to use, she turned to Ruth, who was puffing on another cigarette. 'The boat is late. Perhaps it isn't coming, and we can all go home and forget this foolish idea.'

Ruth spoke sharply. 'It is not foolish, as well you know. Besides, the boat is here. If you look out there, you will see a torch signalling to us.'

Anya peered out into the darkness. After staring for a little while, she spotted a pinprick of light. 'How am I to get out to the boat? I do not swim,' she snapped. Her stomach was so tight with nerves that she felt sick.

'There is a rowing boat on its way. It may be a good idea to remove your shoes and stockings, as you will have to paddle a few feet.'

'Thank goodness,' Anya groaned as she kicked off the shoes. She reached under the heavy tweed skirt to unclip her rough woollen stockings from the suspenders, stuffing them into the worn leather bag that hung over her shoulder.

'Tie the laces together and hang the shoes round your neck so they don't drop into the sea,' Ruth instructed.

Once the shoes were secure, Anya took a few steps forward and dipped her toes into the gently lapping waves, then swore quietly. 'Bloody hell, the water is cold. I hope I do not fall in from the boat,' she said, attempting to laugh. As she spoke the words, her fear returned. 'Promise me you will kiss my son for me. Go to Sea View tomorrow and do just that. Whisper in his ear that his mama and tata love him dearly. You will do that for me?'

'I promise, but you will soon be home to tell him yourself, Anya. Keep your son in your heart and tell yourself you will see him very soon.'

'I will try,' Anya said as she continued to look out to the estuary that led to the sea and to France.

'Ahoy there!' a boy called out, steering a small rowing boat close to the beach. As he approached the shore, they could see that he was wearing a balaclava helmet and was dressed in black, making him harder to see or to identify.

'I hope the boat that is taking me to France is bigger than that,' Anya said.

Ruth tried to match her dry humour. 'You are safe; the boat taking you over the Channel is slightly larger,' she chuckled. She picked up the leather bag and handed it to the lad, who was trying to coax Anya into his boat. 'Godspeed,' Ruth called to them as loud as she dared, watching the boat disappear into the darkness.

'How long will this take?' Anya asked. She didn't like that the boat sat so low in the water; she feared it would sink.

'Only a couple more minutes and we'll be there,' said the boy as he pulled on the oars and breathed deeply.

Anya watched him. 'You are a brave person, doing this.'

'Nah, being out in all weathers fishing is brave. This is easy work,' he said as he stopped rowing and let the small boat glide along until it bumped against the side of a larger vessel. 'Here you are, madam; there's a rope ladder you can climb up to get on board. I'll bring your bag.'

Anya had slipped her feet into her shoes while the lad was rowing. She tied the laces and stood up, trying not to rock the boat too much. With her heart in her mouth, she grabbed the rope ladder and tentatively took a step up, followed by another; one foot after the other, praying she wouldn't slip. As she reached the top of the ladder, a rough hand reached out and hauled her over, whereupon she fell in an inelegant heap onto the deck.

'At least stand up. We can't beat the Jerries with you flat out on the deck like that.'

Anya shook her head to clear her thoughts and looked up. 'Mildred?'

'That's me,' Mildred chuckled. 'You look as gobsmacked as I was when I was told you were my passenger,' she added, taking Anya's hand and helping her to her feet.

The lad in the rowing boat hauled the leather bag over the side and called out to Mildred. 'I'll be off then, boss, if you don't need anything else doing?'

'Cheers, Josh. Don't forget, if anyone asks about me, I've gone off on my holidays to visit family. I'll see you all right for any days' fishing you've missed.'

'Are you sure I can't come with you? We're due some bad weather and you'll be glad of an extra pair of hands.'

'Anya can help me,' Mildred answered as she waved goodbye to the lad.

'I have no knowledge of boats; I don't even like the fish you catch,' Anya said, wrinkling her nose. 'This boat smells of you.'

Mildred roared with laughter. 'This trip is going to be interesting with you not even sounding like a Frenchie, let alone looking like one. Come on, let's go below and have a mug of cocoa before we set off.'

Anya looked about with interest. In all the time she'd lived at Sea View she'd managed not to venture onto Mildred's boat. She would have to get used to the pungent smell of fish. 'And you are to accompany me; are you sure you are up to it?'

'There have been no complaints so far,' Mildred replied as she led the way down a short flight of steps to below deck. Anya spotted a small area containing a stove and a table; there was a bench against the side of the boat. Elsewhere she could see a heap of fishing nets and boxes.

'Am I able to ask how many times . . . ?'

'A dozen or so, and before you ask, yes, I've been off the boat and on foreign soil as well.'

Anya shook her head as she took it all in. 'I had no idea you got up to this kind of thing. I thought you went out to catch fish and sell it – and give Flora enough to feed us. I know I complain about the fish, but I want you to know I am grateful. But how do you get the fish when you are out fighting the enemy?'

Mildred shrugged her shoulders. 'There are a few of us who do this kind of thing, and part of working undercover is to share the catches. Otherwise people would become suspicious.'

'Do you change your clothes when you get to France?' Anya asked, looking at Mildred's attire: oily overalls, wellington boots and a knitted bobble hat that had seen better days.

'Yes, and I scrub up well,' Mildred laughed as she put a can of water onto the small stove and checked the flame underneath. 'That should do,' she said, closing the small door to the stove.

'Are we going to set off, or just sit here in the middle of the sea drinking cocoa? The sooner this is over, the sooner I can be home.'

'I'm giving Josh time to get clear before I fire up the engine. We are still in the estuary now; when we get out into the Channel, that's when it gets dangerous.' Mildred poured hot water into two mugs and, after stirring the liquid frantically with a bent spoon, handed one to Anya.

'Come and sit up on deck and enjoy the view while you can,' she said, once again leading the way.

'The night is as black as coal out here. What is there to see?'

'Sit still and look to the heavens. You will soon see what I see.'

Anya sat down on a wooden bench and leant back against the bridge, staring into the night sky. 'I cannot see the moon, but there are a few pinpoints of twinkling stars. They are too far away to see properly, which is a shame.'

'Thank goodness they are. I'd have preferred a sea mist, or even a heavy fog, so that we could slip through unseen; but there is heavy rain on the way, which will help. It'll be a bit rough, but that means there won't be as many enemy patrol boats on the French side.'

Anya felt squeamish at the thought. 'Perhaps we should go back until the weather is better, then we can try again?'

Mildred laughed heartily again, almost spilling her cocoa. 'Now I will explain to you what we are going to do to get safely across so we can track down this friend of yours.'

'She is not my friend,' Anya snapped. 'I am just to identify someone I once knew at home in Poland.'

'That's as may be, but we must get you there first.' Mildred picked up an overall that had been lying on the floor. 'You will wear this over your clothes, along with a hat like mine – and tuck your hair underneath. I want you to look like one of my helpers. Yes, I know it is dirty,' she said as Anya made a face. 'It smells of fish as well, so you'll have to put up with it. We want to fool the Germans into thinking we are out fishing.'

Anya was aghast. 'You mean you will speak with them?'

'It has been known, and that is why I always have a crate of fish ready to hand over to them.'

'If I had a gun, I would shoot them all,' Anya spat. 'You are a traitor colluding with the enemy. You should be locked up along with your stinky fish.'

Mildred laughed again. 'Bless you, girl. It has taken ages for the Germans in their patrol boats to get used to the fishing vessels. Along with the French fishermen, we've risked life and limb to gradually inch closer, and if it means we hand over some of our catch, all the better. All the time we keep fishing, it is possible for one of our boats to slip through and drop off an agent. Do you understand now?'

Anya was thoughtful. 'You are saying there are other fishermen out here tonight just to help me get through.'

'And me. When we leave this boat, someone will slip on board and take over the *Saucy Milly.*'

'It sounds too easy,' Anya said, not wanting to believe what she had been told.

'It has worked several times before; we just have to hope we will be lucky again.'

'When haven't you been lucky?'

Mildred shook her head, not wanting to mention that one of the agents she had helped had been shot. All she'd brought home on that voyage was the body of a brave young woman.

'How do we get back?'

'The fishing fleet will be out on certain nights when there isn't a full moon; a rowing boat will be waiting at a set time. If we aren't there, they will return twice more . . .'

'Then . . . ?'

'Then they will presume our mission has failed, and will not return.'

Anya shuddered. Ruth had told her nothing of the dangers involved in getting to France, let alone escaping afterwards.

Flora couldn't sleep; she had so many ideas spinning around in her head. In front of her the mug of Camp coffee was going cold while in her hands she held the primrose yellow blanket she'd collected that day from the chemist's. John's follow-up chat with Mr Francis hadn't yielded very much additional information. Even with John adopting the air of someone in authority, Francis had not provided a detailed description of the couple who'd dropped the blanket. One minute he thought she was blonde; the next he wondered if she might have been wearing a headscarf over her hair. The man had apparently worn a mackintosh, like so many others who were not in uniform.

John was apologetic when he returned to Sea View, and Flora could not comfort him very well, as she'd hoped for so much more. He made his apologies, as he had to head back to London, but told Flora and Rose to keep thinking about where the mysterious couple might be. They knew the town better than he did – where would a couple with a child have gone, that's if they hadn't left Thanet?

'Mum?'

'Rose, love; did I wake you?' Flora said, as Rose entered the kitchen. She was wrapped up in the old dressing gown she kept at Sea View for times like this when she didn't go home to her cottage in Pegwell Bay.

'No. I did drop off, then had an awful nightmare where

Tom White was auctioning off baby Alexsy to the highest bidder.'

'Goodness, that must have been frightening.'

'It was, and every time I tried to bid the words wouldn't come out of my mouth. He was standing on a stage and looking down on us all and Alexsy was crying his little heart out. I woke in such a sweat.'

'You look flushed even now. Let me make you a cup of hot milk? It might help you drop off to sleep.'

'No, I'm past feeling tired. I'd rather sit down here with you, that's if you don't mind?'

'Of course not. Let's move over to sit by the stove, it'll be warmer there. It looks like rain is on the way,' Flora remarked, looking out of the window as she moved to her armchair. A flash of lightning lit up the night sky. 'I'd hate to be out at sea on a night like this.'

21

Rose walked along the line of Nippies, checking that their uniforms were worn correctly, without missing buttons or holes in their black stockings. 'Turn around,' she commanded then, inspecting the gas masks ingeniously attached to their belts at the back. 'You would all have heard about the gas exercise in Ramsgate recently – imagine if that had been real, and you'd forgotten to wear your mask? Be vigilant, ladies. And remember not to use the case for anything other than carrying your mask.'

The Nippies voiced their agreement. Once Rose had dismissed them, they all hurried to their workstations.

'I'll be in my office for the next hour,' Rose said, stifling a yawn.

Lily bustled into the office a few minutes later, carrying a tea tray. 'I thought you might need this to keep you awake. Did you have a bad night?'

'You could say that. I sat up with Mum; we were chewing over everything that has happened since Alexsy was snatched by Tom White. Nothing makes sense at all, even though we now have the blanket that was taken at the same time.'

'We need to put our heads together,' Lily said, pinching a biscuit from the tea tray.

Rose sighed. 'It's good of you, but I've been over and over everything with Mum so many times and we've got nowhere.'

'You need fresh eyes, and who could be better than me and Katie to help? You know I feel responsible for Alexsy going missing. Besides, Katie has been so down in the dumps since Jack went back to his ship, she needs to be distracted.'

'I know how Katie feels, as we never seem to see our husbands for long. But tell me, why do you feel responsible?'

'Well, Tom White only came back because of me and Mary, and look what's happened.'

'You can't blame yourself for this. He was on a mission as soon as he walked into the Ramsgate teashop. You weren't there, so he chatted to Jennie, and bingo: he found a link to you. He is a wily so-and-so.'

'You can say that again. So will you come to Captain's Cottage this evening? I can cook,' she grinned.

'Oh please, anything but your cooking,' Rose smiled. 'Why don't I bring fish and chips with me, and we will have longer to chat if no one has to stop and cook?'

'That sounds good to me. I'll let Katie know, in case she starts to cook her Spam fritters. Don't forget there are four of us, as Jennie will be home this evening.'

'Five if we count Mary; she does love to pinch my chips.'

'My daughter does like her food,' Lily chuckled before her smile dropped. 'Just to think it could have been my baby girl Tom White ran off with; I can't bear to imagine it.'

'Then don't. There are customers to serve and we have a new area manager visiting today, so we'd best look sharp.'

Lily picked up the tray. 'You certainly know how to cheer me up. I hope he's a decent sort.'

'Me too, as I've not been able to glean any information about the man – not even a name. Usually someone at head office will tip me off, but I've not heard a thing. Katie promised to let me know if he turns up there first.'

'Oh well, we'd better be on our best behaviour,' Lily grimaced. 'I hope this doesn't mean the day is going downhill.'

Rose gave her a wry smile. 'We will find Alexsy. And as far as the new area manager is concerned, we will have to wait and see . . .'

Rose didn't have to wait long. Only ten minutes later there was a loud knock on the door of her office before it burst open. She looked up from where she was working on next week's staff rota, ready to reprimand whatever Nippy was making such a racket. Her jaw dropped as she recognized the woman standing in front of her.

Miss Butterworth was as frightening a spectacle as she had been when Rose first joined the company as a very young Nippy. The woman had terrified her then and, going by the way she was now shaking, that feeling had never fully gone away.

She rose from her seat. 'Why, Miss Butterworth, how lovely to see you – my goodness, it must be two years since you left the company. Thank you so much for popping by. Please take a seat and I'll order refreshments; I take it you have time for a cup of tea and one of our delicious cakes? Excuse me a moment,' she added as the telephone started to ring. 'Lyons teashop, Margate, how may I help you?'

'Rose, it's Katie. I wanted to warn you our new area manager is on her way to see you. You'll never guess who it is?'

Rose's heart plummeted to her boots as the penny dropped. 'Thank you so much. I'll get back to you later with the information,' she replied.

'Oh my goodness, is she sitting with you now?' Katie asked.

'That's correct,' Rose said, trying hard not to smile as Katie started to laugh. Rose replaced the telephone receiver.

'I'm sorry about that; now let me organize refreshments,' she said, going to the door and calling out to Lily, who was clearing a table nearby. 'Miss Douglas, would you bring tea to the office when you have finished preparing that table, please?'

Lily frowned and looked past Rose to see who her guest was. Her eyes opened in shock as she spotted Miss Butterworth. 'I'll do that at once, Mrs Hargreaves,' she said, giving a small bob before hurrying away.

Rose pinned a smile to her face and returned to her desk. 'I must say how surprised I am to see you back in Thanet. May I ask how your sister is?'

'My sister passed away at the end of last year,' Miss Butterworth replied, 'and since then I have returned to work for Lyons, at the same time being offered promotion. I understand the previous area manager has retired.'

'Mr Grant is a sad loss to the company and the area. He gave me away when I married,' Rose said, looking at her wedding ring and thinking of that happy day.

'I heard you had married into the aristocracy; I must say, you have done very well for yourself. It is usually the

London Nippies who tend to meet the better class of male customer.'

Rose held back the words she really wanted to say to the woman and smiled sweetly. 'Ben's family aren't exactly aristocracy. I look forward to working with you. Do you plan to make many changes?' she asked, praying Miss Butterworth would leave her to run the Margate teashop without too much interference. Mr Grant had been very happy with her work as manageress.

'I do intend to make some changes, but for today I wish only to inspect the teashop and the staff in order to plan what will happen next.'

Rose groaned inwardly, wondering what lay ahead for her and her staff.

'Hello, Miss Butterworth; I thought I spotted you earlier. Are you paying us a visit?' Lily chirped as she placed an overloaded tray on Rose's desk.

'Miss Butterworth is our new area manager – or is that manageress?' Rose asked the stony-faced woman.

'I prefer manager, as it is more professional. Manageress sounds like someone who works in a wool shop.'

Lily sniggered before mouthing 'sorry' to Rose. 'I'll leave you to it,' she said, backing out of the room.

'Miss Douglas, before I hold my staff inspection, would you either change your stockings or darn the rather ugly run below your left knee? I'm surprised you didn't notice it when you had your staff check this morning. That's if there was one,' she added with a glare at Rose, who felt her cheeks start to burn.

Lily stepped back into the room. 'It happened just now, when a customer caught my leg with her shopping basket. I was about to change them when Mrs Hargreaves asked me to fetch tea for you,' she replied, before turning and leaving.

'If you are going to be sick, use the bucket,' Mildred instructed Anya, who was starting to look a little green about the gills. 'There's a rope tied to the handle so you can swing it over the side and rinse it out. Sorry, it does smell a little fishy,' she apologized as Anya heaved, holding it in front of her face.

'How long before we arrive in France? I think I will die from seasickness if I don't put my feet on dry land before long.'

'A little under half an hour should see us meeting the French boats; that's if this weather doesn't get any rougher.'

'Do you mean you are going to have someone row us to the beach, as we did in England?'

'If only we could, but the patrol boats would pick us up before we even reached the shore. We plan to transfer to one of the French fishing boats, and two of their crew will take the *Saucy Milly* back to Ramsgate.'

Anya looked aghast. 'You mean I am to climb onto another boat out here in the sea?'

'Don't worry, I have done it many times. You will have a rope tied around your waist; if you fall in, we will pull you out. It is a bit choppy out there at the moment, so I hope the transfer can take place.'

'This is madness, pure madness,' Anya shouted, forgetting that only moments before she had been feeling seasick. She marched up and down the deck, ranting, until she came face to face with Mildred. 'Take me back. I refuse to go on with this mission. I have a son who needs me; what good am I to him if I drown?'

'Oh, don't be so melodramatic,' Mildred snapped. She pulled Anya over to a pile of rope close to where she had been steering the boat, then pushed her firmly until the sobbing woman was sitting down on the pile. Returning to the wheel, she shouted towards Anya, some of her words being whipped away as the threatening storm sent sheets of rain towards them. 'I would like to be able to put my arms around you and soothe your tears. But not only am I not like that, you know you have to go through with this mission. Many people depend on you.'

'There are others who could do this,' Anya sniffed.

'From what I understand, you are the only person capable of carrying this out. It is a straightforward job; no one is asking you to blow up trains or execute the enemy. They simply want you to be able to say, "Yes, this is the woman," and then I can return you back to your home and your son. However, if you insist, I will turn the boat around and we will return to Ramsgate harbour. I'm more than happy to wash my hands of this and go back to my bed and sleep the sleep of the dead. You, meanwhile, will have to explain to Ruth and the other people who run the SOE that you've let everybody down. The choice is yours, just make up your mind and say the word and I'll signal the French fishing boat that is approaching us now. Men on that boat are risking their lives to help you . . .'

'Cheer up, Katie, it might not happen,' Lily joshed her friend as they helped Rose open the newspaper-wrapped parcels containing their fish suppers. 'Let's eat out of the paper to save on washing up,' she added, going to a drawer to collect cutlery.

'Is there anything I can do to help?' Jennie asked as she joined them in the kitchen. 'Mary is tucked up in her bed, fast asleep; I tired her out running around the garden playing hide and seek.'

'Thank you so much. She does enjoy playing with you; you are like a big sister to her,' Lily smiled, wondering if Mary would ever have siblings. 'I'd best put a few chips on a plate for my darling daughter, or she will complain in the morning. Get the salt and vinegar, Jennie, and we can sit and eat them on our laps in the living room.'

'And pretend we're at the seaside?' Rose grinned. They could hear the sea from where they lived at Captain's Cottage.

'That's something I do miss: walking on the beach and not being confronted by an angry soldier or seeing the sea defences,' Katie said wistfully. 'Shall I butter some bread to have with the meal? I brought home half a loaf from the teashop.'

'That's a good idea,' Rose said as she started to hand out the food to the girls.

Once they were seated, Jennie listened to them all chatting about Thanet and its beaches. 'I've never seen the coast without the defences,' she said, 'as the war had started by the time I came here. It must have been wonderful in the olden times.'

Lily gave her arm a playful slap. 'Hey, not so much of the "olden times", we aren't that much older than you! It's just that we grew up here and know each other from our school days.'

'I grew up in the children's home alongside my Jack. If it hadn't been for Rose's mum, I'd not have known what proper families were like,' Katie said.

'They aren't all they're cracked up to be. That's why I ran away and came here; but I'm happy now,' Jennie grinned.

'And when the war is over, we will be able to show you more of our part of Kent. There's nowhere else like it,' Katie said.

'I love what I've seen so far. I feel as though I've fallen on my feet knowing you all, as well as having such a nice job,' Jennie said, forking chips into her mouth.

'You may change your opinion when you meet our new area manager,' Katie sighed. 'She's going to be hard work. All I could think was, come back Mr Grant.'

'You talk as if you know her, is she a local person?' Jennie asked.

Rose laid down her fork. 'She was our Ramsgate teashop manageress when the three of us started working there as Nippies. She was a domineering person. We girls feared her, and it was a relief when she left to care for her sick sister. I am surprised to see her back working for the company, but I suppose with so many men away fighting in the war they are bound to take on more female managers. A woman I know from school told me it is the same where she works, at the Ramsgate Woolworths: women are moving into management but will have to relinquish their positions when the men return to the workplace. She was offered promotion, but refused as she is expecting her first child.'

A pained look crossed Katie's face, but she kept quiet.

Lily sighed. 'I was the first person she picked on, just

because I'd caught my stocking and hadn't rushed to change them. It was awful.'

'It can't be helped.' Rose shook her head. 'We are just going to have to be careful when we know she is due to visit us. I've already heard from two other teashops, and we are going to tip each other off when she is on the warpath. What was she like at the Ramsgate branch, Katie?'

'The first thing she did was ask me why I wasn't expecting yet, as I'd been married a while. I didn't know where to look. The customers heard her as well as the staff.'

Lily was shocked. 'I'd have told her to mind her own business, whatever did you say?'

Katie's bottom lip trembled as she spoke. 'I told her we hope to have a large family in time,' she said, as several large tears plopped onto the fish and chips in her lap.

'Oh, sweetie,' Lily said as she hurried to Katie's side and flung her arms around her, causing her tears to flow even faster. 'That was a downright awful thing for her to say to you. I feel you should write to head office and lodge a complaint.'

'I don't want to cause any trouble,' Katie sniffed. 'I'll be more aware of her next time she comes to Ramsgate.'

Lily was still fuming. 'She's lucky Anya wasn't at the Margate teashop, as she'd have shown the woman the sharp side of her tongue.'

The girls all laughed, apart from Rose, who was wondering where Anya was and whether Ruth had any news she could share with her. 'Perhaps we should give Miss Butterworth the benefit of the doubt. From what I can remember there was only her and her sister, and she may still be grieving; it can't have been long since she passed away. Everyone acts differently when they lose someone they love.'

Lily agreed. 'I'll try to remember that, as I know it took me a long time to get over the loss of my mum. If it hadn't been for you and Flora taking care of me, goodness knows how I'd have turned out.'

Jennie, who had been listening intently, nodded her head. 'Flora is such a kind lady; she deserves a medal.'

Rose smiled at the young girl. 'My mum is one in a million, but I doubt she would agree she deserves a medal; she is far too modest. However, speaking of Anya, we must remember we were getting together to see what we could come up with to find little Alexsy. I wonder who the woman was with Tom, later on the day Alexsy was taken? When the yellow blanket was dropped by the chemist's shop?'

Katie chewed her bottom lip as she thought. 'Is it worth returning to ask the chemist what he saw?'

Rose shook her head. 'John Bentley has already tried that. He even gave the impression he was a detective and pressed the man as much as possible, but it was no good. He couldn't give any more information.'

They fell silent as they finished their meal. Afterwards, Lily collected the newspaper pages and the cutlery.

'I may know something,' Jennie said, looking frightened. 'I know I'm to blame for all this, but I want to help you all find the little lad; and as soon as possible, before Anya comes home.'

'Oh, Jennie, you're not to blame for any of it,' Rose consoled her.

Katie joined in. 'Anything you can tell us, however trivial, just might lead to Alexsy being found.'

Jennie looked nervous. 'Then I think I know who the woman is.'

22

~

Mildred shook Anya's shoulder. 'Pull yourself together; it is almost time to transfer to the other boat.'

Anya groaned and lifted her head. 'I want to die,' she whispered, her voice echoing into the metal bucket.

'That may well happen if we don't get a move on.' Mildred shook her harder as lightning flashed overhead, illuminating the sky as well as the approaching fishing boats.

Anya got to her feet and sipped at the mug of water Mildred handed to her. 'What is this?' she gagged.

'I've put some brandy in it to buck you up. Knock it back and get yourself ready.'

'Perhaps the Germans will not be about in this terrible weather,' Anya suggested as thunder rumbled around them, followed by more fork lightning.

'We may be lucky and they've fled back to a safe harbour; there again, they could be sniffing about, expecting us to take advantage of the bad weather.'

Anya knocked back the rest of the water and found her way to the lower deck to retrieve her things, holding tight to anything that would keep her upright. She grimaced at the smell of oil and rotting fish as she collected her coat, which was folded up with the bag she carried, and climbed the narrow steps back to where Mildred was hanging on to the wheel. The *Saucy Milly* fought against the wind as she turned off the engine.

'Ahoy, Nancy,' a man called from the French boat as it pulled alongside. Ropes were thrown onto the deck of the *Saucy Milly*, with one brave young fisherman leaping across after them, quickly grabbing each rope and securing them before the two vessels could drift apart in the rough sea.

'Bonjour, Alphonse.' Mildred shook the hand of a second man who leapt on board. Anya was speechless as she looked at the large, broad-shouldered figure dressed from head to toe in oilskins; he spoke to Mildred in French, and she replied sounding equally fluent in the language. Anya recognized very few words apart from the name given to her for the mission, Monique. As it was mentioned, they both looked towards her, and the man scowled.

'We are ready,' Mildred said as she rejoined Anya. 'Alphonse will assist you into their boat. He suggests you speak very little, as your lack of French could give you away or at the very least draw unwanted attention – as could your Polish accent.'

Anya nodded. Her seasickness was driven away by sheer terror as Alphonse lifted her into his strong arms and, leaning over the side of the *Saucy Milly*, threw her across to another man in the French boat. She shrieked, but before she knew it she was standing on two wobbly feet watching Mildred receive the same treatment. Their bags followed and a few minutes later, with Alphonse back on his own boat and a pair of Frenchmen left in charge of the *Saucy Milly*, the ropes were untied and they were on their way.

Anya was shown below deck, out of the driving rain, and given a blanket to wrap around her shoulders. The sickness she'd felt earlier did not return, and in its place was a feeling of fear tinged with excitement. There was no going back now. The sound of the *Saucy Milly* could just be heard, as if it fought against the storm, until it faded away completely. She was here in French waters and must concentrate on the task ahead.

'I will do this for you, Henio, even if it is for your memory. I will succeed to get home to our child and do my part to make the future a safer place for him,' she whispered, before closing her eyes to try to sleep and gain the strength for whatever lay ahead.

'It is time,' Mildred said, leaning close to her ear. 'But there is a problem.'

'What is the problem?' Anya asked as she rubbed the sleep from her eyes. 'Please don't say the mission cannot go ahead.'

'No; it's just that the storm has taken us off course and we are further down the coast, so we will miss our rendez-vous. Alphonse is using the radio to try to make contact, but that is dangerous as the message could be picked up by the enemy.'

'I see. Is it possible for us to walk back to the meeting point? I have no idea where we are going for me to iden-tify Anouska; perhaps we could walk inland . . . ?'

'We will have to wait to hear what Alphonse is told. We are in their hands.'

Anya's mind was turning over their situation. 'Tell me, can we trust this Alphonse?'

'He has been part of my last three missions. I don't have any cause to doubt his judgement or his loyalty. He is a reliable member of the resistance and has no love for the Germans. In that respect you are both alike. However, I cannot speak for the men who work on this boat with him. We learn not to speak to too many people, just in case there are those not as reliable who would sell us to the Germans for a few francs.'

Anya spat out her words. 'Life is cheap to these Germans. I have lost too many family members in Poland, and possibly my husband as well, to be able to collude with these barbaric animals.'

'That is the spirit, madame,' Alphonse said as he joined them. 'I have news, but it is not good. You must make your way back to the original meeting point. Your contact will be there to guide you in forty-eight hours. I wish I could help you more, but if the Germans spot my boat fishing in the wrong area, they will start to ask questions. As it is we must explain about the storm taking us off course during the night, and for that reason you have to be onshore as soon as possible. I will draw a map to guide you; you will have to avoid several villages and stay as close to the shoreline as you possibly can,' he said as he scribbled on a crumpled piece of paper.

Mildred nodded as he explained, while Anya tried to understand but failed. After he handed Mildred the map she turned to Anya. 'It is time to take off the overalls and turn yourself into a French woman, or at least a passable impression of a French woman,' she said, as she unbuttoned her own overall to reveal a creased and faded floral dress. From her canvas bag she pulled out scuffed shoes and an old felt hat. 'Hurry up,' she said, as Anya stood looking astonished at the transformation.

Anya removed her disguise, thankful to be rid of the smelly fishing clothes, and waited to be told what to do next.

'I will help you into the rowing boat,' Alphonse growled as Mildred shoved the map into the pocket of her dress. 'Here is some food to sustain you; it isn't much but will see you through,' he added, holding out a paper bag.

'Thank you,' Mildred said, kissing him on both cheeks. 'You won't be forgotten for this,' she added, as Anya copied her and mumbled her thanks.

'Godspeed,' he called, and the women were rowed towards French soil as dawn began to break.

'When will Anya be back?' Joyce asked, as Rose did her rounds of the teashop.

Ever since Miss Butterworth's arrival the week before, Rose had been on tenterhooks, checking not only the staff but the whole of the premises each morning for any reason the woman could complain. When Joyce asked her question, Rose was on her hands and knees looking under the main counter at the front of the shop for crumbs that might attract vermin. She stood up and brushed down her skirt.

'I have no idea; I plan to ask head office,' she lied. What she really meant was that she was worried beyond belief, and would be speaking to Ruth soon to find out if there was any news of their friend.

'I'm only asking as I know I'm not perfect for this job; Miss Butterworth told me so in no uncertain terms when she noticed I was not as tall as the typical Sally.'

'Why ever would she have said that? I wish I'd known. I'd have told her you are worth two of any of the other Sallys.'

Joyce blushed. 'I wasn't fishing for compliments; I like to do the best job I can.'

'Think no more of it. The only reason Lyons originally wanted taller women as Sallys was because the job involves reaching across the counters and up to the high shelves. Have you found that a problem?'

'No, not at all. When I started, Mildred brought along a small set of steps that fit perfectly behind the counter and can be pulled out when needed. She is such a thoughtful person; in fact, I think she made them herself when she heard I had the job.'

'Hmm – that's another person who seems to have gone missing,' Rose said, thinking aloud. Seeing the questioning look on Joyce's face made her realize she ought not to have spoken.

'I beg your pardon?'

'Don't listen to me, I was being silly. Mildred is enjoying a visit to her family,' she said. It was a shame to deceive Joyce, but she didn't want to say that she had no idea where Mildred had really gone. 'Getting back to your work here, I have no intention of sending you packing when Anya returns; I'd be a fool to do so. In fact, we need to have a chat at some point – I'd like to extend your hours, if you are agreeable?'

Joyce beamed. 'That would be wonderful, thank you. I need to be around for when Pearl isn't at school, but I'd love to work more hours.'

'That's good. Let's have that chat in a couple of days, when you've had time to think about it,' Rose smiled back, pleased that she'd made Joyce happy.

'Any news?' Lily sidled up to Rose as she was nipping to the service area to collect a customer's meal.

'Is this about the war, or something else?' Rose asked.

'About Jennie looking out for that friend of Tom White? I thought she may have spotted her by now, especially as you've transferred her back to the Ramsgate shop while we cover her workstation. Just coming, sir,' she called to a man who was waving in her direction. 'I don't know how long I can cover this many tables.'

Rose returned to her office, her mind on Alexsy and how frightened he must be away from all those he knew and who loved him dearly. It was so frustrating that nothing seemed to be happening to look for him. Each day her mother walked to the police station and enquired about their investigations and each day she listened to how sorry they were and how they were no further forward. Each afternoon she picked up the telephone and asked to speak to the person in charge of the investigation and most days he wasn't there, so she left a message – and no one returned her calls.

It was as if they didn't care. It was explained that they were looking, but Flora and the girls felt it wasn't enough and were doing all they could to find the child before his mother came home to the distressing news. Between them, the Nippies and the Sallys had visited all the shops in Ramsgate and the surrounding area asking them to look out for a woman or couple who suddenly had a child around the age of one year old with them. Flora's phone number was prominently shown on the posters they left with shop owners, but so far very little had happened, apart from a junior journalist arriving to eat cake and spell Alexsy's name wrong when the short piece went to press on page ten of the local newspaper.

Rose reached for the telephone and rang Katie at the Ramsgate branch. 'I have a half day, so I thought I'd pop into your teashop on the way to Mum's house. I think it's time we did more to find Alexsy.'

A little later, Katie greeted Rose at the door of the Ramsgate teashop. 'I have it on good authority that Miss Butterworth isn't in the area today,' she said, 'so we can have tea in my office and talk to Jennie. She was trying to tell me something earlier, but I was busy handling a complaint. Nothing serious,' she added as Rose showed concern. 'Some woman complained her pot of tea was cold. She was only trying to get out of paying,' she shrugged. 'I replaced it and conveniently left it off her bill.'

'Oh, Katie, you'll get the sack if Miss Butterworth finds out.'

'The woman was hard up; I could see it in the way she only ordered for her children and was going without herself. She finished up the few scraps on their plates. It was heart-breaking.'

'Just be careful, all right?'

'I was. Anyway, I spoke to her as she was leaving and mentioned that if she knew of anyone looking for a part-time job, she was to send them to me, as we have a few vacancies.'

'Do you think she will return?'

'She already has,' Katie replied. 'She starts tomorrow in the kitchen.'

'I'm envious that you filled a vacancy so quickly,' Rose sighed. 'Now tell me, how is our Jennie getting along? Has she found any leads to the anonymous woman who was spotted with Tom White?'

'I'll let her tell you herself,' Rose said, going to the office door and waving to the young girl, who hurried into the room.

'Hello, Rose,' she smiled. 'Have you heard the news?'

'I thought I'd let you explain,' Katie said as she indicated for Jennie to sit down. 'In your own time,' she prompted the girl.

'Well, as I said the night we had our fish and chip supper, I thought I'd seen her in the town and, more importantly, in here.'

Rose tried to contain her impatience. 'We know that much, Jennie; that's why we've moved you to this branch, in case you see her again.'

'The thing is, I was chatting to the new woman you took on this afternoon while I served her children with ice cream . . .'

Katie grinned at Rose. 'I treated them.'

'We were standing by the poster we'd stuck up on the wall and I asked her to keep an eye out and gave her some more description. Blow me down, she did better than that: she told us where the woman lives. I was all for going up there straightaway, but Katie said as how we should wait to speak to you and Mrs Neville and plan what to do. I don't think you should wait long, in case she moves on.'

It only took Rose a moment to make her decision. 'I'm going to Mum's from here, but I'd like you both to join us by teatime. Can you arrange that, Katie?'

'Yes, I can ask two or three Nippies to work an extra shift. What about Lily and Joyce at Margate?'

'I'll use Mum's telephone to ring them. I'd best give the afternoon tea a miss and get cracking straightaway,' Rose said, making a move after noting the name of the road Jennie had mentioned.

23
~

Lily placed the telephone receiver down on Rose's desk before going out into the Margate teashop to speak to Joyce. 'Rose has told us to clock off early. We are to go to Sea View; she has some information about Alexsy's whereabouts and wants as many of us as possible to help.'

Joyce stopped wiping down the counter and put her hands on her hips. 'That is good news; at last we can do something to find the poor mite. Give me a shout when you're ready to go. It has been a long day and I will look forward to escaping.'

'And what are you fine ladies up to? Have I caught you chatting while you should be working?' Peter asked as he entered the shop and swung Lily around in his arms.

She bit the inside of her cheek to stop herself laughing out loud. 'For heaven's sake, you will shock the customers,' she said as Joyce gave him a disapproving glare.

'Behave, Peter,' Stew said. 'You'll get the ladies in trouble with their boss if you aren't careful. I do apologize,' he said to Joyce. 'We are just off duty, and it means some of my fellow pilots like to let off steam. We're here to see if you and your friends would like to come out with us?'

Lily straightened her uniform and pulled a sad face. 'Me and Joyce are finishing work early to go to Sea View and help in the search for Alexsy. Rose has been on the phone; they seem to have a lead on someone who may have taken him.'

Stew gave a broad smile. 'That is very good news. What have the police told you?' he asked in his broad Scottish accent.

Lily looked embarrassed. 'The police haven't done much; it was someone at the other teashop who came up with the information of where they thought this woman lived. We're knocking off early and going to help Flora and Rose.'

'Then we will help as well,' Peter said, rolling up his sleeves. 'There may be some fisticuffs involved; you will need the strong arm of the RAF.'

'Now look here,' his fellow officer said. 'I don't think we should go rushing in with all guns blazing. This is a job for the police.'

'By the time they get their backsides into gear, this woman could have disappeared with Alexsy,' Lily hit back.

'Lily is right,' Joyce joined in. 'We must act now before it is too late. Of course we will get the police involved, once the lad is safe and we have the woman.'

'And Tom White,' Lily spat out. 'He won't get away with this if I've got anything to do with it.'

'What if there are other people involved, rather than just this couple?' Stew asked her. 'You could find yourself in trouble if you come face to face with a group of people hell bent on kidnapping children; it could endanger the young lad's life. I'm just trying to imagine what I'd want to do if it was my own son who'd been taken. Of course, I would feel like stringing up the culprits; but the law must be obeyed, and that also means not endangering yourselves.'

'Stew is right,' Peter agreed. 'We need backup, and I know just the chaps. May I use your telephone?'

'Well, I don't know; our area manager might walk in at any moment.'

'There's a telephone box over the road,' Joyce suggested.

'I'll be back in five minutes. Order us some toasted teacakes and tea,' Peter said to Stew before hurrying out the door.

'I'll find you a table,' Lily smiled as she led Stew to a window seat. She liked the affable Scottish airman who had visited Captain's Cottage many times along with Peter. She had the impression he missed his children, as he often spoke of them and was quick to show photographs and news sent by his wife. She wondered if his wife knew about the women who lived in their cottage . . . 'I'll get your tea ordered,' she told him, writing down the order before hurrying away.

A short time later, Peter came back into the teashop with a confident smile on his face that made several of the lady diners smile in return. Lily, who'd been keeping an eye out for him, collected their order and returned to the table. Even though Rose wasn't on duty, Lily didn't want word to get back that she had been shirking and chatting with male customers. God forbid, especially, that Miss Butterworth should hear; that woman had never liked her, and had used the word 'flighty' when mentioning her name on more than one occasion. Lily had annoyed her all the more by smiling sweetly and speaking in a posh accent.

'Here you are, boys,' she grinned as she placed their order on the table. 'Will there be anything else?'

'Apart from your company to go dancing later on, I can't think of anything,' Peter laughed as he bit into a teacake.

She shook her head in disbelief. 'It's only ten minutes since you agreed to help us look for Alexsy, or have you forgotten already?'

He leant back in his seat, wiping the butter from his lips. 'All sorted. I've called up a few chums I know in the army to help us. They are good blokes.' He looked at his watch. 'We'd best be making tracks or they will be at Sea View long before we are, and Mrs Neville will wonder why half the army is on her doorstep.'

'What?' was all Lily could say before calling Joyce and hurrying to the staffroom to change into her outdoor clothes.

'How ever will we all squeeze into that?' Joyce asked, as the two airmen led them outside the teashop to where their lorry was parked.

'If the two of you can fit into the passenger seat, I'll climb into the back,' Stew offered as he helped them up into the cab. From the teashop window, two Sallys who were working behind the counter laughed at the women's discomfort.

'We'll soon be in Ramsgate,' Peter shouted above the din of the noisy engine as he started it up.

'Thank goodness for that,' Joyce exclaimed, grabbing on to Lily for dear life.

*

'I don't know how to thank you all,' Flora said as she and Miss Tibbs handed out mugs of tea to the men who had joined them in the kitchen of Sea View. Peter had exaggerated a little about the number of soldiers he'd called, but the six who had arrived were warmly welcomed. Rose was amazed to find that one of the soldiers knew Ben, and had even attended their wedding.

'In my book that makes you almost family,' she'd grinned before helping Flora to fill in all the details of what had happened when little Alexsy was snatched from the pram.

'Can you repeat the suspect's name?' one of the men asked. Lily quickly answered, explaining more about Tom White working for Lyons before joining the army.

'May I use your telephone?' the sergeant in charge asked Flora. She led him to the hall and showed him where it was before returning to the kitchen and closing the door to give him privacy.

'What exactly is your plan?' Rose asked Flora.

'Oh goodness, I'd not really thought about it. Young Jennie here was told the name of the street and approximately where the house is, and . . . well, I thought it would be a case of turning up and taking Alexsy back.'

Lily laughed, but then her expression became serious. 'We need a better plan than that. What if it is the wrong house? Or the woman hasn't taken Alexsy after all, and has her own child in the house? It wouldn't only be a matter of looking foolish; we could be in trouble with the police for bothering her, and for not giving them all the details of what we think we know.'

'Can they arrest us for holding back information?' Katie

asked, looking worried. Stew assured her that this was highly unlikely, but that they'd all get their knuckles rapped and the men would probably be reported to their commanding officers.

'I can't have that. Perhaps you should leave this to us,' Flora said, giving the men an apologetic look.

'But we have the transport,' one of the soldiers told her. 'We can't have you ladies walking the streets alone.' This made Miss Tibbs give a girlish laugh.

The army sergeant came back into the room just as Rose started to speak. 'I intend to go and look for Alexsy regardless of who else is going to join me. I also want to have a word with Tom White before we call the police. I'm unhappy that he treated Mum like he did and I'll make it clear to him I will be informing the police; just perhaps, that will be enough to have him scarper and never come back to Thanet again.'

'I'll help you,' Lily said, 'as it was my Mary he was after.'

The rest of the women in the room agreed.

The sergeant cleared his throat to get everyone's attention. 'We will be accompanying you; it seems that our Tom White is absent without leave and we need to apprehend him. No doubt the police will have a say in this as well, so we will be working together. Let's drink our tea and decide what is going to happen.'

The women all grinned at each other.

'Well, I never,' Miss Tibbs exclaimed.

'Let's hope he's nabbed and locked up before the day is out,' Flora sighed. 'I just want life to get back to normal. To think he lied to me about his health and his reasons for coming back – and all along he had absconded from the army. What a rotter!'

'It couldn't happen to a nicer chap,' Lily smiled as she raised her teacup to Peter, who grinned back.

Anya held out her hand to Mildred, pulling her to her feet. 'You look tired; would you like to rest a little more?'

'No, we need to keep going or we will be late for our rendezvous; then what will happen?' Mildred muttered, wincing as she took a few steps. 'These shoes are killing me.'

Anya tutted. 'You are not used to wearing shoes.'

'I'd have looked daft wearing my wellington boots with this dress,' Mildred said, looking down at the crumpled floral cotton that had seen better days.

Anya had to agree as she looked at her friend in her unusual garb. 'You should have dressed as a man like you usually do; then you'd have been comfortable during our trek and your feet would not be aching as much.'

Mildred ignored Anya's comment, not wishing to explain that if they'd met German soldiers during their journey, a woman dressed as a man would not have been looked upon favourably. 'I'll cope,' she said. 'At least I refused to wear a corset under this disgusting frock.'

Anya laughed out loud, with Mildred joining in moments later. 'Look,' Anya said, 'there is a footpath over there that must lead down to the sea. Why don't we take a rest, and you can dip your feet in the water to soothe them? It will be better for you than sitting at the edge of the road while being vigilant.'

Mildred agreed. Since being dropped off they had followed the map scribbled on a scrap of paper by Alphonse, sticking close to a road that followed the shoreline towards Lion-sur-Mer, all the time listening out for traffic and being prepared to hide behind a hedge at the slightest sound of approaching potential enemy vehicles. Or indeed collaborators. There had been very few farms or houses, which they were grateful for, although Alphonse had whispered to Mildred that they would have to be extremely careful as a German battalion had recently been spotted in the area. They'd thought it best not to inform Anya of the dangers, with him suggesting they lie low through the night and venture past the buildings where the enemy would be camped out just after dawn, when there would be fewer people about. It would look as though they were on their way to work, but even so, they had to be vigilant. Travelling at night, they might well have been stopped and questioned if there was a local curfew in place.

'We could rest and eat some of the food Alphonse gave us,' Mildred suggested. 'Let me go first in case there's someone about, since I can speak the language.'

As it was they had safe passage down to the edge of the sea, where they were out of view of the road, and settled between a few sand dunes that sheltered them from the wind whipping across the water. Mildred rummaged in the canvas bag she had slung over her shoulder, pulling out a paper bag containing part of a loaf of bread as well as a lump of cheese and sausage wrapped in oilcloth. 'The bread is almost stale, but it will be filling,' she said, tearing it into four and handing a piece to Anya. Taking a small knife from her bag, she next cut into the sausage and cheese, rewrapping the rest for later. 'It should give us one more meal if we are frugal,' she said, before biting into the sausage.

Anya sniffed the meat and wrinkled her nose at its strong garlic odour. Taking Mildred's knife, she thinly sliced the sausage and cheese and placed them between two halves of her bread. 'Just edible,' she said, although Mildred noticed she ate every morsel and licked her fingers afterwards.

Mildred slipped her knife into her pocket, planning to rinse it in the sea, then untied the laces of her shoes and kicked them off with a sigh of relief.

'Your toes are red raw, and there is a blister on your heel. How are you going to continue the journey with feet like that?' Anya asked as she peered closer. 'Go down to the water's edge and soak them; the salt water may help.' She placed her hands under the skirt of her dress and wriggled out of a cotton petticoat, ripping strips from the garment. 'Use this part to dry your feet and then bind them with the bandages I have made. I will come with you to check you do it properly,' she said, standing up and removing her jacket before rolling up the skirt of her dress and tucking it into the elastic in the legs of her knickers. 'I don't wish to get wet,' she explained, seeing Mildred's smile.

'I had a sudden memory of being a child and doing the same when I went paddling in the sea. Come on; let's run into the waves, as they will be cold,' she said, holding out her hand to Anya. The two women ran the twenty yards into the crashing waves, shrieking as the cold water splashed around their legs.

'It is cold but invigorating,' Anya shouted to Mildred to make herself heard above the sound of the waves.

'My feet feel better already. Perhaps when we are back

home in Ramsgate, we should try to dip our toes in the sea more often,' Mildred called back.

'I don't think so,' a man said from behind her in a gruff German accent. 'Put your hands up . . . and turn around slowly.' They heard the unmistakeable click of a gun.

Anya closed her eyes as she turned. She didn't want to look into the eyes of the Nazi bastard whose army had destroyed her home and her family in Poland. She felt a surge of anger at the thought that this would be the end of everything for her: she would never see her son or her Henio again, never serve bread as a Sally. Above all, she'd spent the night on a stinking fishing boat being sick in a bucket, only to be killed by the first German they came across. Beside her, she felt Mildred's elbow nudge her as they stepped forward on the uneven sand. The soldier had stepped behind them and was shouting for them to move forward. Anya opened her eyes just as Mildred stumbled.

'Mildred,' she cried. Ignoring the soldier's shouts, she bent down to help her friend.

Mildred grabbed her arm and pulled her down to her knees while whispering. 'If this fails, his name is Domino, meet him by the boatyard at the designated time. Now stay there.'

Anya was confused. What the hell was going on? She felt rather than saw the gun as the German soldier moved up behind them and bent over Mildred, aiming directly at her head. Mildred let out an almighty roar, startling him. At the same time, she lunged at him with the knife she'd used to cut up their meal.

'Take that . . . and that,' she bellowed as the man staggered, clutching his stomach.

For a moment, Anya's eyes met his. Clear blue and ice cold. 'Is this war worth your hate?' she spat at him as he collapsed in a heap across Mildred's legs.

She struggled onto her feet and rolled him off Mildred, helping her to her feet.

'Check he's dead,' Mildred said, not taking her eyes off the man, who now lay motionless on his stomach.

Anya put her fingers to his throat. 'There is no pulse,' she said in a calm voice. 'What should we do now?'

Mildred looked around, shielding her eyes against the late afternoon sun. 'They don't tend to travel alone. Help me drag him out of view before we're seen; there must be more of them about.'

Holding an arm each, they tugged and dragged until the soldier's body was by a sand dune, hidden behind the remains of a wall that lined the road.

'Take off your jacket and use it to brush over the sand so there's no trace of what happened,' Mildred said. She started to go through the German's pockets and remove anything that might identify him.

'What now?' Anya asked as she bent over, hands on her knees, trying to catch her breath.

'Now we bury him and move on. We have an appointment to keep.'

24

'Is everyone ready and clear about who they are paired with?' Flora asked, looking around the kitchen at the expectant faces.

'As ready as I'll ever be,' Miss Tibbs said as she waved a furled umbrella in the air.

Flora sighed. 'Miss Tibbs, it is far too dangerous for you to come with us. You could be knocked over if things get rough.'

The old woman looked disappointed. 'No one wants you when you are old,' she said quietly, sitting down at the table.

Rose's heart ached for the lady she had known since her childhood days. 'We have a very important role for you,' she said, sitting next to her and sliding a sheet of paper and a pencil in front of Miss Tibbs. 'There are bound to be people ringing here to share their important news while we are out looking for Tom White. We want you not only to keep an eye on the children but to be responsible for collating the telephone calls in case we miss something.

I've written down the telephone number for the Ramsgate teashop and if anything important comes in, you are to ring them and they will pass it on to us as we won't be far away. Do you think you can do that for us?'

Miss Tibbs looked from Rose to the sheet of paper. 'I'll do my best,' she said, a little worried.

'Shall I stay behind and help Miss Tibbs?' Joyce asked. 'I'm not sure I'd be very much help in the group, unlike some of you.'

Miss Tibbs looked relieved. 'Yes, please,' she nodded.

'Good; then let's get going,' Rose said, standing up. 'We all know the parts we must play, but please, everyone: be careful. We don't need the man getting aggressive, and the woman is an unknown quantity.'

'There's also the safety of Alexsy to consider,' Katie chipped in, speaking directly to the men to make sure they understood. 'We don't want this to get out of control.'

The sergeant agreed with her. 'We need Tom White in one piece and not to be knocked about; there are others who will deal with him.' He looked around the room. 'Who needs a lift in one of our vehicles to get into position?'

Peter glanced at Lily and winked. 'My pretend wife and I will walk the short distance, as we have the pram.'

'And I'll walk with them, as I should be able to recognize the woman now that I've seen her a couple of times,' Jennie said, feeling important among the older people in the room.

They all filed out of Sea View with calls of good luck ringing in their ears as Miss Tibbs and Joyce waved them off. 'Why they need to take the pram when the children are all here beats me,' Miss Tibbs said as they went back indoors. She checked the telephone as she passed it. 'And you can behave yourself, too. We don't want anyone ringing us who has nothing to do with rescuing that little lad,' she added, to Joyce's amusement.

'Deep breath,' Lily said as she pushed the pram through the High Street and turned into a side road. 'We are very close to the house now.'

'Do you want to stop and take a breather before we approach?' Peter asked, nudging her arm and nodding across the road to where Flora and Katie stood. Close by were the two vehicles used by the airmen and soldiers.

'I'm fine, thank you. I must say, this feels like one of those spy films where they stake out the building where the villain is hiding; although it feels quite different from sitting and watching in a cinema.'

He laughed and kissed her cheek.

'What was that for?' Lily asked, although she rather liked it.

'For being brave,' he said.

'I'm not sure about being brave; I just want Tom White to get what he's due. It's about time. I pray we have the right house.'

Peter casually glanced around. It was a short street of small properties, the type that were often called two-up, two-downs; all had seen better days, with a gap further up the road where homes had taken a direct hit during a raid. Lily couldn't help thinking she'd visited this street before. Then it hit her like a flash of lightning: this was where the woman lived who offered to get rid of unwanted babies. A small sob escaped as she fought hard to remain composed, telling herself that everything had turned out for the best in the end. She now had a beautiful daughter. But what if . . . ?

Peter reached out and stopped the pram, holding on to the handle. 'You aren't looking so good. Stop here and pretend to check the baby while you take a breather,' he said, concerned at her distraught face.

Without answering, Lily bent over the empty pram and straightened the blankets while taking a few deep breaths. With the hood raised, no one would know there were two cabbages and a bunch of carrots wrapped in a baby's shawl. 'I'm ready to move on,' she said, giving him a sweet smile. 'It is good of you to care; I'll explain later why I was overcome for a moment. I almost made a foolish mistake a couple of years ago . . .'

'We all make mistakes at times; we'd not be human if we didn't. I fear my good friend will be making one soon if he isn't careful.'

Lily frowned as she watched Katie walking on the arm of the Scottish airman. 'They do look rather cosy, but perhaps they are acting their part in this scene we are setting?'

'He does like her a lot,' Peter said as he kicked the brake on the pram so they could move on.

'He has a wife and young children.'

'And your friend has a husband . . .'

'Oh dear; what can we do?'

'We can be ready to pick up the pieces, although I'll try to have a quiet word with him. He has too much to lose for a wartime affair.'

'As does Katie, to have her head turned by a flashy pilot.'

'Ouch! Touché,' he answered, before pointing discreetly

to where Jennie was hiding behind a tall hedge and waving at them.

'It's the house with the black door,' Lily said as she started to cross the road towards the property. 'Don't follow me all the way, but stop to tie up your shoelace.'

She pushed the pram up the short path to the front door and use a blackened brass knocker to rap three times, as loudly as possible. Her heart was thudding so hard in her chest that she almost believed it would be heard.

After a while, as Lily's heartbeat started to settle, footsteps approached the inside of the door and a female voice could be heard speaking loudly. 'Shut that brat up; I swear I'm going to leave him on the doorstep of the church if you don't do something with him.'

The door opened several inches. Lily could smell cigarettes and stale body odour as a thin-faced blonde woman peered through the opening. 'Who are you and what do you want?' she asked, puffing smoke out through the small gap.

Lily wrinkled her nose but resisted the urge to step back. 'I want to see my husband,' she said, meeting the woman's eyes directly.

'You've got the wrong house. There's no one's husband living here, love,' she said, starting to close the door.

'His name is Tom White; does that ring any bells? Our daughter here is called Mary.' Lily nodded towards the pram.

The woman's eyes glinted with malice. 'Hang on a minute,' she said, then closed the door in Lily's face.

'What do we do now?' Anya asked, brushing down her skirt as Mildred used two sticks to make a small cross and stuck it close to the head of the dead soldier.

Mildred stepped back and bowed her head for a moment before answering. Then she said, 'We move on as quickly as possible in case he has a comrade looking for him. Collect your things and try not to leave any footsteps in the sand, as it may attract attention.'

'The cross you planted will do that,' Anya pointed out.

'He may be the enemy, but he still deserves respect,' Mildred said as she started to limp towards the footpath which led to the road. 'We will walk for another hour and find somewhere to sleep for the night. Tomorrow is the day we meet Domino, who will lead us to the target.'

'You are a better woman than I will ever be,' Anya said as she fell in step behind Mildred. 'I would have left him to rot where he fell.'

'I am not a better woman; I have killed many times. I simply hope that when my own time comes, someone will be respectful of my body. You have been through a lot and have reason to hate. For me, it is a job that must be done for us to win this war.'

'Is that why you removed his identity documents?'

'They will be given to someone who can notify his next of kin; somewhere, in the not too distant future, a mother will be grieving. Now, stop talking and concentrate on walking – and keep your eyes peeled.'

After they had walked for most of the hour, Anya insisted they stop so she could bind Mildred's feet again. She made much better progress with just the fabric from Anya's torn petticoat wrapped around the blisters, without her shoes rubbing and cutting into her feet. Instead, she tied their laces together and strung them around her neck.

They resumed walking for a time, until Mildred held

her arm out to stop Anya going any further. Holding a finger to her lips, she pointed to a nearby field where a farmer could be seen herding cows into a barn. 'He will be milking them and then settling them down for the night. Once he has gone, we can hide there until the morning.'

Anya licked her lips at the thought of fresh milk as her stomach rumbled. They settled behind a hedge and waited.

'Come, we can move now, the farmer has gone.' Mildred nodded to where he was pushing a cart containing milk churns across the field away from them.

'I know cows,' Anya said as she entered the barn, whispering words to the creatures to calm them. 'We kept cows when I was younger, before . . . before my world was destroyed. We need to find a container of some kind,' she said to Mildred, who stood back from the animals. 'Don't be frightened; they are big, but they are harmless.'

Mildred grunted a reply, but didn't seem convinced. 'Will this jug do?' she asked, going to a bench at the side of the barn. 'What do you want it for?'

'I need something to contain the milk; I plan to milk a cow for our own refreshment. The farmer was too quick to have milked them properly – ah, it is as I thought,' Anya said, pulling a small stool over to one of the cows. Sitting down, she began to milk the animal and soon had half a jug of milk to go with their supper.

While Anya was busy, Mildred had laid out the remains of their food on the wooden bench. They drank from the jug thirstily as they devoured their meal.

'We have dined well tonight,' Anya said as she wiped her mouth. 'Now to find somewhere comfortable to sleep . . .'

'We'll need somewhere away from the opening of the

barn in case the farmer returns earlier than expected, but that we can easily escape from if need be. And away from them,' Mildred added, giving the cows a wary look.

Anya found enough straw to make them a comfortable bed to rest on. Mildred was soon asleep, oblivious to thoughts of what the following day might bring, but Anya lay awake watching the stars through the gaps in the roof. She was wondering what could have gone wrong in the life of her former friend from Poland, that she was now fraternizing with the enemy. Perhaps she would learn more when they met this Domino person.

She spent a restless night, tossing and turning, listening to sounds outside the barn and watching as night turned slowly to dawn. The few times she dozed off, she had vivid dreams of running through Ramsgate calling out for her son. He was always just out of arm's reach and try as she did, she could never get close to him. As dawn broke she was more than ready to move on, finish the mission and get home to Alexsy.

'Come, we must move on,' she said in a low voice, shaking Mildred awake. 'The farmer will be here soon.'

Mildred groaned as she stretched before stumbling to her feet. 'I'll be fine once we get moving,' she insisted as she stretched her legs and swore under her breath.

'Let me change the dressings on your feet; I have a little more of the fabric left from my petticoat,' Anya said, opening her bag and pulling out the strips. She bent over Mildred's feet and started to unwind the binding carefully until she reached the sores on her toes and heels. 'You need to soak your feet so that we don't tug on the wounds and make them bleed,' she said, looking around in frustration.

'There was a stream not far from the road. Let's walk that way and I can dangle my feet in the water,' Mildred suggested.

'Lean on me,' Anya instructed as they made their way out of the barn, heading back towards the route they'd been on the night before. Anya looked behind them; she'd have liked to enjoy another drink of milk to set her up for the journey ahead, but Mildred's comfort came first.

'How does that feel?' she asked as, after wetting the old dressings and slowly removing them, Mildred dipped her feet into the trickle of water and sighed with relief.

'Blissful,' Mildred sighed. 'Give me a little while, and then we can set off on the last leg of our journey.'

Anya took off the jacket she had been given to wear over her dress. Inside the rough wool there was a lining of cotton that had seen better days. She ripped out as much as she could and handed it to Mildred. 'You can use this to dry your feet. It could be cleaner, but needs must . . .'

Mildred chuckled as she took it from her. 'You are starting to sound like Flora with your "needs must".'

'I wish I was Flora at this moment, standing in her kitchen, making food for the residents of Sea View. What I wouldn't give to enjoy a big bowl of her stew with fluffy dumplings.'

'Not a fish pie?' Mildred chortled.

'At this moment in time, I would gladly eat the smelliest fish you could catch,' Anya replied with a rueful smile.

25

Lily waited for the door to reopen. As the moments passed, she became fidgety; where was the woman? She looked back to the pavement, where Peter was finding it hard to act nonchalant while keeping close enough to step in if Lily had a problem with the inhabitants of the house.

'What can we do?' she mouthed towards him.

He shrugged his shoulders and wandered further up the road to where Jennie was still hiding behind the shrubbery, then bent to tie his laces. 'Could you see that woman?' he asked under his breath.

'I could only see part of her face, but I'd swear she was the one who was in the teashop when I was told she lived here. What will you do if she doesn't open up again? She might've gone out the back way.'

Peter groaned and continued up the road, to where Stew was in a cosy conversation with Katie. 'Look sharp, we haven't thought to cover the back entrance. They may escape that way. I'm going back down the street and will tell the others to keep an eye out.'

'What about Alexsy? Could Lily hear him?'

'I could hear a child crying. It could have been him.'

'Let's hope so,' Katie replied, pushing Stew to get a move on. They set off quickly to find the back of the terraced houses, looking for an alley that might give them access to the property where, hopefully, little Alexsy was safe and well.

As Peter was heading back down the road, trying to look casual, the sound that put the fear of God into every living person could be heard, creeping closer and louder by the minute. He stopped beside Jennie's hiding spot. 'Break cover and get yourself to a shelter,' he hissed. 'Do you know where to go?'

'Yes, there's an entrance to the tunnel shelters in the next street. I'll see you all down there,' she said, jumping a short fence into next door's garden and making her way to safety.

He continued down the street, wanting to get Lily away to safety, but stopped short as he caught a glimpse of her entering the house and closing the door behind her.

Thinking the worst, and imagining her suffering at the hands of the couple inside, he ran to the door and pounded it with his fists until it opened.

'It wasn't locked,' Lily said, letting him in. 'There's nobody in here. They must be heading for the communal shelters.'

'Or using the air raid to scarper,' Peter said as he started to look around the small house. 'Hmm; I wonder . . .' He pulled back the edge of a rug, looking for any sign of access to a cellar.

'If you're looking for a cellar, it can't be under a carpet, as there's no one up here who could've put it back in place,'

Lily pointed out. 'More likely to be under the stairs.' She turned towards a full-height door, unbolted it and pulled it open. 'Here it is; but there's no one down there,' she said, glancing down into the darkness. 'Can't be, as it was bolted on the outside.'

'They must have gone to the shelters,' Peter said, opening the back door. Outside, they saw their fellow searchers congregating on a pathway that ran along the back gardens of the terraced houses.

'They're not here,' he called out. 'Split into two groups and search the surrounding streets; they can't have gone far.' As he moved down the long, narrow garden to speak to the men, he froze to the spot as the whistling of a bomb signalled that enemy planes were close. 'Everybody down,' he bellowed, and they all fell flat to the ground. An explosion in a nearby street had them change their minds about searching for Tom White, instead running hell for leather for the public shelters.

Lily hung on to the pram; it belonged to Flora and was put to many uses. She didn't want to leave it behind in case it was stolen or damaged in the raid.

'Let me take that,' Peter said.

Lily couldn't help but giggle at how he manoeuvred it along the pavement, taking care not to bump into people. 'It's funny to see you pushing a pram. Have you had much practice?'

'I'll have you know I've often pushed my nieces and nephews about when I've visited my parents. I have three sisters, so there are always opportunities for Uncle Peter to help out; and I enjoy it. It's good practice for when I'm a father,' he added as they reached the tunnel entrance.

'You seem to have your life mapped out,' Lily said. 'Is there a young lady you have your eye on to be the mother of these children?'

'I have a shortlist,' he grinned as he allowed an elderly couple to go ahead of them. 'The right woman needs to fit certain criteria. First, she needs to love children; second, be hardworking; third and fourth, make a decent cup of tea and be happy to be my wife. What do you think? Have you got a list of your own?'

'Hmm; my list would include entering a property via the front gate rather than dropping into an apple tree. After that, he needs to love my daughter and have a good sense of humour.' She looked sideways to see the expression on his face just as he leant down to give her a gentle kiss on the lips.

'That was number five,' he said as they moved forward into the tunnels.

Lily was silent as they approached the entrance. She knew relatively little about this man, who had quite liter-ally dropped out of the sky and into her life; but what she did know, she liked very much. After her disastrous ex-periences with men early in life, she had vowed to bring up her daughter on her own, but gradually she could feel her resolution wavering.

They made their way through the narrow tunnels towards the section where the residents of Sea View had set up camp. Even though the girls at Captain's Cottage had an air-raid shelter in their garden, they often preferred the camaraderie of the Ramsgate tunnels. As Lily and Peter walked on they kept a look out for the rest of their group, and also for the woman Lily had encountered at the front door of the suspicious house. She prayed the child who had been crying inside was Alexsy and not some other poor youngster.

'Over here,' Peter called out, waving his arm as he saw Stew and Katie weaving their way through the crowd.

'Have you seen Jennie, Rose and Flora?' Lily asked, concerned for their friends' safety.

'Rose is up ahead of us; she must be at our base by now,' Katie explained. 'We were held up.'

Lily frowned. The light wasn't good, but she could have sworn Katie was blushing. Oh no, she thought, please don't say she really does have feelings for Stew. 'Do you think Tom and his lady friend are down here somewhere?' she asked.

'We were looking for them as we came along, but so far, no luck. Stew thinks we should all regroup and plan a search of the tunnels. Peter's army friends are going to do the same, so I told them to head towards Flora's base. So we should hurry.'

Lily sped up; she was of the opinion that plans for the next step would not get very far without them being present.

'Thank goodness you're here,' Flora said, getting to her feet and giving Lily and Katie a big hug. 'You deserve a mug each of Miss Tibbs' tea for getting my girls to safety,' she said to the two airmen.

'It's always a pleasure,' Peter said, nodding in thanks to Miss Tibbs as she passed him tea in an enamel mug. 'You certainly have a good setup here,' he added, looking about him at the area with its neatly arranged temporary wall and small paraffin stove.

'The bunk beds are allocated to us as well,' Joyce chipped in as she brushed past him with an armful of blankets.

Peter shook his head in disbelief. 'I had no idea that while I was up there in the sky playing my part, all this was going on down here below ground.' He sat down next to Joyce as she explained how the tunnels had been dug out, and all that had gone into making the residents of Ramsgate as safe as possible.

Lily joined Flora and Rose, filling them in on what had happened at the house before the air raid started. 'They're more than likely down here somewhere,' she concluded.

'With Alexsy?' Rose said hopefully.

'I would think so, as we checked the cellar to the house and it was empty. Tom is far too much of a coward not to have run for safety. Do you remember how he was always the first to go down into the cellar at the Margate teashop?'

'And the last to leave,' Rose chipped in.

'You know, this could be the ideal time to find them,' Katie said thoughtfully.

'We must split into groups, with someone in each group who can identify Tom,' Rose said. 'We need to be discreet about it, though, and not give them a reason to flee.'

Lily picked up an enamel cup and tapped it against the stove, just loudly enough to get the attention of the others in their group. 'Rose is going to explain how we will continue the search while we are down here,' she said, passing the floor to her friend, who took great care to explain that they had to be discreet. Once Tom and his lady friend had been spotted, they were to step back and allow the army to take over.

The army sergeant stepped forward. 'Tom White is a

deserter and needs to be apprehended so he can be tried and sentenced. We believe the woman he is living with is the widow of one of his comrades who died in action. White is a coward, but he is an aggressive coward. Twice he has almost been apprehended but escaped after a fight, injuring those who tried to arrest him. He has taken cover in properties where he threatened and coerced house-holders until they feared for their lives . . .'

Flora was aghast to learn about the excesses of Tom's past. To think that such a man had moved among the young women she cared for! 'Is the woman he is currently with in danger?'

The sergeant gave a harsh laugh. 'No, with Deirdre Hope it's a different case completely. Before Kevin Hope died in action, he'd become mates with White and confided in him about Deirdre being in prison for stealing three babies. She was selling them on to women who couldn't have children of their own . . .' He paused, looking around as the penny dropped among his horrified listeners.

'He planned to take my Mary and sell her, didn't he?' Lily snarled. 'If I get my hands on him . . .'

Flora put her arm around Lily. 'Instead, he snatched Alexsy thinking it was Mary; at least he will be safe, if they are planning to sell him on to a couple who dearly want a child.'

'That's if they have a buyer for a young boy. It may be they had a ready market for Mary, but not Alexsy.'

'Gosh,' Joyce said as she sat down quickly. 'We need to find them right now.'

'That's what we are about to do, ma'am,' he said, giving her a reassuring smile. 'I would like to put you into groups of three, with at least one person in each group who would recognize White; and also a man in each group. No disrespect to you ladies, but if he becomes violent, you will be safer if you're in male company.'

Flora and the other women were vocal in their agreement and soon nearly everyone was assigned to a group, with only Miss Tibbs and young Pearl remaining to keep an eye on the sleeping children.

One group was sent up the tunnel that led to the exit where Tom White would have entered. Joyce was relieved she was in this group, and would only have to tip off the two soldiers who went with her.

Flora, accompanied by Peter and Jennie, went to the main entrance to the tunnel network, while Rose headed off with two soldiers, leaving Lily to accompany Katie and Stew through one of the lesser used branches of the tunnels.

'That should give us good coverage, and hopefully we'll winkle him out before the all clear sounds,' Lily said.

'Ooh! I've not had a winkle in ages,' Katie said, licking her lips.

'With pepper and lots of vinegar,' Lily agreed. 'Mildred used to bring them back with her when she'd been to the fish market. Talking of which, has Flora heard from her? It's so unlike Mildred to go away for so long. We've not even had a postcard.'

'Perhaps she has a gentleman friend?' Stew suggested, at which Lily and Katie raised their eyebrows at each other.

'It is very out of character; I do hope she's all right. I'll take a walk down the harbour and ask tomorrow. For today, though, let's concentrate on finding Tom White and getting him locked up,' Lily said as they turned a bend in the tunnel and stopped to look about them.

'I hope you know the way back,' Stew said, sounding a little worried. 'Otherwise we could end up wandering about underground for ever more.'

Lily noticed Katie touch Stew's shoulder to comfort him. She had never been a tactile person, especially with strangers, and they'd not known Stew long enough to call him a family friend. Besides, he was married, and Katie would need to be careful no one noticed her getting pally with another man while her husband was away at sea. 'Don't worry; once the all clear goes off, you can follow the stampede out of here,' she grinned. 'We all felt uncomfortable when we first came down here, as it's not natural to be sheltering underground.'

'Hello, Lily,' a young woman called out. 'We don't usually see you down this tunnel; are you lost?'

Lily laughed, and introduced Stew to the group of women. 'They used to work with us at the Margate teashop before they left to do war work,' she explained. 'That's a thought: do any of you remember Tom White, who used to be an assistant area manager? I heard he was down here somewhere and thought I'd say hello to him.' She smiled sweetly, ignoring the way two of the women nudged each other. They'd no doubt heard the rumours that Tom was Mary's father.

'Funny you should say that; I spotted him further up the tunnel when we first came in. He took me out once,' one of the group smirked. 'He was with a scruffy woman and she was carrying a toddler with dark hair. He was going to ignore me, but then he asked about you. I told him you still worked at the teashop and he should pay you a visit some time,' she added, glancing at the other women. They looked keen to hear what Lily would say in response.

'I must have missed him,' she said easily, pretending to glance around. 'Which way did he go?'

'In the direction you just came from. I told him you'd probably be with Flora Neville and the others from Sea View.'

Katie gasped. 'Miss Tibbs is there alone with the children,' she hissed at Stew and Lily. 'Nice to see you,' she said hastily to the women, as she grabbed Lily and Stew's sleeves and pulled them along. 'Hurry, he could be after Mary,' she said as they worked their way around people standing about chatting. As they hastened away, they heard the ex-Nippy call out, 'How's your husband, Katie?'

'Bugger, there goes the gossip mill,' Lily exclaimed. 'You two have got to be more careful . . . I don't want to know!' she said, as Katie began to protest that Stew was just a good friend. 'Just be careful, as you've got too much to lose for a quick dalliance. And I'm talking to both of you. Now, come on, let's get back to Miss Tibbs.'

Lily ran as fast as possible. She was grateful to be wearing her comfortable shoes.

'Look, up ahead,' Katie panted as they rounded a bend and Flora's part of the tunnel came into view. 'There's someone talking to Miss Tibbs.'

'Is that him?' Stew asked.

'Yes, and that's the woman I saw at the front door of the house,' Lily cried. 'Miss Tibbs looks worried.'

They slowed down and stood quietly, catching their breath and watching the scene from not twenty feet away.

'Katie, you know these tunnels – can you find the army lads and tell the sergeant we've found Tom White and his accomplice?' Stew said. He gave her a kiss on the cheek. 'Whatever you do, be careful.'

'You too,' Katie replied. 'Don't do anything until the soldiers are back here, will you? Otherwise we might lose him for good. He's not going to go back to that house if he knows we're onto him.'

Lily watched their exchange with sadness. Katie and Stew were so comfortable together. This had gone further than a simple friendship. She hurried a little way after her friend. 'Oh, Katie, what have you done? Promise me you'll stop seeing Stew once this is all over and he's gone back to his air base. Think of your Jack.'

'I've not stopped thinking of Jack,' Katie said sadly, 'and in some ways, Stew reminds me of him. I felt so lonely when he went back to his ship . . . Is it possible to love two men at the same time?'

Lily placed her hands on Katie's shoulders, forcing her to meet her eyes. 'The war is to blame for so much of this. But just because Jack's away, you can't take up with any Tom, Dick or Harry. Promise me you'll finish it.'

'I promise; I'll tell him that our friendship is over. I must go,' Katie said, disappearing into the network of tunnels before Lily could say another word.

26

'You need to rest,' Anya insisted. Mildred was wincing with every step she took.

'We can't stop now; we are too close to the meeting point,' she gasped, stopping to lean on a fence and catch her breath. 'Can you see up ahead?'

Anya held a hand up to shield her eyes against the morning sun. 'There seem to be some buildings up ahead that look like warehouses. Is that what you mean?'

'Yes, that was our original destination before the storm took us off course. Domino will be there in just over one hour. He will have news of our target.'

'Target? What is it with these strange words and false names?' Anya huffed. 'I am Anya, not Monique. You are Mildred, not Nancy, and Domino is not a proper name.'

Mildred sighed. 'Believe me, it is important we continue to use our aliases. If the Germans catch up, we need to stay in character and never give anything away. Surely this was drummed into you during your training. You were given certain items to help you if you should be captured, weren't you?'

'I never completed the training; I was required to be here much sooner than anticipated. I learnt a little Morse code, but only up to the F, so that is not much help; I can also scramble over a high wall if there is someone to give me a bunk up. This may be of more aid to me,' Anya said, pulling a long hatpin from her felt hat. 'But no use against a gun or a knife . . .'

'Were you given a pill?'

'With which to kill myself if I'm found in a dangerous position? I threw it overboard on the way here. I am not a coward,' she said, giving Mildred a hard stare.

Mildred was too tired to explain to Anya what could be done to her if she were to be captured. She would do her best to keep the woman safe and get her back to Ramsgate in one piece. It had been a bad idea, she felt, for her to accompany someone she already knew; it risked compromising the mission and putting the whole team in jeopardy. It was bad enough that Domino . . .

She pushed the dark thoughts from her mind. Patting the pocket of her jacket, she took comfort in knowing she had something that would do more to save them than a hatpin ever could. 'Just keep walking,' she huffed, deciding not to continue a conversation she found depressing.

As they approached the cluster of buildings, Anya could see they were set around an inlet of water. Several small vessels were moored nearby, along with rowing boats. The buildings had seen better days, with some of them being little more than slats of wood attached to posts lying at angles.

'It is very quiet,' she said, peering carefully from around a small shed.

'It is Sunday, which is a help; for many it is a day of rest,' Mildred replied while consulting the scribbled map Alphonse had given her. 'I have been here before . . . follow me.' She moved as fast as her injured feet would allow. 'There should be a double gate at the back of one of these buildings, and that is where we have to wait.'

'Out in the open?'

'No, we can tuck ourselves away inside and await his arrival.'

Anya gave a triumphant laugh. 'So it is a man. At last I know something about this person.'

'He is certainly that,' Mildred smiled knowingly. 'After he arrives, I believe it will only be an hour or so before you can identify your friend and we can head for home.'

'I will be home in time to tuck my son up in his bed,' Anya beamed as her spirits lifted.

Mildred didn't say anything as she lowered her ample frame down to sit on a couple of straw-filled sacks. In her opinion, nothing went to plan, and she thought it unlikely that they would really be home in good old Blighty by evening. After gingerly pulling off the rags wrapped around her feet, she closed her eyes, keeping her hand on her pocket. Who knew what dangers lurked nearby?

They sat quietly, and eventually Mildred dozed for a while until Anya nudged her. 'I can hear footsteps,' she murmured close to Mildred's ear.

Mildred got to her feet, forgetting the excruciating pain for a moment as she crept closer to the rickety doors. Putting her ear close to the wooden slats, she listened, putting a finger to her lips in case Anya spoke.

'Nancy . . . it is Domino.'

Mildred kept her hand close to her pocket and pulled the door open slightly. 'Thank goodness you are here,' she said, letting a man inside and closing the door behind him after looking out to see if he was being followed. 'This is Monique,' she said, going through the formalities.

Anya stood with her mouth open in astonishment. 'I know you, but not as Domino. You are John Bentley who used to visit Flora at Sea View – although you were much more presentable in those days,' she added, taking in his unshaven chin, dishevelled hair, and clothing that would have been suited to farm labour.

'I said this wouldn't work,' he told Mildred in exasperation. 'Never have I worked with people I know; it is far too dangerous.'

'We had no choice,' she said, trying to pacify him as she moved back to where she'd been sleeping and sat down; the pain in her feet was getting worse.

'What is wrong?' he said, kneeling in front of her to examine her swollen feet.

'Oh, you know what women are like, wearing the wrong sized shoes.' Mildred tried to laugh, at the same time fighting back tears. 'Domino, I don't know if I'm able to complete the mission; I could hold you back.'

'I tried my best to bandage them for her,' Anya said, looking over his shoulder. 'But we've walked so far . . .'

'You've done a good job,' he replied, inspecting the wounds under the ragged fabric.

'Thank you. What can you do to help her?' Anya asked, wincing at the sight of the sores as he let the air get to them.

'I have a small kit of items that may help.' He pulled a hessian bag from his shoulder. 'It isn't much, but after a night's rest we can hope Mildred – Nancy – feels well enough to continue.'

'Tomorrow?' both women exclaimed.

'I have bad news,' he started to say as he cleaned Mildred's wounds with a bottle of clear liquid, making her curse out loud. 'The pain will lessen now. I will dress the wounds in a little while.' He took a package out of his bag, along with a thermos flask. 'Vegetable soup: not exactly delicious, but warming and filling. The bread is rough but will do.'

'We are used to the bread,' Mildred said, trying to laugh. Her face was pale and her voice weak.

Domino passed them small tin cups of soup and drank his from the lid of the flask. They bit into the lumps of bread he tore from a small loaf.

'When we get back, I will treat you both to a slap-up meal in a Joe Lyons teashop,' Anya said with a faraway look in her eyes. 'Please, tell us what you know and why we cannot continue today for me to identify this woman? Not that Mildred doesn't need the rest.'

'I'm afraid our plans have changed. Anouska moved on today; she is now in Vaux.'

'Blast that storm, it's played havoc with our plans,' Mildred muttered. 'What shall we do now?'

'It will be a half day's journey to Vaux, but I will find transport, never you fear. We will not leave you behind. Now rest and regain your strength; we will need you to get us back across the Channel,' he said, assisting Mildred to relax against the sacks of straw.

He drew Anya across to the other side of the room, where they stood looking out at the darkening sky. 'It is a great service you are doing for England,' he said as he lit a cigarette, offering one to her.

'No, thank you. I was led to believe it would be a simple task,' she said, looking back to where Mildred was starting to nod off. 'I insisted Mildred should rest all day; now I want to get this done and go home to my son.'

He turned away slightly, but not before she saw the expression that flickered across his face.

'Why do you look like that?' she asked, grabbing his sleeve. 'Has something happened that you are not telling me? Is it a bomb – has something happened at Sea View?'

'Nothing has happened to Sea View. As soon as you are back, you'll see that everything is the same as it was when you left,' he said. He hated to deceive her, but a distraught woman would not help the situation. They had a job to do, and he would tell her later what had happened to her boy.

'I am relieved, as I've had such dreams about my son. It has worried me.'

'Just concentrate on the task ahead,' he replied.

'Are you able to tell me more about what will happen?'

'It should not take long once we are in the vicinity of where Anouska is staying. We want you to be able to have a good look at her and be sure she is the same woman you knew back in Poland.'

Anya was pensive. 'It has been a while since I travelled with her when we left our homeland. I hope I can confirm it is her. What I don't understand is why I must do this, and what will happen to her – you don't intend to kill her, do you? I could not be party to murder.'

He shook his head. 'I'm surprised you weren't told more. There again, if you'd been caught, it could have been dangerous for you to know more – and for our target, if you had been interrogated.'

Anya shuddered at the thought. 'What can you tell me now?'

'Very briefly, all we know is that after you left your friend in France she made her way to Paris. She married quickly once she met up with her elderly father. He introduced her to a colleague, an eminent scientist some years older than her, but who could offer her security in this turbulent time.'

'I could never do that . . .' Anya murmured before indicating for him to continue.

'Like many women of her status, she took a lover. In her case, it was a high-ranking German officer.'

Anya was so angry. 'How could she do such a thing after what they did to our beloved country?'

'Lower your voice. We have to be careful in case there is someone nearby.'

'I'm sorry. I cannot believe she would have sold herself to the enemy.'

'She hasn't.'

'What do you mean by that?' Anya hissed back at him.

'She has sent a message to us that she has secrets about army movements that she wishes to share, on the understanding she and her father will be given safe passage to England.'

Anya fell silent, trying to digest what he was saying. 'Why do you need me?'

'This may all be a trick by the enemy, an attempt to have one of their spies infiltrate our circle. That is why we need you to identify her. So few people know her from before the war.'

'And will we be bringing her back to England with us?'

'No; your mission is only to identify her, so that we are sure she is who she claims to be. We won't bring her back until the time is right. It must be planned carefully, so her lover doesn't find out until she is on home soil.'

'Where is she staying in Vaux? Will I be able to see her without being spotted?'

'They are to attend a banquet being held for a high-ranking officer . . . no, I'd rather not say who it is,' he said, as Anya opened her mouth to ask.

'How will I be able to get close enough to identify her?'

'With your training at the Lyons teashop, we plan to have you work at the banquet. There will be two other women working undercover with you, so you will not be alone.'

Anya let out a burst of laughter before slapping her hand over her mouth. 'I am a trained Sally for Joe Lyons,' she said.

'I don't understand?'

'I am trained to sell bread and cakes at the counter in the teashop. I have never been a Nippy or served a single cup of tea, let alone a meal for grandiose people. Besides, I do not speak the language.'

He looked dismayed. 'Someone's made a blunder. I will see what can be done. Now, get some sleep; you have a busy day tomorrow.'

27

Lily couldn't stand by and watch as Stew wandered closer to where Tom White was talking to Miss Tibbs. She followed him, keeping close to the tunnel wall in case Tom turned and spotted her. Much to her alarm, she saw Miss Tibbs lift Mary from her lap and hold him out towards the man; whatever was she doing? She moved closer until she could hear young Pearl speak.

'Why do you want to hold Mary?'

'She reminds me of my sister's daughter; we lost them in the Blitz,' Tom said, putting on a sad voice. 'Just to hold the little girl for a short while would help heal my broken heart,' he continued pitifully.

Lily forced herself to hold back. Where on earth were the soldiers who knew he was AWOL from the army? She prayed that Katie would reach them and bring them back soon. She could see that Stew was poised to move in on the scene, and raised her hand to silently restrain him. All the time Tom was within their sight, all was well.

She chewed her bottom lip as he dangled Mary in his

arms while he spoke to her. Mary waved one of her little hands and smacked Tom's face. Lily smiled; Mary was fussy about who held her at the best of times. He flinched but held on to her, ignoring Pearl's attempt to take her back.

'Please may I have her; she's not at all happy with how you're holding her,' Pearl begged, looking around for help as Miss Tibbs chatted away about the weather.

Lily couldn't step in yet, as she had no idea where his accomplice had gone with little Alexsy. She must be somewhere close by, she thought, scanning the busiest area of the tunnel where it began to widen out. Suddenly she heard a child start to cry and recognized the voice as Alexsy's. Slowly she turned and followed the sound, leaving the main tunnel and heading into one of the smaller ones. The crying became louder with every step she took. *Please keep crying*, she prayed . . . and then there she was, only a few feet away: the woman Lily had seen at the house. And Alexsy was with her!

'I'll take him, thank you very much,' she said in a loud, authoritative voice, moving swiftly in and lifting Alexsy from the woman's arms before stepping back. She hoped Stew had seen where she'd gone, as she would need backup very shortly judging by the thunderous glare Deirdre Hope was giving her.

'Here, what are you doing taking my child?' Deirdre screamed, making Alexsy cry even louder. 'Help, help, someone is stealing my child,' she cried out, attracting attention from people standing nearby.

'What's going on?' an elderly man asked, confronting Lily with his arms crossed. 'You can't go pinching kiddies off other women. What's wrong with you?'

'I'm not . . . I mean, this is my friend's son, Alexsy.

This woman's boyfriend stole him from his pram last week and we've been searching for him ever since.'

'A likely story,' a woman called out, and before she could draw breath Lily found herself surrounded by angry people.

'Give him back!' someone shouted.

'Call the coppers!'

'Grab her before she legs it!'

Lily felt sick and a little giddy. Where were her friends when she needed them? 'Look, some of you will know me. I work at the Lyons teashop in Margate. My friend is Flora Neville from Sea View guesthouse. She will vouch for me and confirm I'm telling the truth. Please, you've got to believe me,' she begged.

A few people stepped away, not wishing to get involved any further, but the most vocal couple remained as Alexsy started to grizzle and call out 'Mama'.

'Give him back!' they insisted.

'Oh, bless him, he wants his mummy,' an older woman said as she pushed through the crowd and pulled Alexsy from Lily's arms.

'Please don't . . . you have no idea . . .' Lily gasped as the woman handed the child back to Deirdre, who immediately disappeared into the crowd. 'Someone help me,' she cried desperately, helpless as the nightmarish situation unfurled. Her head was swimming as she spun frantically round, seeking a friendly face to help her.

'Lily, it's all right. I'm here,' Peter said as he held her close and soothed her frustration until she could think straight.

'It's like a nightmare. I had him in my arms and then the crowd turned on me . . . They've helped that woman get away with him.'

'They thought they were doing the best for the child. I could hear the shouting from where I was.'

'Excuse me, love. I saw what happened,' a young woman said as she tugged on Lily's sleeve. 'I recognize you from the teashop; I go there regularly for a meal with my mother. Doesn't that young kiddie belong to the foreign lady who works on the counter selling bread? I've seen her with him. Why has that old cow got him? I wouldn't trust her as far as I could spit. I wondered if she was up to her old tricks when I spotted her with the boy . . .'

'Old tricks?' Lily asked, trying to get as much information as possible out of the woman even if they already knew some of what Deirdre had been up to.

'She was on the game when her husband was around. She'd do anything to earn a few bob. I've heard some stories about her selling babies when she wasn't helping women in trouble get rid of them, like . . .' the woman said, getting into her stride.

'Lily!' Stew and Pearl rushed over to her. 'Tom White has snatched Mary. We've lost them in the crowd,' Pearl cried.

'That's his name,' the younger woman said. 'Tom – I thought it was funny her being an old tom, and that being his name,' she cackled.

The woman's words buzzed round in Lily's head. Why was she standing here listening to this woman when Mary was in danger? 'Look, I must go, but can you come into the teashop tomorrow and have a chat? I'll stand you a free meal – bring your mum as well,' she added, as she began to walk away before turning. 'Sorry, I didn't catch your name?'

'Thank you, I'm Liz Friend; I hope you find him. I'll keep an eye open.'

Lily turned to follow Peter and Stew, but they had disappeared. 'Pearl, where have they gone?'

The young girl looked white-faced even in the dim lighting. 'They've rushed off after the man who took Mary. What can we do?'

Lily knelt in front of Pearl, even though her every instinct was telling her to follow the others and claw her daughter back from Tom. 'I want you to be a very brave young lady and first check that Miss Tibbs is all right. Then I want you to fetch your mum and Flora. Have you got that?'

'I have,' Pearl said seriously. 'You'd better hurry after them.'

Lily gave the girl a quick hug and then set off, running as fast as she could and swerving around people taking shelter, praying that she would reach her daughter before Tom White vanished with her completely.

As she ran, ignoring shouts of 'slow down' and 'watch where you're going', the wail of the all-clear siren could be heard along with shouts of 'Everybody out' from a group of men who'd been sitting around a card table playing poker. Up ahead, she spotted the back of a man in an RAF uniform who was also pushing through the crowd. They all had the same intention of getting out of the safety of the tunnels and back into the fresh air.

'Peter, Stew, wait for me,' she shouted above the sound of footsteps and people chattering. Somehow they heard her, turned and waited. Leaning against Peter, she gasped for air, her heart thumping in her breast as she tried to speak.

273

'Take your time,' Stew said, helping to hold her upright.

'They've got both the children,' she managed to explain. 'We've got to find them before they get out of the tunnels; anything could happen after that. Peter, can you hurry on ahead?'

They watched as he pushed through the crowd, ignoring the grumbles thrown his way. 'Thank you for helping me,' Lily gasped.

'I'd be the same if it was one of my children who'd been taken. It doesn't bear thinking about.'

Lily wasn't sure it was the right time to talk to him about Katie, but then, when would it be? 'You seem to have made friends with Katie.'

He pondered over her words. 'I like her a lot.'

'She's also a married woman; you will be careful, won't you? Please don't break her heart.'

'I would never hurt her,' he said as they started to push through the crowd. 'There seems to be a hold-up ahead.'

'What's going on?' Lily called out.

'They're saying the coppers have arrested someone up near the entrance,' an elderly man told her. 'There again, I was never good at Chinese whispers, so I might've heard it wrong.'

'That sounds promising. Hold tight to my hand; we're going in,' Stew said, before dragging Lily firmly through the queue of people held up behind whatever was happening. 'Make way, please. This lady is wanted by the police,' he announced in a gravelly Scottish accent that had people stepping back straightaway.

Despite her fear and worry, Lily was impressed at the way he took command and efficiently cleared a path for them.

'I'd never have got through here without you,' she said gratefully as they finally reached Katie, Peter and the soldiers, who were standing with the police inspector and several constables.

'Lily, thank goodness you're here,' Katie said, passing a sobbing Mary into her arms. 'I've done my best to soothe her, but that rat has really upset her.' She glared at Tom White as he was being handcuffed with an army officer overseeing his arrest. 'He was shouting at her to shut up as he came out of the tunnel and walked straight into us. He is not father material,' she snarled, as Tom looked beseechingly towards them. Meanwhile, his female accomplice was being led away screaming and blaspheming at the policemen, who held her by the arms to stop her kicking and punching them.

'Help me, Lily. I don't know why they are doing this to me,' Tom called out.

Lily turned her back on him and concentrated on cuddling her little daughter close until Mary's sobs subsided. 'Where is Alexsy?' she asked anxiously.

'I have him,' Flora said as she joined them. 'Young Pearl did a sterling job finding us and explaining what had happened. I've never run so fast in my life as I did when I thought Tom White had hurt my girls.' There were tears in her eyes.

'Mum, it's all over now,' Rose said as she put her arm around Flora. She gave her mother's shoulders a squeeze and then turned to the senior policeman. 'Inspector, I'm taking everyone back to Sea View. You do remember where that it is, don't you? You visited when Alexsy was first snatched by Tom White, but very little was done. You can take our statements once everyone has recovered from this ordeal.' She fixed him with a look that challenged him to argue. 'Come along, everyone,' she called out. 'I think it's time we had a hot cup of tea and put our feet up.'

'What about work?' Lily asked as she fell into step beside Rose.

'I'll put a call through to head office when we get to Mum's place. I'm sure they will understand if we don't go into work until tomorrow. It's not every day we help to round up a couple of criminals, is it?'

'You can say that again,' Katie said as she caught up with them. 'I'm so relieved it is all over. I feared we would never see little Alexsy ever again. Whatever would we have said to Anya when she returned from London?'

Rose drew in a deep breath. For the past few hours, she had actually been able to forget about Anya and the fact her friend was not working in London. Now it looked as though she would have to contact Ruth and give her an update on the latest developments. Perhaps if she pushed enough, Ruth would tell her where Anya really was? The poor woman deserved to know what had been happening with her son. What if something terrible had happened to him? How would they have been able to let her know? Enough was enough. Anya should be home where she was needed, Rose fumed to herself.

'Rose? Are you all right?' Katie asked, slipping her arm through her friend's. 'You've gone very quiet.'

'I'm fine; it's just been a bit of a shock,' she said, forcing a smile onto her face. 'Thank goodness we're here. Let's get inside and put the kettle on for Mum; I reckon everyone will want feeding as well, don't you?'

'With all hands to the pump, we can soon have a meal on the table,' Katie said as she watched Rose put her key into the lock and open up the front door to Sea View. 'It's good to be home,' she sighed. 'I'll always think of Sea View as my real home, and Flora has been like a mother to me.'

'And you girls are like my daughters,' Flora said as she put her arms around them and ushered them inside.

'That was tasty,' Miss Tibbs said as she wiped her mouth with her handkerchief. 'After all the shenanigans this afternoon, I was ready for a decent meal. Can I help with the washing up, Flora dear?'

Flora shook her head. Dear Miss Tibbs certainly seemed to have bounced back from the events in the tunnel only a few hours earlier. At first she had blamed herself for Tom White taking Mary, after he'd sweet-talked her into letting him hold the child. As she had explained to Flora, he'd seemed like such a charming man. Thank goodness young Pearl had kept her wits about her and alerted everyone when he casually walked off with the child in his arms.

'There are plenty of helping hands; just sit and rest. It has been a strange afternoon,' Flora said, patting the old lady's arm.

'There's someone knocking at the door. Shall I see who it is?' young Pearl offered, knowing that she had to ask permission before allowing anyone into the house.

'I'll go,' Rose said. 'I want to use the telephone to speak to head office.' And speak to Ruth, she thought to herself as she ran up the short flight of stairs from the kitchen to the hall and hurried to the door.

'I apologize for the intrusion if you are still eating,' the police inspector said as he entered the house, followed by the army sergeant who'd been such a help to them.

'Not at all, we are eager to hear what has happened since we left the tunnels,' Rose assured him. 'I hope you don't mind but we are all together in the kitchen; it is warmer in there than the front room. Please follow me.' She led the way down the stairs, glancing longingly at the telephone. She would just have to make her calls later.

Flora made the two men welcome, and chairs were found so they could join everyone around the table. They soon had hot tea in front of them along with slices of an apple pie that Rose had brought home from the teashop the day before.

'I think it's safe to say we are all eager to learn what has happened with Tom White, so our children can sleep safely in their beds tonight,' Flora said once everyone was settled.

The police inspector cleared his throat before speaking; he looked nervous. 'First, I would like to apologize for not treating the case of missing Master Polinski seriously enough. I would also like to thank you all for your perseverance in finding the child.'

'It's a good job we did, young man; otherwise he would still be out there lost and alone,' Miss Tibbs chipped in, wagging her finger at him before being hushed into silence by Flora.

She urged him, 'Please continue.'

'To be honest, I do not have much to say about Mr Thomas White. I will leave that to the army. However, I can confirm that Mrs Deirdre Hope is under arrest for collaborating with the aforementioned gentleman in order to gain money by stealing and selling children.'

'You mean there are others?' Katie gasped.

'I'm afraid so. However, evidence found at her premises has given us a good indication of where these children are now. I can assure you all that they will be recovered and returned to their rightful parents.'

'Why haven't you charged Tom White with child abduction?' Lily demanded.

'All in good time,' he said. 'First, Tom White is being taken to a military prison – perhaps you would like to take over?' he said, turning to the sergeant.

The sergeant nodded. 'I can confirm the man in question was absent without leave and we have been looking for him since the end of February. He has committed a number of crimes during that time, and these will all be taken into consideration when he is charged.'

'Prison is too good for him,' Joyce said, with Miss Tibbs agreeing wholeheartedly.

'I just can't stop thinking about the parents who have had their children stolen; the loss must be so painful.' Katie pulled out her handkerchief and dabbed at her eyes. 'If I were in their position, I'd be inconsolable. Please assure me, Inspector, that you will move faster to help them than you did while looking for our Alexsy?'

Flora noticed how Stew placed an arm on Katie's shoulder to console her. She frowned, and he quickly stepped away.

'Thank you both for coming here to give us an update,' she said to the two officials. 'I for one am greatly relieved to hear that Tom White is out of our lives once and for all.'

'We can only hope so, madam,' the inspector said. 'There is, however, the small problem of young Mary's parentage. White seems to think he has a right to access to the child, as he is her father. Is that the case, Miss . . . ?'

All eyes turned to Lily as she took a deep breath and crossed her fingers behind her back before speaking. 'He is not the father of my daughter; if he was, I would have his name on Mary's birth certificate, would I not? I will bring it to your office tomorrow to show you,' she promised.

'Thank you. Then we can go ahead and include the abduction of your daughter with his other charges,' the inspector said, getting to his feet. 'We will leave you to your evening; thank you again for your help,' he said, before he and the sergeant were shown out by Flora.

'Lily?' Katie said, raising her eyebrows at her friend.

Lily grinned. 'For once I've got my own back on that creep Tom White.'

Miss Tibbs carefully stood up. 'I for one am going to celebrate. Who else would like a sherry? Rose, get the glasses out, and Joyce, you can pour.'

The rest of the evening was spent in mellow contemplation of the day's events. It wasn't until Rose headed to her bed that she remembered she'd yet to make her telephone calls. 'They can wait until tomorrow,' she murmured as she laid her head on the pillow, and within seconds she was fast asleep.

28

Anya peered into a cracked mirror and frowned at the dowdy waitress uniform she'd been given to wear. It was old and itchy and seemed to be well worn. The waist was tight, and she feared such was the state of the fabric that it might tear at the seams while she was working. The white apron was no better, having been washed many times, yet still there were yellow stains. The stockings were black, and that was all you could say about them; they were held together with thick darning wool, and going by the stiffness around the toes, she had to wonder whether they'd ever been washed. As for the white cap, her only thought was that the people in charge of banqueting arrangements in this building could learn a thing or two from Joe Lyons.

'Are you ready, Monique?' an elderly woman whispered in perfect English, glancing around first in case anyone was nearby. 'I will have you working alongside me as I serve the soup course. Just copy what I do and you cannot go far wrong. Follow me with the tureen; I will nudge you when we are close to the person you wish to identify.'

'Thank you, Natalie,' Anya whispered back, 'that doesn't sound too hard. I will soon learn the layout of the tables.'

'There are over four hundred people sitting down to dine; this is why we considered it safe for you to work here, as the employers have had to call in every member of staff along with extra people they do not know in order to serve all the guests on time. It is imperative that we act professionally and do not make any comments on what we see or hear.'

'I understand. I just wish to see this woman and then leave.'

'I'm not sure that will be possible, as leaving early could draw attention to you. However, don't worry about that. We will think of a way to discreetly get you out of the building.'

Anya nodded, trying not to worry about the long evening stretching ahead of her.

'I have told people you are my cousin, and that you have come to visit an ageing relative for a couple of weeks,' Natalie continued. 'You were not only glad to be able to help this evening, but the money you will be paid will come in handy. I gave your name to the banqueting manager; with him being so busy, he simply noted it and took my word that you could do this job blindfolded – even though you are mute.'

Anya nodded her head. She peered down into the tureen of insipid-looking liquid she had been asked to carry. 'Whatever is it?' she whispered back.

'Onion,' Natalie replied, grimacing.

'They forgot to add the onion,' Anya sniffed.

'Hurry up, Natalie. No dawdling, or there will be complaints and the soup will become cold.' A stern-looking man in black formal attire waved them through a set of double doors into the vast hall.

Anya froze to the spot, causing waitresses behind her to bump into each other as she took in the sight before her. The vast wood-panelled hall was decorated on each wall with ceiling-to-floor swags of red fabric decorated with the Nazi swastika. She had stepped into the viper's nest.

'Come along,' Natalie hissed. 'You need to keep going. Concentrate on the soup and not on the people in uniform,' she instructed as they headed for the first row of white-covered tables.

Uniforms? Anya hadn't even looked at who was seated at the tables, as she had been mesmerized by the symbol of the people she had come to hate long before she fled from Poland. Dragging her gaze away from the red banners, she gazed at the guests, and her anger increased. Almost every man in the room wore the uniform of the Third Reich. Most were enjoying jovial conversations with their fellow officers while the women, dressed in formal evening attire, paid attention to their partners. A noise in her head, rather like the roar of thunder, threatened to overwhelm her senses to the point she could hardly think.

'Concentrate,' Natalie hissed as she picked up the first soup plate and dipped her ladle into the tureen. 'And smile,' she added, seeing the grim expression on Anya's face. 'People are here to enjoy themselves; it is not our place to make them miserable. Now, let us speed up with this soup before there are complaints that it is cold.'

Anya pinned a fixed smile onto her face and, doing her best to ignore the room and the people in it, walked carefully behind Natalie with the heavy tureen. 'Can you see her yet?' she whispered, as Natalie turned to fill another soup plate.

'No, she is somewhere near the top table where the dignitaries are sitting. We will fetch another tureen and continue to serve. There are five courses, so there is still time for you to have a good look at her.'

Anya thought her feet would hurt almost as much as Mildred's did by the time she'd continued with her task. Already, a darned patch near her toes was rubbing uncomfortably.

Once they'd served six tureens of soup, it was time to clear away the plates ready for the next course. Anya wrinkled her nose at the smell of the fish with its accompanying strange mix of vegetables. It was so foul that she promised herself she would never again complain about Flora's fish pie, or indeed the smell of Mildred's boat, the *Saucy Milly* – if they ever saw it again.

This time, Anya also carried plates of food to the hungry guests. Copying Natalie, she was able to serve it correctly, and for a little while she even started to enjoy her work; at least, when she managed to forget who she was serving. She avoided eye contact with the guests in case someone asked her a question. The fish course was soon consumed and the plates cleared away.

Back at the serving station where they collected the food, Natalie leant close to Anya to speak. 'I might try some of that duck they're having for the next course.'

Anya frowned. 'Are we allowed? The last thing I need is to be caught by the enemy for stealing their food.'

Natalie laughed ironically. 'This is why we eat their food and steal as much as we can to take home to our families; we must look out for each other. However, be careful. There is bound to be someone among the staff who would happily give us away in order to curry favour with this scum.'

'In that case, I will be careful. I would like to take some of that cheese with me, and perhaps some tarte tatin for my friends; they've not eaten properly for a few days. They are relying on me to complete the mission this evening.'

'It will be done,' Natalie smiled. 'Come, let us start to take out the main course; the food is plated up. We're moving on to serve a different section of the table so that you can seek out the person you are looking for.'

'I thought you knew where she was sitting?' Anya asked as they took the hot dinner plates from a serving table at one end of the hall. She copied Natalie by carefully balancing two plates in each hand.

'She is near the top table; that is all I know. I suggest you look discreetly at those at the top, then work your way down each time we bring food to the table. But don't stare too long, in case someone notices.'

'I understand,' Anya replied, determined to serve the food as quickly as possible so that she would have time to look at the women sitting close to the top table. Four times she moved at a fast pace up and down the banqueting hall, serving food and checking the guests. She was about to return for a fifth time when the banqueting manager caught her by the arm. Anya froze, fearing the worst.

'Woman, take this tray to the top table and serve our distinguished guest. Be quick, as he is waiting.'

It was clear from the way he nodded towards the top table that she was expected to go there immediately and serve on her own. For a moment, she froze. What if someone spoke to her?

Natalie stepped in to take the tray from her, but was pushed aside by the manager. He pointed to Anya.

She had no choice but to nod her head in agreement and turn away, carrying the tray. Hurrying the length of the hall once again, she decided this would be her chance to have a good look for the woman she was seeking. She glanced to the left as she passed the diners, quickly ruling out certain women by their size and age. The woman she sought was slim and around her own age. Try as she might, she couldn't remember much else about her – but then an idea came to her. She'd been told the woman had married a much older man. Perhaps if she looked for older men, not in uniform, it would help her? There again, perhaps the woman was here tonight with someone else . . . a rapid stream of thoughts rushed through Anya's head as she approached the top table.

Deep in thought, she held out the tray to one of the uniformed men standing at either side of the main guest. After checking what was on it, he stepped back to allow her to set down the plate. It was then that Anya came face to face with Adolf Hitler.

She dropped the tray with a shriek, causing silence to fall throughout the enormous room. All eyes turned towards her . . .

The Führer looked at Anya through ice cold eyes for what felt like a lifetime. Then, to her astonishment, he began to laugh. She stood frozen to the spot as he laughed and laughed, pointing at the mess she had made of her uniform with food splashed down the front.

Inside, Anya was grappling with her emotions. She wanted to fly at Hitler's throat and shake the life out of him, but an image of her son flashed before her. How would Alexsy live his life without either of his parents? There was no guarantee that Henio would ever return from wherever he was. If Anya were to perish here, at the hand of the most hated man in the world, would it serve any higher purpose?

She felt sick as she realized what she would have to do.

She curtseyed and lowered her eyes, trying to look deeply ashamed of what she had done; trying to behave as if what she felt was awe and respect for a great leader.

Hitler brushed her away with a careless wave of his hand, still laughing.

She turned and fled from the hall, heading for the nearest ladies' cloakroom, not caring whether staff were allowed to use it. Locking herself in one of the cubicles, she sat down and tried to compose herself. Shaking from head to toe, she did her best to think logically about what to do next. She knew she could not go back into that room and risk drawing Hitler's attention.

As she thought about the consequences of her actions, there was a knock on the door. A whispered voice called her name. 'Anya? Is that you? Please let me in, I beg you . . .'

Anya knew it wasn't Natalie, but the voice was familiar – a safe familiar – a voice from her homeland. She opened the door of her cubicle. 'Hello, Anouska. It has been a while.'

Anouska Bartkowicz closed the door behind her and wedged one of the cloakroom's elaborate little chairs under the handle to stop anyone else entering. Then she all but collapsed into one of the other chairs, gazing at Anya.

'Are you here to help me? I can think of no other reason

you would have returned to France, as when we parted you were going to England to find your husband . . . Henry?'

'Henio,' Anya corrected her. 'My husband's name is Henio.'

'I need your help, Anya,' Anouska said. 'I was told that someone would attempt to get me away from France to safety. When I spotted you at the Führer's table, I just knew you were here for a reason.'

'That wasn't the plan. I am here only to confirm who you are. Later . . . well, others will help you.'

'There's no time,' Anouska said, looking frantic. 'They already know I am not to be trusted; I fear for my father's life. Please, Anya, you have got to help me escape right now; if we wait another day, it may be too late.'

Anya looked at the friend with whom she'd escaped her homeland years earlier. Beneath the painted face and fancy clothes was someone she had once been close to; she was caught up with troubling thoughts of what could happen to Anouska if she refused to help.

'As much as I'd like to take you with me right now, it's not possible. It could be dangerous for both of us,' she replied, seeing fear cross the woman's face. 'Can you tell me why it is so dangerous for you to stay here? I have been told very little.'

Anouska stared hard into Anya's face. 'I will have to trust you, although you were very harsh with me when we left Poland together. You told me no good would come of me staying in France. You were right.'

'I'm sorry if I appeared hard. I know it is my nature to be serious – it is only because I care and worry so much about others. What has put you in so much danger?' Anya asked again, before giving a harsh laugh.

Anouska frowned. 'What is so funny?'

'I laugh only because here we are hiding in the ladies' washroom, and out there is the vilest monster walking this earth. If we had an ounce of bravery, we would attempt to kill him even if we lost our own lives in the process.'

A smile flitted across Anouska's face. 'I like your humour, Anya. The danger for me is connected with my father; he is a scientist and was planning to escape to America before the fall of Paris, but the attempt failed when he became ill. I stayed to nurse him, and it was decided that I should marry one of his Polish colleagues – for my own protection, you understand? It was a marriage of convenience only. Tomek is much older than I am, and not much younger than my father. He is a dear man and I respect him greatly. However, he too has an illness, a terminal illness. And with my father still being frail I needed help for both.'

Anya was sympathetic. 'I imagine you would, but how do I come into all of this?'

'I took a lover . . . a German officer. He helped me with medicines and food to support them both. In return, I . . .' She looked ashamed.

'You don't have to continue if you don't wish to.'

'But I do; you need to know. How else can you help me?' Anouska begged.

'Then continue, but please be quick before someone misses us and comes looking.'

Anouska nodded, looking weary. 'Henrick, the German officer, is being sent back to Berlin. If it hadn't been for Hitler's visit, he would have gone today. As it is, he is leaving tomorrow afternoon.'

'Surely that is good, isn't it?'

'No, as he plans to take me with him. The fool is en-amoured of me. If I refuse, he says he will put Tomek and my father in front of a firing squad and the world will lose two eminent scientists . . .'

29

'I'm exhausted after yesterday,' Lily said as she stretched her arms above her head and yawned. 'Are you really going to do a staff inspection this morning?'

'I feel the same and can only think that Miss Tibbs' sherry must have been awfully potent,' Rose laughed. 'As for your question about a staff inspection: that's what I'm here in the staffroom for, so look lively.'

'I thought you'd say that,' Lily said, rummaging in her locker. 'I'm sure I had a new pair of stockings in here . . . Oh well, the ones I have on will have to do.'

Rose went to her own locker and took out a pristine pair. 'Here you are, but please hurry up and put them on. I have a feeling we are due a visit from you-know-who.'

Lily groaned as she started to unfasten her damaged stockings.

A young Nippy dashed into the staffroom. 'Mrs Hargreaves? There's a telephone call for you from the Ramsgate teashop, and I was told to say it's urgent.'

'Oh God; that can only mean one thing,' Rose sighed as

she hurried through the teashop to her small office, where she found the telephone receiver lying on the desk. 'Hello, Katie. I'm sorry to keep you waiting – I was in the staffroom and just about to start an inspection. How are you feeling today? I'm fit for nothing.'

'Thank goodness somebody answered your telephone; I've been ringing for ages! You'd best look lively, as Miss Butterworth is on her way to you. Would you believe she was camped out on our doorstep before we even opened this morning? Talk about catching us on the hop. I feel as though she's chewed me up and spat me out; I've been left with ever such a long list of things to do. She even mumbled something about finding a replacement manageress.'

'I'm sure she didn't mean it,' Rose replied, concerned by how down Katie sounded. 'I still think her bark is worse than her bite, but thank you for letting me know. Will you be going along to the dance at the West Cliff Hall this evening?'

'Try to stop me,' Katie said. 'I'll need cheering up after I've worked my way through all these jobs Butterworth left me with.'

'Good luck with that. I'll see you later,' Rose smiled as she replaced the receiver. Glancing around her office, she thought she'd better spend half an hour tidying it up. As a rule, no other staff members were allowed in the room, but with her having had the morning off yesterday and then not come in for the rest of the day, it didn't look its best. Post had been left piled on the desk and the room needing a good dusting.

'Oh God,' she groaned. 'I forgot to ring head office to say we wouldn't be back in work yesterday afternoon.' She sat down and put her head in her hands, then sighed as she heard somebody enter the room. 'If that is you, Lily, could you arrange a cup of coffee, please? I need to clear my head before I start going through this work. You can also tell the staff I'll be skipping inspection this morning after all, as I need to catch up in here.'

A sharp cough brought her to her senses. 'Mrs Hargreaves, are you shirking your duties?'

Rose raised her head to see Miss Butterworth standing before her. 'Good morning. How lovely to see you,' she said, even though it pained her to do so. She imagined what the teashop, her office, and the uninspected staff must look like through the new area manager's eyes. No doubt Rose too would have a very long list of work given to her by Miss Butterworth today, going by the stony look on her face.

Miss Butterworth placed her briefcase on the desk, pulling over a seat that Rose kept for visitors. She sat down opposite Rose and waited for her to speak. 'I haven't got all day, Mrs Hargreaves; I believe you have something to tell me?'

'I'm sorry . . . I . . .'

Miss Butterworth raised a hand to stop her stammering. 'I do not have time to watch you as you fail to remember the most basic of your duties. Answer me this: where were you yesterday?'

Rose felt her stomach turn inside out. So, Butterworth had heard she'd failed to return to her duties after the air raid. She could have kicked herself for not putting through a call to head office to explain. She straightaway blamed the police inspector for arriving at Sea View just at the wrong moment, but knew in her heart of hearts that she was the only one who was truly responsible. Furthermore, her mistake meant the other teashop staff who had been with her would be in trouble too, since they'd been relying on her to clear the situation with head office.

'I can explain, but first, can I fetch you a cup of tea?' she asked, hoping to soothe the savage beast as she stood up to leave the office. With luck, she could tip off Lily, who could then keep the staff on their toes before an inspection.

'Sit down. I require an answer to my question. Then I will inspect the teashop and staff before making my recommendations to head office.'

'Recommendations?' Rose asked, forgetting that she was supposed to answer Miss Butterworth.

'I will be implementing changes. I believe you would refer to it as a new broom sweeping clean? I will decide once I have completed what I came here to do. Your career very much hangs in the balance, depending on your explanation for having disregarded your duties yesterday. I take it alcohol and Lily Douglas were involved?'

Rose felt her cheeks start to burn. 'Of course not. For your information, I hardly ever drink. I had one sherry last night after a rather upsetting day. If I may, I'd like to explain what happened.' She took a deep breath to compose herself. 'Yes, Lily was involved, as was Joyce Hannigan, and Katie from the Ramsgate teashop. I am the one at fault, as I told them I would place a call to head office and explain why we could not return to work in the afternoon, following the air raid. I'm afraid that with the police visiting my mother's home, it completely left my head. I'm sorry,' she added, fearing she would cry if she said much more. She imagined her failure to fulfil her promise to her friends had cost them their jobs at the Lyons teashops.

Miss Butterworth peered at Rose over the top of the spectacles she wore for paperwork. After a moment, she removed them. 'Why would the police be visiting your mother's home?'

Rose sighed. 'If you will allow me, I'd like to start at the beginning.'

'Go ahead.'

Rose started by telling her about Anya taking leave from the Ramsgate branch to work in London training the Sallys; then, shortly afterwards, her son being abducted. 'Her friends were caring for Alexsy, as Anya's husband is still missing in action,' she added.

'It must be hard for her,' Miss Butterworth said without showing any form of compassion. 'Continue.'

Rose cleared her throat before explaining how, with no police action, they had heard that the man they believed had snatched Alexsy had been seen in town. 'We had no choice but to meet at my mother's and head to the house. Of course, then there was an air-raid warning and we rushed to the tunnels, and the man snatched Lily's little girl as well . . .'

Miss Butterworth shook her head. 'This is worse than a penny dreadful. Next you will be telling me he is the father of these children.'

'No, only Lily's daughter,' Rose replied before slapping a hand over her mouth, realizing she had added that last piece of information without Lily's consent. 'Both the children are now safe thanks to the army getting involved, along with our friends in the RAF.'

'Where is the navy when you need them?' Miss Butterworth said scathingly.

Rose bit her lip, not sure whether the older woman was joking. 'We were grateful for their help.'

'What happened to the man who abducted the children?'

'He is safely locked up and cannot do any more harm. We were informed he was absent without leave from the army and, along with the widow of another soldier, was planning to sell the stolen children to childless couples.'

For the first time, Miss Butterworth's face showed a flicker of emotion. 'It must have been traumatic for all concerned. How are the children?'

'After a good night's rest they are as right as rain, thank goodness. The adults involved aren't as relaxed, as it has been an awful time. It was the police inspector along with the army officers arriving yesterday that put all thought of notifying head office out of my mind. I can't apologize enough,' she said miserably, bracing herself to hear the worst about her position with the Lyons company.

'Thank goodness for that. You may think I am a hard woman, Mrs Hargreaves, but I do have a heart. I lost a child myself when I was only a young woman and can sympathize with the parents of Mary and Alexsy. Tell me, does Mrs Polinski know about everything that has happened?'

Crikey, Rose thought, whatever could she say that wouldn't make Anya look like a bad mother who could not be bothered to come back to Ramsgate and help search for her child? 'It is rather difficult, as Anya is doing a very special job that involves the government; I only found this out because I went to look for her at the training school in London. Please, can you keep that information to yourself? I'd hate anyone to get into trouble, and that includes Anya.'

'You are a trusted friend; I'll not be putting this into my report. However, may I ask if the man who is at the bottom of all this trouble is our ex-employee Thomas White?'

Rose nodded. 'It is,' she whispered. 'And I hope we never have to set eyes on him again. I've never met such an odious person, capable of treating people in such a despicable way.'

Miss Butterworth got to her feet. Going to the door of the office, she caught the attention of a passing Nippy. 'Tea and toasted teacakes for two, in here as soon as possible, please,' she said before returning to her seat.

'What happens next?' Rose asked, feeling herself tremble all over. Her fate lay in the hands of Miss Butterworth.

'The way I see it, you need to tidy your office and inspect your staff, as well as the kitchen. I shall enjoy my tea and be on my way,' the area manager said, closing her notebook and placing it in her briefcase.

'But my job . . .'

'Your job is also to care for the wellbeing of your staff, as well as being on top of your position as manageress. You are a loyal friend, and your staff should be grateful that you care; that is something I wasn't always very good at in my own time as a manageress. Don't dare argue with me,' she said, raising her hand as Rose went to speak. 'Now, let's have our refreshments and then I will leave you to get on with your work – and no doubt to speak to Mrs Jones at the Ramsgate teashop,' she added, giving Rose a smile. 'Ah, good, here they are. I don't know about you, but drinking sherry always leaves me feeling hungry the next morning. Will you be mother, or shall I?'

Rose couldn't have spoken if she'd tried. She knew she didn't deserve the outcome of this meeting. When times got tough in her job, she would look back on this day and remind herself never to think the worst of Joe Lyons' management.

The girls spent the evening at the West Cliff Hall, Ramsgate, as the guests of Peter and Stew; the regular dances there were hosted by the staff of nearby Manston airfield.

'You have no idea how much I enjoyed that,' Lily said breathlessly as she sat down next to Rose. 'After all we've been through with that bloody Tom White, it's about time we got ourselves dressed up and had some fun. I didn't expect so many people here,' she added, looking out at the dance floor where couples were squashed together, dancing shoulder to shoulder. There was a mixture of civilians and service personnel in the crowd, all enjoying a rare night out.

Rose smiled. 'You and Peter make a lovely couple on the dance floor. How do you feel about him?'

'Why are you asking? Do you fancy being a bridesmaid?' Lily sniggered as she reached for her glass, finishing the port and lemon in one gulp.

'I just wondered. He does seem keen on you, and it's not every day a handsome pilot drops into your garden on the end of a parachute.'

Lily chuckled. 'It wasn't that romantic, as we had to cut him down from where he was dangling in the apple tree. To be honest, I don't know how I feel about Peter. He's a decent enough bloke, but I don't think I could go through however long the rest of this war will be worrying about whether my husband will come home at the end of the day. You know, Anya puts on a brave face, but you can tell that deep inside she is grieving for her Henio. I can't be like her; I just know I can't. So, I'll enjoy Peter's company and see how things go from there.'

'I understand completely. If I didn't know Ben was safely ensconced behind a desk running some department or other for the army, I too would be tearing my hair out and praying for the war to end.'

Lily snorted with laughter. 'I'm sorry; I'm not laughing at you. It's more that here we are, dancing and all dressed up in our best frocks, and you're acting as miserable as sin. Look, Peter's bringing over more drinks. After that, why don't you get up with the band and give us a song or two? You know you want to. I saw your face light up when the bandleader asked you to sing as we came in. What do you say?'

'I'll have that drink and then I'll get on that stage and sing my heart out, just as you suggest. Life's too short to be miserable,' Rose grinned.

'It looks like those two are having a good time,' Lily nodded towards the dance floor, where Katie and Stew were attempting a quickstep. 'They make a good-looking couple. It's a shame the pair of them are married . . .'

'To other people,' Rose added. 'That is something to be worried about.'

'I say let her have some fun; he's a decent chap and won't mess her about. You know, they talk for hours about his family and her Jack; it's quite sweet.'

'Sweet it may be, but it isn't right. We're going to have to watch them as Katie's quite an innocent, and I'd hate her to be hurt if Jack should find out. It's best if she decides not to see Stew any more.'

'She's going to tell us to mind our own business,' Lily said. 'We will have to take it carefully. Perhaps you could come to Captain's Cottage one evening for supper and we could bring up the subject . . . ?'

'I'll do that,' Rose promised, as Peter arrived with the tray of drinks. She hastily changed the subject. 'I wonder what I should sing?'

'I don't mind, as long as it's something by Helen Forrest that we can dance to,' Lily said as she snuggled up to Peter. 'Something that tugs at the heartstrings.'

'I know just the song,' Rose said as she squeezed past the couple and headed towards the stage.

Katie and Lily watched as Rose spoke to the leader of the band before standing in front of the microphone and wating for her cue as the saxophonist played the first moody notes.

'. . . *You made me love you, I didn't want to do it, I didn't want to do it . . .*'

She closed her eyes and swayed to the music, cupping the microphone in her hands as she poured her heart out in the song. '. . . *I want some love that is true . . . give me, give me, give me, give me, what I sigh for . . .*' She imagined she was in Ben's arms as he steered her around the dance floor. '. . . *You know you made me love you . . .*'

Rose opened her eyes as the song ended to a round of applause from the dancing couples, who had all stopped at the edge of the stage to hear her sing.

'Ladies and gentlemen, give your applause to Ramsgate's answer to Helen Forrest,' the bandleader called out as he helped her down from the stage, and she returned to her friends.

'I know I say this every time you sing, but you are wasted working for Joe Lyons,' Lily said as she gave Rose a hug.

'I agree,' Stew said. 'This is the first time I've heard you sing, and you are up there with the best of the singers with the big bands.'

'I'm happy as I am, thank you,' Rose replied, suddenly feeling shy. 'I met my Ben at a dance like this,' she added a little sadly, looking around her. 'Who will dance with this neglected married woman?'

'I'd be honoured,' Peter said as a foxtrot started to play, and he took her hand.

'Hmm, one song and she has the pick of the men; perhaps I should learn how to sing,' Lily grinned.

'Don't even try; you are tone deaf,' Katie laughed as she stood up to dance with Stew, leaving Lily to watch her friends on the dance floor.

'I'm the only single woman here and I'm a wallflower . . .' she said, shaking her head until a soldier stepped forward and asked her to dance. She took his hand willingly and continued to dance the night away – until the evening was cut short by the arrival of Moaning Minnie, and they all headed down to the public shelters once more.

30

Anya was shocked by what Anouska had told her. 'Scientists? Why are they here in France, living among the enemy? It doesn't make sense.'

'I know it is ludicrous, but my father has lived here for many years and was of the opinion the Germans were not interested in him. I've begged him to leave; we could have been safe in America by now.'

'What does your husband say about this?' Anya asked as she went to the door, placing her ear against it to check if anyone was nearby. She nodded to Anouska to continue speaking.

'He is old and no longer cares about the war as long as I am with him. He has friends here and thought he would live out his final days here in France,' she said, looking troubled.

'How old is he?'

'Seventy-six. He is three years younger than my father.'

Anya found it difficult to imagine having a husband so much older than her. But then, if it was a match made mainly for security and companionship, why did it matter?

'Is he ready to leave with you and your father, if we can get you away from France?' she asked. She knew she was talking out of turn, but even so, she couldn't just stand by and watch as Anouska and her loved ones from the old country suffered at the hands of the enemy.

Anouska couldn't look at Anya as she replied. 'I don't know, but we could try.'

They fell silent as Anya thought carefully about what could be done. 'There may be a way . . .'

'I'll do anything,' Anouska promised, holding on to Anya's hand and imploring her, 'Please help us.'

'First, I need to speak to the people who brought me here. I am in their hands, as I will need their help to get back to where my courier is waiting to take me back to England. Where are you staying?'

'We have an apartment a few streets away from here. We plan to go back there tonight when the dancing has finished.'

'Is it possible you could return earlier? My comrade will expect me to leave once the dinner service has finished.' Anya didn't add that once she had identified Anouska, she would be able to return to where Mildred was hiding. Their journey from the coast to Vaux had been slow as a result of Mildred being incapacitated, and she expected the return trip to be equally slow.

'I can pretend to have a headache. I do suffer with them, so my father will understand.'

'Will he be agreeable to leaving France with you?'

'He will. I'm not so sure about Tomek, but he loves me in his way, so I think he will agree.'

Anya closed her eyes and took a deep breath. She wasn't sure Domino would be impressed with her returning with three people in tow, all of whom had to be transported across the Channel to safety. 'You will have to travel light, so dress in clothes that will keep you warm and dry. Tell your husband and father to do likewise. Now, go back to the banquet and try to act as though nothing has happened – perhaps your head is starting to ache?'

Anouska went to the door and removed the chair that was wedging it closed. 'Thank you, Anya,' she said before hurrying from the room, her skirts floating around her in a rustle of silk and organza.

'God, what have I done?' Anya muttered to herself as she turned towards the mirror. She ran cold water into the white marble sink and splashed her face until she felt refreshed before doing her best to clean the mess from the front of her uniform. Then she readied herself to face Natalie and tell her what she'd promised Anouska.

'You've what?' bellowed Natalie when Anya found her in the busy kitchens and explained. Around them, pots and pans crashed and staff shouted over the din.

'I said we would take Anouska, her father and her husband back to England and safety. Why is that so wrong?'

'You have no idea what you have done.' Natalie shook her head in disbelief. 'Get back to your work and I will speak to you later,' she scowled.

Anya slunk back to the banqueting hall and helped to collected dirty crockery, keeping well away from the top table and avoiding the gaze of the demon who was holding court over his fawning followers. She also suppressed all thoughts of picking up a sharp knife and freeing the world of the tyrant, reminding herself that she had to think of her son and getting back to him.

For the next hour, she worked hard while wondering what had been decided about helping Anouska and her family get to safety before she was whisked away to Berlin by her lover. What must it be like to have a high-ranking lover who provided one with beautiful gowns and invitations to important social functions?

She thought about what Anouska had been like as a child, back home in Poland. Anya couldn't remember much, apart from that the girl had been popular and top of the class; meanwhile, Anya herself had simply done her best to stay caught up at school and to be a good daughter and, later, a good wife. It was only after their village was decimated by the invading Germans that the two women had found themselves thrown together, fleeing for their lives. They had parted ways in France when Anouska had gone to search for her father in Paris, while Anya had found someone to smuggle her into England. She had been following her husband to an unknown Kent airfield, where she had heard that he flew planes alongside other Polish pilots who had escaped capture or death during the invasion of their homeland.

Feeling fit to drop, she returned to the kitchens, where she hoped to find Natalie and learn whether a decision had been made about what they should do next.

As she looked around the vast room full of preparation tables, ovens and people in white overalls, she gradually realized that Natalie had left without her. She would have to find her own way back to Mildred. A chill spread through her body as she fought to quell the panic clutching at her throat. She was alone in France, and Adolf Hitler was in the building.

After going back into the banqueting hall and continuing

to help the waiters and waitresses clear the tables, Anya decided she ought to at least try finding her way back to where she and Mildred had spent the night. Domino had taken them to a small hostelry where he seemed to know the landlord. The room they had been given was in the loft of the building, with two small cot-like beds, one coarse blanket on each covering a straw-filled mattress. They had been offered a meal of some kind of stew with hard, almost black bread – it had been warm, filling and very welcome after their journey, although Mildred reckoned it was horse-meat. Anya had slept for a while before being taken by Domino to where Natalie was waiting for her. She had never expected to come face to face with Hitler.

She took a quick glance over towards the evil man, who was making his way towards a pair of double doors leading onto a ballroom. Wasn't this when Anouska had said she was planning to leave, blaming a headache for not wishing to dance? Moving over to the long table where the Polish woman was seated, Anya pottered about, collecting silver cruet sets and placing them on a tray as she had seen other waiting staff do. After a few moments, Anouska rose to leave. She walked past Anya, brushing against her. Anya felt something pushed into her hand and quickly slipped it into her pocket; it felt like a piece of paper.

Bobbing a curtsey, she hurried away to the staffroom and took her outdoor clothes from the locker. She was about to get changed when she thought better of it: if she was stopped while walking back alone, it would be better to be dressed in a waitress's uniform than in her everyday clothes. Looking around, she found a discarded bag made of rough sacking and used it to hold her usual clothing.

She'd just stepped out of the staff entrance when a man's voice called after her, causing her to freeze mid-step.

She turned. The head waiter was waving a pay packet. Anya took it from him and bobbed her head in thanks before walking away at a brisk pace. She wanted to run, but there were too many people about and she didn't wish to draw attention to herself. In the distance she could hear sirens and hurried as best she could.

Unlike in England, where the streets would have been in darkness, there was a lamp at the corner of the street which helped her identify the way back to her lodgings. With her heart beating rapidly and her head pounding with fear, she counted each step back to the relative safety of the hostelry, breathing a sigh of relief as the building came into view. Using the side door, she slipped inside and ran up the three flights of stairs to their room.

'Thank goodness you're back,' Mildred said, turning away from the window. 'Did you have any problems? There are a great many soldiers on the street.'

Anya sank onto her bed and kicked off her shoes. 'It was hell. I never wish to spend another evening like it,' she said, before relating every detail of her experience.

Mildred sat and listened without interrupting, only shaking her head and whispering, 'Well, I never,' a few times.

'What news of Domino?' she asked eventually. 'I thought he would accompany you back from the banquet.'

Anya shook her head. 'After I explained to Natalie that I had promised we would try to help Anouska, I returned to my duties. Later on, I found that there was no one about to help me find my way home. It seemed as though they had deserted me because I'd done something wrong; that's why I came back here alone.'

'You made the right choice. But are you sure you were not followed?'

Anya was honest in her reply. 'I never thought about being followed, as I was hell bent on getting away from the banqueting hall. I am worried about Anouska. How are we going to help her, especially now that Domino and Natalie have disappeared?'

'Your part in this mission was never about rescuing Anouska; it was to identify her and report back. Someone else was always meant to take over after that. She has put you in a difficult position.'

Anya put her head into her hands, trying to concentrate on Mildred's words. Then she remembered something. She reached into her pocket and pulled out the scrap of paper Anouska had passed to her on leaving. 'This is her address,' she said, holding out the note. 'I'm going to see if I can help her.'

'Don't be a fool; you are interfering with the mission.'

'I have to help her. She is Polish, as am I, and we have to help our fellow countrymen. Goodness knows what will happen to her if I don't do something.'

'On your head be it,' Mildred said as she bent to put on the shoes Domino had found for her. They appeared to have once belonged to a man and they were two sizes too large, but they greatly helped her to walk.

'I'll be quicker on my own,' Anya protested.

'And I will never forgive myself if something happens to you, so please do not argue with me. Collect all your belongings and let's get moving.'

'Why are we taking everything with us?'

Mildred shook her head. 'We dare not leave anything behind that could get the landlord into trouble with the Gestapo. Besides, we may not be able to make it back here again if . . .'

Anya frowned. 'If what? Please don't talk in riddles.'

'If we are separated . . . if we are followed . . . if we are arrested – does that make my comment clearer?'

'I'm sorry. I never understood what you meant.'

'That's the trouble with you,' Mildred huffed. 'You never think – do you?'

'I don't understand,' Anya said, hurt and confused. 'Have I offended you? I know your feet are hurting, but I have done everything requested of me.'

'And more,' Mildred muttered as she pulled on an old coat over her crumpled cotton dress. 'Come on. Let's get this finished, and then we can go home.'

Anya prayed liked she'd never prayed before as they worked their way back through the now deserted streets. Deserted, that was, apart from the numerous soldiers on patrol, who stopped them on two occasions to check their papers and ask where they were heading.

Mildred answered in perfect French, pointing to Anya's uniform and waving her hand in the vague direction of the banqueting rooms, which Anya thought meant they'd both been working and were on their way home. Each time, she studied Mildred's face for any sign that she should be ready to defend herself, or indeed to run away. If we get out of this alive, she promised herself, I will learn to speak the French language.

31

'This is the building; they are on the second floor,' Anya said as she pointed to a brass plate on the wall by the large double doors. Even late at night, they'd been able to find their way with the help of the street lighting. Anya had found herself stopping from time to time to look up at the tall properties with their decorative iron balconies on each floor. Facades were damaged in places and the buildings looked tired, but even so, she thought they had a special quality about them and must have looked magnificent in their heyday.

'You'd better go first, as the woman knows you. She may panic and wonder what is happening if she sees me at her door,' Mildred said as she pushed Anya into the building and towards the wide staircase. 'Wait here a moment . . .' She checked where two doors in the passageway led.

The inside of the building was as tired as the outside, with chipped plaster and fading paintwork. The wooden balustrade needed attention and a good polish, Anya thought, as she started to climb the stairs. Behind her she could hear Mildred puffing and stopping to catch her breath on each landing. It was evident she still wasn't back to her usual level of good health after injuring her feet.

'Perhaps we should wait a couple of minutes before we knock on the door?'

Mildred nodded. They waited until they heard the front door of the building open and close, then footsteps on the stairs. 'Hurry, in case we are spotted,' she hissed, prodding Anya in the small of the back.

Anya knocked on Anouska's door and waited. After a minute, Mildred leant over her shoulder and knocked harder. They heard someone approaching the door from inside.

'Why Anya, how lovely to see you,' Anouska said in perfect English, embracing her friend and inviting her inside.

Anya wished they could speak in Polish, but then Mildred would not have understood. 'This is my friend Nancy; we are travelling together,' she explained as Mildred stepped forward and shook hands.

'I'm delighted to meet you,' Anouska said, although she looked nervous. 'Please come in.'

They followed her into a large room that looked fit for a king, with plush carpets and stylish furnishings. Ornate gold-framed mirrors hung on every wall. Two matching chandeliers were suspended from the ceiling and tinkled slightly in the breeze coming from double doors that opened onto a balcony. This was a different world from Anya's life in Ramsgate.

'You have a very nice home,' she said politely.

Anouska shrugged her shoulders. 'It is mine for as long as . . .' She let the sentence trail off.

'Please continue,' Anya prompted her. 'I would like to know more of your life since we last met.'

'I will do anything to survive this war,' was all Anouska said before going to a decorative side table and taking a cigarette from a gold-encrusted box. She lit it with a matching lighter that rested on the table. 'Do either of you . . . ?'

Both women refused her offer.

'Please sit.' She nodded towards a long, deep blue velvet-covered sofa that faced into the room.

They sat down, Anya shivering slightly as the night breeze came in through the curtained French windows. 'You will have to wear something more practical if you wish to travel with us to England,' she pointed out to Anouska, who was still wearing her evening gown.

'I have a travelling costume and sturdier shoes; it will not take me long to change. May I ask who else will be with us?'

Anya opened her mouth to answer as Mildred cut in. 'It does not concern you,' she said in a sharp voice, which shocked Anya. 'However, we leave in ten minutes, so please hurry.'

Anouska didn't reply, but fixed Mildred with a brief stare and then left the room.

'That was rather pointed,' Anya scolded Mildred.

'There's no time for pleasantries. Besides, I don't trust her as far as I can spit,' Mildred replied, getting to her feet to check the room.

'What are you . . .'

'Sshh,' Mildred put a finger to her lips as she crept towards the heavy curtains that covered the entrance to the balcony. Reaching into her pocket, she pulled out a small pearl-handled revolver and held it in front of her.

Anya was wide-eyed as she watched Mildred; this was completely ludicrous. Whatever was Mildred up to? She felt she should say something, but then decided to humour her friend for now and kept quiet.

Mildred reached out and quietly grasped the edge of one of the curtains while pointing her gun at whoever she expected to be on the balcony. 'Come out with your hands up,' she said loudly, at the same time pulling back the curtain.

Anya gasped as one of the German officers she'd seen at the banquet stepped forward with his hands raised high above his head. 'Do not shoot,' he said. 'I am unarmed.'

'Over there. Sit down,' Mildred hissed as she waved her gun, directing him to a desk and chair not far from where Anya was sitting.

'But *I* am armed,' a suited man said, stepping through the door Anouska had passed through minutes earlier.

Fear gripped Anya's stomach. Who was he? She'd seen him recently ... Of course, he had been seated beside Anouska during the banquet. Was this her father or her husband? It was hard to tell, with them being so similar in age. This man was wearing a black dinner jacket with his bow tie undone; his tall frame, slicked-back silver hair and high cheekbones gave him a sinister air.

'Get over there, both of you,' he snapped at Anya and Mildred, indicating that they should move to stand in front of a large fireplace. 'Throw your gun to the floor,' he said to Mildred, 'and no tricks.'

'What is going on? Anouska, where are you?' Anya called out, fearing her friend was in danger but showing no fear of the man holding the gun.

'Shut up,' the suited man said, waving the gun in Anya's direction. 'My wife will come out when I tell her to,' he snarled.

So this is the husband, Anya thought. He wasn't quite the weak, elderly man she had imagined him to be and didn't look at all sickly. She'd expected him to be bent over his plate, having his food cut up for him and being spoon-fed by a nurse. She gave a cynical smile, causing him to bark at her: 'What do you find so funny?'

'You are not what I imagined you to be when Anouska told me she'd married an older man.'

'As if I care what you think; you are just another Polish peasant girl.'

'Who came from the same village as your wife,' Anya spat back at him. 'At least I married a man who is fighting for his country.'

'Shut up, before your brave husband is standing over the grave of his wife,' he snarled. 'Anouska, are you ready?' he called over his shoulder. 'The train to Berlin will be leaving soon.'

Anouska appeared at the bedroom door, dressed in a tailored black travelling ensemble with a leather clutch bag and matching shoes. 'Will these shoes do for the journey?' she asked her husband. 'Or there are the ones I left on the bed . . .'

He turned to glance into the bedroom and she snatched the gun, shoving him through the door and quickly turning the key in the lock. 'You,' she said, waving the gun at the German officer, who was watching the scene unfold with barely concealed mirth. 'Don't move.' She stepped sideways towards the windows, keeping her eyes on the man, and tugged at the plaited silk ropes holding back the drapes. Throwing them towards Mildred and Anya, she instructed them to tie him up securely.

'What about gagging him? He may shout for help.'

'No one is likely to hear him.' She shrugged her shoulders. 'Now, let's get out of here before my father gets home.'

'Now I am confused. I thought you wished us to help you and your father escape from enemy-occupied France?'

Anouska's expression was one of contempt. 'He is as bad as the rest of them; he as good as sold me to the highest bidder. First the old husband, and then the Nazi bastards who would keep him in riches until the war was over. If they are to lose the war, and God I hope they do, then he will use anything he can to wheedle his way in with the Americans or the Russians.'

'Not the English?' Anya asked.

'Who knows?' she smiled. 'He has skills that these countries require, and they will pay handsomely; I don't wish to be involved any more. That is why you must take me with you. I can pay you well for my passage and my keep once I am in London,' she said, opening her jacket and patting a thick fabric package wrapped around her waist. 'I have waited a long time for this day.'

'Then we must hurry,' Mildred said, going to the door of the apartment.

'Not that way; my father will be here any moment. He is a creature of habit. We must jump.' Anouska nodded towards the balcony, tucking the gun into the waistband of her skirt.

'God, this is going to kill me,' Anya swore as she sat on the balcony and lowered herself over the edge. On a count of three she let herself drop to the ground, her fall broken by the shrubbery that surrounded the building. 'It is not too bad,' she called up to Mildred. 'Do as I did, and you will be fine.'

Mildred landed with a grunt and lay still among the shrubbery for several moments before Anya helped pull her away in case Anouska fell onto her prostrate body in the dark.

'Are you injured?' Anya whispered.

'No, just winded. My old body won't allow me to do much of this kind of thing without complaining.'

Anouska jumped after them, throwing her shoes down first. She stood up and straightened her skirt, pulling the shoes back on. 'This way,' she whispered, leading them away from the building's main entrance. 'We must be careful in case my father is nearby.'

They walked in silence until they were some distance away; then Anouska paused and looked at Anya. 'Where do we go?'

Anya looked to Mildred, who shrugged her shoulders. 'We need to find Domino. He's the one who knows the way back to our rendezvous point.'

Anya was exhausted and her head was throbbing. She hadn't slept well since their arrival in France and she had been working hard all evening. 'The last time I saw him was when he walked with me and Natalie to the banqueting hall. I thought they'd be waiting for me when I left, but there was no sign of them. That's why I went back to our lodgings alone.'

'Then we go back to the hostelry and we wait,' Mildred said, looking around to get her bearings. After a couple of minutes she took a compass from her pocket and pored over it, eventually giving a satisfied grunt. 'This way,' she pointed as the two women fell in step behind her.

'She grunts a lot,' Anouska said.

'She certainly does,' Anya agreed.

The women walked on in silence, glancing back now and then in case they were being followed. They stayed close to the sides of buildings, not wanting to be challenged for being out after curfew. Anya gave a sigh of relief when she recognized the hostelry where they had hidden away.

While Anya showed Anouska the way to their room up in the eaves of the building, Mildred stopped to speak to the landlord. Their conversation took place in hushed tones before money changed hands and she joined the others.

'What news of Domino and Natalie?' Anya asked, noticing Mildred's downcast face.

'Nothing of Domino, but Natalie is dead.'

Anya felt sick. 'How can that be? She was with me earlier this evening, making sure I could see Anouska . . . ?'

'See me – what do you mean?' Anouska turned to her.

Anya shook her head, unable to explain why she'd been there. She couldn't help but think she might have alerted the Germans to Natalie by aiding her to identify Anouska. Perhaps it had been when she made a fool of herself in front of Hitler, she thought to herself, before pushing the memory away. She had a job to do so she could get home to her son. She could only pray the news about Natalie was not true.

'I just wanted to help you,' she said to Anouska.

A smile crossed Anouska's face. 'And you have. But tell me, who is this Domino, and why is he important?'

Mildred didn't speak for a moment before shrugging off the question. 'Just a French person who helped us.' She fell silent as there was a knock on the door. It was the landlord, bringing them a tray of food. Again he whispered quietly to Mildred before she thanked him and carried the tray into their room. 'Tomorrow, people will help move us towards the coast. For tonight, we eat and sleep. Anouska, you may have my bed and I will sleep in the armchair.'

'No, you can have my bed; you need to regain your strength,' Anya insisted, and would not be swayed however much Mildred argued.

Later, as she tried to sleep in the lumpy horsehair-stuffed chair, Anya thought about John Bentley and prayed he had not perished at the hands of the Germans. She would never again be able to look Flora in the eye if it turned out that John had met his fate while helping her. She thought hard about where he might be. She replayed the memory of him walking with her to the banqueting hall before handing her over to Natalie. The last thing he'd said to her had been, 'I'll be close by in case I am needed.' But he hadn't been there when she needed him. What had happened?

She looked over at the two women who shared her room. Moonlight was coming in through the window and outlining their beds. Mildred seemed to be sleeping soundly, with the occasional snore coming from below her blanket. It was Anouska who caught Anya's attention, slipping silently from her bed and moving towards the one small window, her movements smooth and catlike. For a moment Anya wondered if she might be sleepwalking, and held still as she watched rather than risk waking her;

Anouska had been through so much, it was not surprising if her sleep was affected.

Anouska stood looking out for a few minutes, as if she was seeking something or someone, before raising her hand and then turning to go back to her bed. She stopped close to Anya – so close, Anya could hear her soft breathing and smell the lingering echo of her perfume. She froze, still not wanting Anouska to know she was awake, before giving a silent sigh of relief at hearing the bed creak as the woman returned to her slumber.

32

June 1942

'I've made a decision,' Rose said. She spread a towel out on the rough grass in the back garden of Captain's Cottage and lay down flat, enjoying the warmth of the sun on her body. She was wearing a pale blue floral sundress and had removed the matching bolero to warm her arms and shoulders.

'I hope it's not to do some gardening. I'm exhausted after three long shifts in a row,' Lily said from where she lay in red shorts and a skimpy top, with a straw sunhat over her face.

'The only decision I've made is to get us a glass each of cold lemonade from the pantry; that's when I can be bothered to move,' Katie said, stretching out in the one deck chair they possessed. She looked pretty in her yellow flared skirt and matching headband that pulled her hair back from her face.

'Mmm, that sounds delicious,' Lily almost purred. 'Aren't we lucky to all have leave on the same day? And the sun to be shining as well.'

'And no air raids,' Katie said, touching the rough wooden frame of the deck chair for luck. 'So, what is your decision, Rose?'

'I'm going to London to find Anya. It is time she returned home.'

Katie looked perturbed. 'You told us you went once before and had no luck. Its seems such a waste of time. Could you not write a letter to head office and ask their advice? Perhaps tell them little Alexsy is missing his mummy,' she said, looking over to where he was sitting on the grass watching Mary dig holes in the border with her bucket and spade.

'I've tried that already. I addressed the letter to the person who sent the original instructions to send Anya to the training school in London.'

'It does seem rather fishy,' Lily said, leaning up on one elbow and pushing back her sunhat to look at her friends.

Rose rolled onto her tummy and rested her chin in her hands. Heaving a big sigh, she made the decision to confide in Lily and Katie, as she knew they could keep a secret. 'There is something else; I've known about it for a while now. Ruth is involved. I'm not sure how much, but she seems to know where Anya is. Only she's saying very little.'

Katie screwed her eyes up against the midday sun. 'Anya said something very strange to me when she left Alexsy in my care. She told me that Jack and I would be the perfect parents for her son. I shrugged it off, because you know how strangely she puts things at times; I put it down to her lack of English. Now I wish I'd asked her what she meant.'

'Mildred spoke to me in a similar way when I caught her having a good clear-out in her bedroom,' Rose recalled.

'Not that she has a child who needs taking care of. But when I mentioned it to Mum, she told me that Mildred had asked her to take care of her affairs if anything should happen to her.'

'What does Mildred have to do with it, though?' Lily asked. 'It's Anya who seems to have been away for an age now.'

Rose put her straight. 'I reckon their whereabouts are connected. Mildred went away around the same time as Anya, and now her boat is back in the harbour, but there's no sign of her.'

'Gosh, I hope they're all right. This is giving me the shivers,' Katie said, turning pale. 'I do agree that something needs to be done. They've both been away far too long. I would never forgive myself if it turned out they were in some kind of trouble, and we did nothing.'

'I think we should all go to London, and why not do it tomorrow?' Lily said, jumping to her feet. 'I'll get our drinks and a notebook so we can plan what we are going to do; keep an eye on Mary, would you? She seems to be eating the earth in the flower border.' Mary looked up at the mention of her name and gave a muddy grin.

The girls added their thoughts as Lily jotted down everything that concerned them about Anya being away for so long. 'Don't forget to note down how we feel about Mildred vanishing at the same time,' Rose said as she chewed her fingernail.

Katie looked over Lily's shoulder. 'I feel we should ask Flora what she thinks as well. Anya and Mildred live at Sea View, so she must have picked up on how they were acting before they left.'

'You talk as if they'd disappeared together,' Lily said.

'Mildred is supposed to have gone to visit a friend – or was it a family member? – and supposedly Anya is training Sallys in London.'

'I know it is confusing, but we can't start making assumptions about what's happened,' Rose said. 'We must keep to the facts. Don't forget that Mildred has gone off to visit family and friends in the past . . .'

'But wherever she goes, the *Saucy Milly* goes with her. It doesn't return to the harbour without her,' Katie argued. 'Someone needs to go and speak to the other boat owners to see what they know.'

'We could do that this afternoon, then pop in to see Mum and ask her what else she knows,' Rose suggested.

'Yes, and see if someone can look after the children. We can't trudge all the way up town with a pram, and the kiddies are too young to really enjoy the journey,' Lily said.

'Good thinking. We can't really barge into the Lyons training office with a pram,' Katie agreed. 'This little man needs his mum home safe and sound, wherever she may be.' She hurried over to pick Alexsy up and cuddle him until he complained loudly, before looking at Katie and saying 'Mum' as clear as a bell.

'They were covering up for Mildred,' Lily fumed as they sat around the kitchen table at Sea View. 'And who were those two French chaps on the deck of the *Saucy Milly*? I've never seen them working in the harbour before. Something smells extremely fishy, and it's not Mildred's overalls. What do you think, Flora?'

'I'm inclined to believe you, but it is imperative we don't go charging in like a bull in a china shop. Let me look at your notes,' Flora said. Lily slid them across the table. 'I just wish we knew who it was Mildred had gone to visit. I know so little about her family background, apart from what she told you girls about her relationship with her late father.'

'She doesn't have any living relatives,' Miss Tibbs said from where she had been dozing in her armchair.

'Are you sure, dear?'

'I've not lost my marbles, if that's what you think,' the old lady tittered. 'Honestly, girls, when you get to my age, everyone assumes you've forgotten everything. I may forget where I've left my knitting, but I'm as sharp as a knife with older memories.'

Rose went over to the old lady and knelt by her chair. 'What did Mildred tell you?'

'It was while we were talking one day about my sister; I mentioned how she'd died, and I told Mildred that I don't have any living relatives. She reminded me that friends are worth their weight in gold, and here at Sea View, with such good friends, we have a vault full of gold.'

'That was so kind of her,' Flora sniffed, rubbing her eyes.

Miss Tibbs raised her eyebrows at the interruption. 'I will continue. I asked Mildred about her own family and apart from what you all know about her acrimonious relationship with her father, she told me there were no living relatives. I can only assume you heard her wrong when you thought she said she was visiting family.' She looked at the girls' expectant faces before turning to Flora. 'You may have the answer, as I believe you are the executor of her will.'

'My goodness, I'd not given that a thought. However, the paperwork is with her solicitor.'

'Then I suggest you use your telephone and ask him. Must I think of everything around here?' Miss Tibbs sniffed, before checking her empty cup. 'A cup of tea and a biscuit would be very nice.'

'I'll make the tea and you make that telephone call, Mum; it will help us with our investigations,' Rose said as she went to the stove to slide the kettle over the hot part of the plate. Flora hastily left the kitchen to do as her daughter suggested.

'You're starting to sound like Sherlock Holmes,' Lily joshed.

'You may laugh, but the more we know, the easier it will be to find our friends.'

'You're right, I shouldn't be joking,' Lily apologized. 'But you know, Mildred was right about what she said. Friends are so important. Katie and I are lacking in the blood relative department and we value our friends very much.'

Katie's eyes welled up and she was unable to reply for a while. 'Goodness, I don't know what has come over me. I've done nothing but weep these past few weeks. Just ignore me.'

Lily gave Katie a questioning look, but decided now was not the time to say any more. They helped to wash the cups and lay a fresh tea tray, although Miss Tibbs had now dropped off to sleep again.

'Flora . . . I wonder if John Bentley knows anything about what has been going on?' Lily asked when Flora came back into the room.

'Why do you say that, dear?' Flora asked.

'Well, Rose told us Ruth knows more than she is letting on about Anya's disappearance. And didn't he come here the same night Ruth visited to speak with Anya?'

'Pure conjecture,' Flora said, shaking her head, although try as hard as she might, she couldn't get John from her mind. 'Perhaps speak to Ruth.'

'We will. How did you get on telephoning the solicitor?'

'What he told me is not supposed to be shared, but I trust you will not let this go any further . . .'

The girls all voiced their agreement, waiting to hear what Flora had to say.

'There's no family mentioned in Mildred's last will and testament,' she started.

'Told you so,' Miss Tibbs responded, without opening her eyes.

'However, she has made bequests to a few friends from long ago. Her solicitor told me that they will be difficult to trace without Mildred's help, and he had hoped she would get back in touch to assist him. It was his opinion that some of them may have passed away.'

'So we're none the wiser about who she could be visiting?' Rose said sadly.

'Not exactly. He did mention Mildred has left a large donation to the Seaman's Mission, and also to a fisherman, Jake Singleton, for his help and support these past few years.'

'Perhaps she is visiting him?' Lily beamed. 'Let's go find him. Where does he live?'

Flora shook her head. 'That's the strange thing; he lives here in Ramsgate. She's not likely to have paid an extended visit to someone living a few streets away.' Seeing the girls' disappointed faces, she spoke again. 'What I suggest is you all go to London as planned and revisit the training school to try to get more out of them. Also, go to see Ruth and have it out with her. Tell her that you won't leave until you have answers. It's a shame Lady Diana is still in Scotland; I feel she would have been a great help to us in wheedling information out of Ruth.'

'I don't understand what Ruth has to do with all this?' Katie said.

'I have a suspicion, but cannot say,' Flora replied. 'With three of you confronting her, though, you may have some success. Now, why don't I sort out a meal for us, and then you all get an early night?'

'I'm rather worried about what we might find out,' Katie said.

'Don't be,' Flora said. 'I plan to take the children with me tomorrow and pay a visit to Jake Singleton. You never know, he may be able to shine a light on the mystery of the missing Mildred.'

'That's a good idea,' they all agreed.

Flora was still thoughtful. 'Rose, I've been thinking about Miss Butterworth. Do you feel that now she has warmed to you a little, she would be willing to help?'

'In what way?'

'I've been wondering how Anya knew she was going to work in London before you were informed the next day by letter. What if that official letter never came from Lyons' head office at all, and this was concocted by Ruth . . . ?'

'But I rang them . . .'

'You rang the telephone number printed on the letter,' Lily butted in.

'Gosh,' was all Rose could think to say.

'I suggest you place a call through to Miss Butterworth and ask for her advice. She could at least investigate the problem. It may be that a different department, or person, sent that letter . . .' Flora let the sentence trail away with a meaningful look.

'Don't forget to mention that man at the training school who you thought knew something, and then he told you to speak to someone in your family, and you thought he meant Ben, but then Ruth all but said she knew more than she was letting on . . .' Lily reminded Rose as she checked what she'd written in her notebook.

'I'll do that right now. I know which teashop she's visiting this afternoon, so it will be easy to locate her,' Rose said as she reached for her handbag and pulled out the small diary where she kept important telephone numbers for her work.

'We can start afternoon tea while you do that. I have some eggs, so let's have fried eggs on toast. The kiddies can have theirs boiled with soldiers. We don't have to worry about Joyce and Pearl, as they're visiting friends,' Flora added.

The others were thoughtful as they cleared the kitchen table and helped Flora prepare the tea.

'Didn't any of you girls bring some cake home with you?' Miss Tibbs asked as she awoke at the mention of teatime.

'Sorry, we had a day off from work and came over here to speak to Flora. I'll bring you some gypsy tart next time I visit, courtesy of Joe Lyons,' Katie promised.

Miss Tibbs licked her lips. 'That's worth waiting for.'

The girls giggled at the old woman's words. When Rose rejoined them, she was greeted by a cheerful atmosphere rather than the subdued one she'd left fifteen minutes earlier.

33

'What did the dragon lady have to say?' Lily asked as they sat down to eat.

Rose smiled at everyone sat around the table. 'I was worried she would bite my head off, but in fact she was extremely sympathetic and agreed something didn't sound right. She has promised to see what she can find out at head office. I told her the three of us want to go to London to see if we can find anything out, and she has given us another day off – she suggested we take in a show, and she will book us into the Lyons ladies' hostel for the night.'

Lily couldn't believe her ears. 'Blimey, is she ill or something?'

'I think it is very sweet of her, and I for one will work twice as hard when we get back,' Katie said. 'Oh dear; what about the children, and the staff rotas?'

'You are to go and enjoy yourself once you have found out all you can about Anya.' Flora was adamant. 'Don't give the children a second thought. I'll take care of them, and perhaps if you give Jennie and Joyce full shifts it will help fill the gaps?'

'Thank you, Mum. Miss Butterworth did say she would go to both teashops and check the remaining staff weren't overstretched. I think she has a soft spot for Thanet; after all, this is where she used to work when she was a Nippy. Oh, and she said she would arrange travel permits as we will be visiting the Lyons training school, and drop them into Captain's Cottage tomorrow morning.'

'Blimey, she really has been helpful,' Lily said as she raised her cup. 'A toast to Miss Butterworth, and long may she reign.'

'Then I suggest we eat up and you girls get yourselves off home and into your beds. You have a busy few days ahead of you. I do hope you enjoy yourselves,' Flora smiled.

'But most importantly, we must find out where Anya and Mildred have disappeared to,' Rose reminded them.

Flora pushed the pram through the hot streets of Ramsgate. Even the lure of the harbour did nothing to soothe her; she had too much on her mind to enjoy the early summer day. Her mood wasn't helped by the weight of the pram. At nearly three years of age, Daisy was getting too heavy to sit on the special seat that fitted on top while Alexsy slept in the body of the pram. Now that he was so mobile and full of energy, he wanted to sit up and look about rather than snooze.

'It's time we changed your mode of transport,' Flora remarked to the fractious Daisy, who wanted to get down and walk. 'Here we are . . .' She pulled the pram backwards up a short path and put on the brakes. 'Now, you do your best to be quiet for a little while, as I must talk to the man who lives here,' she told the little girl as she lifted the blackened knocker and brought it down with a bang. 'Oh my goodness, that was loud,' she said as the door opened.

'It takes everyone like that,' smiled a white-haired man. 'The postman has had more than one heart attack delivering my parcels; you'd think he'd have learnt by now.' He chuckled as he peered more closely at Flora. 'Aren't you the lady who owns the boarding house on the other side of the harbour? Where Mildred Dalrymple lives?'

'The guesthouse, Sea View. Yes, I'm Flora Neville,' she smiled back, thankful that he recognized her. That would make it easier to broach the subject of Mildred's disappearance. 'And you must be Jake Singleton. I wonder if you could spare me a few minutes? It's about Mildred . . .'

'Of course I can; I hope there's nothing wrong with her? I can't say I've seen her in a while. I hope she's keeping well?'

'There is a problem,' Flora said, glancing at Daisy, who was hell bent on escaping from her pram seat.

'Why don't you bring the kiddies inside? Better still, let's go through to the back garden and that one can run herself ragged. Can the little one walk yet?' he asked, as Flora let Daisy free and picked up Alexsy.

'In a fashion; he tends to shuffle about on his backside and pull himself up by grabbing at tablecloths and cushions. You need eyes on the back of your head with him around,' she grinned, giving Alexsy a kiss on the top of his head.

'I can see you've got your hands full,' he chuckled as he led the way through a small front room full of knick-knacks and past a tidy kitchen, through a door that led into a garden that to Flora seemed longer than all the rooms in the house.

'You have a lovely home,' she said politely, thinking that she could easily imagine retiring to a property like this and leaving Rose to run the guesthouse.

'It suits me,' he said, pointing for Flora to sit on a carved wooden bench while he took a chair beside a small table. 'The kiddies can go where they please, no need to worry about them damaging anything,' he added as Flora set them down, vowing to keep an eye on them both and be ready to stop Alexsy picking the bright blooms. 'Now, tell me what is wrong with Mildred.'

'I'm not sure there is anything wrong with her. It's just that she's gone missing, and we have no idea where she could be.'

He nodded thoughtfully. 'What makes you think I can be of help?'

'Mildred told us just after Easter that she was going to visit family, and it's only now some time has passed that we've realized she doesn't have any family left alive. It is so out of character, but as she put her affairs in order before she left and made me the executor of her will, I have started to wonder whether she has done something silly.'

'Mildred Dalrymple has never done a silly thing in her life,' he barked at her. 'I've known her since we were children and she is the most sensible person I've had the good fortune to meet. Now, if you were to say she does some foolhardy things at times, then I'd agree with you.'

Why, he is in love with Mildred, Flora thought as she watched his worried face. 'This is why I need your help,' she said. 'As the executor of Mildred's will I happen to know that you are mentioned as one of the few beneficiaries. I've been hoping – no, I've been praying that you might be able to shed some light on what has happened.'

She waited for him to speak as he sat looking out over the garden, down to where the sea could be seen sparkling in the sunshine.

'Where is the *Saucy Milly*?'

'Back in the harbour. It wasn't there for a while,' she answered, watching his face carefully.

'And she definitely isn't on board?'

'My daughter, Rose, and her friends went to look and told me there were two French lads on board. They didn't speak to Rose, and she has very little French to be able to ask questions.'

He nodded thoughtfully. 'It is as I thought. When the *Saucy Milly* next sails it will return with Mildred, as it has done in the past.'

Flora shivered. 'You are talking in riddles; please, you've got to tell me what is happening,' she begged. 'Surely, if she went fishing, then she must have returned with the boat. And in that case, where has she gone since she came back?'

He raised a hand and pointed towards the sea. 'Rivers run deep with Mildred, and she is loyal to her country. Did she happen to leave on the night of the storm?'

'Why, yes, there was a storm around the time she went away. Could she have gone overboard, do you think? Perhaps I should speak to the police or ask around the fishermen in the harbour?'

Jake shook his head, smiling. 'She will return from wherever she is, you have no need to worry. The fishing fraternity is a close family and will not divulge its secrets, but its members will rally round if she needs help. Now, would you like a cup of tea?' he asked, slapping the side of his leg as he stood up, so loudly that he gave Flora the fright of her life.

Half an hour later, Flora walked back to Sea View deep in thought. From what she could understand, Jake Singleton had been hinting that Mildred was over on the other side of the Channel on some kind of mission. But what could that be, and why Mildred?

She stopped to look at the busy harbour, thinking back to 1940, when so many soldiers had been brought back half drowned from Dunkirk – and then it hit her. If Mildred was somewhere over the Channel, it meant she was in enemy-occupied France.

She raced back to Sea View and sat by the telephone, praying she wasn't too late. Rose had promised to ring her from a telephone box and let her know when the girls had arrived in London. She needed Rose to go and see Ruth, to ask her to get in touch with John Bentley: he was the only person Flora could think of who would know what to do to get Mildred back. She recalled him saying he had been well travelled before war broke out and he might just know how to track down her dear friend. If not, he could at least speak to the two French lads on the *Saucy Milly* and find out what they knew.

Rose stopped Lily and Katie as they left Victoria train station. 'I want to speak to Mum to see how she got on visiting Mildred's friend, Jake,' she said, opening her purse. 'Drat, do either of you have some coppers I can borrow?'

Both dug about in their purses, coming up with some loose change. 'Will it do?' Katie asked.

'Just about, if I speak quickly and Miss Tibbs doesn't answer the telephone,' Rose grinned. 'Here's an empty phone box. I'll only be a tick.' She hurried inside.

Lily and Katie stood beside the box, out of the way of the crowds, and watched as Rose spoke for a few minutes before putting down the receiver. When she rejoined her friends she looked serious.

'Mum seems to think Mildred could be in France, but has no idea why. She wants us to visit Ruth and ask her to get in touch with John Bentley, as she reckons he can help.'

'Crikey; I knew Flora had it bad for John, but thinking he can find Mildred is taking it a bit far . . .' Lily laughed.

Rose froze on the spot and turned on her friend. 'It's not like that at all; it was something the old fisherman said to her that got her thinking. I agree with her that John is the right person to ask for help,' she said firmly as they started walking again. Then she smiled. 'I do think she likes him, though . . .'

They stopped for a drink and a bite to eat at the Corner House near to the Strand, and watched the Nippies dash about serving the hundreds of diners while they decided what to eat.

'Blimey, this place is massive,' Lily said as she looked about her. 'To think at one time, I wanted to come to London and work in a Corner House. I'd have got lost in here. How about some fried fish?' she asked as she read the menu.

Katie made a face. 'I'd rather not, if you don't mind; I'm feeling a little sick. It must have been the train journey. Perhaps I'll just have a cup of tea.'

'You do look a bit green around the gills,' Rose said as she put the back of her hand against Katie's forehead. 'You feel a little warm; take your coat off and take a few deep breaths. I'll ask for a glass of cold water for you to sip. You'll be as right as rain before too long.'

Lily watched thoughtfully without saying a word.

34

'Well, that was a waste of time,' Rose said as she joined Lily and Katie, who were waiting outside the building that held the training school for Nippies and Sallys. 'I was told Mr Montgomery wasn't there, but that was only after the receptionist recognized me. Perhaps one of you two could enquire?'

Lily was thoughtful. 'Katie, do you happen to have your spectacles on you?'

'You know I always carry them in case I can't read something, but I hate to wear them; why do you ask?'

'May I borrow them? And Rose, can we swap handbags? Yours doesn't look as frivolous as mine. Hang on a minute, let me take out my notebook and pen.'

'Whatever are you up to?' Rose asked, frowning as Lily put the spectacles on the end of her nose and swung the black leather handbag over her arm. Poised with the notebook in her hand, she faced her friends.

'Do I look like a serious person who could well be a police officer, or perhaps a restaurant inspector?'

'You can't,' Katie gasped, while Rose shook her head in disapproval.

'Just you watch me,' Lily said as she walked towards the entrance to the training school. 'Why not go for a walk and window shop? I intend to be a while.'

With her friends telling her to come back, Lily pushed open the heavy doors and entered the building. She was pleased that she had worn her best outfit, a navy blue skirt and matching jacket; with her hair freshly washed and wearing her best shoes, she felt a million dollars.

'May I help you, madam?' a young receptionist asked from behind a high counter where she oversaw the entrance area.

'I'm here to speak to whoever is in charge of personnel for the company,' Lily said, peering over the rims of her spectacles. It was useless looking through the lenses, as she couldn't see a thing. 'It concerns a highly confidential matter.'

'If you take a seat, I will find the person you wish to speak to. Who may I ask is enquiring . . . ?'

'Sergeant Dalrymple from the Kent police,' Lily said, giving the girl a look that discouraged questions. She mentally patted herself on the back for using Mildred's surname, which she felt somehow demanded respect.

She sat down, facing in the direction the receptionist had vanished so as to be prepared for her return along with whoever accompanied her. While waiting, she took the opportunity to write a few questions in her notebook and fold the corner of the page over; that way she wouldn't open it in the wrong place and show Katie's notes for a dress pattern.

She was just beginning to think no one would be coming when she heard voices and the receptionist reappeared, accompanied by a rather nondescript man in a grey suit.

'Sergeant Dalrymple, how do you do,' he said, extending a hand to Lily as the receptionist returned to her counter. 'I am Percival Montgomery. What can I do for you?'

'Is there somewhere we can talk privately? The matter I wish to discuss is rather delicate.'

'Certainly. Follow me,' he said. Lily noticed him covertly looking her up and down as he gestured her ahead of him towards a door leading into a small office. Dirty bugger, she thought to herself; I can deal with your type.

Once they were inside and seated, she opened her notebook with a confident air and glanced down at it as if it contained copious notes. 'I'm here to ask you about a woman who went missing recently. Her family are concerned, as are we,' she said, hoping her tone was pitched at the right official level.

'I'll help if I can,' Montgomery said earnestly. 'May I offer you tea?'

'Not for me, thank you. I would rather get to the bottom of the disappearance of the wife of a war hero.'

He raised his eyebrows with interest. 'Tell me more.'

'The lady worked for one of the Lyons teashops until recently; her name is Anya Polinski.'

'Oh, her,' he said, looking immediately less interested. 'I have had one of her colleagues here before, enquiring about the lady. She seemed to think Mrs Polinski was working here as a trainer, which is highly unlikely with her being a foreigner.'

Lily held back from putting the man straight, as it would have blown her cover. 'I have spoken to her manager and

339

it seems the lady is highly thought of and an asset to Lyons. Now, I would like to draw your attention to a letter that was sent to the manager of the Margate teashop, a Mrs Hargreaves, whose husband is related to the aristocracy . . .'

It was as she'd thought: Montgomery was suddenly interested again.

'She was the one who came to see me a little while ago looking for Mrs Polinski.'

'Yes, she said as much when I interviewed her,' Lily replied, flicking though her notebook as if looking for notes on the interview. She had to try hard not to smile when she spotted a drawing made by Daisy. 'Ah, yes. You advised her to speak to someone in her family . . . I put it to you, Mr Montgomery, that you have knowledge of where Mrs Polinski might be. Am I correct?'

He shifted in his seat, looking uncomfortable. 'What I have to tell you is highly confidential and should go no further.'

'I am a police officer, Mr Montgomery. Anything I am told in an interview is treated with the appropriate discretion.'

'Of course,' he apologized. 'On occasion, we are asked to give an identity or cover up for a staff member who has to do . . . let us say, work for the government. Do you understand?'

'Yes, I get your drift,' Lily said, sitting forward in her chair.

'That was the case with Mrs Polinski; she never did work here as a staff trainer.'

Lily fought hard to maintain her police officer's demeanour, when all she wanted to do was jump up and down with excitement. At last she was getting somewhere. 'But I understand you told Mrs Hargreaves to look to her family.

Are you saying that you risked giving away a government secret by . . . showing off to the lady?'

His face turned red as he tried to loosen his collar. 'No, not at all. I simply advised her to ask elsewhere.'

'Who were you thinking of when you advised Mrs Hargreaves to ask elsewhere?'

'Miss Ruth Hargreaves.'

Lily closed her notebook with a snap and rose to her feet. 'Thank you for your time, Mr Montgomery,' she said, before escaping from the building as rapidly as possible to find her friends and share the news.

Rose stirred her coffee for the umpteenth time. 'So Ruth has known all along? To be fair, she has hinted, but if only she could have told us where Anya was, it would have saved so much worry on our part.'

'Do you think Anya and Mildred are together?' Katie asked.

'I'd bet my bottom dollar,' Lily said in an American drawl, before glancing up at a clock on the wall of the small cafe where they sat. 'Is there time to confront Ruth before we head off to the theatre? Katie spotted a show she'd like to see while we were waiting for you earlier,' she said, waving a copy of the *Evening News*, 'and I must say it sounds a hoot.'

Rose looked over her shoulder. '*Blithe Spirit*, I'd adore to see it, if you think we can pick up tickets on the door. Margaret Rutherford is supposed to be very funny. Come on, let's grab a taxi and get over to Ruth's; it shouldn't take long to confront her and get an answer.'

*

'Miss Ruth is in; shall I tell her you are on your way up, ma'am?'

Rose gave the doorman a big smile. 'No thank you, we will go straight up and surprise her. Come along, girls.'

She used her own key to enter the apartment and they found Ruth lounging on a sofa with a cocktail in her hand. 'What a lovely surprise, come along in. I'll make you all one of these,' she smiled. 'Are you here for a reason?'

'We are going to take in a show,' Katie said, rather shy in the opulent surroundings.

'But first we need to talk to you about Anya Polinski,' Rose said, without smiling or going towards her sister-in-law for her customary welcoming kiss. 'We know what's been going on.'

The look on Ruth's face showed she knew the game was up. 'At least sit down and have a drink,' she sighed as she went to the cocktail cupboard. 'Be assured we had no choice but to send Anya out to France.'

'Ah, so she is in France. Along with Mildred,' Lily said accusingly.

Ruth dropped a glass and it shattered into hundreds of pieces on the marble floor. 'Bugger,' she swore, pushing a brass button on the wall. A bell could be heard ringing in another room and a maid came running. 'I'm sorry, Grace, I've made an awful mess.'

'Not to worry, miss, I'll have it cleaned up in a jiffy. Would you like me to bring some food through for your guests? Oh, hello, Mrs Hargreaves, I didn't see you there.'

'Hello, Grace,' Rose smiled at the maid. 'Please don't bother on our account as we are off to the theatre shortly.'

Grace bobbed a small curtsey. 'Very well, ma'am. I hope

you have a lovely evening,' she said before hurrying away, returning moments later with a broom and dustpan.

The women discussed the show the girls hoped to see until Grace left the room, whereupon all eyes turned to Ruth.

'Please tell us as much as you possibly can,' Rose urged her. 'You know we are trustworthy.' She went on to explain how they had discovered that Anya's disappearance was connected to Mildred's, and that there were two young Frenchmen looking after the *Saucy Milly* in Ramsgate harbour. 'Mum discovered it is an open secret among the local fishermen that Mildred is more than playing her part rescuing people from France. It's about time someone rescued her and Anya.'

'Has something gone wrong?' Lily chipped in.

Ruth ignored Lily's question and spoke directly to Rose. 'You say her boat is in the harbour? That doesn't seem right at all . . .'

'It was still there when we left for London this morning. I spotted it from Sea View.'

Ruth looked shocked. 'The last I heard, it should have gone back to pick them up. What the hell has gone wrong . . . ?'

Katie was angrier than her friends had ever seen her. 'But it's been weeks. Haven't you wondered what happened to them?'

'Well . . . I . . .' Ruth looked ashamed. 'We have a number of operatives out in the field at any one time and . . .'

'And you forgot about them. Even though they are friends of your family.'

'That's a bit harsh,' Ruth said. 'But I do understand how you feel.'

'What are you going to do to get them back here?' Lily demanded. 'That's if it isn't too late.'

Katie burst into tears. 'This is why she was adamant that Jack and I should look after Alexsy if anything should happen to her and Henio. I can't bear it,' she sobbed into her handkerchief.

Ruth looked between the three friends, wishing she could tell them the truth about Anya and Mildred's mission and what had really become of them. To begin with, it had seemed so straightforward . . .

'Look, I want you to go off and see your show and then come back here. There's plenty of room for you all to stay the night. I'm not listening to your protests,' she said as the girls started to argue. 'I'll not only have some supper ready for you, but will have got things moving to bring them home. I promise I will put this right. Now, who's for a cocktail before you head off to the theatre?' she asked, almost certain that before long she would find herself delivering the worst possible news about their missing friends.

35

Ruth sat deep in thought for over an hour until there was a knock on her door. She'd been shocked and angry to learn that John Bentley had returned only a few days before, and Kenneth had not informed her.

'John; thank you for coming so quickly,' she said, letting him into the apartment. 'How's the leg?' she added, seeing how heavily he was leaning on a walking stick.

'Getting better, thanks. I'm told I could have lost it, so can't complain.'

'I've grateful you made it back in once piece, at least,' she said as he sat down in an armchair. 'Drink?'

He declined. 'What's going on?'

Ruth sighed. 'I had a visit from Ben's wife, Rose, and her two friends. It seems that, along with Flora, they've been digging about and have put two and two together. They had already worked out that Mildred and Anya must be together, and they turned up here this evening wanting me to do something.'

'Did you tell them?' he asked.

'. . . That we believe them to be dead? How could I do that to them? It didn't seem the right time, what with me sitting here drinking cocktails when they arrived. I sent them off to the theatre and then spoke to Kenneth. He will be here shortly. I thought you'd better hear what he has to say.'

'If you brought me here to listen to how two brave women perished at the hands of the Gestapo, I don't want to know. It was bad enough losing Natalie, but Anya and Mildred . . . I blame myself as I should have done more – as should you.'

'Oh, for God's sake, you were lucky to get away from there with your life. You walked right into the trap, and with so many Nazis about . . . You know we have to rely on information and nothing concrete had come through the usual channels. You are letting your heart rule your head as you know these women.'

'I owe my life to a few brave people in the underground; it's just that I should have gone back for them, rather than leave Anya in that hellhole and Mildred back at the lodging house. I should have done more to find them,' he said, looking wretched. 'If it wasn't for me falling into the trap outside the banquet hall . . .'

'But the lodging house was bombed the day after you were injured. And unconscious. You can't blame yourself; they'd never have escaped with their lives, even if Anya had managed to make her way back to Mildred.'

'We left a naive woman who doesn't speak a word of French alone in occupied France. She should never have been sent on the mission,' John said angrily as there was a knock on the door.

'I must answer that. I gave Grace the evening off so we wouldn't be disturbed; or more to the point, so she wouldn't hear anything she shouldn't.'

'It's a bit late now to be thinking about those walls having ears,' he said bitterly as she led Colonel Kenneth Parry into the room.

'Bentley, it's good to see you,' he said, shaking John's hand. 'On the mend?'

'You could say that,' John replied.

'Kenneth has news,' Ruth said, although she couldn't look John in the eye.

They all sat down while Kenneth took out his pipe, holding it in his hands while he prepared to talk. 'I've had word the three women are alive . . .'

'Three?' Ruth and John said in unison.

'They have Anouska Bartkowicz with them.'

John got to his feet, wincing. 'We need to get them out of there – right now. Why ever is that murdering woman with them?'

Ruth shook her head. 'This is our fault; we never told Anya the real reason she was to identify Bartkowicz, and now look at what has happened. How new is this information?' she asked Kenneth.

'A few days since the encrypted message came through. It reached me this afternoon.'

John paced the floor, leaning heavily on his stick. 'I'm going back to get them. Can you drive me to Ramsgate?' he asked Ruth. 'I'll find a fishing boat even if I have to steal one.'

'There's no need, as the *Saucy Milly* is in the harbour with two French fishermen on board,' Ruth said, pleased she was able to contribute some useful information.

'They will be Alphonse's men, and trustworthy,' Kenneth said. 'I'll get back to the office and arrange cover for you. When do you reckon you will head off?'

'With luck, in the early hours, depending on the tide,' John said as a grin crossed his face. He'd avoided Flora for too long, first being injured, and then not being able to face telling her he had left her friends behind in France. He intended to put that straight as soon as possible.

'I'll get dressed and leave a note for the girls, since we'll have left before they get home from the theatre,' Ruth said as the heaviness in her heart started to lift.

'Thank goodness for no air raids,' Ruth said as they headed through Thanet towards Ramsgate. 'And we've made really good time,' she added, looking at John's pale face. 'What's the matter? I thought you'd enjoy the journey.'

'I prefer driving limousines at a sedate speed, rather than hanging on for grim death in a sports car while you have your foot flat on the floor,' he grimaced.

She laughed out loud. 'Stop your moaning; we're nearly there and in one piece. Shall we go straight to the harbour once we arrive?'

'No, I plan to stop at Sea View and ask Flora for her help. She knows people who can help me get the *Saucy Milly* over the Channel without sinking her. It's been a few years since I've handled a boat and nothing of her size.'

'That's a good plan, although I'm coming with you even if I can only swab the decks and be company. I'm a dab hand with a gun as well,' she added, expecting him to object.

'Then consider yourself hired. You started this business, so you ought to be here at the end of it. I also want someone to keep an eye on the two French hands, as I'm not sure I trust them, and we need at least one person who can get us to the point on the French coast where we can pick up Anya and Mildred.'

'Not Bartkowicz?'

'Hopefully not,' he replied.

Before long, they were both standing on the doorstep at Sea View waiting for Flora to answer the door. It was ten to two in the morning and the house was locked up for the night.

It was a bleary-eyed Flora who opened the door, wrapped in her old candlewick dressing gown and suppressing a yawn. She peered out of the doorway, trying to identify the two people standing there in the black of night. 'Ruth?'

'And John,' Ruth replied as they entered the guesthouse. Flora closed the door and pulled the blackout curtain across before turning on a light.

'Whatever brings you here at this time of night? It's not the girls, is it?' she asked, putting her hand to her heart fearfully.

'No, the girls are fine and fast asleep back at the apartment after seeing a show. A few things occurred last night, after Rose gave me a piece of her mind about abandoning Anya and Mildred . . .'

'Oh dear. Yes, I knew they were going to London to have a word with you.'

'I deserved it – we all did,' Ruth apologized. 'Anyhow, there is news, and we have come down here to take the *Saucy Milly* back to France to rescue them.'

Flora beamed with delight. 'Thank the Lord they are well. Come through to the kitchen, it will be warmer down there; this night air can still be chilly even though it's June.'

She bustled about, putting the kettle on the stove, while Ruth and John took off their coats. 'Oh, have you hurt yourself?' she asked him, noticing the walking stick.

'It's nothing,' he said, searching her face for any sign that she was angry with him for vanishing yet again, but seeing nothing.

'It's a war wound,' Ruth was quick to say. 'You may as well know that John was part of the mission with Anya and Mildred when everything went pear-shaped, and he was brought back injured.'

'Oh dear,' Flora said again. 'It is very much as we thought; although I've been surprised to learn that Mildred is part of this.'

Ruth chose not to say anything, as Mildred had been one of her most successful recruits. 'This tea is most welcome,' she said as she cupped the mug with both hands and sipped the hot liquid.

'I can make some toast if you are hungry?' Flora asked, thinking that tea alone was not enough.

'No thank you, but we do need your help,' Ruth said, indicating for her to sit down with them. 'We're both going over to France with the *Saucy Milly*, but we aren't sure about the two French lads that are on the boat. Have you heard anything about them?'

'Not a dickie bird,' Flora said. 'They seem to have kept themselves to themselves. Personally, I'd not want them with me if I were on the boat, as there's no way to be sure whether they're for or against the British. Why, they could be spies,' she said, warming to her point.

'I'd rather go over there with a British crew, and at least one who would know the *Saucy Milly*,' John said.

'I know the right person. He's getting on a bit, but is a friend of Mildred's as well,' Flora said, thinking of Jake. 'He would know the tides as well as the Channel.'

'He sounds ideal. When would be a good time to speak to him?'

'Let's leave it until six o'clock, as I reckon he will be up by then. Do either of you know anything about first aid?' Flora asked tentatively.

'I usually carry a few essential items,' John said, thinking of Mildred's feet, 'but I'm no expert.'

'In that case, consider me part of the crew. I've had a fair amount of training as an air-raid warden since the war started and can bring along my first aid kit.'

'I don't want you put in any danger,' John said.

'I'm coming, so please don't object,' she said, giving him a stern look.

'I can have the two Frenchmen brought in for an interview, which will leave us free to use the boat,' Ruth said.

'That would be good,' John nodded.

'You haven't mentioned how to find them when we get there,' Flora said.

'Don't worry about that; I know the exact place where they will be hiding. Mildred knows what to do if something like this should occur. If this Jake is half the man you say he is, then with my directions we won't have a problem.' He didn't mention the likelihood of patrolling gunboats or enemy action over the Channel.

When the three girls arrived back at Lady Diana's London apartment to a note from Ruth explaining briefly where she had gone, they decided to go straight to bed and catch the milk train back to Ramsgate the next morning. They hoped they would find that something was happening, at long last, to bring Anya and Mildred safely home.

'Let's all go back to Sea View,' Rose said. 'I feel sure Mum will know what's going on.'

'We'll get a decent breakfast as well as seeing my lovely daughter,' Lily added with a fond smile.

But hold-ups on the line, as well as an air-raid warning, meant that it was late morning by the time they eventually reached Sea View. They found the guesthouse in a flurry of excitement.

'I'm taking Miss Tibbs and the children up to the teashop to get them out of the house while your mum is busy,' Joyce explained excitedly as they passed her in the hall. 'She's going to France, would you believe?'

Rose didn't ask Joyce to explain but hurried through to the kitchen, where she found John Bentley and another gentleman poring over maps and navigation charts spread out on the table; meanwhile, Ruth and Flora were making sandwiches.

'What's going on?' Rose asked, not daring to hope that her friends would be on their way home soon.

'Hello, darling. Can you make yourself a drink? We are rather busy with a plan to rescue Anya and Mildred. Did you have a nice time at the theatre?'

'It was a glorious production and we laughed until we ached, as Margaret Rutherford was so funny,' Rose replied, as if her mother running off to rescue her friends was nothing out of the usual.

'I'm glad you enjoyed yourselves,' Flora said distractedly as she checked a box on the floor. 'What food do you usually take on a boat trip?' she asked Jake.

'Hardly anything,' Jake replied. 'We are out catching fish so will cook some of that if we're hungry.'

Rose wrinkled her nose. 'I do feel you should take a few towels and a change of clothes as Anya and Mildred must be in dire need of feeling clean by now, unless they've found somewhere to wash.'

'I doubt they have, as there's only a small stream if they are where I expect them to be,' John said, looking up from the map he was studying.

'If you've known this all along, why wait until now to go and fetch them?' Katie asked, sounding more than a little angry.

Ruth was embarrassed by the accusation. 'John was injured. Otherwise he'd have brought them back before now, wouldn't you, John?'

Katie apologized, but John was ashamed. 'If I'd not been injured and almost comatose until I was back in England, I could have done more. However, with what was happening, we thought they'd been killed.'

Flora was shocked by his words. How could they not have warned them this was possibly the case? She wanted to discuss this more, but there was so much to do. Her mind was on the present. 'We are heading down to the *Saucy Milly* later this afternoon. Jake reckons there will be maintenance work to do, as she's sat on the water not being used for a few weeks. Will you stay here for a little while and keep an eye on things, Rose?'

Rose had followed the conversation not liking what she'd heard. Had this wretched war cheapened life that much? Flora gave her a look that said now was not the time to start an argument. 'Of course, but I will have to go into work tomorrow morning. I can't expect Miss Butterworth to give us another day off.'

'Come back to Captain's Cottage with us this afternoon,' Lily suggested. 'We can leave everyone to get organized. I fear we'll only be under their feet here.'

'That's fine,' Flora nodded. 'Joyce and Miss Tibbs will be here then, and I daresay we will be back during the day tomorrow. It won't take very long to cross the Channel and then return, will it, Jake?'

Jake chuckled but didn't give her a direct answer.

36

'I'm going upstairs to sort out some of the clothes I've stored here,' Rose said when the three girls arrived at Captain's Cottage later that afternoon. 'I need to pass some on to the church for the women who have been bombed out of their homes. I feel quite guilty about having clothing not just here but at Sea View, and over in Pegwell Bay. Besides, I'm forever losing things.'

'If there's anything you don't want, leave it in my room,' Lily called after her as she joined Katie, who was sitting on a bench by the corner of their cottage looking out over the sea. 'Phew, what a day! And to think Flora will be setting off over the Channel once it gets dark; rather her than me.'

'I can't take it all in,' Katie said, looking confused. 'So much has happened; this whole business feels like a jigsaw puzzle with a piece missing. I just want everyone home and safe, then I can breathe properly once more. I think that's why I've been feeling out of sorts lately.'

They both leant back, enjoying the warm sunshine.

'I could easily doze off, especially as I don't have Mary

to care for while she's staying with Joyce,' Lily murmured. 'I might just have a bath and relax for the evening, even if I can't have the water very deep.'

'You may have to change your plans; it looks as though we have visitors,' Katie said, sounding more than a little excited as they heard the click of the front gate. She grinned at Lily as Peter appeared around the side of the house. 'Hello, Peter, are you on your own?' She looked past the pilot to see if Stew was with him.

Rather than answer with his usual wit, he sat down between them and put his head in his hands. Lily slid her arm around his shoulders. 'Has it been a bad day?'

He raised his head and she saw tears in his eyes. 'We lost a plane this afternoon . . . the whole crew . . .'

Lily had her heart in her mouth. 'Please don't say . . .'

'Yes, Stew was a member of the crew. I'm sorry,' he said, turning to Katie, who sat frozen with shock.

'No, it can't be true,' she whispered. 'It can't be true . . .'

Peter put his arms around both girls as they wept for the lovely Scottish man who had brightened their days at Captain's Cottage.

'His poor family,' Lily sniffed as she wiped her eyes. 'I can't begin to imagine how it will be for them. From what he told us, his children are very young.'

A car horn beeped from the front of the cottage. 'That'll be the men. They dropped me off so I could let you know what's happened before you heard it elsewhere,' Peter said, getting to his feet.

'That's very kind of you. Please raise a glass in his memory for us,' Lily said, knowing the men would be off to drown their sorrows. She was aware that Peter would need the companionship of his comrades. 'I know I'll miss him and so will the children.'

'It never gets any easier,' he sighed.

'If I wrote a letter to his wife, would you send it on to her?' Lily asked. She was sure the woman would like to know what a good and helpful friend Stew had been to them all.

'I'm sure she would appreciate it, in time. Perhaps if you have a photograph of the get-together at Easter, you could include it in your letter?'

She looked at his red-rimmed eyes and nodded, unable to speak. At that moment she couldn't have loved him more, and selfishly prayed he would survive the war and be hers for eternity.

'I'll see you soon,' he said, giving Lily a brief kiss before gently touching Katie's cheek. 'He valued your friendship,' he told her.

Katie nodded her head but said nothing.

Lily walked him to the gate and watched as he was driven away before returning to Katie. She might take this very badly indeed if what Lily feared was true.

Lily sat back down beside her without speaking; she would leave it to Katie to say something first, and take it from there.

After a while, Katie spoke. 'I'm pretty certain I'm pregnant,' she said quite calmly.

Lily reached sideways and took her hand. 'It's Stew's, isn't it?'

'How did you guess?'

'Don't you remember you told me how you'd had a visitor just after your Jack went back to his ship?' A thought came to her. 'You didn't tell Jack, did you?'

'No, he's a bit old-fashioned with women's things; we never speak of my monthlies.'

'Then there is no need to tell him the baby might be Stew's. For all we know, it could be your Jack's. These things can happen, no matter the time of the month.'

'But what if it is Stew's? I already feel so guilty about the one time we were together. He did as well, but we couldn't stop our friendship. Oh, this bloody war,' she cried out before hiding her face in her hands.

'No one need ever know. This baby is a blessing in disguise; perhaps Stew was meant to come along and leave you pregnant.'

'Do you think so?' Katie said as she looked up at Lily. 'I'm not sure I can keep this to myself. I've never lied to my Jack before . . .'

Lily laid her hand on Katie's and gave it a squeeze. 'Sometimes it is best to have secrets just to save your marriage. Jack is a lovely chap, but men cannot always accept these things.'

'He is a lovely man. I'd die rather than disappoint him and have him leave me. I love him so much.'

'Then take this baby as a gift and enjoy your child. There was one thing I learnt when I was expecting my Mary and that was, whatever life threw at me, I still had my baby – just you remember that,' she said, getting up to leave Katie alone with her thoughts.

'How much longer must we wait? I cannot keep walking and walking,' Anouska complained. 'I thought by coming with you we would be picked up immediately, but it seems an age since the banquet.'

Mildred rolled her eyes. If she wasn't careful, she would tell the woman exactly what she thought of her. When Anouska wasn't moaning about having to walk everywhere to stay one step ahead of the Germans, she was whining about the food they found.

'Before too long we will be picked up by a boat and taken home to Blighty; then you can go to London and live the life of Riley,' she said through gritted teeth. And I will be rid of you, she thought to herself.

'I have no idea what this Blighty is. I thought the English were better organized when picking up someone important?'

'We thought we were picking up your father, the eminent scientist,' Anya said, feeling very much the same as Mildred. 'I want to be home with my son rather than here, wet-nursing you,' she muttered. 'Now, I am going to see if I can find some eggs and milk. Would you like to join me?'

Mildred mouthed 'Thank you' and relaxed as the younger women left the old barn where they were now hiding out. This was where they'd first met Domino all those weeks ago, and Mildred knew it was where they would be rescued at some point. She and Anya had been taking it in turns to walk to the shoreline and look out for a boat but so far they'd not seen anything remotely friendly.

Mildred had wondered if word would get to Alphonse; he might attempt a rescue, but if he were to come to this area it would raise suspicion. She was torn. Perhaps if they returned to where Alphonse had dropped them off, they might spot him? There again, they could meet the enemy, or even miss a British boat.

She sighed. She was tired and fed up, and they'd hardly done a thing. Anouska was such draining company and made things so difficult for them, always wanting to go off on her own with no regard for their safety . . .

Mildred must have dozed off, as she woke to find Anya's excited face close to hers.

'I walked down to the shore before going to find food. There's a boat: it is still far out but even in the darkening sky it looks to me like the *Saucy Milly*. I'd know her anywhere. We should move closer to the sea to be ready. Now is the time to move to the empty warehouse at the water's edge that you told us would be better for getting aboard the boat when it arrives.'

'Where's Anouska? We don't want to lose her now,' Mildred said, staggering to her feet. Sleeping on the cold ground and not eating well for all these weeks had done her no favours.

'I left her wandering about when I spotted the boat; I told her not to go far. She should have been back here by now.'

'Go find her. I don't trust her as far as I can spit,' Mildred growled as she started to collect their few possessions.

Anya hurried away, following the path away from the shore. She pulled up short when she heard voices, stepping to one side of the path to hide. Peering out carefully from behind a tree, she saw Anouska standing in the moonlight with two German soldiers on motorbikes. As Anya watched, Anouska turned and pointed back towards the barn.

She bent down and crept closer. The two men seemed to know Anouska and she was talking to them, first angry, then grateful when they handed her a chocolate bar. After a while the men drove away and Anouska began walking slowly back towards the barn, passing Anya, who leapt out from behind her tree.

'What are you playing at, talking to the enemy?' she asked, grabbing Anouska by the arm and shaking her. 'I could slap you.' She held up her hand with thumb and forefinger an inch apart. 'We are this close to being rescued, and you do this. What is your game?'

Anouska laughed close to her face. 'If you haven't worked it out by now, you are a stupid peasant woman.'

'Then I am a stupid peasant woman,' Anya said furiously, 'as I have no idea.'

'It is you we want; or should I say, the people who come from England under cover and rescue those held by my comrades – the Nazi Party,' Anouska said, as she pulled a gun from her pocket and aimed it at Anya.

Anya was shocked to her core by the idea of a woman from her own village working hand in glove with the Nazis. 'But why me? How did I come to be pulled into this?' she asked, looking around for a way to escape.

'Oh, that part was easy; we had been watching. We had been planning to kill Nancy and Domino, along with their comrades, for some time, and we set a trap to say I wanted to be rescued by the British. But then they sent you. When I recognized you, we quickly changed our plans and it was decided that I would fool you all into taking me to London, where I could spy for the fatherland.'

Anya was aghast. 'So, just because you happened to remember me, Natalie has died, and no doubt other people as well – just so that you can try to stop brave individuals from fighting the tyrants of this world?'

'Well done, peasant girl, you understand it perfectly.'

'What is to happen now? Will you shoot me?' Anya asked. She made a show of looking round wildly and cast a glance towards the *Saucy Milly*, checking her progress towards the shore.

'Now we set the trap.'

'Trap?'

Anouska puffed herself up, looking important. 'You are going to bring the flies into my web; the flies who are currently on that boat.' She gave a harsh laugh. 'Now, start walking back to Nancy, or Mildred, or whatever you wish to call her. We need to be in place for when the boat gets close to the old warehouse. Then I set my trap . . . Walk,' she said, poking Anya with her gun. 'Don't think for one moment I won't use this. It is no skin off my nose whether you live or die.'

Anya stumbled on, thinking about how she could warn Mildred. As the barn loomed closer there was just enough light for her to make out her friend with a sack slung over one shoulder, waiting for them.

Mildred did a double take as she spotted Anya stumbling in front of Anouska, and reached inside her coat to withdraw her pearl-handled gun.

'Let her go or I'll use this,' she barked.

Anya's stumble threw Anouska's aim and her bullet only scraped the side of Mildred's head, but it was enough to knock her to the ground. She lay there, dazed, with blood gushing from her small cut.

'What have you done?' Anya screamed as fury took hold of her. She turned on Anouska, not caring that the woman still had hold of her gun. There was a struggle, with Anouska's gun flying from her hand into a dark corner of the barn.

Anouska stepped back, casting about for the best

escape route, but as she hesitated Anya clenched a fist and flew at her, knocking her out cold with a punch to the jaw. 'You can lie there and rot,' she spat, before hurrying over to Mildred. 'Please, you can't be dead – not now, when the *Saucy Milly* is close by and we are going home,' she pleaded. 'I can't go back to Ramsgate without you.'

She knelt beside Mildred, feeling for a pulse. 'You aren't dead, thank goodness,' she said, cradling her friend's head in her arms.

Mildred groaned. 'Leave me here. You must go to the boat and tell them where we are.'

'No, I am going to get you closer to the shore. There are Germans in the vicinity and Anouska is in contact with them.'

'She would be,' Mildred muttered, adding something unrepeatable that surprised Anya. 'If it hadn't all gone wrong, Domino would have had her back in London by now and handed her over to the authorities. She's a nasty bit of work. You were only supposed to have identified her, not taken pity on the woman.'

'Forget her; I want you looked after. She is out cold and won't be moving anywhere soon.'

Mildred tried to prop herself up on one elbow and cursed as the pain caused her to fall back. 'Don't trust her. Leave me here and take her to the boat. She mustn't get away now. She's no friend of the British; she needs locking up and questioning.'

'I will not leave you behind,' Anya said, pulling Mildred to her feet and heaving her over one shoulder. 'I am strong enough to do this,' she said through gritted teeth before staggering forward in the direction of the shoreline and the empty warehouse.

'You need to rest,' Mildred told her after they'd covered a hundred yards or so. 'It's dark, so we won't be found by the enemy.'

'Just a few more feet and we can stop,' Anya said, refusing to put down the injured woman.

'I think I can stand,' Mildred whispered.

Anya stood her on her feet and Mildred hung on to her arm as they moved slowly forward. 'Fifty more steps and we will be there,' she said, urging her on until they reached the warehouse. It was open at one end, facing the sea, close enough to the *Saucy Milly* that the pair could surely have been seen on shore, if only the moonlight was brighter. Anya pulled off her jacket and waved it, desperately trying to get the attention of anyone on board.

'We need to be ready to climb aboard as soon as possible,' she urged Mildred, leading her further on until they were close to the landing stage at the seaward end of the warehouse.

Once there, Mildred staggered for a moment and then fell into a dead faint. Anya dropped down beside her, fearing the worst.

'I will never again complain about unpleasant customers who tell me the bread is stale and neither will I tell Flora I hate the fish pie when she serves it up at Sea View. In fact, I will ask for second helpings and eat it with a smile on my face,' she told Mildred as she held her hand.

Mildred did not reply. Anya stroked her face and tried hard to remember the good times at Sea View with the wonderful people she thought of as her family. The moon appeared from behind the clouds and shone through a hole in the wooden roof. 'Are you watching the moon and thinking of me, Henio? My thoughts are often of you, and if you are safe,' she whispered.

The sound of waves lapping against the building made her think of Ramsgate somewhere across the sea. What would her friends be doing now? Perhaps Lily had taken them dancing and they had stopped on the way home to buy a bag of chips; she could almost smell the vinegar and taste the salt on her lips. Why, oh why, did this have to happen?

Angrily she closed her eyes. Now was not the time for tears. 'Do not cry,' she hissed to herself through gritted teeth. 'We will come through this; there are people who rely upon us both to return. To fail is not an option.'

Footsteps approached from behind them. 'It is too late, Anya; it is too late for you both,' a familiar voice called out. 'I will have the chance of a new life, but you and your friend will not.'

Anya turned to see a gun pointing at her head from only a few feet away. Her nose wrinkled as a familiar perfume reached her, and she closed her eyes. If she could have fought back, she would have done, but there was no time. She swore, thinking that she should have found a hiding place where they wouldn't have been discovered. Life was for living and she had failed. There was no time even to pray as the gun fired . . .

'I can smell fish,' Anya declared as she sat up and sniffed deeply. 'Mildred, I'm on your bloody boat,' she said, wincing as pain shot through her arm. 'I'm not dead, then?' she asked, as someone sat by her side and held a cup of water to her lips.

'Drink this, it will help you feel better,' Flora said. 'It is only a flesh wound, but enough to be painful. You took a nasty fall when John pushed you onto the deck to avoid the German gunshots as we set off.'

'Flora? What are you doing here . . . ? And John is alive?'

'He is,' Flora said.

'Thank goodness. Will I be all right?'

'Yes, nothing a day or two in bed won't cure,' Flora assured her. 'I'm overjoyed to see both you and Mildred. You have no idea how hard we've tried to find you; no one would give up.' She smiled as she tucked a blanket around her friend.

'What about that Anouska, such a horrid woman – she tricked us all. I recall hearing her voice and then nothing . . .'

'She had Mildred's gun and tried to use it on you both. I'm told it was because you know too much about her. She was downed with just one shot, although she isn't dead; Ruth needs her alive as there are people who want to talk to her about her associates.'

'So, it is over? I'm on my way home to my son?'

'You are; indeed, you can see Ramsgate on the horizon,' Ruth said as she joined them. 'Are you up to hearing some news?'

'As long as is it good news. I need good news right now, along with a decent cup of English tea.'

'Just before we set off to rescue you, we had word that Henio is alive. He was picked up after his plane went down over occupied France; he is in a prisoner of war camp, but is well.'

'Oh, that is wonderful news,' Flora exclaimed, giving both women a hug.

Anya was thoughtful. 'France, you say. I wonder if we can get there in Mildred's boat . . .'

Acknowledgements

Gosh, it is always so hard to thank those who have played a part in bringing my latest book to life, as well as those who have supported me through the six months it takes to research and write.

Fellow historical saga authors are a joy to know and such loyal friends. Spread around the world, we meet online to chat, laugh, moan and cry. If you ever need a shoulder to lean on, you can do no better than a saga author.

I always end this part of my book thanking my husband, Michael, as well as Henry, our much-loved dog. Henry, a Polish Lowland Sheepdog, is getting older and starting to slow down and his eyesight is fading fast. Halfway to his twelfth birthday, he is immortalized in my Teashop Girls books as Henio, Anya's Polish pilot husband. Part of Henry's registered pedigree name is Henio – my research always stays close to home! I couldn't write these books without the support and help from my husband of fifty-one years (how did that happen?). Time passes so fast, but memories linger – and make great stories.

Bloggers and reviewers are so important in an author's life, so thank you one and all.

My agent, Caroline Sheldon, is a constant in my writing life and I thank her again for not only her professional help, but also for going above and beyond to cheer me on. Thank you, Caroline.

My amazingly wonderful publisher, Wayne Brookes; I am lucky to have you supporting my writing and being such a good sport when I ask the impossible when discussing plots, covers, the publishing world and so much more.

The whole Pan Macmillan team are great at what they do, from waving the flag for my books to editing and making corrections. I'd be lost without you all.

I can't leave this page without mentioning Annie Aldington, who has narrated all my books to date and does such a wonderful job of bringing my girls and my stories to life. Having had the pleasure of seeing her in action, and having a go myself, I'm in awe of what she does. Thank you, Annie.

Last but not least, thank you to my loyal readers as I'd be nothing without your support x

A Letter from Elaine

Dear reader,

It seems only a short time since I sat down to write to you. Here we are in the first months of 2024 and looking forward to the spring. It has been a joy to write a third Teashop book and visit again the beautiful Kent coast, albeit in wartime.

Have you visited Margate or Ramsgate? I have many happy memories of visiting both towns for holidays with my parents when I was a child. Later, day trips taking the Brownies for days out – that was hectic and fun! In recent years, I have spent many happy times in Ramsgate with writing friends Natalie, Ann, Rosemary, Francesca and Elaine R., where we would spend a week working hard and enjoying visiting the Ramsgate Tunnels, many teashops, as well as the historical harbour that has featured in my books. We are blessed in Kent to have so many historical places to visit and enjoy. Happy memories!

In this book, you would have read how some of 'the girls' leave the shores of England to play their part in bringing the Second World War to an end. This has taken my research to a new level, which means I can purchase more books – I need to move to a larger house, although my husband seems to think we need to downsize . . .

If you have enjoyed my books, please do let me know by popping to my 'Elaine Everest Author' page on Facebook and joining in with our chats. I would also appreciate a short review on Amazon, even if you purchased the book elsewhere or borrowed it from your library. Just a few words will suffice.

Thank you again for being such loyal readers.

Until next time,

Elaine xx

Christmas with the Teashop Girls

It is late 1940 and the war feels closer to home than ever for Rose Neville and her staff at the Lyons teashop in Margate. The worry of rationing hangs overhead as the Nippies do their best to provide a happy smile and a hot cup of tea for their customers. When a heavy bombing raid targets the Kent coastline, Lyons is badly hit, throwing the future of the cafe into jeopardy.

The light in Rose's life is her dashing fiancé, Captain Ben Hargreaves, and planning their Christmas Day wedding. But she must also prepare to take two new step-daughters into her life and get on the right side of her wealthy mother-in-law, Lady Diana. Is Rose ready to become a mother so soon?

When Rose's half-sister, Eileen, makes contact, it seems that Rose's dreams of having a sibling are coming true at long last. But her friends begin to suspect that something is not right about Eileen and her husband: just what are they hiding?

As the Christmas Day wedding draws near, the bombings intensify in Kent and London, putting everything and everyone Rose loves in danger. Only one thing is for sure: it will be a Christmas she never forgets . . .

Keep in Touch

I love to hear from readers, and there are many ways you can not only follow me but contact me to chat, as well as enter competitions.

Twitter:
Find me as @ElaineEverest
I will often tweet book news, so if you follow Twitter, look out for me.

Facebook author page:
Come and chat and hear my news on Facebook.
www.facebook.com/ElaineEverestAuthor

Instagram:
I have an account on Instagram, so why not find me and say hello?
www.instagram.com/elaine.everest

Website:
This is where you can not only read about me and all my books, but also read my blog posts where I chat about my life and everything to do with my books.
Go to www.elaineeverest.com

My newsletter:
Sign up to receive a copy of my monthly newsletter, where I not only give you the latest news about my books but also run some fab competitions. In the past there have been competitions to win a sewing machine, leather handbag, hampers, jewellery and signed copies of my books. You will find the link to sign up on my website: www.elaineeverest.com

The People's Friend

If you enjoy quality fiction, you'll love *The People's Friend* magazine. Every weekly issue contains seven original short stories and two exclusively written serial instalments.

On sale every Wednesday, the *Friend* also includes travel, puzzles, health advice, knitting and craft projects and recipes.

It's the magazine for women who love reading!